THE BROKEN PROTECTOR

A SMALL TOWN ENEMIES TO LOVERS ROMANCE

NICOLE SNOW

ABOUT THE BOOK

My fresh start turned into a dumpster fire.

Awesome new job. Small town heaven. Friendly faces galore.

Then I strolled into my new home and found the unspeakable.

Just when I'm sure it can't get worse, I'm "rescued" by a man who makes me see red for miles.

Enter Lucas Graves.

A bossy grump with a badge who's sworn to keep me safe.

He rocks the scary-hot vibe, he reads too much, and he never misses a chance to give me crap for being a nerdy little cactus who mouths back.

Not the type of man I'd go for in my right mind.

Definitely not the type I should keep trading bruising kisses with.

Redhaven, North Carolina has driven me insane.

Why else does my heart race when Lucas gets jealous and overprotective?

How could I think he'll ever share more than another reckless night?

He guards his own battered heart as fiercely as he watches over me.

It can't get more complicated.

Oh, but then it does.

There's a razor-thin line between heartbreak and hope with a broken protector.

He's so wrong for me I could scream.

But I'm not losing sleep over the very real danger I'm in.

I'm terrified that Lucas Graves might be the best thing that's ever happened—if he'd let us happen at all.

I: LADY IN RED (DELILAH)

*N*o one ever totally captures the stillness of a desolate highway leading far, far away from the only city you know.

Oh, they might try.

They'll tell you about the streaming cars slowing to a trickle, and then to crawling ants scattered few and far between.

They'll tell you about the wide-open sky, the way the yellow dotted line on the road runs together into a single liquid stream.

They'll tell you about the forests, the grass, the countless fences drifting by.

And they'll always mention the silence. Nothing but your tires grinding on tarry asphalt and the occasional bump when you veer too close to the shoulder.

What they won't tell you, though?

What it feels like to be alone for the first time in your life.

What the stillness is when you can't hear anyone else.

No slamming doors.

No whistles from the street below.

No phones blaring down the narrow halls of an apartment building full of disjointed lives crammed together, each one insulated in its own little bubble of humming refrigerators and televisions and notifications.

There's just nothing.

Nothing but quiet stretching on for so long, so deep, that you start to hear your own pulse.

It's unlike anything I've ever known.

Somehow, it feels like a shower, rinsing off the dirt of big-city life and making me ready to step into a whole new chapter of me.

I'm not sure if that's what's waiting in North Carolina.

I couldn't even tell you what really made me take a job in a tiny town I've never heard of, close enough to Raleigh to get decent internet but too far to make a day drive to the beach worth the commute.

When I responded to the postage-stamp-sized ad in my neighborhood circular for a K-4 teacher, I wasn't actually expecting to get the job.

I have the degrees, but not much experience beyond a few supervised part-time and substitute teaching gigs in inner-city schools.

Something like this—a full-time position with room and board covered—would be a pipe dream back in New York.

Sure, I worked my ass off.

Perfect grades. Awards. Extracurriculars. Internships.

So maybe I was the most qualified candidate willing to move to a town that's barely a dot on the map and probably doesn't have a single Uber.

But maybe, just maybe, no one else could stand the thought of living in this much stillness.

Me? I could ride like this forever.

Just me and my ratty old Kia Sportage with everything I own piled in the back, cruising into an endless red sunset.

It's barely late afternoon, the light brassy and thick, by the time Google Maps chirps and tells me to take the next exit.

There's not a single building around. No gas stations, no rest

"You'll do fine, hon. Everyone gets used to Redhaven's quirks eventually. If you stay here long enough, you become part of it."

I don't know what to say to that.

There's something about her statement that makes me a tad uneasy. That stifling feeling strikes again, the same tension that hit when I saw that house on the hill.

Part of me wants to ask about it, but I don't know where to start.

Janelle takes the problem out of my hands, though, dusting her hands together briskly with a no-nonsense smile. "But listen to me, chattering on. I'm sure you'll be wanting to get settled in, won't you?" She leans back, peering under the glossy reception counter and fishing around. "Jeez. I know I put those keys some-where—*ah*, there we go."

She comes up with a little key ring with a red plastic fob shaped like a guitar pick. She separates out one brassy-colored key.

"Front door," she says, then the next, a silver one, "back door," and then last, a smaller silver key, "storage shed." She holds them out to me. "You'll want to take a left on the next street and follow it all the way to the end, right where the tree line breaks. It's the old Crowder house at the end of the lane. You've got your own yard and a lovely lake view for fall. I think you'll enjoy."

I have no idea what that means—the old Crowder house— but I guess it would make sense to someone from here.

I smile again as I take the keys, folding them into my palm.

"Thanks!" I tilt my head. "Do you own the house, Janelle?"

"Heaven's no. That's the Arrendells. You spoke to Lucia for your interview, didn't you?"

I nod.

It was a short interview. The woman on the other end spoke with a refined accent and a certain culturedness that made me feel like a gum wrapper stuck to her shoe, even if she was perfectly pleasant and professional.

She'd asked me to send a photograph. I guess to prove I can clean up well enough to fit in a small-town classroom rather than coming all the way down to North Carolina for an interview only to have to go home.

Imagine my surprise when the hiring paperwork landed in my email the next day.

"She's the First Selectman in this town. Her husband, Montero, is number two. They tend to order things like that around here. If you have any problems with the house, they'll take care of it or send one of the boys out to help."

"The boys?"

"Oh, their sons." Janelle snickers, her fingertips pressed to her lips. "I think it's just Ulysses in town right now. Those boys do love to keep busy, jetting all over the place. But I'm sure he'll be happy to take care of you if his folks are busy. And if *anyone* gives you any trouble, you come see me ASAP." She leans across the counter, one hand splayed against the wood. "There are perks to being married to the police chief, after all."

Again, I'm at a loss for words.

I've been here five minutes and I already know more about this town than I do about my own father.

I'm not in a horror movie... right?

The overly friendly, curious townsfolk won't turn out to be radioactive cannibals, or ninja robots that suck the life out of newborns. Sacrifices up in the hills, haunted mansions, Blair Witch dolls in the trees, etc.

Nah.

Me not knowing what to do with someone being this nice, that's my damage.

And isn't that part of why I came here?

There's an excuse caught on my tongue, something angling to let me escape so I can stop being awkward, but I stop and frown. "Hey, Janelle?"

"Yes, hon?"

"Wasn't there anyone else around to take this job?" I ask her because I couldn't exactly ask the woman hiring me, or she might have thought I didn't want it. "I mean, don't get me wrong, it's a nice gig. My own house, my own classroom, decent pay. I just thought it was a little funny that Mrs. Arrendell up and hired me over the phone."

"Yes, well, about that..." Janelle lets out a long sigh. "There's nobody local qualified. And when someone comes in from the city, well..." She frets her hands together. "They never do last too long. If it's not the fact that we only have pizza delivery three days a week, it's all manner of inconveniences. No public transit, touchy cell reception, y'know." Her smile is tight. "Some folks just can't give up city life."

Hmmm.

I'm not sure I buy it.

But I do need this paycheck, not to mention a strong experience on my résumé that's near impossible to come by back home.

So I'm not complaining.

If it turns out I'm one of those big-city girls who can't adapt to small-town life?

Baby, I'll *learn*.

I can at least stick it out long enough to walk away with a good reference for my next job.

"I'm sure I'll be fine." I try to offer what I hope is a warm, reassuring smile. "I'm used to roughing it on my own."

"Good. I hope so! We could do with a strong young lady around here to brighten things up. Good role model for the kids, you know." Janelle beams. "Do call up if you need any help with anything—anything at all. I finally put our number on Google a couple weeks ago!"

"Awesome. And thank you, ma'am." I offer my hand again. "Nice meeting you."

She gives my hand another firm shake before letting go with a little wave. "Welcome to Redhaven, Delilah. I hope you're here to stay."

Me too.

I could use somewhere to cool my heels for a while.

I walk out into the fading afternoon light and pack myself into my Kia again.

Left at the next street and down toward the woods, huh?

Ugh, small-town directions.

Still, it's not hard to find.

I enjoy the picturesque drive down a winding street dotted with signs depicting children on bicycles and a twenty-mile-per-hour speed limit. People are just coming home from work and rolling into their two-car garages. A few scruffy fathers in shorts and loafers without socks are already on their lawns with hoses while their kids run in and out of the spray like puppies.

It's all very Pleasantville.

A girl could get used to this.

I'll probably be meeting a few of those puppies soon, too. Many of them look young enough to be in my classes.

I try not to be obvious about getting a peek at their faces so I can remember them later.

They're cute kids. They look *happy*, and the more happy little troublemakers I see cavorting around with their parents, the more I smile.

The more I think I might've made the right decision.

A sigh full of relief slips out of me as the road tapers off and leads me up to the new rental.

The 'Crowder' house at the end of the lane.

My house.

It's a homey cottage painted a pretty cerulean blue.

Black shutters and a row of three dormer windows set into the peaked black roof.

The door is an eye-popping red.

The well-trimmed yard looks huge, complete with brick-lined dirt beds just waiting to be flush with flowers or vegetables next spring.

No garage, but plenty of room for street parking. Plus, a

squat little storage shed in the same blue shade off to one corner of the backyard.

A raw wood fence that isn't falling down hugs everything. Through the break in the boards and the trees beyond, I can make out the shimmering lake in the distance.

Deep breath.

I wonder if I've died and gone to heaven.

Best of all, the house is set off the street for a little more privacy from nosy neighbors. Three steps welcome me up to an open porch.

I could see myself sitting out here on warm evenings, sipping iced tea while I grade papers.

With one more smile that might break my face, I park and get out.

The gate opens at the lightest touch, unlatched, the hinges squealing a little—I almost miss the dull thud of footsteps on grass.

Wait, what?

I freeze.

My heart thumps the same way it did in college when I'd have to walk back to my dorm after midnight alone, just barely escaping the university library at closing time.

I'm being paranoid.

I *know* I'm being paranoid.

City girl, overly suspicious, imaginary danger lurking around every corner.

Still, I shift the keys clutched in my hand so they point out like sharp little blades through my knuckles. Then I slowly creep around the side of the house.

"Hello?" I call softly. "Hello!"

Nothing.

No one along this side of the house.

I swallow thickly and tiptoe around the back.

I'm just in time to glimpse a dark, blurry shadow vanishing around the other side of the house. It's a hint of motion, something that looks like an arm before it's gone like it was never there.

Was it?

Are you feeling okay?

My chest turns to lead as I decide my eyes aren't playing tricks.

"Hey, wait!" I shout, sprinting across the backyard.

I'm racing toward the point where that flicker of motion disappeared, careening around the other side of the house.

Nope.

Nothing again.

But there's a weird rustle in the trees beyond the fence.

Trunks of slender poplars waving.

Almost like someone hopped the fence and bolted into the woods.

I fall against the fence, panting hard as I grip the wood, staring into the trees, straining to see something.

But I can't make out anything.

Maybe it really was a hallucination caused by my own excitement and the long drive. Or I just startled a coyote or a raccoon or something.

"Calm the hell down, girl." Closing my eyes, I blow out a rough breath.

This is probably what Janelle was talking about.

City girls getting all spooked by nature, freaking out at every tiny sound.

I don't want to be like them.

I shake my head sharply, annoyed with myself, and push away from the fence. I step around the front of the house again and climb the porch.

This might've dampened that little thrill I had at coming here, but it's not ruined yet.

That happens exactly three seconds later.

I fit the key in the lock and the door swings open at the lightest touch, unlatched.

That last second feels like an eternity.

I stop and gaze into the house as the door opens on squares of sunlight falling through the uncurtained windows onto the glossy hardwood floors.

And a panicked scream lodges in my throat.

Shafts of gold light fall down like crosses over a twisted hand, revealing the ugly secret I'll never get out of my head.

The body of a woman lying face down on the floor.

II: RED EYE (LUCAS)

$\mathcal{I}$ think I've read this book over thirty times by now.
Ender's Game.

Genius boy, strange aliens, weird technology, interstellar conquest. I probably know every line by heart. You could turn a page, cover it with your hand, ask me what's on it, and I could recite it for you word for word.

Guess I should get myself some new books.

Not like there's much to do on shift but read.

Hell, there's no point in even being out on patrol right now. There's rarely any good reason in sleepy Redhaven, which is why right now my version of 'on duty' involves lounging in a chair in the back office of the police station and reading my bored ass off.

My boots are propped up on the captain's unused desk while I keep an ear open for any incoming calls.

Over at the dispatch desk, Mallory's filing her nails and playing a game that occasionally makes her phone spit something in Korean.

I don't know a word of Korean.

Still, judging from the tone of the male voices and the way she's blushing, I'd guess it's awful dirty.

To each their own.

I read old books till my eyes turn red, and Mallory plays games where Korean guys purr at her and make her feel like she's twenty again.

What the hell? It passes the time.

Maybe when my shift's over, I'll head out to the gym and break a sweat.

Normally, when a 911 call comes in, I don't even look up.

Around here, *what's your emergency* is usually more of a 'pig caught in someone's clothesline' situation. Half the time I wind up feeling less like a cop and more like Redhaven animal control.

For some reason I can't explain, though, this time my head snaps up when the phone goes off.

There's this tingling on the back of my neck, prickling and cold and inexplicable.

Maybe I've just been uneasy all day, knowing that new teacher they hired is coming into town. We don't get new folks that often, not the kind that settle in to stay.

Despite how Redhaven looks, your everyday person can't afford the housing around here. You were either born here, or you're vacationing.

Someone new always leaves the vibe a little unsettled.

Of course, it might also be the fact that she was hired by the Arrendells—or so I've heard through the town grapevine.

That's enough to set me on edge all by itself.

I snap my book shut with my thumb as a bookmark and listen in while Mallory switches on the headset tucked against her salt-and-pepper hair.

"9-1-1, what's your emergency?" she chirps.

I can't make out what's happening on the other end of the line.

There's a faint distressed voice and it's not one I recognize.

A woman.

And apparently, she's making poor Mallory go pale.

"Miss, can you please repeat that one more time?" she strains, her voice breathless. "I... yes, of course. Of course, miss, and could you give me your name? Thank you. Yes. I'll send someone right out. Don't touch anything, please. No, don't go inside the house. Yes, yes. Thank you."

I jump up and snag a sticky note, tucking it into my book before tossing it on the desk.

"Trouble, Mallory?"

Her wide eyes dart to me as she jots something down on a notepad, then murmurs something reassuring into her headset before ripping the paper off and thrusting it at me like a bomb.

"There's a body," she announces, just as Chief Bowden plods in from the little closet he's claimed as his private office. His thumbs are tucked into his belt loops, dragging his uniform pants down below his belly. "It's at the Crowder house. The new teacher, she said she opened her door and found a dead girl inside."

"You're shitting me," I whisper, raking a hand over my face.

My stomach flips over as the numbness on Mallory's white face says she's not.

I snatch the piece of paper away and frown at the name written there.

Delilah Clarendon?

Fuck.

Even her name smells like trouble—and I already wonder what the hell kind she's brought with her to our little town.

* * *

I'M NOT ALARMED till I see the body for myself.

Tense, yeah, but part of being a police officer is keeping it cool as a cucumber until there's reason not to be.

Sometimes all it takes is one person keeping their shit together to help everybody else hold it together, too. I learned that in some sticky situations.

Still, as Chief Bowden and I settle into my patrol car and hit the road, this ugly premonition sinks into my bones, harsh and cutting.

Why does it feel like I've been waiting for something to happen?

It's been too quiet around Redhaven for ages. Certain people learned to take their dirty business somewhere else.

You know the old saying—don't shit where you eat.

Well, sooner or later, somebody was bound to slip up.

And if there's really a dead body at the new teacher's house, it might just be my chance to catch them in the act.

As we head out to that little blue house at the edge of town, I'm expecting to pull up on this frazzled kitten collapsed in a mess of tears, flipping her fancy latte and throwing a fit, demanding to speak to—who knows?

The mayor, which we don't have when it's just a town council of selectmen.

The manager?

Some manager. Any manager.

Whatever authority figure she can complain to about how we could possibly let this catastrophe happen to her. As if we're not just as shell-shocked as she is.

I'm not trying to be a dick. I've just got a feeling this stranger could make a nasty situation worse.

That's what I'm assuming till the second we pull up and spot her.

This eerily calm, motionless figure waiting for us on the front porch. Not what I expected.

My first impression is that she's kind of an old soul.

Young, for sure. Early to mid-twenties, maybe.

She's tiny.

So damn small I could pick her up with one hand.

Leggy as hell with thick hips and a slender waist, all of her looking real casual in a dark-blue tank top and jeans.

Lightly tanned skin. From the thin white tan lines on her shoulders, it looks pretty natural, not sprayed-on or burned into her by tanning beds.

Her face starts with a tumble of black hair cascading over her shoulders and back. High cheekbones render her expressionless, stone-cold, her full lips set in an unrevealing line of horror.

Then there's the tattoo.

That stylized dragon tattoo coiling over her shoulder and down her arm, its black ink crisp and fluid, hinting there's a little something more to her behind that hard-set mask.

Shit.

She doesn't look like the sort of girl who'd pack up her big-city life and come down here to teach a bunch of munchkins in a town that doesn't know her from Adam.

Which makes it extra weird that the day she shows up, so does a body.

The girl lifts her head as I park my patrol car.

Her eyes are just faint shimmers in the shadows under the porch, watching us warily.

"Think she's gonna be a problem? Looks skittish as hell." In the passenger seat, Bowden clucks his tongue.

"We should talk to her before we make any kind of assessments, Chief." I check my sidearm at my hip, make sure the safety's locked, then toss my head. "Come on."

We step out of the car.

Our new arrival instantly goes tense, but holds her ground.

The chief is half-right.

I haven't spoken one word to her, yet the girl makes me think of an alley cat, guarded and feral but ever ready to defend her territory. I take it slow as I push the gate open and walk up with Bowden behind me.

Look, I'm no stranger to women turning to stone around me.

I'm a big guy. To some folks, that means safety.

To others, that just makes me a bigger threat.

So I stop at a safe distance, close to the steps. I don't want to crowd her, make her feel unsafe, and I keep my hands well away from my weapon as I take a slow look around.

The front door is hanging open.

Can't see inside at this angle, but I'm guessing that's where our problem is.

Looks like there's been a disturbance around the house. Grass in the side yard bent and broken, freshly crushed, probably by somebody running to dig into it that hard.

Was it her just taking a look around?

Or maybe someone fled the crime scene?

"Miss Clarendon, right?" My gaze snaps back to her.

She narrows her eyes. Now I can see they're blue, indigo-like, a kind of dark night-sky shade.

"Yes. That's me," she whispers.

"Lieutenant Graves. Lucas." I nod at the chief. "And this is Chief Bowden."

"Think you met my wife," Bowden pipes up in his slow, sleepy drawl. He's staring off at the woods and doesn't seem all that interested.

I hold in a sigh. Man's getting close to retirement, and honestly, it's a bit overdue.

"Janelle?" he asks.

"Um, yeah," Delilah says coldly. "She gave me the keys. Don't think she left me the dead girl, though."

"Absolutely not," I agree. Hell, I've known Janelle Bowden my whole life, and she can't even swat a bee. "Mind if we take a quick look?"

"I doubt she's going anywhere," Delilah bites off before her face smooths. "I mean... I'm sorry. I think I'm still in shock. Yeah, take your time."

I step up on the porch. The boards creak under me.

She immediately stiffens as I draw closer. I stop, keeping my gaze fixed on her and not looking inside just yet.

"You can breathe," I say. "I doubt you're a suspect. No need to panic. There's a sidewalk over there if you don't want to be here."

I point my thumb over my shoulder.

Her lips thin.

For the briefest second, I think I'm about to get that city-girl freakout I expected.

Then she looks away, hugging her arms to her chest. "I'm not worried about that."

I tilt my head. "You stressing about something else?"

"Like why there's a body in my new living room, you mean?" Her shoulders jerk sharply in something that's less like a shrug and more of a flinch. "But also, where I come from, you wonder how much you should say to cops. Even if you didn't do a thing. You wonder how much they even care."

"Fair enough, I guess," I agree. "Where you from?"

"Queens. New York, I mean."

"New York City?" I whistle softly. "Well, if you can give me a few minutes, Miss New York, maybe we can get this sorted."

Her head snaps up and she glares at me, slightly baring her teeth.

I'm okay with that.

Rather have her pissed at me than panicked over finding the body.

See, that's the thing with being a cop.

You get to see the front people put up. Right now, she's putting up one hell of a wall, all alley cat bravado with her tail frizzed up and back arched, ready to claw me to pieces if I get too close or say the wrong thing.

It's the body language that gives her away.

The way she holds her arms in close, making herself compact, shielding herself.

The way her fingers dig into her inner elbows until her knuckles show white through the skin.

For just a second, the way her lips tremble.

She's holding it together out of sheer stubborn pride, I think, but it's taking an iron will.

Deep down, the girl's scared as hell, and who can blame her?

Who wouldn't be, showing up in a strange new town and finding a body before they can even move into their new digs?

"Chief," I say.

Bowden grunts back, climbing up on the porch behind me.

"Ma'am." The chief tips his cap to Delilah before following me inside.

I hold my breath while my eyes adjust to the dimmer light.

Yep.

That's a dead body, all right.

I stop just past the threshold, moving to one side to let the chief inside but going no further. I don't want to disturb a single goddamned thing, just in case we're dealing with a proper crime scene and not some freak accident.

I swallow hard, my throat going as dry as the Mojave.

At first blush, it looks like there's blood all over the floor, spiraling out in liquid pools across the wood.

Actually, it's not blood—it's silk.

A red dress the same rusty color as half-dried blood, the bodice belted with a streaming scarlet sash, the skirt spread around the body of a once-pretty slender girl with gold skin and a twist of black hair pinned behind her head.

One arm sprawls out and the other rests against her side.

She's young, judging by her build and porcelain-smooth skin. Face down, I can't make out an identity just yet, but at first glance I don't pick up on anything I recognize.

My heart sinks.

Who is she, and what the hell happened to her?

"You recognize her?" I ask Bowden.

He shakes his head, clucking his tongue in that annoying habit he has.

"Don't look like nobody I seen around," he says. "You wanna turn her over?"

"Not yet." I fish my phone out from my pocket. "Don't move anything until I get a few good pictures. Might have to bring in the Feds and they always appreciate the extra camerawork."

I open my camera app, adjust the lighting, and start snapping photos, carefully circling the body at a distance. There's no furniture in this room to move with the house still mostly bare, making it easy to keep an eye out for anything of interest.

Fucking shame I already know I won't find anything.

Probably wasn't meant to find this body, either.

Only, something happened.

Somebody made a big damn boo-boo.

I can't imagine anyone leaving her here on purpose.

I step closer, crouching down and taking a few more detailed shots.

She's definitely dead—no respiration at all—but she couldn't have been gone for more than a day when there's no sign of decomposition. If not for the awkward angle of her body and the total motionlessness, I'd think she was just passed out cold, sleeping pretty as a picture.

Just to be doubly certain, I stow my phone and fish out a pair of nitrile gloves from my pocket, then snap them on and press two fingers to her throat.

No pulse.

Wouldn't that have been a lovely surprise.

Tell the new teacher her dead girl's actually a drunk girl who stumbled into her house, and everything's okay.

"Anything?" Bowden asks.

I shake my head. "She's cold. Help me turn her over, Chief. Careful, now."

I catch her shoulders.

Bowden catches her feet and we gently flip her over onto her back. Her limbs flop limply, her head lolling in this sad nod.

Once she's repositioned, I crane my head, frowning down at her face.

Damn.

No signs of bruising, injury, nothing.

Just a little puffiness around her eyes, which is normal as the body shuts down. She's Instagram model pretty, but she doesn't look like anyone I've ever seen, even with the summer tourists who invade our growing handful of Airbnbs and rentals.

"No broken bones, no contusions," I mutter. "No ligature marks on the neck. Any thoughts?"

Bowden hitches his belt. "Can't say. We'll need the coroner in on this."

"Have Mallory call it in. I'm gonna take a look around."

I straighten, pulling myself up—only for a shadow to fall across the dead girl, blocking the fading sunlight from the doorway.

Delilah stands behind us, her arms still tucked around her, her eyes clouded as she looks down at the girl's body with her brows in a troubled line.

"Who is she?" she asks softly.

"I don't know yet."

It's like the room goes quiet as the grave, the air somber, this nameless dead girl between us and a million questions I don't have answers for. Underneath those midnight-blue eyes, there's a searching need.

Almost like Delilah's looking at that girl's empty face and seeing herself.

Herself, or else every Jane Doe heartbreaker who ever died without anybody knowing her.

I shake my head, running a hand through my hair. "She's not a local, I can tell you that much. There's no sign she was assaulted or injured from any external trauma. It's possible she had some kind of medical condition."

"And that medical condition magically landed her in my *house?*" For just a second, Delilah's voice cracks. A tiny break in that tough exterior. "You don't think that's a little weird?"

"It is," I say carefully. "You're a teacher, right? I bet you can think of a dozen reasons she'd wind up here if something happened and she wasn't feeling right. People aren't always thinking straight when their body goes haywire."

Delilah's mouth twists in a sour line, waiting for an explanation I can't give her.

Shit.

I've got to watch my mouth. No need to disclose too many details.

Not even theories, and not just because if this is a murder, I can't fuck up the investigation.

I definitely don't want to start the small-town rumor mill spinning.

"Stranger coincidences have happened," I say with a shrug.

"But I—" Delilah stops and turns, staring outside, her delicate face caught in profile with the light highlighting all her fragile edges. She's like a cannon made of glass, frailty and fire. "I just thought..."

"What did you think?"

"I thought I saw someone when I pulled up. They were around the side of the house, gone before you could blink. Over the fence and then into the woods, I think." She shakes her head. "I told myself it was a wild animal and I was just getting spooked too easily. But now..."

"Could be."

Or it could be something else entirely.

Did someone dump this body here and run when Delilah caught them in the act?

Or was the body never meant to be found, and New York accidentally interrupted something worse?

I glance at the chief—but he's moved to the side window looking out toward the fence, the forest. He's just staring, chewing the inside of his cheek.

Goddammit.

He's checked out again.

He hasn't even made the call to dispatch like I asked.

I get that this job is pretty lazy ninety percent of the time, but this is the time when I'd expect any officer worth his salt to wake the hell up and *pay attention.*

Sighing, I step closer to Delilah. "Listen. Is there anyone you know who might want to hurt you?"

She stiffens and slowly looks up at me.

"Not here. I only arrived an hour ago. I don't even know anyone in town. Lucia Arrendell hired me through a phone interview."

Lucia damn Arrendell.

I have to hold back the urge to snarl at that name.

Keep it casual, Graves.

Still, I can't help saying, "Odd way to hire somebody, don't you think?"

"I don't know. Eccentric rich people, or whatever, right? And it sounds like you guys need new teachers bad." She shakes her head, her inky hair falling against her bare shoulders, blending with that tattoo. "There's this one guy, back in New York... But he wouldn't know I was here. He couldn't have followed me or gotten here ahead of me."

My interest sharpens.

"You want to elaborate on 'one guy?'"

Her lips curl bitterly. "Creepy ex. Kind of stalker-y. Every girl's got one, you know." She glances past me at the dead girl on the floor. "Maybe she did, too."

"That's one possibility." I glance at Bowden again, the back of his buzz-cut head, before gesturing to Delilah and taking another step closer. "Mind coming out to my car to talk for a bit? I'd like to get this guy's name and information. Consider it due diligence."

And I'm doing some more as my eyes rake over her, trying not to let myself get too smitten with her looks.

I don't know her, and a pretty face doesn't mean she's just a witness.

Delilah resists for a moment, uncertainty clouding her face—there's that alley cat look again—before she retreats, putting distance between us.

"You mean," she whispers over her shoulder as she steps onto the lawn, "you want to get me away from the crime scene. Especially if I'm a potential suspect."

Damn.

I don't know this girl.

She's as much of a stranger as that dead girl on the floor.

Still, something about the way she holds herself and bows her head like she's grieving the loss of a life she never even knew trips something primal.

It makes me want to wrap her up in a safe cocoon and protect her, even if I can't rule her out as a suspect just yet.

Sure, she might be putting on a brave front or one hell of an act, but I won't blame her for being rattled.

She's got a car, a dusty old Kia, parked out on the curb. I can make out moving boxes and laundry baskets piled with her stuff inside.

Fuck, this sucks.

The girl threw her whole life into the back of a ratty SUV. Showed up in a new town where she's got no kin, no friends. Took on a job with folks she's never met, sight unseen.

Then she walked right into this fucking mess.

Lots of people would be breaking down right now.

Somehow, Miss Delilah's spine is still stiff, her expression composed. She's trying her damnedest to keep it together.

I follow her down the steps.

"You're not under arrest. Until the county coroner gives us a cause of death, we've got no firm reason to suspect foul play," I say. "I will have to ask you to make other accommodations for a few nights, though. Even if she died of natural causes, we need to preserve the scene and gather evidence before moving the body, and we can't do that if you're moving in."

She whirls on me in a lash of black, her hair like smoke, billowing around her.

She glares at me, all burning blue eyes.

"And just where am I supposed to stay?" she snaps.

"I've got a sofa." It's out before I can stop it, a dumb joke rising in answer to her sparking glare. "Little bit of hometown hospitality. Welcome to Redhaven. Pillows cost extra, Miss New York."

Me and my big mouth.

She's not amused in the slightest.

A scowl settles over her face and her *fuck-you* gaze just hardens.

"I bet you think you're real funny, cracking shitty jokes at a murder scene," she spits.

When she says it like that, it ain't my smartest move. She doesn't see I'm trying to lighten the mood, mostly for her sake.

"Never thought about doing stand-up, but I keep myself entertained," I throw back.

Delilah's eyes narrow, right on the verge of shooting flames now.

One slender tanned middle finger pops up in a proper New York salute.

I can't help grinning. "That how you say hello where you're from, New York?"

"It's how we say a lot of things, you prick."

My eyebrows dart up.

"I'll take it as a declaration of your undying love," I grumble. Then I skirt around her and pull the driver's side door of the patrol car open so I can snag the notebook tucked into the sun visor. "Now, if I could get that name and contact information, I'll follow up and make sure your ex didn't trail you out here and have anything to do with this."

Delilah goes dead silent for a moment.

That middle finger disappears and her hand goes back to gripping her elbow in a death hold.

"Please don't—just don't tell him where I am," she whispers. "Go ahead, make sure he's still in New York and all that, but don't tell him I'm in Redhaven."

"I won't," I promise. "You're safe here, Miss Clarendon. I wouldn't dare joke about that."

Her gaze flicks to me, then to the open door of the blue cottage house.

"Am I?" she asks sharply.

Knife, meet guts.

I wish I could make her believe me, but she's got good reason to feel skeptical.

Sure, I can promise her I won't let anything bad happen till I'm blue in the face, but that won't make her believe it.

I'll just have to do my job, and make sure she doesn't have any reason to regret coming to our little town.

She's subdued as she gives me a name, a number, a last known address.

Roger Strunk, age twenty-six, an HVAC repairman from Queens.

That's one lead.

The chief steps outside then and tells Delilah she's welcome to stay at The Rookery's main property, free of charge. I know he means it when he says Janelle would be happy to have her.

Delilah warily accepts, but thank fuck she does.

That means I know where to find her.

I hate that it all feels a little too easy. Too neat. Too simple.

Maybe her paranoia is starting to infect me now.

Then again, I've got my own good reasons for finding this whole ugly business a little fishy.

The simplest explanation isn't always the right one.

Usually, when things look too simple in Redhaven, it means one thing.

Trouble.

* * *

I CAN'T GET that girl off my mind.

Both of them, really, but mostly, Miss New York.

I can't bring that poor dead girl back to life. I'll certainly do my best by her—make sure we get her IDed and start bringing her some justice. But justice won't bring her back.

Delilah, though, she's still alive.

And here I am, still thinking about the stiffness of her spine, the way her mouth was set in this grim line like she was trying not to break down in front of me.

I just had to run my mouth and upset her more, even if she flashed me her claws.

So I can't help wondering if there's something I should do for her, too.

'Course, that might be because I'm parked across the town square from The Rookery, settled in my car for my patrol shift.

While everyone else in this God-fearing town is sound asleep, there's lights on in the house up the hill—and in a single room in The Rookery.

I can make out a feminine silhouette, settled against the window seat, backlit by gold.

She must've been there for hours.

Barely moving, just staring into space.

I don't think she's noticed me.

Will she get any sleep tonight at all?

Fuck.

For about two seconds, I try to talk myself out of it.

Good thing I don't listen very well. Because next thing I know, I'm stepping onto the sidewalk, locking my vehicle behind me.

Screw it.

As of now, the Redhaven PD does house calls.

I head up the walk and I don't even make it to the door before I hear a window opening above me, and then a soft hiss.

"Lieutenant Graves?"

I stop, craning my head up to look at her.

She's perched on the sill in a little babydoll tee and shorts, her hair tumbling over her shoulder.

"Evening, Miss Clarendon," I call up.

"It's almost morning," she whispers. "What are you doing here?"

I shrug, tucking my hands in my pockets. "Thought I'd check

up on you. You look like you're having a bit of trouble, ma'am. Mind if I come up?"

Her expression darkens into a scowl. "I mind a lot, thank you. I'm not having more trouble, and unless you're officially here to question me or you've got a warrant, *no,* you can't come up. I don't want to wake up Janelle."

I try not to let my jaw set.

"She sleeps in the house out back with the chief, you know. They wouldn't even hear you." It's damn hard not to smile at this girl when she gets her hackles up, and I'm glad for her attitude. If she's using it as a shield, it'll hold her strong till she's past this crap. "Don't worry, New York. We're not so old-fashioned that she'd go talking behind your back for having a man in your room at midnight."

Her blue eyes dagger me like icicles. "You're right. You did the world a favor when you didn't go for that career in comedy."

I can't help the way my lips twitch up. "Wow. I thought you New Yorkers spoke fluent sarcasm."

"And I thought you townies only spoke hillbilly, but you actually pronounce the ends of your words. I'm shocked."

"Nah. Hillfolk live a bit higher up in the woods. Not people."

She blinks. "Hillfolk?"

"You'll meet the Jacobins when they're ready and not a minute sooner. They're the kind of folks who can't be found unless they want to be." I rock on my heels, studying her face. "You sure you're gonna be all right? You don't have to worry. I'm just out here on patrol all night, and I tend to settle in around the town square. If anyone comes by this place, I'll see it from there. Thought you should know."

There it is.

That New York glower, coming back in full force. "I don't *need* you to watch over me, Officer. You insisted I'm safe... aren't I?"

She's got me there.

"Just doing my job, lady. You happen to be where my job is."

"Wow, the full cop chaperone experience. Haven't seen that since high school. I feel so special!"

"You were the one who said you didn't need me," I growl. But there's no point in riling her up, either, no matter how sweetly it makes her flush and her eyes glitter. I just nod firmly and lift a hand. "I won't keep you up. You need me, I'm parked right across the way. Have a good night, New York."

"Not likely, Officer Limpdick," she mutters.

Snorting, I ignore that comically wrong insult to my manhood and start to turn away, but this odd hunch turns me back.

Right on time to see her New York salute again, her slim middle finger thrust to the night sky, jabbed in my direction.

Two one-gun salutes in one day?

This is going great.

Before the window slams shut, there's nothing left but the lash of her hair before she vanishes from view.

There you have it.

It's gonna be a long-ass night, the kind that leaves you red-eyed and questioning your own life the next morning.

At least New York's gonna be fine, attitude and all.

And me?

I fight back a shit-eating grin and shake my head.

All the way back to my damn car.

III: RED LIGHT (DELILAH)

*S*he's coming.

I'm back at the blue house, the interior lit red, the girl rising up off the floor like she's being lifted by strings, her hair unbound and streaming, her limbs hanging limply, her face hidden.

She's still dead, but I can *feel* her glaring at me like it's my fault.

Like I'm the one who killed her.

Knowing it's a dream doesn't ease my sick fright as I stumble back.

As she twitches.

As that nightmare dress flares around her like a blood-drenched rose.

With an unholy scream, she throws herself at me, her dead fingers reaching for my throat.

I snap awake just as those cold, clammy hands find my neck.

When I open my eyes, I realize the hand around my neck is my own.

God.

I'm panting myself hoarse. My heart feels like a panicked hummingbird, and I'm staring at the ceiling of the suite while my hand grips my throat like I can force my racing pulse back down.

Oh, crap.

Closing my eyes, I slump back into the sweat-soaked sheets, moving my hand down over my chest, trying to get a grip on reality again.

Nightmares shouldn't surprise me after what happened yesterday afternoon.

The house.

The body.

That girl.

I just didn't want to show the cops how much the whole thing shook me.

Especially when the older one—the police chief—barely seemed to care, smiling that dopey grin of his like I just called him to deal with kids playing a prank.

Then there's the other guy.

Lieutenant Joker Limpdick.

I *hate* smarmy assholes like him.

Too big for his own good.

Too aware how handsome he is with his cocky, one-sided smile broadcasting his ego to everybody else.

His face cut perfectly, all chiseled masculine planes.

His green eyes look like spring, starkness against a suntanned brow and a sweep of night-black hair.

He has this slow, calm way of speaking that's not quite a Southern drawl. More like he's taking his sweet time tasting every word in a deep, gravel-tumbling voice.

A voice that keeps calling me Miss New York.

Holy hell.

He's lucky all I did was flip him off.

You can't ever show weakness in front of a man like him.

Right now, though, I'm anything but strong.

I'm alone.

I hug my knees to my chest, pressing my palm against my mouth and stifling a whimper.

That poor, poor girl.

Who *is* she?

Did someone slaughter her, and then leave her there for me to find the moment I rolled into town?

Jesus.

Why?

Common sense says not to stick around and find out.

Usually when you find a dead body, you should get the hell out of Dodge before you wind up being the next victim or The Last Girl in a horror movie—if you're lucky.

But where would I even go?

Back to the career black hole of New York?

Crawling home in failure with nothing to show for it?

No job, no prospects, and there's no way in hell any school would hire someone like me without the right connections. Especially not for this kind of pay and the lower cost of living.

Oh, plus there's Roger.

Before I closed out my lease and turned in my keys, he hadn't done anything the police considered serious enough to bring him in.

Parking his car at the end of my street, watching me come and go.

Always 'coincidentally' being in the same shops I was at the same time.

Slipping up and liking a few of my Facebook posts when he was supposed to be blocked, and the idiot didn't have enough sense to give his burner account a name I wouldn't recognize.

Nothing criminal.

There's no law against being on public streets or pinging your ex on social media under creepy anonymous accounts. Nothing the police could bust him on.

All too typical.

A tale as old as time.

They can never act until it's too late and the worst has already happened.

But would Roger escalate? Would he even dream of going this far?

To the point of killing some random girl just to scare me back home?

I shake my head so violently my hair whips my shoulders.

No way.

I don't want to believe it.

Roger was always more passive-aggressive, the boyish dependent type.

That's partly what ended us.

He wanted to be codependent, cutting out our other friendships until we only had each other, always in contact. It got to the point where I couldn't even study because if we weren't together, he just had to be on the phone with me.

He always swore we could sit there in silence, only to erupt at his dumb games on the TV when I was trying to concentrate.

Sleeping on the phone on the nights he didn't stay over, too. When I started having neck pain from the headset, he just told me to get a better pillow.

At first it was weird, but flattering.

That little thrill of being the sole focus of someone's crazy obsession.

Of course, it got really old, really fast.

Then it got *controlling*.

After that, a little stalking would be right in character.

But murder?

That's hard to buy, even for a man who angrily rejected therapy and desperately needs it.

Which means I'm walking into someone else's problems and possibly making them mine.

Or maybe Officer Horsedick was right.

Maybe the girl truly died of natural causes.

She was young and pretty, but young people can have heart

conditions, high blood pressure, who knows. Then there's drinking and overdoses.

That doesn't make her death any less sad.

But it does make it a bit easier to look at this as wretched bad luck, and not me making a *massively bad decision* to stay here.

Don't cry, don't cry.

But my nose is stinging as I lift my head.

My worn reflection in the vanity mirror across the cozy bedroom of the two-room suite gazes back at me.

I look like hell. No surprise.

Lines under my eyes, red around the edges, nose pink.

Looks like concealer's going to be my best friend today.

Especially since I need to get off my butt and get dressed for a meeting with my employers—something that feels more like a real job interview than the brief call and paperwork that led me out here.

I can't let them think one brutal shock will chase me out of town.

Six a.m., the clock says.

Perfect.

I always wake up with the sunrise, no alarm, even when I want to sleep in.

Sometimes it's annoying. This time, I'm grateful.

What would have happened in my dream if that girl finished pressing down on my throat?

My meeting's not until nine o'clock sharp, so I've got time to take a long shower and breathe in the steam. It helps calm the jitters.

I take my sweet time getting dressed, putting on my camouflage to face the day.

It's not that I'm pretending to be someone I'm not.

I just know the assumptions some parents might make about girls in tight jeans with visible tattoos in remote little towns.

I'm definitely not giving anyone reasons to reject me before I have a chance to prove I can be a good teacher to their kids.

Believe me, I *want* to be a good teacher.

I want to be the reason these kids smile, just like how so many of my teachers stepped up for me when my childhood wasn't great.

And no, that's not something I like to dwell on.

So I blow-dry my hair, do my makeup until I look just a little too doe-eyed and innocent, and then throw on a comfy pair of black fitted pants, a white sleeveless silk blouse, and a loose slate-blue knit cardigan. Thick enough to conceal my tattoo but not so thick I'll sweat half to death in the late August heat.

Perfect.

With one last nod in the mirror for good luck, I grab my purse and head downstairs.

Janelle intercepts me as I step into the lobby, pulling me into a warm hug before I can say anything besides "Oof!"

I should've expected this.

She did it last night, too, after her police chief hubby turned me over and explained the situation. All hugs and apologies, like she was somehow responsible for the gruesome discovery in that house.

I pat her back a little stiffly, waiting for her to let me go.

"Good morning to you, too," I manage around a near mouthful of her shoulder.

"Oh, good morning, hon." She pulls back, gripping my shoulders, her worried eyes searching my face. "Are you all right? No bad dreams?"

I smile faintly. "Tiny nightmare. Probably to be expected, but I promise you I'm fine."

The look she gives me, I can't quite figure out what it is.

Either she doesn't believe me... or she pities me terribly.

"They really do raise them tougher in the city, don't they?" She smiles. Before I can ask what she means by that, she squeezes my upper arms. "Come on. I just finished putting out breakfast. Complimentary with the stay."

"Oh, I'm not—"

I start to say *I'm not hungry.*

I never get the chance.

Next thing I know, I'm sitting in a hardback chair with a lake view and a steaming cup of coffee. There's a plate piled high with eggs, scones, and sausage in front of me.

Janelle Bowden is a whirlwind. The summer tourists must love her.

I don't know what to think, honestly, but it's comforting.

A little bit of forced normalcy after yesterday's—well, *everything.*

Murmuring my thanks, it gets easier to smile like I mean it as I tuck in.

Breakfast is divine.

Good enough that I've cleaned my plate without realizing it. Maybe Janelle knew what I needed more than I did because I hadn't recognized just how shaky I felt until the sensation starts to settle down with a full belly.

My hands are less trembly, the unease in the pit of my stomach a smidge faded.

I know. I *know* it's normal to feel this way right now.

I'm just not very good at forgiving myself.

But I feel less like a nervous wreck and more like I'm about to split my zipper as I thank Janelle one more time and head out to my car with a little note in her loopy handwriting, telling me how to get to the town hall.

It's easy enough to find, this big white building with a red roof and a steeple like a church, shingles gleaming in the morning sun.

To hell with it.

It's a gorgeous morning, and I need to walk off the ten pounds I just ate.

It's strange how the town smells like wildflowers. All I see are neatly maintained streets and a few sidewalk hedges.

Where is that scent *coming* from?

It's almost like rose water, and it's strongest at the center of the plaza, where that bronze statue of the guy on horseback stabs up at the sky.

I stop and stare at the monument. The marble base alone stands taller than I do.

It's a pretty dramatic pose, the horse rearing up, the rider's cape flaring out. A handsome sculpture of a man with bony cheekbones and a fierce face. His garb makes me think of revolutionary era minutemen.

There's a plaque at the base with a name.

Frederick Arrendell, 1750-1833. Honorable Founder.

I trace my fingertips over the engraving, then slowly circle the statue with my nostrils tingling.

On the other side, I find fresh roses resting against the base on the cobblestones. Their crispness says they couldn't have been here for more than a few hours.

They're a soft sunset-pink with green leaves and thorny stems. They're woven together, not really a wreath, more just a giant sheaf stretching from one side of the marble to the other.

Weird.

Maybe this is one of *those* towns, though.

Long, deep history going back to the colonial days with a reverence for its founders that can only be found in these old communities where half the family names were established before North Carolina was even a state.

No wonder Lucia Arrendell spoke to me like she was royalty deigning to address a mere mortal.

I linger for another minute—I'm early, anyway—before pushing away and letting my wandering steps take me to the town hall.

Under the shade of the little overhang above the door, I knock briefly, then push the door open, tentatively peeking inside.

The entryway is lushly carpeted, decorated heavily with marble columns and floral arrangements and flagpoles draped with the American flag, the North Carolina state flag, and a red thing with a circular symbol I don't recognize. Paintings of more men in colonial style line the walls, including a few with the same fearsome face as the statue.

There's no one behind the broad wood reception desk, but at the far end of the room, standing before a heavy set of oak double doors, I spot three people who look less like small-town royalty and more like they just stepped off the runway in the NYC fashion scene.

The one who catches my attention first is the woman.

She's tall, rail-thin, wearing a couture black gown with a plunging neckline and a lazy drape to the silk fabric. Her shoulders and arms are bare and her fingers are cloaked in black gloves, delicately holding an unlit cigarette.

She carries herself with a hips-forward slouch and a quiet sensuality that's faded gracefully with age.

She's got cheekbones like razors. A mouth like a curving fruit. Eyes as grey as deep mist, her elegant features framed in a white-streaked bob of platinum-blonde hair.

I'd guess she's a very well-aging mid-sixties, along with the man at her side.

He has a sort of 1930s charm, right down to his three-piece suit and pocket watch on a gold chain.

He makes me think of Clark Gable with his black hair swept back and silver touches at the temples, his thin mustache and a certain arrogant twist to his brows. His eyes are jade-green.

For a split second, I can't help but think of Lucas Graves.

Their eyes are almost the same shade, this translucent green that's almost glassy.

Yet Lucas' eyes are so warm they remind me of spring.

This man's eyes are unreadable, a foggy glass I can't quite see through.

I'm guessing the other man with the same eyes is probably their son. Maybe early thirties, impeccably dressed in a stylish Italian suit. He has her blond hair, his green eyes, and the face of a fallen angel.

Yep.

I think I've just found the Arrendells.

They lean in close, murmuring to each other. Just a soft buzz of voices in airy accents—but as the door creaks, they go quiet, lifting their heads simultaneously.

Three sets of sharp eyes fall on me.

I freeze in my tracks.

There's something about them.

This crackling presence that electrifies the whole room.

The most intense one is the son. He studies me with a widening, unblinking interest that makes me feel like he's forgotten how to see anything else.

Jeez.

If I'd stayed in NYC, I'd probably have avoided eye contact at my own wedding.

Being gawked at like this makes me feel *naked.*

I glance away quickly, finding a spot just over his shoulder to look at instead of meeting those intense eyes again.

The woman breaks the stillness and her slim face relaxes with a small, thoughtful smile.

"Ah, the lady of the hour," she lilts in an accent that's more New Hampshire than North Carolina. She lifts her unlit cigarette to her lips like she's taking a coy little drag. "Miss Clarendon, is it not?"

"I... yes." I take a deep breath, scrub my hands against my thighs, and straighten up. No need for me to be so nervous just because I'm not used to dealing with rich people who are also like my boss' boss. Donning my most professional smile, I step closer, offering a hand. "You must be Lucia Arrendell."

"And my worse half, Montero." She lays her hand in mine like a feather, just barely touching, before turning her head languidly to her son. "My youngest and least responsible son, Ulysses."

Both Montero and Ulysses chuckle.

"Welcome, Miss Clarendon." Montero reaches for my hand, grasping it firmly.

His eyes dip over me, assessing me like he's looking to buy a horse before he looks away just as fast, dropping my hand like he's lost interest.

"I do hope you'll find our town more welcoming after yesterday's distressing encounter," he rumbles.

Distressing?

That's what you call it?

God, rich people are weird and overly polite.

That goes double when Ulysses steps up and takes my hand in both of his before I have a chance to respond.

"Delilah." He practically breathes my name. "I've been waiting to meet you."

What?

I blink. My fingers curl helplessly in his. His fingers are hard, his touch vaguely cool.

"...you have?"

"Entirely. I owe you an apology after what happened yesterday."

Ulysses bows over my hand—and I realize almost too late that he means to kiss my knuckles.

Oh my God.

Maybe he's just being gentlemanly and cultured in a way a dumpster rat like me can't comprehend, but I jerk my hand free before he can, tucking it against my inner elbow as I hug my arms to myself.

I forget how to breathe.

Way to make it awkward, Lilah.

Ulysses studies me, his gaze too curious before he straightens like it didn't happen and offers me a disarming smile.

"You see," he says, "it was my responsibility to prep the house for your arrival. I left it in the hands of a good cleaning crew, but I should have made a point of checking in personally. I could've spared you the horror. Have the police identified the girl yet?"

"No," I say flatly, shaking my head.

I wasn't expecting him to just bring it up like that.

For an instant, all I can see is the red of Lucia's brightly colored mouth. It's almost the same red as the dead girl's dress.

My breath rattles as I inhale. "But it's not your fault."

That makes me wonder, though.

That cleaning crew, should I tell Lucas?

Maybe if he finds out who they were, they can tell him something that might lead to more clues.

But Ulysses is talking again, relaxed and laughing. "You're too kind, and apparently, you're a resilient young thing. But come." His gaze sharpens as he gestures toward the double doors. "We shouldn't keep the council waiting."

...the council?

I'm meeting the whole town council?

Oh, hell.

There's no time to protest or make excuses.

The Arrendells are like peacocks, closing in around me. They usher me into a wood-paneled conference room.

A good half dozen people are already seated at a U-shaped table, dressed much more plainly, older men and women who already look bored and ready to be done with this.

I feel like I've stepped into a Tim Burton film.

The Arrendells are just surreal, their colors more vivid than reality, cast against the drab backdrop of everyday life.

After meeting them, the rest of it's pretty boring.

Names pass over my head I'll probably remember after hearing them a few more times.

Pleasant greetings all around.

I'm shown to a chair, and there's talk about the education budget, holidays, and zoning.

All things I have no say in but end up listening to intently anyway.

The council members make proposals, and every time Lucia and Montero have the final say, yeas and nays gliding off their tongues.

Meanwhile, Ulysses never takes his eyes off me.

I don't even know how to feel about it.

It doesn't quite feel like flirting, but it's definitely *intense.*

Every time I glance up and catch those jade eyes on me from across the room, my heart skips.

I'm so ready for this day to be over.

After a few more yeas and nays, the meeting adjourns.

Thank God.

As I stand, a few more people give their welcomes and make small talk before I'm free.

The sunlight feels heavenly as I burst outside and take a deep, shaky breath of fresh air.

Only to stiffen when a warm voice purrs at my back.

"Are you all right, Miss Clarendon?"

I whip around to find Ulysses standing in the doorway behind me. He's so tall and he's got this odd way of standing out yet also blending into the background.

Also, he's *still freaking watching me.*

But there's concern in his eyes and his brows are drawn together.

I clear my throat, forcing another smile.

"I'm fine!" I insist. "I just didn't sleep well last night. I'm sure you can imagine... Oh, and I'm sorry if I made a rough impression today."

"Not at all. I expected you to be more upset, honestly, considering the whole—" He stops and waves a hand. "—the whole *situation.*"

I can't help a tired bark of laughter. "That's one way to put it."

"I try not to be insensitive." With an almost conspiratorial smile, he steps into the sun, the brilliance reflecting off his pale hair and casting his eyes in shadow. He offers me his arm. "Let me make up for the shock yesterday—and for meeting my parents. They're a bit much. I'll show you around the schoolhouse."

For a moment, I balk.

But there's nothing in his smile besides friendly reassurance.

Okay, okay.

I'm being paranoid and jumpy.

This is a good time to calm down and stop making a big deal out of everything.

So I slip my hand into Ulysses' arm and nod. "Thank you. Though I'm guessing in a town this size, there's not that much to show."

"You'd be right, but at least we can say we have *amazing* scenery for a walk." He leans toward me with a chuckle and tosses his head toward the plaza. "Right this way."

Ulysses leads me down the sidewalk of one of the broad paved streets, trees dotting the walk and the morning filled with crisp smells of late summer. Although now and then I hear car engines, lawn mowers, children playing, the sounds of shop doors opening and closing, laughter...

It's still so *quiet.*

Silent in a way that makes the day feel peaceful and slow beneath the cloudless blue shell of sky.

Ulysses points out the town as we walk, all the little shops selling everything from locally bottled wine to a pub he swears has the best cheese fondue east of the Rockies.

A little convenience store that closes at ten p.m.—so not that convenient.

The grocery store, the secondhand shop, the barber's.

Every store is a quaint thing that looks like it was plucked out of a doll village and sized up to make Redhaven.

He seems proud of his town. I guess that's a good sign.

There's a warmth to the way he speaks as he tells me about how the cheese shop on the corner has been owned by the same family for six generations.

I feel a little bad about being so on edge earlier.

Especially since he's stopped staring at me, and it's easier to relax.

The road ends at the school, opening up on a broad, grassy lawn shaded by pine and oak trees. The building is long and low with rows upon rows of windows against brick, topped with a mossy green roof and a playground off to the side.

A sign announces *REDHAVEN* on a bronze plaque. I blink as we stop outside the fence.

"This is the elementary school?"

"This is the school. Period." With an amused sound, Ulysses swings the gate open for me. "From kindergarten through high school, we grow up in these hallowed halls."

I eye him, half smiling. "You went to school here, huh?"

"Nah, my mother shipped me off to boarding school as soon as she could get rid of me. I spent most of my years abroad in Switzerland and Italy." He lifts his brows with a self-mocking little sniff. "You can't expect wealthy parents to actually *raise* their children, Miss Clarendon."

"Heaven forbid." I throw my hands up with a relieved laugh.

He's not as stiff as he seemed at first.

The air's easier between us as he gives me the tour.

Every school I ever visited in New York easily dwarfs this place.

There aren't many classrooms because there's not many classes.

I'll be teaching rotating kindergarten through fourth grade, scheduling my times around periods with teachers who handle things like PE, art, and electives that aren't under my umbrella.

The backbone of the school's C-shape is the 5-8 wing, and as Ulysses guides me through tiled halls, we're ambushed by a curvy woman with a messy ponytail of strawberry-blonde hair.

I barely glimpse her through the window in the door while she's settled at a table in yoga pants, cutting out bits of poster board. The instant she sees us, she's out the door, pulling me away from Ulysses with both hands.

"You're Delilah, right?" Bright, chirpy, excitable, her brown eyes lit. She's got a slight drawl that's not quite country and not quite East Coast, giving her voice a pleasant burr. "I'm Nora.

Nora Greenweather. I can tell you I've been looking forward to you for the longest time!"

I practically squeak, taken aback.

"Me?"

Ulysses starts to say something, but Nora shoots him an amused look. "Don't start. Not even a chance for you to roll out one of your lines, you devil." She leans into me, both hands grasping mine. "He's the town flirt. Watch out for this one." Then she squeezes my hands, grinning. "And yeah, we've all been waiting. Someone's gotta take care of the little ones, and I did double duty for the second half of the last spring semester. I'm not cut out to deal with them until they're old enough to take 'no' seriously. I don't know how you stand it."

It's a torrent of words, open and honest and sweet.

I smile.

"I love kids," I say. "There's just something about watching them start to develop their own personalities, and having the privilege of shaping that."

"Well, aren't you a sweet thing." She says it closer to *thang*. Her eyes soften. "I hope you won't let that whole crazy business scare you off. I'm still in shock—everybody is, really—but I'd like it if you stuck around. We don't usually get random bodies around here, I swear."

I snort. "Word travels fast."

"Faster than the speed of light. Them NASA scientists ever figure out how to harness the speed of a small-town rumor, we'll be on Pluto in a year." Nora laughs and finally lets go of my hands as she gives Ulysses a *look*. "You take good care of her, you hear?"

"Miss Greenweather," Ulysses says grandly, slipping an arm around my shoulders. "I'll gladly make sure Miss Clarendon has everything she could ever dream of."

* * *

BY THE TIME I finish the grand tour with the high school wing, I'm ready for a little alone time.

Everyone's been so nice. But I can only deal with people above the age of ten for so long before I need to escape and blow off some tension.

Kids make sense to me.

Kids are easy.

They're honest about what they want and free and open with their feelings. They're still too innocent to understand why people lie, cheat, and twist relations into such a tangled mess of hurt and misunderstandings.

For me, it's always been adults who are hard to understand.

The town's only gym seems like a great place to avoid other grown-ups for a while.

The nice thing about gyms is that everyone just minds their own business. The place can be packed, and I'll still feel completely alone.

I need that right now.

I never thought I'd get so addicted, so quickly, to the charm of small-town peace and quiet.

Sweet solitude.

And I really didn't need to worry.

I throw Ulysses a few excuses, swing by The Rookery to snag my gym bag, then cross the plaza to the single-room gym. There's no one there except a teenage girl behind the counter.

There's not much to the place at all. No surprise.

A row of treadmills, ellipticals, and other miscellaneous machines. There's a mirrored wall by the weight sets, a big flatscreen TV, and two locker doors on both sides of the stair climbers for men and women. They're all empty today as I change.

Even better.

The girl behind the counter is on her phone, twirling her hair like she's flirting with a special someone.

But as I step up, she offers me a smile, her blonde ponytail bouncing. "Welcome to *Work It!* Do you have a membership card?"

She knows I don't.

I feel like a dossier on me was passed around secretly before I even arrived in Redhaven.

"Not yet," I say, adjusting the strap of my bag and smiling. "But I'd be interested in getting one. What kind of plans do you have?"

She opens her mouth to give me a sales spiel, but stops as the door jingles again behind me. I glance over my shoulder and get an eyeful I need like a hole in the head.

Lieutenant Lucas damn Graves comes striding in, cockier than ever.

The last time I saw him, he was in uniform—dark navy blue bordering on black, crisply stitched, streamlined to make him look sleek and powerful and intimidating.

And yes, *obscenely sexual.*

Even if he acted like an elephant dick, there was a professional front behind the façade of the uniform.

Now, off duty, the man looks downright bestial.

He's a lion-man in his translucently tight white A-shirt and black track pants with their thin white racing stripes. They match the black stripes on his white tennis shoes.

He's built like a tank. At least six and a half feet tall, solid brick shoulders, arms as thick and hard as oak branches.

I can even see his chest and a thin nest of black hair showing in dark shadow through the shirt.

God help me.

Before, he was clean-shaven, but now he's sporting a proper five o'clock shadow.

His dark hair is messy, tossed to one side and falling into his eyes, turning them cat-green in their shadow.

One punishing arm flexes as he adjusts the heavy-looking bag over his shoulder.

Then he stops mid-stride as his gaze lands on me.

Just great.

I freeze.

My stomach flips with irritation, and damn him, his lips twitch in a subtle smirk, tossing my insides around again.

The girl behind the counter isn't nearly so dumbstruck.

She smiles brightly, her cheeks flushed pink. "Mr. Graves! Hi."

He nods at her, but those stark green eyes stay pinned to me.

"Afternoon, Trisha," he rumbles.

He doesn't even say hello.

Why can't I decide if that pisses me off or feels like a relief?

He just dips his head, lifting two fingers in a mocking salute before turning and strutting off with a prowling stride to the men's locker room.

I can't stop scowling at his back, pathetically speechless.

Yeah, I've got to find a better way to say *dick.*

I'm not even sure why he riles me up so much.

Probably that juvenile *Miss New York* nickname and the way he always shows up without warning. Or it's the laughably inappropriate way he got me to stop fixating on the dead girl by teasing me about sleeping on his sofa.

Or maybe it's just that he's so flipping tall.

I've been a short stack my whole life.

And I've had more than one person try to make me feel small, crowding me out of daring to take up space.

"...hello? Miss?"

Oh.

Trisha's talking to me.

My face goes hot and I whip my eyes back to her, clearing my throat. "Sorry. So, about those membership plans?"

It doesn't take long before I'm set up with a monthly trial plan. I'm almost shocked at how cheap it is when I'm used to NYC markups on everything.

I could've saved even more if I'd committed to a quarterly plan. But maybe I'm thinking about dead bodies, quietly wondering just what my limit is for how many I'm cool with before I panic and hightail it out of town.

Or I'm just being dramatic, and what's actually on my mind is tree-lined lanes and how nice it would be to jog down them at sunrise, no membership required.

Sighing, I do a quick five-minute set of stretches before I claim one of the treadmills with *House Hunters* on TV for company.

I've barely started a light jog when the men's locker room door swings open and Lucas Graves stalks back out, sans gym bag.

He takes one glance at me—a glance that lingers too long, making me nearly trip on my own feet—before he looks at the television.

Somehow, he switches the channel over to *Better Call Saul* before climbing on the treadmill next to mine and gliding into a steady, pounding pace.

Holy hell.

The man goes from nothing to a strong, violent run in under five seconds. Almost like a racehorse bursting out of the gate.

He runs for two solid minutes without even huffing.

This. Is. So. Bad.

My mind goes terrible places, wondering what else his body can do with gym-freak stamina like that.

"I was watching that, you know," I mutter when I can't stand it any longer.

He doesn't look at me, his mile-wide chest rising and falling in deep, steady breaths.

"So change it back. You've got thumbs, right?" His gaze stays on his digital readouts as he shrugs.

"Um, yes. I have thumbs. Very observant." Glaring, I manage to hold up a thumb instead of another middle finger salute. I'm being nice today.

I shake my head, ready for more of his crap, but apparently he's holding back too.

"So change it back," I mouth, scowling, but then slow the tread-mill and step off it.

I brace my burning feet on the floor for a second before I stomp over, grab the remote on a little console table under the TV, and flick the channel back to my show.

I don't even make it back to my machine before the sound changes, and Bob Odenkirk starts yelling at a couple cartel guys who look like they eat kittens for breakfast.

Yep.

Looks like I'm going to get arrested for assaulting a cop today.

I whip my head up, glaring at the TV, then at Lucas.

He's got his phone out, not even missing a stride as he taps his screen. I catch a glimpse of the Roku logo.

Oh, that absolute *jerk*. He's got an app synced to this TV, and he just—

Argh!

A little growl slips up my throat. Still gripping the remote, I punch the button back to *House Hunters*, staring at him pointedly the entire time.

He's still got his head bowed, his face unreadable as the TV changes again.

"Oops," he whispers. "Butterfingers."

"Butterfingers, my ass!" I hiss back, stabbing the button again. "Dude, do you mind?"

He spreads his hands.

With his long, easy stride, the motion makes the muscles in his waist pull dangerously tight against his A-shirt that's finally starting to darken with sweat.

"Don't know what's wrong with this damn thing," he lies. "It's busted today. Just keeps switching back on its own."

Right as he taps his phone again, watching me with a mock-innocent look.

Right on cue, the TV flicks back to his stupid suspense show despite me *mashing the button down* like my life depends on it.

"You don't know what's wrong with it, huh?" I can't believe I'm this annoyed and yet somehow smirking helplessly.

Idiot.

I jab the button again—really fast this time, stabbing it with my fingertip—just as he hits the button on his screen. The TV starts flickering back and forth like a psychedelic kaleidoscope of noise and color.

"Maybe your thumb's broken," I say. "Mine are working, last I checked."

He glances at his hand languidly then, lifting his thumb off his phone. "Must be. Would you look at that. It should stay now."

I snort and hit my channel again, shaking my head as I try to pick up the pace and try to have a normal workout.

I point two fingers at my eyes and then at him.

I'm watching you.

Is that thunder or is it a low rumble of laughter in his throat?

At least the channel stays as I pick up speed again.

I wonder how long it'll take before I'm too tired to fume over his shenanigans. And here I thought the kids would be the ones pranking me.

"You always watch shows about big houses nobody on a normal salary can afford?" he asks.

"Are you always this much of a judgmental prick?" I ask. I don't even bother keeping my voice down.

There's no one here but us and Trisha, and Trisha's not making any secrets about her eavesdropping.

"Only to the pretty girls," Lucas snaps without missing a beat.

I almost trip on the machine.

I have to grasp the bars to catch myself before I go flopping off the treadmill.

"Jeez. You really are shameless."

Lucas jogs on with a blank face, but his eyes give away everything, flashing amusement.

When he glances at me, I'm struck yet again by just how warm his eyes are compared to Ulysses.

It's weird how two people can have similar eyes, but what's inside them makes it night or day.

As the laughter fades from his eyes, his gaze sharpens. "Don't worry, New York. I'm just trying to be accommodating since you seem to enjoy being pissed at me so much."

I bare my teeth. "Don't. Not today, *Officer Dick*," I add under my breath.

"Officer Graves. Not Richard. My name's Lucas Graves, in case you forgot."

Holy hell.

"...you know exactly what I meant."

"Reckon I do, but wouldn't be polite to say it in a lady's company."

God.

That slow drawl of his is like molasses, sweetness and mockery melted together. And I don't know what to do with it, especially when he's still watching me with eyes that go right through me.

I scrunch my nose at him.

"I'm not a lady, and I'm not Miss New York. I've always been too short for the pageant circuit, anyway."

He snorts. "Who says that's why I'm calling you that?" But his undertone says that's exactly why he's calling me that, though it fades as he sobers. "By the way, I wanted to talk to you about that. New York, I mean."

I've only been half watching House Hunters with the world's most annoying man in my ear, but now he has my full attention, my run slowing to a speed walk. "What? Did you find something out about my ex?"

For a moment, there's just the pad of our footsteps against the treadmills, impacts alternating in rhythm.

Lucas frowns.

His hands settle on his grips like he needs support before he says what's next.

"Not necessarily anything to do with the girl," he says. "I did call him, though. Pretended to be a car warranty sales rep. You know, the usual scammy stuff. Makes it real easy to think up reasons to keep him talking."

I want to laugh, imagining how he must've pissed Roger off, but the nauseous feeling in the pit of my stomach won't let me. "He hates that stuff. Did he hang up on you?"

"Not before cussing up a hell of a storm. He sounded pretty agitated, and not just by me hounding him." He shakes his head. "Still, it kept him on the line long enough to try to get a trace on the call. Nothing too sophisticated—we're not the NSA here—but we've got a few apps that can help pinpoint locations." His eyes latch on and hold mine. "This time, I couldn't. He's wise to that stuff, I guess. Which means we don't know where he is, and the man must have a reason for hiding his whereabouts."

I suck in a breath and stumble so sharply I have to step off the belt.

"Wait, you... you think he's here?" My fingers dig into the grips as I stare at him.

"Can't say with confidence, Miss Clarendon. Could be he followed you, or could be he's somewhere else entirely." He taps the treadmill's interface and his steady run eases to a light jog, then to a halt as he turns to face me. "Can you think of anyone else he'd want to hide from?"

"Maybe," I say dubiously.

I hate the way my voice nearly breaks.

I don't want to be afraid of a creeper like Roger.

"He was really controlling. He always wanted to know everything I was doing every waking minute, but you can guess it didn't go both ways. He was pretty secretive about where he was whenever he wasn't with me. Sometimes I'd catch things, though. Matchbooks and cards from casinos and clubs."

Lucas' jaw tightens. "So, you're saying he might've had some gambling problems, then? Makes sense. Some asshole obsessed enough to control his girlfriend that way with stalker tendencies, it'd fit the profile with compulsive gambling in the mix.

Maybe he got in with some bad high rollers who might want to track him down."

I swallow hard. "So you think he's just laying low and it has nothing to do with me? Or he's getting out of town ahead of some mafia loan sharks or whatever and stalking me out here is a perfect excuse to leave?"

"Two good possibilities," Lucas admits. "It's also possible he's just a paranoid little shit and nothing's going on in his lonely-ass life."

Whoa.

I'm not expecting the sudden harshness in his tone or that shine in his stare.

He almost sounds jealous. Overprotective.

And I almost don't hate it.

"Well, okay." I lick my dry lips. "What happens next?"

"We stay vigilant and keep watching," he rumbles. "And you call me if anything out of the ordinary happens, New York. Don't hesitate. If I'm not in, you can trust my guys. We've got a damn good team out here, even if we're smaller than a wolf pack."

"Delilah," I say pointedly. "If you want me to call you, it's *Delilah.*" I force a weak smile. "*Not* Miss Clarendon. Definitely not New York."

"Delilah." He purrs my name deeply like the huge cat he is with his hot, raspy tongue.

Anyway.

I look away, smoothing my hair back from my sweat-dotted brow. "So, when we're talking out of the ordinary, do you mean things that go bump in the night or another dead body?"

"Either, or anywhere in between."

"Got it." I curl my hands tighter against the grips, staring at the screen on the treadmill. Suddenly running doesn't have much appeal when my heart keeps racing just fine on its own.

I take a minute to figure out how to ask the question burning at the back of my brain. "Did you find out anything else about her?"

Lucas heaves a deep, slow sigh. "I can't be disclosing case details, New York. You know that."

"Please." I'm so desperate I ignore the fact that he's still using that stupid nickname. "I know I didn't know her, but... I need to know."

He considers it gravely, rubbing his knuckles against his dark-shadowed jaw, raking them over faint stubble.

"There's not much to tell yet, honestly," he says. "Though I'm due on shift in a couple hours, and we might have more in from the coroner's office then. While we still don't have a positive ID on her, initial toxicology and examination indicates an overdose."

"Overdose? Oh, God." I slowly exhale until I feel deflated. "So she wasn't... she wasn't murdered?"

"Not that we can tell. As far as the chief is concerned, your house is cleared as a crime scene. We didn't find anything interesting on a full sweep. You can probably move in again soon— assuming you still want to. Can't blame you if you'd rather pitch a tent on the street than spend another second in that place after all that."

"I mean, that's not what I'm worried about. I'm fine at The Rookery." I shake my head. "But I still don't get it. If there's no foul play, then how did she end up there?"

"Most likely scenario?" Lucas glances over his shoulder toward Trisha, who's at least being a bit more subtle about watching us past her phone now. His voice drops as he looks back at me. "The girl was probably involved with the folks on the hill. Every so often, they throw these big lavish parties, and now and then the guests get up to a little of their own dirty recreation on the side. Wouldn't be surprised if she got herself high and wandered down to your house, found her way in somehow, then died there."

I blink. "The people on the hill—what hill? I don't—oh." When it hits me, I gasp. "That big house? You mean..."

"Yeah. The Arrendells," Lucas answers reluctantly, working his jaw.

Holy shit!

"The people who hired me," I rush out, eyeing him skeptically. "The people who told me during my interview they were looking for someone with *family values.*"

"Different families got different values." He shakes his head, watching me almost warily. "Maybe they got mixed up with the wrong people. Who the hell knows. A few bad errors in judgment, some shit nobody meant to happen, only it happened anyway. That's how it works sometimes."

I frown, starting to feel dizzy.

I'm having serious trouble reconciling any drug-fueled debauchery with the buttoned-down Ulysses Arrendell I met. Sure, he was a little too nice, but mostly he was just charming—even if the way he talks is a little odd. Too formal, I guess, the kind of speech you pick up when your parents ship you to crazy expensive boarding schools overseas.

Holding my tongue, I eye Lucas.

I don't know what to believe.

I don't know either of these men.

I don't know whether Lucas would lie to me for some reason, and I also don't know whether Ulysses would put up a charming front to hide the fact that his little party got a girl killed.

Then again, if I could trust first impressions, I'd have never dated Roger Strunk.

My silence must speak volumes because Lucas shrugs his broad shoulders. "Believe me, don't believe me, that's your choice. I'm just giving you a theory."

He powers up his treadmill again, settling back into that ground-eating run that tells me he's had training somewhere besides the police academy. I doubt small-town boot camp trains his kind of stamina.

But I don't say anything as I settle back into my own distracted jog.

The silence between us isn't what I'd call uneasy.

I can't block out his presence, and he's aware of me too.

It eats at me for the next five minutes, this steady tension that somehow feels like a truce, too.

Not just because he's killing my workout zen. But because he's been—I don't know, *decent* today.

Even if it's just doing his job and I don't know if I can trust him.

After a few more minutes running, pacing my steps to my thrumming heartbeat, I clear my throat and force myself to speak.

"I'm sorry for earlier." It feels like pulling teeth. I've always had trouble with apologies. That's why I have to make myself say them when it's truly necessary. "The other day. You were checking up on me and I was kind of a fire-breathing bitch. I'm sorry."

Now he does miss a beat, his sneakers squeaking before he recovers.

He slows and gives me a long, hard look. His perma-grumpy face softens into something handsomely understanding, almost graceful.

"Nobody's at their best with the shit you stumbled into," he says. "You didn't hurt my feelings one bit. I can recognize when someone's lashing out because they're in shock and not completely in control versus when they're a *real* asshole. Don't worry."

Smirking, I toss my ponytail back over my shoulder. "How do you know I'm not a real asshole?"

"I don't." He snorts loudly. "But if you are, New York, I reckon we might just get along."

"You reckon you can keep calling me that and not die, too?"

"I do, Miss Delilah." His eyes flash brighter.

Oh my God, no.

...I think we're having a moment.

"You're so ridiculous!" I shout. I can't help laughing, shaking my head.

At least now it's easier to breathe, even as I force my lungs to work.

I used to be a really crappy runner.

I'd always breathe through my mouth and wonder why I got so winded that my lungs gave up long before my body did. My mom taught me that I have to breathe through my nose, pace it, control it, and once I got that down, the rest comes easy. She learned that because she was a bad runner, too, for all the same reasons.

It's weird having so much in common with a parent you didn't know for most of your life.

But I guess blood runs thick and true.

Thinking about blood brings me back to a flash of scarlet, that poor girl—and my thoughts freeze in place. I stare down at the screen with my speed, my distance, my heart rate, and it's probably no surprise that whenever I think of that poor girl, everything ticks up.

"Lucas?" His name sticks in my mouth.

"Yeah?"

"Will you..." I bite the inside of my cheek. "Will you just keep me updated if you find out who she is? I just feel like I should know her name."

He lets out a hesitant sigh. "New York—"

"I know, I *know*." I close my eyes, cursing myself.

Why am I getting so attached? Why am I prying him, asking for information I can't have, letting this eat at me like acid?

"If the family doesn't want her name released, legally you can't, right? I get that. But if you can. If you can, please. I've decided to go back to the house soon. I could use the extra space and I don't want one rotten memory chasing me off. Also, I'm going to be living with her ghost." I pause, sighing before I say, "Shouldn't I at least respect her enough to know who she was?"

I feel him looking at me, cool and assessing, but I keep my eyes on the screen, the numbers.

"Okay, Miss Delilah. I'll do what I can," he says finally.

"Oh. Oh, thank you!" I cannot believe I'm smiling as hard as I am at this stubborn caveman with a badge.

Of course, he says nothing.

We just run on for a little while longer, silent, together and apart, each of us moving to the rhythm of our own thoughts.

IV: RED WITH ENVY (LUCAS)

*G*otta say, Delilah Clarendon's one peculiar girl.

Living with ghosts?

Then again, aren't we all?

I slouch down in the driver's seat of my patrol car, parked in my usual spot on the corner of the square. I'm keeping an eye on things over the top of my book.

The Great Alone by Kristin Hannah today.

I'm not picky about genre as long as the writing's good.

Only, I'm struggling to slip into the fine Alaskan drama and it's got nothing to do with the writing.

On the surface, today looks like any other.

Lazy afternoon light spilling through town, people strolling around running errands. The town square's the beating heart of Redhaven.

It's not unusual to see half the folks who live here passing through—and if a mild-mannered police officer wants to keep an eye on things, it's the best place to perch.

What I'm watching is The Rookery.

Delilah hasn't come out today, not while I've been on shift.

I don't know why that bothers me, besides the general concern for how she's holding up.

She's not a suspect.

A nagging voice in the back of my head wonders if she should be.

If I let a pretty face and her damsel-in-distress defensive vibe cloud my common sense.

It'd be pretty damn clever.

Skip town, run away from the Big Apple before she gets pegged for murder. Bring the body with her. Strip the ID and dump the girl's corpse in the house before calling it in and claiming she found Jane Doe there.

And here I fell for it because I just wasn't seeing her as conniving enough.

Not when all I see is another woman caught in an impossible predicament, proud and stubborn and refusing to see it.

My first thought wasn't suspicion.

Maybe I can save this one.

That's what I thought instead.

Fuck.

Delilah's nothing like Celeste, and she made it crystal clear she doesn't need any saving. I'd almost think she was too calm at the crime scene.

Except I know she wasn't, deep down.

All those little telltale markers of fear and sharp words that made me wish I could hold her trembling fingers and banish the stark fear in her eyes.

Besides, I'd like to think I've been at this long enough to be a mighty good judge of character.

That girl's guarded.

Not guilty.

She's also currently emerging from the sliding double doors of our local hardware store, which explains why I never saw her leave The Rookery. From the fat bags she's hauling, she's been up and running errands since before my patrol shift even started.

Damn.

Also, she's got company.

Double damn.

Ulysses Arrendell hovers like a hawk as he helps grab several bulging bags from her hands with a warm smile. Together, they make their way to the Kia parked across the square at The Rookery.

She's smiling back, too.

Laughing, shaking her head like he's the harmless town ham and not a walking scandal waiting to happen.

Is that a hint of jealousy?

Fuck, yes.

I also don't care that it shouldn't be searing my blood.

I'm eyeballing the pretty boy weirdo fit to break my face.

Don't like *that*.

Don't like that shit one bit.

It's not my place, I know. She's the new girl and she's gonna meet people, make friends. If it were anyone else except this fresh-faced vampire fuck boy—

Fuck!

The growl I'm holding in scrapes my throat.

So does the urge to dart out of the patrol car and zoom over for a little talk.

No abusing the badge for personal reasons, of course.

But is it really personal?

Or is it my cop instinct screaming *danger* at the top of its lungs?

Even if I'm the only crazy asshole who thinks so.

If I shared my thoughts about the Arrendells with anyone else, they'd send me straight to a shrink, or maybe put me on leave.

I come two seconds away from giving in.

Two damn seconds from making up a half-cocked reason to walk over there and grunt hello, even if it's just to tell Delilah what she already knows: I have no new intel on the case, and I probably won't for a while.

Even if I really want to remind pretty boy I'm there.

Luckily, my phone saves me from making a bad decision, vibrating violently on the dash. A quick glance at the caller ID says it's the coroner's office.

Well, shit.

Maybe I'll have some new info after all.

It probably says a lot that they're calling me and not Chief Bowden.

I snag my phone and swipe it. "Lieutenant Graves."

"Lucas?" The friendly voice of Dr. Nicholas Morales comes over the line. We don't work with him much, small place like this with no active murder cases, but he's always professional and a little chatty when we cross paths. "I hope I'm not interrupting anything? We've got her." I sit up sharply in my seat as he finishes. "We've got a positive ID and we've figured out the cause of death."

* * *

EMMA SANTOS.

Hours later, I still can't get that name out of my head.

Emma Santos of Los Angeles, California. Only twenty-two.

Hell of an age to die.

I'm off street patrol and back at the office, closing out my day by once again stealing my captain's desk—this time to work on my case reports. Her name is right there on the top of the page, prints of my crime scene photos clipped on top. Got the autopsy report from Morales via email, too, along with a few photos.

Preliminary toxicology results confirmed.

Drug overdose. Cocaine.

Enough blow in her system to drop a bison. It just stopped her heart cold, right there on Delilah's shiny new floor.

I gnaw the tip of my pen, staring down at the pages.

Damn, this doesn't feel right.

On the surface, it makes perfect sense. It's an easy story.

The younger Arrendell brat throws another private charity gala, bringing in outsiders from God only knows where. Then this girl shows up with her junk or gets it from a coked-up stranger, goes a little too hard, gets herself way too high, and stumbles down the hill to Delilah's house, barges in, collapses and dies when the drugs hit her heart.

I can even picture the path she'd have taken. The mansion looms over where the streets blend into the forest on that side of town, and there are a few spots that make for good hiking trails.

Wouldn't be hard to navigate even if it was a dark, steep, strange place.

But what the hell was she doing here from LA?

Oh, and she was wearing *heels.*

If that's our story, then technically it'd be a suicide by overdose, accidental or not.

The problem is, it's too easy.

Plus, there's the fact that Delilah said she saw somebody running away the minute she pulled up to the house. Maybe someone who knew that body was in there and wanted to cover it up.

Hell, maybe somebody who *put* that body there in the first place.

I've been thinking about that ever since she told me about glimpsing someone on the property, and that instinct drags me to a theory that just keeps getting stronger.

Technically, Emma Santos' case should be cut and dry.

Nothing left to do but track down her next of kin, notify them, and officially declare this an accidental death by OD.

Only, the dead girl's heels are stuck in my brain like pointed daggers.

Stumbling down from that big old house through the woods wouldn't have been easy in those shoes—not without breaking an ankle first—especially in a drug haze.

Yeah, fuck it.

I'll leave the case open a little while longer.

Do a little digging of my own.

Keep things quiet for now.

I type a note in the digital case file and leave a matching sticky note on top of the printout in the folder.

Unsolved. Investigating potential theories, suspects. Maintain confidentiality and wait to notify next of kin.

I'll have to get the captain or Chief Bowden to sign off on that, but I doubt that'll be a problem.

My hunches rarely miss the mark and they know it.

I should be getting home now, though. Maybe swing by The Rookery to check on Miss New York. Something tells me to keep a closer eye on her.

That clingy ex of hers could be a problem in more ways than one, even if he's not connected to Emma's murder.

Plus, I don't like the fact that Ulysses Arrendell won't stop orbiting her. I need to question him about Emma, too, even if that's like talking to the wall.

If she was one of his dates, sugar baby, evening fling, that's important. Especially if he knows which one of his guests could've supplied her with cocaine.

With the way the Arrendell brothers jet around in high society with models and actresses, it's plausible. Doesn't make him culpable.

I'm sure he'll wiggle out of any drug charges by claiming it was all her. That they were just having a nice little how-do-you-do when she broke out the hard drugs.

Still.

It'll paint a clearer picture of what the hell happened.

Maybe it'll even help me get over this urge to pick him up and chuck him as far away from Delilah Clarendon as possible.

Something ain't right about that man.

Hell, the whole family.

Trouble is, big money helps them be discreet and bribe their way into hearts and minds, throwing around fat donations everywhere and aligning themselves with just the right causes so the world lines up to kiss their rich asses.

The most you hear are rumors and gossip and conspiracies that make them out to be the spiritual heirs to the Marquis de Sade. Thrilling dungeons, orgies, mock human sacrifices, that kind of thing.

Nothing realistic enough to put any stock in.

Definitely nothing you can prove.

The tabloids come calling every year and they've never turned up anything but breathless whispers.

All word of mouth, threads by people acting like teenagers on Twitter—if they aren't really teens to start with.

I think the bastards like it.

The imaginary scandals give their reputation a touch of naughty excitement that makes every single girl—and a few not so single ladies—shiver a little when they're in town. That's what the brothers are after more than anything. More bad boy cred.

Lord knows the Arrendells never invite any locals to those all-night soirees.

Anyway, whoever they want to fuck in their little leather dungeons is *their* business.

I don't care about that.

I care about the people they hurt and sweep under the rug.

I care about the people I've lost because of them.

I can't prove shit. *I can't.*

I got nothing. Not even a body.

But I promise you, no matter how crazy it sounds, they fucked me over.

Once upon a time, Montero Arrendell killed my sister.

What kind of sons do you think a man like that raises?

Snarling, I force my mind off this morbid track before it can drag me down memory lane, save the last of my work, and lunge out of the chair.

On my way out, I blow Mallory a kiss that always makes her laugh and say my goodbyes. She waves me off, fixated on her phone with a dreamy look while some Korean guy in a suit gives her the flirtiest grin.

Weird game.

My thoughts are still on Delilah, though.

Wondering if she'll chase me off like my tail is on fire, those star-filled blue eyes flashing with pure prideful spite and a flash of indigo.

It almost makes me smile.

Damn, I'm screwed up.

And who else should I see when I step out of the station but New York herself, her Kia cruising down the street with boxes piled so high in the back I'm sure she can't see out the rearview mirror.

It's worse than before.

Looks like a hell of a lot more than just the flimsy stack of moving boxes she showed up with.

I ought to pull her over and give her a friendly warning about that.

Instead, I slip into my cruiser and pull out after her.

There are only a few cars between us, a couple soccer moms in almost identical RAV4s—one in misty sea green, one in misty sea blue—passing by with their back seats full of kids.

I'm probably being goddamned obvious about following her, but maybe the soccer moms are blocking her view—or maybe she hasn't caught sight of me past those boxes, despite the tanned, tattooed arm I see leaning out of the open driver's side window as she angles her head out to squint at the side mirror like that's going to make up for it.

That how they drive where you're from, New York? I wonder.

Once we hit the town square, the soccer moms peel off to the left along the roundabout, while I hang a right and stop behind Delilah just as she parks in front of The Rookery. She's already climbing out by the time I cut the brakes and open the door, pulling the back hatch of her Kia Sportage open.

And unleashing a total avalanche.

Fuck!

Yelping, she covers her head as several big boxes topple over on her. Cursing up a blue streak, I launch myself out of my car and push her aside with my shoulder, slamming my back against the wall of cardboard and catching it with my shoulders.

I get bonked in the back of the head with a sharp corner for my trouble, but luckily whatever's in it doesn't hurt.

Much.

Delilah stumbled to one side, her swirl of dark hair lashing around her. Now she straightens up, just blinking at me.

She looks at me first before she looks back at my patrol car, her expression red with one question.

Where the hell did you come from?

"Um," she fumbles awkwardly. "You okay?"

"Not gonna have 'falling box' on my death certificate," I say. "But if you could straighten this mess right out, please, ma'am. I'm not cut out to be Atlas."

There's a suspicious little twitch to her lips. Like she wants to laugh but she won't give me the satisfaction.

She does hurry to reach around me, rebalancing the boxes, standing up on her toes to shove them back as far as she can until the weight eases off me.

This close, it's impossible not to notice how *tiny* she is.

It's easy to forget. Her bold personality takes up a lot of space, daring you to find her small and frail, but in reality she's just a kitten—more legs than anything.

Legs and the kind of round, curving hips that could fit just right in a man's hands.

My hard-on loves the image.

She's almost pressed against me, wedged in tight.

Fuck, I can feel her warmth.

Under that hard exterior, she radiates a soft heat, making

my skin prickle as I watch how the dragon coiling over her shoulder stretches with each motion, the way she sinks her teeth into her lower lip in focus. It highlights that perfect round little bud where the bow of her smile meets in the middle.

And god*damn*, does she smell good today.

Something fruity, sweet and light—pear, I think, and a touch of something floral. This heated scent that's all insufferable woman.

The way it hits me nearly knocks my legs out from under me, my knees going weak just as my gut tightens.

What the *fuck?*

Now is not the time.

Not when she's either a potential suspect or a potential stalker victim, or worse.

Dammit, man.

Screw your fucking head back on.

My head's listening.

My cock sure as hell ain't.

It's a small relief when she steps back, giving me an odd look before murmuring, "Should be safe to let go now."

I ease away, glad when nothing else comes tumbling down. "You trying to get all of this out, or anything specific?"

"Just a few little things. The electric hot pot, the toiletries in this bag here—" She reaches past me and snags a bloated plastic bag sporting the logo for a little locally owned bed and bath boutique that prides itself on handmade soaps and fragrances. Then she snags something else, but I don't get to see what it is before it hits the ground.

A slender box busts open.

Out rolls a purple fucking vibrator.

I must be grinning like a lunatic.

Delilah stares in horror, her eyes wide and glassy. She's just waiting for me to skin her alive with all the smart-assed remarks hanging on my tongue.

"Um..." she stammers, frozen in place, straining to clear her throat.

"You dropped this," I growl, forcing back every last shitty, teasing comment I want to make.

I just sweep down, pick it up along with the box, and pass them back to her.

Don't know how I ignore the fact that this could've been inside her days ago. I don't have enough wits to look closely and figure out if it's brand new.

Her brows almost fly right off her face.

I'm not sure who's more surprised that I'm skipping out on giving her hell about it.

Pity.

Still, my eyes linger on the toy as she brushes her long hair back from her blushing face and shoves it back into the bag. "Um, if you wouldn't mind getting the hot pot? I don't want to knock anything else over trying to get at it..."

Just like that, we pretend to have a normal interaction.

I'm not daydreaming about her pressing that little bullet between her legs and coming fireworks.

She's not flushing a dozen kinds of red, knowing that *I* know what she fucks herself with.

I'm not mentally counting a hundred ways I could make her come so much harder.

I half expect her to rip my head off just for staying quiet—and for being tall enough to reach the top of her stack.

"Since you asked so nicely. Glad you saved the bigger armful for me." I smirk at her slit-eyed *fuck-you* look. Then I catch the box with the hot pot and tuck it under my arm. "Anything else, boss lady?"

She snorts. "No. I don't think so."

She loops her bag over her arm and stretches up on her toes to grab the Kia's hatch, giving me a view of her tanned stomach as her shirt lifts. All while the thin tank top pulls just a little too tight against her breasts.

Stop frigging looking.

I damn near have to grab my own head and twist around to jerk my gaze away, looking at the fence for the B&B instead while she slams the hatch shut.

"Lead the way," I say.

"You don't have to," Delilah protests. "The box isn't that heavy. I can carry it from here. I just couldn't *reach* it."

"Then how're you going to open the door to your room?" I shrug. "Like you said. It's not that heavy. I've got it."

"There's this thing called a floor, Officer. You can set stuff down to free your hands for things like, oh, keys," she says in her most sarcastic tone.

"You think you're funny? There's something called muscle so you don't have to waste time."

"Whatever you say, Hercules." She rolls her eyes and nods, smiling all the while.

I don't like the little pang that shoots through me. Because her smile came a lot easier when Ulysses Arrendell was helping her out.

Is that why I'm all goddamned prickly with venom?

I'm nursing a crush like a damn boy who got a peek in the girl's locker room, and now I'm getting all jealous 'cause she likes the dude who smiles at her instead of the jackass who pulls her pigtails?

Grow the hell up, man.

Blame the Emma Santos case for demolishing my head—or that purple little rocket I bet makes her a screamer.

She turns to lead me inside the gate, up the walk, and into the cool shaded interior of the B&B. We trudge upstairs to her room. There's a second of hesitation before she unlocks the door with another guarded expression.

What does she see when she looks at me?

I've never met a girl who's so hard to read.

So hard to know if she hates me constantly, likes me for a minute every two hours, or just feels completely indifferent.

At least I can tell when I'm irritating the hell out of her.

I can't help it. I'm not good at small talk.

It's either straight facts or I find a way to fill the silence with a dumbass joke, but I guess some folks don't like that small-town sense of humor.

She doesn't stop me from following her inside.

The room's a suite, decorated cottage style with ruffles and doilies everywhere in Janelle's homey style. The door leading into the bedroom is closed but the living and kitchen area look pretty comfortably lived in.

I set the box down on the polished wood dining table. "Looks like you're half settled in. You staying a bit longer before moving on to the house?"

Delilah vanishes into the bathroom, disappearing with a switch of her hips and a flick of her hair.

Her voice floats back with the rustling bag.

"Just for a day or two, I guess," she says. "Ulysses offered to get the house cleaned again for me, and he said he'll help me move in."

Fuck, fuck, also, *fuck.*

There's no stopping the growl that boils up my throat, sharp and sudden and vibrating.

Delilah's head pokes out from around the doorframe. She blinks at me.

"What was *that?*"

"Nothing," I mutter, zipping my damn mouth shut.

I do not need to be wondering why that Arrendell boy is pushing so hard to get close to Delilah.

Should be obvious, anyway.

She's a gorgeous woman. She's new. That makes her exciting.

Fortunately, I doubt she's his type.

I've seen more than one Hollywood actress disappear inside that big damned mansion, gliding up the winding lane up the hill in their cars with blackout windows. The Arrendells rub elbows with money and fame. Women who wear dresses that cost more than Delilah will make in her life as a teacher, just to slum around for the weekend at some rich asshole's palace.

A tough little New York brawler girl like Delilah?

Nah.

Not unless Ulysses is in it for the challenge—now there's an ugly thought.

It just pisses me off more.

Imagining him working her over like a conquest, then tossing her aside like a piece of fucking trash when he 'wins.'

I shouldn't be here.

I did my duty, brought her things up, and now I'm just hovering at her kitchen table while she saunters out of the bathroom, this time minus the shopping bag.

She stops with her hands on her hips.

"So. Anything new with the case? There's a cold beer in it for you." Her indigo-blue eyes drift over me. "I mean, you look like a beer guy. Stout, am I right?"

I raise a brow.

"You sure you're not a cop yourself? Good call." Still, there's something hiding behind her sardonic tone and her wry look. Something troubled that makes me frown. "You're invested in this, aren't you?"

Damn right she is, the cop in me says. *She's probing you to see if you've figured her out yet.*

I ignore that voice.

This job teaches you to be suspicious, sometimes for all the wrong reasons. You sink into that mentality too hard and soon every interaction, every relationship, becomes us vs. them, with us or against us.

That's how you wind up hurting people without meaning to if you can't control it.

That's who I never want to be.

"Wouldn't you be, in my situation?" Delilah shrugs stiffly.

"Yeah, but it's more than that," I say. "C'mon, New York.

Forget the beer. How 'bout I trade you an answer for an answer? You tell me why, and I'll tell you what I can."

Why do I feel like I'm looking in a mirror?

Her walls rise instantly, this quiet discomfort like she's in pain at the thought of being vulnerable.

Shit.

Maybe I hide it better behind a little sarcasm, deflecting the intimate questions. I know what it's like to fear people getting close enough to actually *know* you.

So why the hell does that make me want to know her more?

She turns her face away, staring at the sunny window on the far side of the room with its plush blue-upholstered window seat, the same little nook where I've seen her curled up before. Doesn't seem like she's really seeing it, though.

After a minute she says, "Back in New York, people die every day. Nameless. Unloved." Her face is expressionless, but her voice is raw emotion. Soft, heavy, lost, and sorrowful. "It's such a beautiful city, but there's so much death. So much *indifference*. I hate it, Lucas. I hate seeing lives thrown away every day, and people shrugging it off because that's just how it is. If I could change one thing about the world, it's that. Give everybody someone who loves them enough to come claim their body if the worst ever happens."

Ah, hell.

No wonder it's hurting her so much, seeing that girl dumped on the floor with no one coming to say they knew her.

"Did you lose someone like that?" I venture.

"No. Not really." Her mouth creases in a bitter, self-mocking smile. "I'm sure I sound dramatic, right? But I can't help thinking that before I found my mother... She was all alone. If I hadn't gone looking for her, then one day my mom would have died like that. Alone. Anonymous. No one to claim her. And I'd have never known her."

I don't understand.

"What do you mean you found her?"

Those are the magic words.

Delilah doesn't say anything.

If I thought her expression was closed off before, it's a fortress now, sealed tight behind a cynical quirk of her lips.

She moves quickly to the little fridge in the kitchenette. Her long hair grabs my attention, this feathery mass pouring down her back. I wonder how long she's been growing it out.

It's enough to distract me from realizing what she's doing until she's pulled out two bottles of our very own local Red House Breweries stout.

I'm almost impressed when she twists the caps off with her bare hands—no bottle opener needed—then thunks one down on the table in front of me before taking a swig from her own.

She exhales as she lowers the bottle.

"Your turn." She points at one of the empty chairs around the table. "Sit. Drink your beer. Talk to me like a normal human being."

Damn her.

I think if I smile right now, I might be the next Redhaven homicide case, so I hold it in.

"Yes, ma'am."

I sit and take a pull off the bottle.

The beer's good. Thick, dark, and foamy with a hint of cocoa sweetness.

I linger over a few sips, watching her, turning my thoughts over to figure out what I can slip her when I've still got so many doubts of my own about this case.

"The county coroner IDed her off dental records," I say. "It took a while since he had to do a national search. She's from Los Angeles. Emma Santos is the name. She's twenty-two and an Instagram model. Toxicology found a big damn mess of cocaine in her system. Enough to kill several people. She died of an overdose. Stopped her heart cold." I take a long pull off my beer, waiting for her reaction. "Rules out foul play, at least."

That last fragment of suspicion quiets when she doesn't

betray a hint of relief, or any delayed reactions that say she's schooling herself so she doesn't betray any prior knowledge.

Mostly, she looks confused—and worried.

"...I just don't get it. How did a model from LA end up in the backwoods of North Carolina?"

"That, Miss Delilah," I say around another swig, "is the million-dollar question. Especially since there's only one group of people in Redhaven known for rubbing elbows with models and actresses."

Her brows wrinkle. "Let me guess, the Arrendells? But if she overdosed on her own, they're not liable for any charges, are they?"

"No. I have to wonder why Ulysses didn't mention anything, if he knew her. He's the only one of the brothers who's been in town recently."

"Are you going to ask him about it?" Her lips purse.

"Him and his old man, yeah. Montero Arrendell has certain *tastes*."

I don't mention that Delilah is a pretty good match when it comes to the types of women Montero keeps around.

"Hmmm." Her mouth twists. "So it may not have anything to do with Ulysses at all?"

There it is.

That bristling irritation, that spark of jealousy, that fear that she might be relieved that her pretty boy white knight just might be clean.

I need to get this shit under control, stat.

She's not fucking mine.

She's not even someone I know with more than passing interest in a nasty death case, so I'd better get my goddamned focus back now.

She doesn't need me to rescue her.

Not from Ulysses Arrendell and not from anything else.

I'm as neutral as possible when I say, "Until I dig up more, I'd advise you to be a little wary of any strangers in town."

Delilah blinks before she offers me her familiar sad smile again, the one that makes my heart ache for her even if I can't quite put my finger on why. "But everyone's a stranger to me. I'm new to Redhaven."

"Then maybe you ought to be wary of everyone, Miss Delilah."

V: RUBY RED (DELILAH)

ou know what's annoying?

I should be thinking about my first day of classroom prep the minute I wake up.

But my brain is stuck on Lucas flipping Graves.

I'm still stuck on last night, everything he told me about Emma Santos and being wary of strangers. Plus, everything I told him about me.

After we finished talking, we just sat there together, drinking our beers in this comfortable silence that only weirded me out because it felt too easy.

It *should've* been uncomfortable, and it wasn't.

It was like that peaceful stillness I only experienced for the first time in my life a few days ago—only this time, I wasn't alone.

Who knew the most annoying man alive could make me feel safe?

Who knew we could just talk, enjoy a few drinks, and just *be?*

When he finished his beer, he got up and left. One nod, a wave of one large hand, a lingering glance from feral green eyes that hid whatever he was really thinking.

Then he was gone into the night.

Nope.

Not thinking about this today—or him.

I've got the keys to the school and a whole free day, so I'm going to scope out my classroom, tidy up a bit, and do a little shopping before the real work begins.

So I shower off, dress light and casual, and head out, stopping by the mini-mart first for a few cleaning supplies.

Good thing I saved my summer tips from part-time shifts at Mom's diner. You have no idea how many school supplies wind up coming out of teachers' pockets.

It's a short trip to the tree-shaded school. From the scattering of cars in the faculty lot, I guess a few other staff had the same idea.

I tie my hair up in a loose bun and head up the walk to unlock the main entrance.

When I get there, the door won't budge.

Ugh.

I fit my key into the lock and twist hard, but the latch doesn't slide a millimeter.

The whole thing feels jammed.

Frowning, I try it again.

Again.

God, what now?

Am I made of bad luck or is Redhaven just the Twilight Zone where nothing is ever predictable?

I wonder if Ulysses gave me the wrong key. Was there some mix-up when they copied it? Am I doing something wrong or—

"Here."

A familiar voice growls over my shoulder—gruff, deep, drawling with that hint of sweet molasses—just as a looming shadow falls over me.

There's no helping how my heart thumps as I turn, backing against the door.

It's just nerves.

Everything in this town makes me jumpier than a grasshopper.

Totally nothing special about the sight of Lucas Graves standing over me, powerful and sleek in his uniform, this giant prowling beast with jade eyes and a rare hint of a lazy smile.

His gaze feels almost friendly and teasing, falling to the keys in my hand.

I just notice I'm clutching them defensively, their sharp edges bristling between my knuckles.

"Mind if I take those?" he asks, holding out his hand. "The door sticks. You gotta work it, jiggle it just right. Let me show you."

My brain goes to horrible, innuendo-filled places.

I eye him before I reluctantly hand over the keys. "...what are you even doing here?"

What I really mean is, how did he conveniently happen to be right here, right when I needed him when I was trying so hard *not* to think about him?

"Before you even ask, no, I'm not following you."

He flashes me a look that makes my face burn. It's like he can read my mind.

He certainly stole a lifetime of dirty thoughts yesterday during that mortifying minute when my little toy was out in the open.

I'm still amazed I didn't shrivel up and die.

And I'm more stunned he had the restraint and the courtesy not to go full raging jackass. The man saved his reputation and saved me from a little cell. I would've punched this cop without hesitation if he took his chance to humiliate me.

But he didn't.

And that has me feeling more pleasantly uncertain about Lucas Graves than ever.

With a stifled grumble, I step aside so he can reach the door.

He fits the key to the lock too perfectly—and before he turns it, he grips the knob, lifting it sharply. He pulls it in with a little tug that makes the door rattle in the frame.

I watch the muscles in his forearm flex, straining all the way up to the cuffed sleeve of his sharply tailored navy-blue uniform shirt.

The door swings open a second later like it obeys his touch.

He releases the handle, then drops the keys into my outstretched palm.

"Way to show me up." I try to sound playful so he doesn't catch the admiration bristling behind my annoyed tone.

"It's what I do, Miss New York. Just pull it in, lift, and you're good to go," he says. "And to answer your question, Captain Faircross sent me out here to talk to the principal. Somebody's gotta handle crossing guard duty and school security for the coming year. We try to plan assignments around patrol shifts."

A little pang strums my heart.

So, he wasn't here for me.

Why isn't that a bigger relief?

I curl the keys against my palm and narrow my eyes. "School security even here? I didn't see any metal detectors."

Shame.

So much for hoping I'd run far enough away from schools built like prisons. Metal detectors everywhere, wanding students down, mandatory drills preparing students for the worst, and everyone breathlessly praying it never happens.

Lucas gives me a long look as grave as his name. "We're not quite there yet. If I have my way, we never will be."

He steps inside then and waves goodbye.

Leaving me looking after him, watching the way his powerful frame moves with a certain swagger—and a certain awareness, too, I think.

Almost like he knows how to handle all two hundred pounds of muscle with poise, harnessing his power like the fine-tuned machine he is.

The hyperprotective edge in his words when he made that

last comment about guarding the kids sends a shiver up my spine. I just have one question.

How big is a giant's heart?

* * *

I AM DIRTY, sweaty, and sore as hell.

But I'm also smiling until it hurts.

It's been a good day.

A little meeting with the principal helps me settle in. It turns out I'd met him at the town assembly without realizing it.

Scott Archer. Late fifties, balding, friendly eyes, and a fatherly smile.

He showered me with kind words and questions as we talked about lesson plans and told me I could come to him with any problems.

He left me feeling better after my first few surreal days in Redhaven. Just a nice slice of the ordinary to remind me why I came here in the first place and that I'm actually *happy* to be starting my first job as a teacher, mysterious dead girl aside.

So by the time I started cleaning my space, I was basically Snow White. Whistling while I work, giving the whole neglected old classroom a good spit and polish until it shines.

Leaving the windows open brings in a pleasant late summer breeze, already tinged with that hint of autumn crispness.

By afternoon, I have help.

Nora drops in and picks up a bottle of disinfecting wipes without even being asked. Next thing I know, we're chatting away while we scrub.

I think I've made my first true friend in Redhaven.

Lucas doesn't count.

The man *bothers* me, presses buttons I don't want to admit I have, and I still can't put my finger on why.

I don't count Ulysses either. He may be friendly enough, but I don't call someone who signs my paycheck and owns my house a *friend*.

Nora, though, she's great company. After our cleaning jam, we stroll down the street to a cute little café with outdoor seating and one of the most amazing mocha latte milkshakes I've ever tasted. Something they proudly advertise as made with blonde roast beans from a shop I've never heard of called The Nest in Heart's Edge, Montana.

Nora leans across the table, just as disheveled as I am, her eyes glittering over the rim of her massive mug.

"You didn't hear it from me," she says, "but little Carly Hansen's dad likes to get handsy with anyone in a skirt ever since his divorce. So don't go wearing anything above knee-length for a parent-teacher conference."

"Oh." My eyes widen. "I'm actually surprised the dress code isn't pure Amish for a town like this."

"Hey, we're not *that* backward. A little rustic, sure, but we keep up with the times." She laughs. "Besides. Lucia and Montero set the dress code. I think Montero might start whining if the skirts ever got too long."

I stare at her for a second.

"Everything I hear about them makes them sound like something out of *The Great Gatsby*." I shake my head. "Is every small town a scandal magnet? We've got old money with good intentions and bad habits, a grabby single dad, and—did you say it was Rachel Black's mother who's a kleptomaniac?"

"Rachel *White*. Rachel Black's mother is the one who stabbed her hubby in the foot with a fork because he was staring at the neighbor girl in a bathing suit." Nora giggles. "What's hilarious is that their marriage has never been stronger since."

I burst out laughing. "God, that's funny. Every girl needs a man who'll wise up after you stab him."

True story, even if I mostly mean stabbing with my tongue.

I'm not violent. *I swear.*

"So, you're saying there's no one in the picture?" Nora leans across the table with an accusing smile. "No one you even have your eye on, girlie?"

"I've only been here for a few days and half of them have been spent worrying about a dead girl." I offer a dry smile. "Dating isn't exactly at the top of my list, Nora."

"Oh, yeah. Of course. After something so crazy, I don't blame you for not even thinking about the gorgeous men who've been hanging all over you since you showed up." With that, leaving my mouth hanging open, Nora grins wickedly and pops out of her kitschy iron chair and pats my shoulder. "But I need to go let my own gorgeous boys hang all over me, actually. My husband never burps the twins right, so I should be getting home. Let's do this again soon."

"Okay." I swallow a million protests building up in my throat and force a smile. For some reason, I'm not ready to be alone. "Will you be around the school tomorrow?"

"Every day until we start. There's always so much to do. See you there?"

"Absolutely."

I prop my chin on my knuckles and watch her walk away. I think I could like her a lot, and she's definitely helping me feel more at ease.

Like Redhaven could become my new normal.

Like I could shake off all the initial horror and freakiness and eventually call this place home.

Eventually.

That wouldn't be so bad, would it?

I linger at the café a little while longer, watching as the traffic clears out and the sunset fades into twilight.

The streetlamps switch on like fireflies around the town square. They're electric, but made to resemble old-timey glass-globed gaslights.

I smile.

Out here, I'm surrounded by people, their quiet chatter, and the cool evening breeze. But it's still so quiet compared to the New York bustle I'm used to.

I think I can even make out a few chirping crickets and a distant owl calling.

I'm so relaxed I almost don't ping on something that should set every hair on my body on end—a dark shadow moving across the town square, too close to my car.

I almost missed it in the deepening night, but no.

No, there's someone there. A tall male shape?

I jump to my feet with a snarl.

Stupid Lucas Graves.

As if him showing up at the school to rescue me from a finicky door was just a coincidence.

Like hell.

I grumble and stalk back inside the café just to cool down, before I fly out there and make a liar of myself and end up getting pretty dang *violent*, after all.

The last thing I need are more strange men shadowing my every move.

Yes, I get that he's a cop.

Yes, he's probably got good intentions.

But he also slides under my skin way too effortlessly and he's squatting in my head, rent free.

I order another frappe shake to go, counting to one hundred under my breath until my blood pressure drops, then thank the barista and turn to leave.

Then someone pulls the door open from outside just as I'm pushing through it, and I'm yanked off my feet.

I smack right into a warm, hard chest.

Or not so warm anymore, considering I lose my grip on my shake and all sixteen ounces of sugary coffee splashes all over the stranger.

Spluttering, I shove back, swiping at my face. "Oh my God, I'm sorry. I didn't—"

My tongue locks up when I see who's wearing my drink.

NICOLE SNOW

Go ahead. Guess.

He stands there with a dead expression, the front of his tight grey t-shirt soaked down to the waist of his jeans, specks of whipped cream in his glossy black hair, more froth dripping off his jaw from the tip of a chiseled nose.

Blinking slowly, he swipes his thumb over a dollop of whipped cream along his cheekbone and then licks it off.

I didn't know a tongue could be so lazy and so obscene simultaneously.

"Thanks for the free drink, New York," he says flatly. "Hell of a way to deliver it, though."

And I crumple halfway to the ground in a laughing fit, clutching my aching sides.

His eyes dip down, waiting patiently until I'm over my little manic fit.

That's when I realize I'm also soaked—and wearing a thin white babydoll tee.

Oh, boy.

It wasn't translucent before, but now, I'm scared there's a shadowy suggestion of my black lace bra underneath visible to everyone.

Especially the lion-man grumpily eyeballing me into the ground.

I glance down in horror.

Yep, he's getting a freaking peepshow with my cleavage soaked. Even the color of my skin shows through.

"Son of a—"

"Better take that off," he drawls in that same bored tone that can't be anything but sarcasm. "Miss Janelle can help you get that stain out before it sets, if you hurry."

"Oh, sure. Let me just rip my shirt off right here in the middle of the café!" I bite off, glaring at him. "What the hell are you doing here? Are *you* stalking me now?"

"Could've sworn I just came in for an evening coffee, but

88

sure. I'm after you, New York. Left my Michael Myers mask in my car."

"Why you—"

"Miss Delilah." Lucas sighs, his expression hardening. "Fine, I'll fess up. I've been watching out for you a little bit when I can. No peeping at you through windows or eyeing you every waking second. I'm just double-checking to make sure you're safe. Also, we're blocking the door."

"Then *move*," I snap, trying to shove past him. Good luck. It's like pushing a brick wall. All I get is a handful of rock-hard abs slicked in wet, sticky cotton. "And stay the hell away from my car."

Lucas steps aside with an odd look.

"Wasn't anywhere near your car, lady. You seeing shit?"

I do a double take, refusing to let my nerves set in.

"Look. If you're going to be honest about stalking me, don't lie about the rest." I flash him another middle finger salute, then sail past as quickly as I can, lifting my chin like I don't care about the few people still in their outdoor seats staring at us.

Like I don't already feel stripped naked, flushed from my face down.

"Go to hell, Lucas Graves."

"Already there," he calls after me.

I ignore him as I fold my arms over my exposed chest and try sprinting across the square without breaking into a full humiliating run. Especially when I feel Lucas' eyes practically burning between my shoulder blades.

It's like having your bra strap snapped by someone's stare.

I so don't need more drama with him right now.

Tomorrow, I'm moving back into the murder house.

It's less than ideal and a lot crazy, but I'm determined to make it mine.

I try to focus on that so I don't dwell on the last cryptic remark he threw at me.

Already there.

What the actual hell does that mean?

At least Lucas won't have such an easy time keeping tabs on me in public once school starts, whatever his motivations might be.

* * *

BY NIGHTFALL, I come to my senses, watching the lazy fireflies darting around outside. Their little lights always make this place feel cozier at night.

Okay, yes, maybe I was a tad harsh to Officer Horsedick.

He's not Roger Strunk.

I *know* he's not Roger.

I also know my gross ex left scars that keep me easily triggered, spitting mad at other people, and I hate it.

Curled up in the window seat of my suite, I hug my steaming mug of chamomile tea to my chest and sip it slowly, watching the quiet outside now that the whole town has gone to bed.

Out there, it's just the fuzzy glow of lamps.

I'm a little warm in the muggy evening after showering off the sticky coffee from earlier, but Lucas was right.

Miss Janelle—*Janelle*, dammit, I'm even starting to think like him—leaped into action the second she saw me, attacking my shirt with baking soda and her stain stick before I could say one word.

Now that's customer service.

I need to talk to Lucas and grind out an apology, though.

I'm still not sure why he sets me off so much and makes me a little volcano of emotion.

Maybe it's his lazy sarcasm. His slow drawl. His razor-sharp looks, powerful and handsome and too toned to ignore.

There's also that expression he always wears, somewhere between announcing *I have a severe allergy to smiling* and cockiest man alive.

Deep down, I feel like he's secretly laughing at me all the time, when I really want him to just shut up and—

No, not that.

No.

I want him to take me seriously. I know that's hard when the first time we met I was a shaking wreck, and he's probably labeled me as some big-city damsel in distress.

Well, if he's Hercules, I'll be Meg.

I'm a damsel and I'm in distress, but you'd better believe I can handle this.

God, I loved that movie growing up.

I drove my first set of foster parents nuts spinning around singing off-key songs. They bought the DVD, and they were thrilled to let it go with me when they sent me off to another foster family without a goodbye.

Defective out of the box, return to sender.

I still have that DVD somewhere in the moving boxes.

Maybe once I'm unpacked and moved in, I'll have a little solo watch party to welcome myself home.

Even if I won't really be alone, will I?

I'm worried I'll always feel like Emma's there in the house, looking over my shoulder, watching everything I do.

I hope ghosts like Disney musicals and my godawful singing. Otherwise, it's going to be a hell of an afterlife, stuck there with me.

I should get to bed.

Once school starts, it'll be an early to bed, early to rise situation. I won't have the luxury of brooding out of my window like a gothic heroine until midnight.

I toss back the rest of my tea, letting it soothe my nerves— right up until they jerk like snapping violin strings.

I gasp.

There's someone standing under my window.

They're creepily still, carefully positioned to avoid the light from the streetlamps.

Nothing but a man-shaped shadow, his head tilted back, looking up at my window.

It's hard to make him out when he's standing too close to the house, partly obscured by crisscrossing shadows and light that won't quite reach far enough.

Fucking Lucas Graves.

But it's not, I realize coldly.

Then I discover a different kind of stillness.

The horrible insta-freeze that glazes your entire body over when your heart just *stops*.

That shape... it's wrong for Lucas.

Tall, yes, but thin. Stooped.

The shoulders are narrower than his, the body language all wrong. It's more like watching a scarecrow or a ruffled raven than a lion-man.

Who?

I don't think.

I'm just gripped by fury and confusion and desperation.

This sick feeling like Emma won't wait for me to move back to the house. She wants to drag me outside by the ear right now because that shadow, that wraith, has something to do with her death.

In my bare feet and pajama shorts, I bolt out of the room.

I'm almost airborne, pouncing down the stairs.

I only slow down when I hit the front door, trying not to wake Janelle or any of the other renters left here when most of the tourists have gone home.

My breath turns to lead, crushing my lungs as I pop outside, peering across the lawn.

Of course, there's no one there.

Did I imagine it? The whole thing?

Inhaling slowly, I walk carefully across the lawn, feeling the cool grass crunching under my feet and poking between my bare toes.

The cozy cricket chirps become a muffled scream of warning all around me.

Just below my window, I stop.

Right where the grass is already crushed in the shape of a large bootprint.

Nope.

Definitely *no*t my imagination.

Neither is the far less subtle sight I don't expect.

My heart restarts, thrashing against my ribs as what I'm seeing sinks in.

It's sprayed on the wall right below my room.

A giant red X, and the paint is still wet and dripping.

VI: RED HERRINGS (LUCAS)

*T*here's proud. Independent. Guarded.

Then there's damn fool stubborn as a mule in a carrot field.

I know too well Delilah's the first three, and now she's leaving less doubt about the fourth one, too.

I'm outside The Rookery, keeping my feet planted just outside the evidence markers in the grass surrounding the footprints we could make out.

They trace a path around the back of the building toward the lake.

It's not the footprints I'm glaring at, though.

It's that ugly honking X painted on the wall, glaring blood-red in the morning sun.

"So you say the paint was wet when you saw it last night? Fresh?" I ask, trying my damnedest to keep my voice neutral as I snap another photo and tuck my phone away. "And less than sixty seconds after you saw a stranger under your window?"

A few feet away on the walk, Delilah leans against a standing roller suitcase, tapping her keys restlessly against one tanned, lush thigh in a pair of ragged denim cutoff shorts.

She's avoiding the grass religiously, like she doesn't want to tamper with evidence. I'm grateful for that.

Little less grateful for a few other things, and it's taking every ounce of restraint I have to keep my temper in check.

Especially when Delilah just shrugs and gives me a one-word answer.

"Yes."

This is going mighty fucking well.

"And you didn't think to call me last night?" I demand. "Call *anyone*? What if the asshole who did this hurt you?"

I can't keep the worry in my chest from clawing its way out.

"Well, I guess then I wouldn't be here to call you at all," she shoots back, her indigo-blue eyes snapping and her mouth set in that obstinate line that tells me I'm in for a fight.

"Goddammit, Delilah," I huff out. "I don't get what the hell you were thinking. Leaving it like this, not only did you scare Miss Janelle half to death when she woke up and found it, but—"

"Boys, I'm fine!" Janelle calls from where she's hovering behind Delilah. "Just a bit startled is all."

I sigh. "Now the scene's gone cold. There's probably accidental evidence tampering from groundskeepers, wild animals... hell, maybe the guy who did this shit himself. I don't know which of these footprints are from him, or which ones are from Waylon when he showed up to mow the lawn this morning. Why didn't you call me?"

She actually looks sheepish for a second, hunched into her bare shoulders. The slitted eyes of her dragon tattoo seem to glare at me.

She mumbles something I can't hear.

"Sorry, didn't catch that," I clip, leaning in. "And woman, you make one wisecrack about small towns closing up shop at nine p.m. and I will take you over my goddamned knee."

That gets her attention.

She shoots me a hot-eyed glare.

"Try it and you'll limp away with a nub for fun," she hisses. "I'm not discussing my kinks with you, Officer Horse Cock."

My brows go up.

If it were any other situation, I'd thank her for guessing half right about my size.

But Miss Janelle's here and her face is burning hot. She clutches her hands as she sputters "E-excuse me!"

"Sorry!" We both belt it out at the same time.

I look down.

Delilah clears her throat, still scowling at me. "I just didn't want to bother anyone, okay? No point in starting a mad panic."

"New York, we're the *cops*. It's our job to get bothered by things like this. Fuck's sake, I spend most days sitting on my ass and doing ride-alongs for teenagers. You could at least give me something important."

"Oh, my bad. Didn't realize I was cutting into your productivity metrics—or your ego." Grumbling, Delilah wraps her arms around herself in that guarded way she has, jerking her face to the side in a flare of wispy hair.

She's looking at that big red X instead of me now.

There's a nervous fury vibrating off her. I wonder how much is just masking her fear.

"Look," she says more slowly. "I get it. I know it was a dumb move and I was being ridiculous. I wasn't thinking. But if this is my problem, why can't it stay that way, Lucas? It shouldn't be anyone else's."

I eye her. "How is it *your* problem, specifically?"

She stays silent, her teeth clamped together so hard I hear them *click*.

Fuck it, I can't help myself.

Crossing the lawn, I give the evidence markers a wide berth and catch her chin lightly.

Her skin feels so soft it's almost startling, like velvet under my fingertips.

Nothing like her hardened exterior.

I coax her to look at me, nudging her chin up.

Her breath catches and her eyes flick over my face.

For a heady moment, her scowl fades behind pure surprise. Her pink lips part in ways that make me forget all about the damn crime scene.

"Hey," I whisper, fighting the urge to run my thumb over her lower lip. I've already lost control once with my outburst and I've got to rein myself in. "Talk to me, Delilah. What's going on? Because right now, we've just got possible trespassing, a little petty vandalism. Likely just some kids fucking with the new teacher in town. Or you think it's something more?"

She swallows, darts her tongue over her lips, leaves them gleaming—but she doesn't pull away from me this time.

"I mean, you sure seem to," she almost whispers, her voice low and throaty. "You're acting like we just found another body here."

Dammit.

I hate to say she's right.

I blew my stack like someone attacked her, tried to kill her, and my own words come flying back in my face.

Petty vandalism. A little trespassing. A prank.

No, it's not life or death, yet here I am yelling at her like a drunken chimp.

Like I care about her safety a hell of a lot more than I would for any other citizen.

Clearing my throat, I make myself let go, and glance at the vivid red X—all the while pretending Miss Janelle isn't watching us *both* after that little dustup.

"Dunno about you," I say softly. "But that looks pretty damn threatening to me."

"That's the thing." She looks at me for a few trembling seconds before she retreats—both emotionally and physically. Her face closes off as she steps back, putting distance between us. "It's a threat to *me*. Which means one thing."

"Your ex, Roger," I finish. "You think he did it."

97

"Who else?"

Sadly, I could name about six people in town off the top of my head, starting with a few punk teens known for getting in trouble with graffiti. Last fall, they even climbed all the way up to the top spire of that ugly mansion looming over the town like a dragon, jealously guarding its secrets.

The Arrendells had a complete shit fit and stopped short of pressing charges when they found out one of them was the judge's kid.

But I don't say that.

No point in spooking her till I've got something concrete.

"Can you tell me more about the person you saw?"

"No. Not really." She shakes her head. "He knew just where to stand so he was in the shadows, barely any hint of light. I know he was tall. Thin. Really wide shoulders. He was walking kind of hunched over like he was trying to make himself smaller. Like he wanted to change his body language, his stride, so he wouldn't be recognized. Kind of looked like a scarecrow, almost."

"And Roger?"

"...yeah. He's a runner. Tall guy." Delilah bites her bottom lip. "Not that thin, but yeah, he's got a lean build. So in the dark, if he was hunched over... Maybe. Maybe it could've been him."

"Okay. I'm going to give you my personal number, not just the police line."

"What?" Delilah's brows pull together. "Why?"

"Because I want you to text me every single photo you have saved in your camera roll with Roger Strunk." I smile faintly. "Unless you wiped them all out."

"I specifically didn't because I was trying to get the cops to take him seriously back in New York, and they wouldn't," she answers. There's a flicker of a smile there again. "I won't promise I didn't print several out and *burn* them in effigy, though."

"Ouch. Hope you don't believe in voodoo, New York."

"Only a little. I already go full Carrie on the guys who really upset me." She puffs her chest out.

I chuckle.

Goddamn, she's a little fucking cactus with curves and I'm too easily amused.

"Here. Let me see your phone." I hold out my hand.

She shoves her hand into the pocket of that denim mess masquerading as shorts, rummaging around. The waistline slips down, baring a strip of velvety skin below the crinkled hem of her ruffled tank top.

Then it disappears again as she lifts her phone out, unlocks the screen, and passes it over to me without protest.

I punch my number into her address book, save it, and pass it back.

"For now, let's assume your ex is in town," I say. "And he's possibly a person of interest with Emma Santos, though toxicology makes that a long shot." There's a theory building in my head, and I don't like it one bit. "So I'm going to ask you again— please be careful. Don't go anywhere alone after dark. Try to keep some company around during the day, too. Stay alert, and if you ever feel like you're being watched or followed, trust your instincts. Get to safety as soon as possible and this time, you call me, Delilah. Understood?"

She locks eyes with me and nods like I've finally broken through to her.

"We tend to pick up on things subconsciously without realizing it all the time. Even if you think it's silly, you hit me up."

"Okay, okay." Her lips quirk up. "Or what? Daddy's going to yell at me again?"

I stare at her.

Every single word in my brain twists into a garbled mess because between talking about taking her over my knee before and now her calling me *Daddy*, I'm pretty sure any hint of a rational thought just rolled out of my goddamned ears and hit the ground.

NICOLE SNOW

Miss Janelle laughs, resting a thin hand on Delilah's arm.

I remember when her hands used to be smooth. Now they're starting to wrinkle, stretching thinner between the tendons with every passing year.

"Don't mind Lucas," Janelle says. "He's always been like this, ever since he was a kidlet. He's like a cherry bomb. Big old bang, then he fizzles out."

"Hey now." My face goes hot. I scrub a hand over the back of my neck, grunting and looking away. "Ma'am, I'm on duty. Kindly don't file my edge off."

"And you're still Lucas Graves, fancy uniform or not. Same boy I've known since you were knee-high to a sunflower," she answers with tart amusement. "I love you, boy, but I won't have this girl thinking you're some sort of big bad wolf with a badge."

"Oh, trust me," Delilah trills, her eyes glittering with *delight*, "I don't see any wolf. I'm not afraid of him."

"Don't you start, too, dammit." I grumble. "Look, I don't care if it's two in the morning and I'm flat on my back from a plate of bad nachos. Call me. I'll come."

For a moment, Delilah falters.

She glances at me with those long, fringed lashes around her wide eyes. I wonder how young she really is when that cynical façade makes her seem wise beyond her years.

Even if she's only twenty-something, she's still a girl—too young for my thirty-six-year-old ass, that's for sure. She's also flushed, startled, and so wickedly pretty I want to hoist her up like a fresh plucked wildflower and inhale her.

Better, *devour* her.

My eyes are still glued to her as she looks away.

"I'll remember that," she says softly. "Does my house include 'lonely places?'"

Shit.

That's a good question.

"It's awful isolated," I say slowly. "Not sure I like you being halfway in the woods, though you're still in sight of your neighbors. Make sure you lock up tight at night. Maybe put in an alarm system. It wouldn't hurt to get a friend to come stay with you, if Miss Nora or someone else doesn't mind." That's when the meaning of the suitcase propped against her hits me. "Hold up. You're planning on moving in today?"

She pats the suitcase with one hand.

"All packed and ready to go." With a rueful glance at that hateful X on the wall, she adds, "Sorry I'm leaving a mess in my wake. Janelle, I can give you something to have that painted over if you—"

"Absolutely not, hon," Miss Janelle says sharply. "It's covered in the town repair budget. This is a historical building."

"Oh, nice!" She beams back an uneasy smile.

It's not hard to tell Delilah doesn't know what to do with kindness. Seems like it flusters her far more than rudeness or aggression or the shit I keep giving her. Why?

She fumbles out a "Thank you."

I'm about to fluster her some more, though.

"How about I head out to the house with you and take a good look around? I can help you carry some of the heavier stuff inside while I'm there." I flex my bicep for good measure until she laughs.

Then for some odd reason, she won't look at me, her cheeks still pink and her lower lip caught between her teeth.

"If I say no, you'll just follow me out there for my own protection, won't you?" she throws back.

"Maybe, maybe not. Hard to be sneaky if I admit it out loud."

"Hard to be sneaky if you walk into another latte shake, too."

Damn her, I laugh, shaking my head and reaching for her suitcase. "C'mon. Let me get that for you."

I'm actually surprised she listens.

We say goodbye to Janelle, and Delilah doesn't escape without a mama bear hug that winds her. I don't get away without getting my ear tweaked as Janelle demands a stern promise to protect "our girl."

Gotta say something for Redhaven hospitality.

Once we decide you're one of our pack, you're family.

As I haul Delilah's suitcase into her packed Kia and find a spot to wedge it in, she frowns at me.

"Lucas?"

"Yeah?"

"Do you really think Roger has anything to do with Emma's death?" she asks. "Or do you think it's something else?"

Something else, I think instantly, but I keep my mouth shut.

Things carry a little too far in this town.

They also carry too fast when you get loose with your lips, and I'd rather keep certain craziness to myself.

"I think," I say, "we had two bad coincidences at once. I'd bet poor Emma overdosed at one of the Arrendells' big parties and they're trying to avoid having it linked to them, even if they wouldn't be criminally liable. I think you showed up just in time to stumble into bad fucking coincidence number one, and bad coincidence number two happened to follow you here."

"Sometimes the simplest explanation really works, huh?" She says it like she wants to believe it, but there's obvious doubt in her question.

"Pretty much." I slam the hatchback of the Kia down, putting my shoulder into it until it latches, before I blow out a breath and step back, dusting my hands off. "Let's go get you moved in."

I wait till she's settled in the driver's seat of her car before I climb in my own. It's ridiculous, almost like I'm afraid someone's going to snatch her out from under my nose in the two seconds it takes me to get behind the wheel.

"Relax, you moose," I growl to myself.

It's not a long drive from The Rookery to Delilah's little cottage, but then nothing's a long drive in Redhaven. Before long, we're turning down that winding lane that ends at her house and the cozy embrace of trees.

I'm worried about her being ready for this. Getting over a

frigging corpse on the floor sucks more out of you mentally than you'd ever imagine.

Not for long, though.

Soon, I'm far more worried about the man standing on the porch in his glossy steel-grey Armani suit. His wine-red Benz is parked right outside Delilah's gate.

He's leaning against one of the porch posts like he's posing for a magazine shoot, so casual I could punch him right in his ugly little face.

Ulysses.

Fucking.

Arrendell.

What the hell's he doing here?

And how do I get him real damned gone, real damned fast?

VII: RED HANDED (DELILAH)

I haven't seen this much testosterone bristling in one place in ages—and I used to walk past construction sites every day, full of men who didn't get the message that in the twenty-first century, we don't catcall girls on the street and make obscene gestures with our—erm, *jackhammers.*

Not anymore.

When I agreed to let Lucas help, I forgot all about Ulysses wanting to help me move in, too.

I guess it's his way of apologizing for failing to protect me from my move-in horror.

Honestly, I feel like I'm being smothered in kindness lately. Everyone wants to help me, coddle me, treat me like a delicate little flower who'll crumple at the slightest breeze.

But I'm not a delicate flower at all.

I'm not wilting.

I also don't want to turn down any hospitality since I'm grateful for the sentiment behind it. I just don't like wallowing when I can pick myself up and get things done.

But *getting things done* would sure go a lot faster if Lucas and Ulysses would stop taking potshots at each other. Especially since right now they're currently locked in a staring contest for the ages over my flatscreen TV.

It's the one expensive thing I own, considering it's almost sixty inches—no size queen jokes, thank you very much.

Instead of cardboard boxes salvaged from the corner bodega in my old neighborhood, the TV is inside a huge reinforced wooden shipping crate with enough room for plenty of padding inside, adding to its weight.

It's not a one-man job.

They're trying to make it one anyway.

Ulysses shucked out of his nice, expensive-looking suit coat and rolled up the sleeves of his silk dress shirt. It's already ruined, I think, little bits of threads torn and tatty from catching on things.

I'd feel worse about it if he wasn't currently gripping one end of the TV crate and glaring at Lucas down the length of it.

"You can let go now, *Officer*," he grits out past a smile that's all teeth, his eyes jade daggers. "I've got this."

"The hell you do," Lucas snarls back with the exact same smile.

Oh my God.

He's holding the other end, standing on the sidewalk outside the fence with his back to the house, his whole wall of a body a roadblock. I think it stops Ulysses from using the TV crate like a bulldozer and just shoving the whole tangled mess of men and crate inside.

Lucas also stripped out of his uniform shirt earlier. Underneath, there's nothing but a paper-thin white undershirt that's gone almost completely see-through with sweat, matted to his skin over packed muscle—the kind that can't possibly be real.

But apparently, here I am, seeing my first real *eight-pack* out in the wild in the most awkward dick-measuring contest ever.

"You know," Ulysses grinds out, "just because I'm rich doesn't mean I'm weak."

"Did I say that?" Lucas snaps. His chiseled forearms flex as he shifts the crate. "You fishing for compliments, Ollie? I hear narcissists do that. Need me to tell you your arms are pretty jacked?"

"Call me Ollie again and I'll—oh, never mind." Ulysses stops just short of threatening a policeman.

Holy hell.

I slip past with two boxes labeled *Kitchen* stacked in my arms.

They're not heavy, but they are tall. I can barely see to navigate and these two dolts are in the way.

"If you guys are done flirting," I snap, "you could both just carry the damn thing inside. It's too heavy for one person. Even if that person is a huge meathead determined to swing his dick everywhere."

Ulysses blinks at me before I'm past them, ducking into the house.

"...was that for him or for me?" he calls mournfully.

I almost smile even though they're irritating the hell out of me.

Really, when he tries to stop sounding so posh and sophisticated, he's just kind of a hot mess and a little dorky.

"*Friend,*" Lucas says, "I'm pretty sure she meant both of us. You gonna move or what?"

Rolling my eyes, I drop my boxes on the kitchen counter, then lean against the sill of the little dining nook window I've left open to let the place air out.

"I mean that if *either* of you lunks drop my TV, I have zero shame about making you buy me a new one," I say, watching them through the screen. "It took me a year of tips to buy that thing. So stop being assholes with the one nice thing I own."

Ulysses cocks his head at Lucas. "Together on three?"

"Yeah," Lucas agrees. I think he might almost be close to smiling—if only his pride and whatever weird grudge he has with Ulysses would let him.

They finally manhandle the TV through the gate and up the walk.

I race out to catch the gate and hold it open for them.

As they pass by, I hear Ulysses whispering, "She's rather sweet when she's threatening us, isn't she?"

"Whatever," Lucas mocks. "Guess it brings out the beautiful spark of violence in her eyes."

"*Hey!*" I point at them as I duck around and head back to the car. "Stick to sniping at each other. Start aiming it at me and I'll bite you both."

"Threesomes ain't my thing, New York," Lucas says distractedly as he backs his way up the porch steps.

I freeze midstep, already dead.

"I figured as much, but I hoped you'd surprise me, Graves." Ulysses honestly sounds baffled. "Are you really so dull in the sheets?"

If Lucas' eyes could shoot death rays, Ulysses' head would be vaporized.

"Keep in mind that I'm in a position to use this thing to shove you flat on your ass, Ollie," Lucas snarls.

"Only if you remember I'm in a position to have you fired and run out of town, Graves," Ulysses answers just as pleasantly, right before they both vanish into the house.

Jeez. Too harsh.

My whole body tenses.

There's a deadly silence, this brief moment of levity evaporating like a scarce raindrop in the desert.

Then I hear Lucas grind out, "I'm well aware."

Ulysses doesn't answer.

He just smiles strangely.

It's the last I see of them before the shadows of the living room swallow them up and they hang a left out of sight inside the house.

I just keep staring.

I can't.

I can't even process a flipping thing that just happened.

Lucas and threesomes and Ulysses' vicious threats and—

Somebody save me.

Now.

Especially when there was no third wheel in my imagination.

Just a single hard, flexing body drenched with sweat, eclipsing me completely.

Warm spring-green eyes so hot with passion, a rough voice dragging out low, sugar-sweet groans and filthy promises—

Yikes.

I think I'm having a hot flash.

Can you start menopause at twenty-four?

Nope.

Nah.

Nada.

Nyet.

I go through a global litany of ways to say *hell no* as I throw myself back into work—and into pointedly ignoring whatever's going on with those two big idiots while they keep sniping at each other.

It's the most Southern passive-aggressive nice-nasty fight I've ever seen.

I don't even know what they're fighting about, only that they don't like each other, and the sizzle in every glance between them makes me think I'm about to witness a new murder.

As I head outside for another box—we're working practically in a relay at this point, always one at the car, one in the house, one somewhere in between—I stop in the entryway from the dining nook to the living room.

There's no blood on the floor now.

No chalked outline of a body.

No yellow crime tape.

Nothing to show Emma Santos ever died here, rudely upending my new life.

But I can feel her anyway, like she left an impression where the air feels colder every time I walk by.

Just my imagination, I'm sure. It still makes me hustle along faster.

I step back outside and grab another box. The back of the Kia's almost empty now, and as much as they're annoying me, I appreciate the fact that they've cut my unpacking time down to a third and saved me a horribly sore back.

It's not my back I need to worry about, though.

It's how well these old creaky porch boards hold up after hours of two large men and one small woman tramping up and down them with heavy boxes.

When I'm halfway up the wooden steps, something tilts under my feet—the board wobbling loose—and next thing I know I'm pitched backward.

Everything flips upside down, including my stomach.

I'm vaguely aware of the box flying out of my hands and blurs of motion on both sides of me in colors that resemble Lucas and Ulysses.

The rest of me is focused on gravity.

Because gravity means bonking my head on the paving stone on the walkway right behind me.

Some part of my lizard brain tries to save me. Windmilling arms, stumbling legs, grasping at empty air to regain my balance, but it's far too late.

I'm falling, falling, and—

Strong arms materialize under me, snatching me away from doom.

They wrap me up, pulling me firmly away from the ground.

Gasping, heart thundering, adrenaline becoming a fever, I stare up into sharp green eyes.

Lucas?

No.

Ulysses.

I'm clutched against his chest as he bends over me, holding

on with one arm around my waist and another behind my shoulders, lifting me off the ground. His green eyes are oddly intense, drilling into me in a way I can't help but notice when shock strips away my defenses.

My stomach flips over with confusion.

Especially when I realize he's still smiling.

It's the same charming, easy smile he always has, but I don't get why he's smiling like that right now.

With a shaky sound, I press my hands to his chest, pushing lightly and hoping he'll get the message. "Thanks! Sorry, one of the steps is loose, I guess..."

"No, I owe you an apology, Miss Clarendon. Seems I've made another oversight, and now I have a few stern words for the handyman," he says lightly as he turns me loose.

I shake off the dizziness once I'm on my feet again.

As he lets me go, I realize I'm practically boxed in between him and Lucas.

And Lucas has turned into this ginormous shadow falling over both of us, looking down at me with his eyes stark and darkened with—

What? Worry?

Something else?

"Hey," he says. "You okay? You didn't hit anything, did you? Sprain your leg?"

"No. I just scared the crap out of myself for half a second, but I'm fine." Well, besides feeling like I'm trapped between the two wild men, and part of me wants to hide behind Lucas to escape the strangeness. The rest of me wants to run away from them both. I clear my throat. "Clumsy feet. That's me."

Lucas just looks at me for a long second, his brows furrowed.

It feels like he can tell what I'm not saying, just like that evening at The Rookery where we sat with our beers. That heavy silence was welcoming.

Especially when he pulls back, giving me breathing space,

and circles around me to crouch down next to the box I dropped.

Thankfully, it landed flat on its bottom. The impact split the corners vertically, busting them out while still leaving the top flap closed, bits and pieces of my belongings popping out through the seams.

"Doesn't look like anything in here got too banged up," he says, prying delicately at something protruding from one split. "Damn. Looks like the glass in this frame busted out, though."

I don't keep many photo frames, not really.

Just this one.

So I know exactly what he's talking about before I even see it.

My heart tumbles like it wants to make up for my missed date with the concrete. I pull away from Ulysses and dash to the box, dropping to my knees next to Lucas—and groan when I see what's cradled in his hands.

A rectangular pewter picture frame in a floral design. It's handmade, every thread-fine detail created with such loving care that the frame itself is a masterpiece.

But it's not the most precious thing.

It's the photo inside, an old Polaroid of my mom when she was about my age, trimmed to fit the oval opening in the picture frame. We look so much alike it could almost be an old photo of me, except I never had kids of my own—and there's a tiny baby in my mother's arms, swaddled up and sleeping peacefully with a wild thatch of black hair puffed out everywhere.

Me.

That's the only photo that exists of my mother with me before I was eighteen.

The glass covering it has shattered out, leaving several shards threatening to scratch the photo's delicate thin film.

I reach for the frame, then stop.

There's an irrational fear inside me, a terror that I might damage it more somehow.

Lucas cradles the frame protectively, like he knows how important it is to me.

It must be etched on my face. Brilliant green eyes search mine, slowly dropping to the photo.

"That your mama?" he asks softly.

"I... Yes. And me." I swallow. Why do I suddenly want to cry? So much has happened in just a few short days, but it's a broken freaking picture frame that breaks me? "She... she gave it to me. I'll have to replace it, though. The picture's the important thing."

"Nah," Lucas says. "You can just replace the glass and keep the frame. I might know a thing or two about that." He offers me an easy smile, warm and reassuring, that makes his eyes crease at the corners. "Let me take care of it, Miss Delilah."

What. Is. Happening?

There's a touch of warmth slipping through me and spreading. "Lucas, why would you—"

"Because it needs to be done, New York, and I can. You need a better reason?" Lucas answers without hesitation, but there's a certain steeliness in his voice that makes it feel like something else.

I start to say something—until Ulysses clears his throat behind us.

Oof.

I jump, instinctively clutching at my arms.

I almost forgot he was there.

"Since that's taken care of," he says sharply, "shall we finish this move before the evening sun burns us to a crisp?"

Welp. Captain Poshness is back.

Lucas and I trade amused, almost conspiratorial glances and stand. He's still holding my photo frame like it means as much to him as it does to me.

"He's right. C'mon," I say, tossing my head toward the house. "I'll find something to wrap that up, and then I'll get you guys something cold to drink."

"Delightful," Ulysses clips.

I shoot him an odd look.

What's he so annoyed about?

God, I swear, men are just *weird* sometimes.

Alien creatures from Mars.

But there's nothing alien about Lucas' grin as he follows me up the porch, both of us skipping conspicuously over the one loose step that tried to dump me on my butt.

"Got any more of that beer?" he asks hopefully.

VIII: RED SKY AT MORNING (LUCAS)

I don't think Miss Delilah's a morning person.

When I show up at her house bright and early the next day, holding my tools, she's still in her pajamas when she answers the door.

If you can call *that* outfit pajamas.

Gym shorts saved from being panties by half an inch of flimsy fabric skimming her upper thighs, the curve of her hips threatening to break through, too many glimpses of the lower creases of her ass.

Plus, an oversized tank top that's only saved from completely falling off her by those generous hips, offering glimpses of smooth curves, dusky skin, a black sports bra.

Her hair's a damn mess, too, falling all over her in this black fountain.

My cock instantly hijacks the rest of me.

Of course, she's unfazed with all the skin she's flashing as she blinks at me sleepily, yawning and dragging her hair back from her face.

"Lucas? What time is it?"

"Seven a.m. Rise and shine."

I pry my gaze away from her shoulder.

Something about the way that tempting hint of black bra strap against her skin fucks with me hardcore.

I get like that with pretty women, I guess.

Just like any other guy, I home in like a hungry dog on long legs, curves, lush breasts, kissable lips. She's sure as hell got every last one of those assets in spades.

I also wind up noticing the little things.

The curve of her shoulder.

The teasing dip of her collarbone and the way her lips flutter when she wets them.

The tender hollow on the underside of her wrist, so sensitive to ruthless kisses.

Fuck me blind.

It's those little things that make me trip on a woman damn *hard*.

Blame it on being a cop. Being trained to notice all the finer points, even when I try not to.

Even when I've got zero business getting stuck on Delilah Clarendon and falling down a bottomless abyss of pure lust.

"Want me to come back later?" I force my gaze over her shoulder.

"It's fine. I should've set my alarm anyway. Normally, I wake up with the sunrise, but usually I'm not this worn out." In my peripheral vision, she lets out another lengthy yawn.

The way she stretches up on her toes with her arms over her head cuts me in two.

Little Miss Everything leaving Little Miss Nothing to a man's imagination.

Then she turns away, the lash of her hair beckoning me.

"I'll put on some coffee. How do you like it?"

Darlin', you're fucking it.

"Black," I grunt out, following her inside and hooking the door with my ankle to pull it shut behind me.

We left the living room a war zone of piled boxes and overflowing laundry baskets yesterday—but to say it's a disaster now is an understatement.

God. Damn.

Just boxes splayed open for days like they exploded, their contents bursting out all over the place.

Clothes. Appliances. Books.

I think there's a laptop buried in there somewhere, but it's hard to tell surrounded by a nest of USB cables and other cords.

Old DVDs. Guess she's not much for streaming.

A PS5 game system.

I stop, blinking at that one.

"You play?" I ask.

She's disappeared into the kitchen and now she leans back out, following my line of sight and laughing.

"The kids in my last teaching residency got me pretty hooked." Her voice goes a little distant as she ducks into the kitchen again. "You can put your stuff down, by the way. What is all that?"

"Toolbox." I set the big busted-up fishing tackle box I use for my tools down at my feet. I keep the smaller box from the hardware store tucked under my arm, shifting it to my hands. "Figured I'd take care of that ratty step while I'm here, and then put in an alarm for you."

Her head pops around the kitchen doorframe again like a little meerkat—in and out, only this time she's holding a can of coffee grounds in one hand. The lid is already popped off and the aroma wafts toward me.

"You don't have to do all that."

I answer with a shrug, making myself look away again.

Because goddamn, the way her neck curves into her shoulder is *murder.*

"Felt like I had to do something to make it up to you after bickering so much with Ollie. Needs to be done anyway, right?"

"I, yes, but..." She trails off.

Pink stains her skin, darkening her cheeks. She gives me a look that's almost consternation, and I try like hell not to smile.

There's her little thing with accepting help again.

"Thanks," she manages.

Then she vanishes right back into the kitchen again.

"To answer your other question," I call after her, smiling under my breath, "I've got no idea what a teaching residency is. Always thought residencies were for doctors."

"They are," she calls back, mixed with the sounds of running water and something clattering around. "But that's what they call it for teachers now, too. You're basically an assistant shadowing real teachers to find your footing, then you graduate to teaching unsupervised."

"So how'd that land you a fancy gaming system?"

"One of the kids in my last residency—her Dad worked for Sony. It's all she ever talked about and her parents generously donated a system to the school. When his daughter found out I wasn't planning to stay in New York forever, she cried and said maybe I'd stay if he gave me a PS5." Her laughter spills out of the kitchen, fond with memories. Not her usual cynical bursts of quiet laughter. "He gave it to me and said, 'I know a bribe won't work and you'll go where you want to anyway. But it makes her happy to give you something, so please take it. For her.' So I did. Mostly because I knew it would make Roger mad. He accused me of sleeping with the guy. I threw one of the controllers at his *head*." She snickers. "I've barely played it for more than a few hours, honestly. I like games, but I just haven't had the time."

"Maybe you'll find some now, New York. Smaller classes, less work outside school hours."

I scan the room, and this time the detail that jumps out isn't connected to Delilah's little firecracker body.

It's the area just inside the entryway, on a direct path to the hall leading into the back.

One spot in the living room without a single thing piled on it or spilling over it.

Could just be she left that spot clear so she could make her way through the house while unpacking.

I wish it was just that.

It hits like a sledgehammer when it sinks in.

That's the spot where we found Emma Santos.

"Hey, Delilah?" I swallow, shifting my mind to another topic.

"Yeah?"

"If they wanted you to stay in New York, why *did* you come out here?"

She's quiet for a minute. There's nothing but a gently growling coffeepot percolating and that ever-stronger coffee smell.

Then she leans around the doorframe, folding her arms over her chest, graceful as she props her shoulder against the wood.

She nibbles at her lower lip, wearing a thoughtful frown.

"I won't lie," she says softly. "Some of it was money. Full room and board covered, plus a good salary? That's hard to pass up. I've never had that much security in my life. But the rest of it, well..." Her eyes darken. She looks past me toward the front windows, her gaze pensive. "I guess I was afraid of being used up before I had a chance to find myself and settle into what I really love about teaching. The schools in New York—they're *brutal*. Just one impossible situation after the next. All those poor kids and teachers trying so hard to make something out of what they're given, but you can't really make a silk purse out of a sow's ear when the whole system's designed to fail." There's guilt in her eyes as they finally shift to me, stars swimming in midnight-blue, making constellations of emotion. "Call it cowardly, maybe. But I've seen too many fresh-faced, hopeful teachers wind up broken and disconnected. Then they're just tossed aside once they're drained."

"Damn," I whisper.

"Yeah. I didn't want that to be me. I wanted to go somewhere where I could actually *do* something for the kids. Maybe one day when I'm more experienced—when I'm stronger—I'll go back.

Then I'll know how to make things better. Or if I don't, at least I can use what I've learned to fight for something better for kids everywhere."

So, this is what's under all those cactus thorns.

A soulful young woman who cares so damn much she'll prick and bleed on someone else's pain.

All because she worries about what she *can't do.*

All because she doesn't realize her own strength.

"Wouldn't call that cowardly at all," I say gruffly. "I think that's a smart move, mapping out a way you can do the best for the folks you care about."

"Sure. For people who don't even know who I am..."

"That's what makes it smart, Miss Delilah. You care enough to plan your future around kids you won't meet for years."

Her startled eyes fix on me. That blush returns, and I think I'm starting to enjoy finding different reasons to coax it out of her.

She glances at the slim cardboard box in my hands, changing the subject. I expected as much.

"Hey, is that...?"

"Come see for yourself." With a smile, I hold it out to her.

She moves so delicately, shifting her weight as she goes. It gives her steps a dancer's grace as she walks around that empty spot on the floor.

My brows pull down.

Even as she reaches for the box, I ask, "You doing that on purpose?"

"Doing what?" She freezes, looking at me oddly, and our fingertips almost touch against the cardboard.

I nod at the open space. "Only empty spot in the room, Delilah, and you're avoiding it like a lava pit."

There's a shiver of her lashes. Sadness flashes across her face.

Still holding on to the box, she looks at the floor.

"Oh, I... I hadn't even realized I was—I mean, sometimes it's like I can *feel* her there. I know it sounds crazy. But I hadn't noticed I was doing it." Her breath hitches. "Have you found out anything new? About Emma, I mean."

"Sorry. Nothing yet."

Her face falls.

Damn, I don't want to push her anymore.

There's something fragile in her face today.

Something that could break just as easily as the glass in her pretty picture frame.

I just nudge the box into her hands gently and bend to pick up my toolbox with a half smile.

"I'll go get started on firming up those steps," I tell her. "Let me know if the replacement glass isn't good enough, and I'll have another go at it."

She blinks up at me, then glances inside the box, smoothing her thumbs over its surface.

"Thank you," she whispers. "I'll bring your coffee out when it's done."

"Perfect."

She's still standing there, looking so damn lost while I duck out into the morning sunlight.

Her closest neighbors, the Greelys, are out in the driveway of their two-story brick house, herding their kids into their minivan. All four munchkins hop around in swimming trunks and goggles, holding their paddleboards and inner tubes.

When they catch sight of me, they belt out greetings.

I wave back, then crouch down to have a good look at the steps.

They're a mess, all right.

Think I'm gonna have to replace the whole damn thing. Plenty of wet winters and baking North Carolina summers have taken their toll. Looks like a minor miracle the steps haven't crumbled away completely.

Good thing I brought a stack of planks and a miter saw. I had a feeling this was gonna be a serious job.

By the time I finish unloading fresh pine planks from my

trunk and get my saw hooked up, Delilah emerges from the house. She's traded her short-shorts for another pair of cutoffs that barely hide an inch more of flesh.

Fuck.

I think there's a strategic hint of black lace peeking through.

You know the worst part?

She damned well isn't doing it to get my attention.

It might be easier for me to ignore it if she was.

Nah, she's just being her little manic pixie self, insanely comfortable in her own skin, casual and easy and free.

I'm the uptight asshole whose balls are turning into the world's biggest pair of flash frozen blueberries.

Why can't I just stop *noticing?*

While I settle down with my measuring tape, willing my eyes not to roam, she drops down on the edge of the porch close by, swinging her legs over it.

She's brought a matching pair of *Nightmare* mugs with her. One Jack Skellington, the other Sally.

She nudges the Jack mug toward me. Steam rises with the scent of good strong coffee, and my stomach growls for caffeine.

She blows on hers, pink lips pursing as she takes a sip. "Here you go. Least I can do since you fixed my frame."

I shouldn't feel so pleased at one little compliment.

"No trouble," I grind out with a nod, slurping my coffee.

"Pretty sure it was, Lucas. Don't be modest. You must be busy with everything happening," she says. "I took a good look. You had to custom cut the glass to fit the setting, didn't you?"

"I mean, if you want a step-by-step breakdown, yeah. Old Max gave me a few pointers. He runs the antique mall in town." I glower at her, suddenly feeling too damn hot under my collar.

"Yeah. Okay." Her smile is so shy, peeking out playfully over the rim of her mug. "I can still tell you put a lot of time into it, crankyface. Instead of just grabbing a cheap glass sheet and slapping it on there and calling it a day, you went the full mile. I appreciate it."

Hiding a grin, I mark off a few more measurements, then stand back to take stock and make sure I've got enough wood to pull this off.

"Happy to help. Miss Lilah, you might want to scoot over a little. I'm gonna have to knock this whole staircase out and put in a new one, and I don't want to get any splinters on those pretty legs of yours."

Her eyes widen.

I don't think it's because I called her legs pretty.

She stares at me, vulnerability softening her face before she inches over a foot to the side, scooting herself with one hand while the other clutches her mug.

I snap my toolbox open and snag my hammer, but I'm still watching her.

"Sorry. Didn't mean to make you feel uncomfortable."

"No, it's not that." She shakes her head quickly. "It's just... no one calls me Lilah but my mom. It startled me, that's all."

"If it bothers you, I'll knock it off."

"...I hate to say it, but Miss New York was kinda growing on me." Her lips quirk up, but there's something haunting her eyes. She looks down into her mug. "It's not a bad thing, really."

I don't know what the hell to say to that.

So for once, I don't say anything at all.

Fine by me.

Don't mind being quiet here in the sun, stealing sips of strong black coffee with Lilah for company while I figure out the best place to knock the old boards loose.

I'm just not expecting her to break the silence with her voice soft and thoughtful.

"You were right, Lucas," she says. "The woman in the picture, that's my mother. The first time I ever saw her was in that picture when I was eighteen. That's when the state finally unsealed my foster records so I could find out who my birth mom was." She takes a shaky breath. "Her name is Mitsi. The state, they took me away from her when I was just a baby. So young I have no memories of her at all. They said she was unfit, living in poverty, and she didn't even know who my father was. She begged to keep me. They said no. I'm surprised they let her put that photo in my file. It's like it was just waiting for me until I was old enough."

I look up and stare like a damn fool.

This time, my silence isn't because I'm lost for words.

It's out of respect for the precious thing she's giving me right now.

This story.

This memory.

This need to know more.

To know more about what makes the wild, beautiful heart of Delilah Clarendon tick and razz up my whole world.

Her fingers tighten around her mug. She stares into it like she can see her future in that bitter brew.

"Those state people, maybe they were just doing their jobs, I get it. But they treated my mom like a throwaway. Someone they could just cut out of my life. And for the longest time, I wondered if my father did that, too. If he just used her and threw her away. If that's what people *do*, because I felt like a throwaway kid." She stops and sighs.

I nod slowly, urging her on.

"When I was younger, I was lonely. Mad at the world. I didn't know anything about my mother's side of things. And then the families I was stuck with... *God.*" She shakes her head. "I burned right through them. They tossed me away because I was too angry. Too restless. Too extra. I wasn't the perfect little angel right out of the box, so I wasn't worth the time to let me get used to them. They just sent me packing, right back to the foster center more times than I can count."

Knife, meet heart.

Fuck this.

I drop my crowbar.

The goddamned stairs can wait.

I set the hammer back in my toolbox, stand, and sit next to her on the edge of the porch. Our arms almost touch.

I can't erase old pains, no. Can't make that shit go away when it's already made her hurt.

But I can be here in the present and make sure she's not alone.

Not while she's opening her heart like a bleeding wound.

She lifts her head, looking up at me so sweetly.

There's a tremor in her lips, a thickness in her voice.

"Maybe that's why Emma gets to me so much, you know?" It's like she's pleading with me to understand. "Because somebody just up and threw her away, whether they know it or not. Whoever gave her the drugs that night. Whoever got her hooked on them in the first place. I dunno. So I want to hold on to her memory so she's not just totally discarded. Just like I wanted to find my mother so bad so she wouldn't be lost forever..."

She trails off, and that's the moment I realize two things.

One, Delilah Clarendon doesn't believe Emma's death was an accident any more than I do.

Two, there's no way in hell this woman could have done it.

Not when I can practically smell the salty tears she's fighting back.

I won't believe it.

I won't believe this is just a spectacular lie.

Maybe I still believe a little too much that people, deep down, are fundamentally good—most of them, anyway.

That no one with even the slightest heart could fake this much emotion. It's coming so heavy now it pulls me closer, almost magnetic, until I can feel her warmth as her arm brushes mine.

Every hair on my body bristles.

"How?" I ask. "How'd you find her? Your ma, I mean?"

"Oh, it was all right there." She swallows a heavy breath. "In my file. Her name, last known address, phone number. All those years wondering who she was and where she went, and it was just sitting there, being kept from me because of some stupid fucking *rules*." She closes her eyes, pressing her mouth to the mug, just breathing the steam. When she speaks again, she's more composed. "She wasn't at that address anymore, of course, but her old neighbors knew her. They talked about her like they loved her when I came knocking. Their info helped me track her down." Her smile trembles so sweetly. "And she took one look at me and burst into tears. Hugged me harder than I've ever been hugged in my life. That was when I found out the truth. She never wanted to give me up... and she'd been working herself crazy all those years, hoping I'd find her so she could be there for me when I was ready."

"Sounds like a great lady," I say gently.

"The most amazing ever," Delilah says fiercely. "She got back on her feet and opened her own diner after they took me away. Mom went from having nothing to owning her own restaurant, and she'd been saving every penny for years. All for me, Lucas. For *me*. She... she gave me my first job at that diner. The extra shifts helped me pay my way through school. All for a daughter she hadn't seen for eighteen years. She's the real reason I took this job, I think. All these big companies are coming into her neighborhood, buying things out, 'upscaling,' and I can't stand for her to lose the diner. So I'm going to help her like she helped me and send every bit of money home I can manage. I'll make sure she has a choice—the most comfortable retirement ever, or at least a lot of helpers to lighten the load if she never wants to give up the diner."

Fucking hell.

I don't think I have any hope left of *not* noticing Miss Delilah Clarendon every waking minute.

She's so goddamned beautiful in this moment.

Full of so much heart that she's nearly breaking mine, her eyes shining and fierce with love for her mother. The devotion spills through her delicate face.

I feel like I've taken a brick to the head and I'm seeing stars.

How the fuck does it happen?

How is it that a man only needs five damn minutes to go from *she's pretty cute and feisty* to falling head over heels?

And I just landed on my face like that old porch step caught me and pitched me down on my ass.

Look the fuck away, man.

Right now.

I have to.

Or else she might look up at me and see something too naked in my eyes. Something I'm not even sure is real or just me getting caught up in her emotional storm, in this *presence* that can put a man under its spell so easily.

Her head starts turning toward me.

Heart thumping, I glance away, trying to be casual about it and failing miserably.

I stare up at the sky, all bright late summer blue, watching the distinctive shape of a grasshopper hawk circling the sun without really seeing it at all.

"Sounds to me," I say, "like you let your heart decide. That can't be a bad decision at all."

"I hope not," she breathes. "I really do."

We're quiet for a spell then.

I'm okay with that.

Gives me a minute to collect myself, and I feel like she could use it, too.

When my voice finds its way up my throat again without the slightest bit of permission, I don't know what's coming over me.

"I get what it's like," I say quietly. "Feeling a bond with family you haven't seen in years. You feel connected to them, even when they're long gone."

"Yeah?"

"Yeah," I grind out.

I can feel her waiting for me in the silence, but I can't do it.

I can't talk about this, even if it feels a little unfair when she just gave me so much of her, piling her feelings in my hands like glittering jewels.

"I wonder if there's someone out there feeling Emma that way," she whispers after a heavy moment. "Missing her, needing to know where she is."

"If there is," I promise, "I'll make sure they get the closure they deserve."

I hate like hell that I can't keep that promise yet.

Because I feel like Emma Santos' death has more dirt behind it.

I don't want to call the people who love her until I can tell them the whole truth about what happened to her.

They deserve that, too.

Just as much as Delilah deserved to be loved by a family who understood her, even if it took her the first eighteen years of her life to find it.

We settle back into a cozy silence, drinking our coffee in the hot morning sun.

When our mugs are empty, I go back to work on the porch.

We're still quiet, and it's good.

It's easy.

Hell, I like it.

I like how comfortable it feels while I do the teardown, while Delilah slips back into the house to wash the mugs. She comes back later with a cold glass of lemonade for me, and it's always refilled just when the sawdust coating the back of my mouth gets to be too much.

She leaves the front door open while she works at unpacking, asking if I need anything every now and then.

I'm definitely not expecting her to feed me later, after I'm done with the steps. They're a little out of place with the fresh yellow pine against the grey-weathered planks of the porch, but it's sturdy enough.

I'm halfway through wiring in the new alarm system. It's this state-of-the-art thing from Home Shepherd, this big security company out west.

But I won't turn down a thick, hearty sandwich, either. She laughs and swipes a little dot of mayonnaise off my nose.

Damn, I could stay like this.

It's warm and easy in a way I've never had before.

I never thought I'd feel this prickly around a woman I usually piss off purely by breathing.

Still don't know what made her decide to let me in today. But it feels like I've been given something precious and completely unique.

That something can't last forever, though.

And just as I'm testing the sensor wired to her bedroom window, I catch the telltale sound of my radio crackling from the dash of my patrol car.

It's parked all the way past her fence on the opposite side of the yard, but I'm hard-wired to hear that sound from a hundred feet away. I give the window one last check to make sure it won't stick before I jog out to my car, lifting my sweat-drenched t-shirt to swipe at my dripping face before ducking inside.

The leather seats almost burn me alive after baking in the sun all day.

Every time.

Every damn time, I forget the seats turn into griddles in the summer.

Swearing, I grab the CB radio handset and roll back out of the car, stretching the cord behind me. "Graves in, what's going on?"

"Oh, there you are," Mallory says. "We've got a pink problem again, Lucas."

"Pink problem?" I groan, dropping my face into my hand. "Aw, hell. Can't Henri take it today? Or Micah?"

"They're already on the scene *with* Captain Faircross. It's not a three-man job," she replies tartly.

In the background, I hear the little *ping* that means Mallory just unlocked something new in her flirty game. "Do be a dear and go help them, would you?"

Snarling, I pull my phone back and check the little app that lets us track each other on GPS. Sure enough, my crew is all piled up in one location.

Damnation.

Sighing, I bring the phone to my mouth again.

"I'll be there in twenty. Ten-four, Graves out."

I don't want to deal with this.

As I drop the radio back into the car, Delilah slips out of the house. Even though she's been in the shade most of the day, she's just as much a sweaty mess as I am, her hair clinging to her face, her shirt so soaked I can make out the stitching on that black sports bra right down to the finest detail.

Goddamn, I'm a dead man walking, and I don't mean the humidity.

Propping herself against a porch post, she flaps the front of her shirt, fanning her belly. "Everything okay?"

"Yep, just the damn Jacobins' pigs again. Orneriest little monsters on the planet. Those things got out on old Maurice Norton's property again, and now Maurice is threatening to shoot them and the Jacobins too for his trouble." I snort. "Shit happens so often we call it the pink problem."

She laughs. "Sounds like they need better fences. Who are the Jacobins again?"

"Remember me telling you about the hillfolk?"

"I remember you being a huge sarcastic prick about the hill-folk." Delilah grins.

"Just my default setting, darlin'." Still, a smile escapes as I trudge back up the walk to pack up my toolbox and start picking up the debris I've left behind. "That's the Jacobins. They don't live in town proper. They've got this big sprawling farm that's practically a small village on its own, way up in the hills past the woods. They've been there before there was a Redhaven, but they don't truck around much with townsfolk and never have.

Think they're happier out there with their pigs and their moonshine and their endless bullshit."

A glitter of interest darkens her eyes as she cocks her head. "Moonshine? Seriously? You'd think the police might want to do something about that."

"Lotta woods out here, New York." I laugh. "Not that hard to lose a person—or a whole distillery. Usually, we don't bother the Jacobins and the Jacobins don't bother us. It works. But right now, I gotta go wrangle their frigging hogs before they plow my guys into the ground."

"Well then." There's something so tempting about the teasing curve of her lips as she stretches up on her toes and drops down again, swaying as she laces her hands behind her back. "Thanks again for today. I mean it. Now go have fun with your pigs. I bet they're shaking in terror."

I'd rather stay here.

That feeling punches me hard in the gut, and there's not a damned thing I can do about it.

"See? Miss Janelle told you I'm not the big bad wolf." I raise a hand, waving as I head back to my car with my toolbox under my arm and a cardboard box I'd stolen dangling from my fingers, filled with wood scraps. "You call me if you need anything else, Miss Lilah. Anything at all."

IX: RED SKY AT NIGHT (DELILAH)

I think I may have busted a rib.

Because yesterday I've never laughed so hard in my *life*.

After Lucas left, I finished unpacking a few more boxes before calling it quits for the day and headed out to run some errands, picking up odds and ends I needed for furniture and wall mountings.

When I heard sirens as soon as I stepped out of the hardware store, for half a second, I was worried. It sounded like multiple cop cars, and I wondered if the noise was announcing another body found.

But I shouldn't have worried.

Two seconds later, two patrol cars went ripping down the street, packed to the brim with—

Hogs?

Yep.

The ginormous pigs in the back seat raised total hell, squealing louder than the sirens, throwing themselves around like they were trying to have a stampede in the cramped space.

I didn't recognize the two men in the front seat of the first car, one white-blond-haired and pale, the other a gruff-looking older man with a forbidding—and very irritated—scowl.

But I definitely caught Lucas behind the wheel of the other vehicle.

His car almost tilted while he fought to keep it steady, his strong hands fused to the steering wheel behind his stone-faced expression.

The pig behind him nosing at the back of his head didn't faze him one bit, rooting around like it was hunting for truffles in his thick black hair.

Another giant hog practically plopped its butt on the head of the other guy in the passenger seat, twisting its curly tail into his long brown hair.

I just stared in stunned silence, watching as Lucas sped through traffic.

A second later, I almost hit the ground.

Laughing so hard I had to set my bag down and touch the sidewalk, clutching my sides, howling so loud I'm sure I risked a few bystanders wondering if the new teacher's all right upstairs.

No, she's not.

Not when Lucas flipping Graves is such a magnificent *dork*.

He's a dangerously cute one, too.

God, I need to get him out of my head.

Once I got myself together, I headed back home.

At least I didn't attract much of an audience.

I guess the 'pink problem' is so common hardly anyone else in this little town bats an eye at pigs losing their shit in squad cars. I hope they understand why a newcomer might think it's the funniest thing in ages.

I was still grinning by the time I went to bed.

Sleep came so much easier with that alarm armed and protecting me. That extra little bit of security feels nice.

It almost makes me feel like Lucas is still here, watching over me, even when he's not.

I wish I was still laughing this morning, but real life isn't so funny.

Especially not when I'm calculating what's left in my bank account and how much I've spent of the moving stipend the town paid me, and how much more I can stretch from now until I get my first official paycheck.

It's just enough for one more big shopping trip.

Later that evening, I've got an overflowing cartload of school supplies.

Nora shops along next to me as we prowl the aisle of Redhaven's lonely superstore that looks entirely out of place, faring no better than me.

I've loaded up on coloring books and water-soluble markers —no angry parents over ruined clothes here—and crayons and puzzles and activity books. She's stocking up on raw materials like poster board and glue. She loves to make these big colorful boards to help keep her rambunctious preteens occupied.

"You know what still gets me after all these years?" she says, wrestling her cart for a few seconds just to keep it moving on one loose, squeaky wheel. "Every year the town council holds a big donation drive for school expenses. I know for a fact the Arrendells toss in five figures, plus a few other families around here with money to burn." She snorts and tosses a pack of multi-colored star stickers into her cart, pauses, then narrows her eyes and sweeps the entire rack of stickers into her cart. "So, how is it every year I spend all my money on this stuff? Where does it all *go?*"

"Athletics?" I venture.

I've seen a ton of schools spend their budgets on the local football team as a matter of town pride and donors with deep pockets who only care about one thing.

Nora gives me a wry look. "We have *one* lacrosse team that isn't even technically part of the school. There are no sports to spend it on in Redhaven. Everything else, the kids get mixed in with other schools from the county."

"I don't know then." That is weird. "The grounds look pretty well maintained, I guess? The buildings, too. Maintenance adds up. Are your textbooks new?"

"Fairly. They're usually about a year or two out of date, but that's *another thing*." She's got a sharp tongue, but she loves to talk. She jabs a finger at some invisible person she's accusing. "There's a new edition every year now! Textbooks used to be good for about a decade, and now every year we've got updates on old things that were wrong, updates on new things... Updates, updates, everywhere, and not a drop to think! How do we even try to keep up?"

"If only we could stop time," I tease, laughing as I drop a few containers of finger paint into my cart. I might try making slime in class since the younger kids love a little tactile play—but the idea of cleaning up that much slime filled with dirt and crumbs is already making me cringe. "No, seriously. The world just changes at light speed now. Blame the interwebs, I guess."

That wins me a gently amused look. "You sound older than me, Delilah. Complaining about the internet? Woof."

"*Hey.*" I bump her with my shoulder. "I'm only twenty-four."

"But is it like cats?" she asks innocently. "You know, a New York twenty-four is like a Redhaven fifty? So world-wise from the streets, right?"

"Oh, don't *you* start too. I'm from New York, not Mars." I laugh harshly. "Lucas keeps calling me Miss New York."

"And you're calling Lieutenant Graves by his first name. Scandalous," she retorts.

Oh, crap.

I nearly squeak.

I hadn't meant to let that slip, but then again, I hadn't realized I'd slipped into calling him *Lucas*, either, just as easily as he calls me New York and now *Miss Lilah*.

"I-I mean," I stammer. "He, um, helped me move. Lucas and Ulysses. Wouldn't it be rude to keep calling him Lieutenant Graves?"

Nora purses her lips in a soft, appreciative whistle. "*Both* of them? Hot damn, girl."

"It'snotlikethat!" I rush out, horrified. My voice carries over the aisles. I cough into my arm and drop my volume. "Oh my God, they just helped me move, Nora. They were only being nice."

"Sure they were, sweetie." Her voice is solemn, her mouth set in a grave line while her eyes are laughing up a storm. "Suuure they were."

Feeling so hot I must be beet red up to my hairline, I shove her lightly again, making her giggle as she sways to the side. It turns into a playful pushing contest as we maneuver our way to the checkout and then pile our things into our cars before tail-gating each other out of the giant lot. We head back to the more intimately packed shopping district, where we can park and just walk to the shops for the smaller things we need.

Or in my case, one big enchilada.

Last on my list is a decent bed and a mattress.

One night on an air mattress is more than enough, and a bed was the one thing I couldn't just buy flat-packed and smushed into the back of my Kia.

There must be like a dozen furniture stores in town—more than any town this size could possibly need—but Nora says they mostly export to other markets, or sometimes build stock for tourist season, when people come in droves just to shop.

She's very proud when she says *North Carolina's the furniture capital of the world, you know.* Apparently, the good craftsfolk of Redhaven are just as much a part of the town's history as stout beer, minutemen statues, moonshining hillfolk, rampaging pigs, hot cops, and fabulously rich weirdos.

It's all getting expensive.

I'm starting to think I might end up living the air mattress life for a little bit longer—but when something grabs my attention, it's not a bed.

It's a gorgeous desk in shiny cherrywood, the color so deep

and rich it's like a horse's hide. The craftsmanship is so beautiful it looks like it belongs in an ancient library full of literary wonders.

I stop dead in my tracks, resting my fingertips over the window.

I can see that desk in my classroom.

Me, standing behind it, smiling at my kids. That desk sets the tone of the entire room, turning it warm, welcoming, somewhere everybody loves to be. Such a pretty place to grade papers, too.

"Gorgeous, ain't it?" Nora says with a touch of pride, stopping next to me. "This is why luxury furniture brands buy from Redhaven. You can't beat anything from A Touch of Grey."

I glance up at the store's name on the little sign above.

"It's so cool it's almost ridiculous," I whisper, beyond awestruck. "No piece of furniture should have its own aura."

I want it.

And I can't possibly afford it.

The price tag says the desk is $3,800.

Almost more than I even earn in a month, pre-tax.

It's not the disappointment that makes my stomach sink, though. I'm used to window-shopping, seeing something I love and knowing I can never have it before moving on with fond regret.

It's the sudden feeling of eyes on me.

Not the usual quick, curious glances of someone realizing I'm the new girl in town.

This feels too *heavy.*

Too familiar.

Almost the way I used to feel when I'd stagger home to my apartment dog-tired and just *know* that Roger was around, watching me, hidden and inescapable.

I don't want to turn around.

That red X sprayed on the wall bleeds into my mind.

...what if Roger's waiting there, just waiting for me to look?

What if he's standing on the sidewalk, staring at me with his saccharine smile, just watching with that eerie obsession I didn't recognize until it was almost too late?

No.

He wouldn't dare be so open.

Would he?

I don't know if I'm scared or pissed, but I swear to God Almighty I'm going to kick him square in the nuts if I catch him creeping on me again. I swallow hard, balling up my nerves like I'm winding them up for a pitch, then make myself turn around sharply, pivoting on my heel like a soldier doing an about-face.

No Roger after all.

But I don't know *who* it is.

There are two strangers, actually.

They're standing on the other side of the road, under a thin maple tree in a sidewalk planter, the leaves starting to yellow. Even though there's not enough foliage on the spindly branches to cast a real shadow, the pair seem to stand in their own plot of darkness.

Two tall, gaunt men wearing worn, but clean clothing that looks long out of date, thick homespun shirts and jeans with work boots.

The older man wears a wide-brimmed hat, shadowing his face and flinty eyes. There's not much of him to see past a bearish beard in black and iron-grey that cascades down his chest, obscuring most of his face except for that creepy stare.

And his eyes are locked on me in grim fascination.

The other man is younger, clean-shaven, his black hair short and a bit messy, but he's got a vacant look to him. Like he's checked out of his own body and it's still stuck on autopilot with this empty, eerie smile.

His eyes are so black, just like the older man's.

I shiver, wrapping my arms around myself like they can hide me from the weight of those combined stares. "Um, Nora? Who the hell are they?"

"Hm?" Nora glances away from the display window. "Oh, them? That's Ephraim Jacobin and his son, Culver. You don't see them in town much. Surprised they're here today."

"O-oh," I say. "Are those the hillfolk Lucas told me about?"

"Yep." She leans in closer to me, dropping her voice. "They're not as creepy as they look, I promise. Just don't go traipsing around in the woods at night on their turf. Then they might snap you right up and sacrifice you to the elder owl gods or something."

I snap my head up, staring at her.

That was a joke, right?

"They might—what?" My chest pulls roughly.

She doubles over, her laughter bouncing off the walls.

"Oh my God, your face, I'm—I'm sorry, D. I wasn't serious." Nora smiles apologetically and pushes me gently. "Lighten up, lady. Figured you were too city smart to fall for that. No, they're harmless. They're just hillbillies in the proper sense who don't like townsfolk too much and keep to themselves. The rest is all silly legends and ghost stories. Our own little Roanoke mysteries, I guess."

"Rude," I say, wrinkling my nose.

But she's right.

If I wasn't already so jittery from everything else, I'd have seen right through that in an instant.

"So, you wanna tell me why they're staring like they've never seen a real live woman before?"

"Because," a voice interrupts from behind me, "you're new in town, and it takes a while to warm up to strangers."

Another weird inkling hits just then, urging me to look back.

This time, when I turn around, I know what I'll find.

Ulysses Arrendell, looking like he just stepped off the cover of a men's fashion magazine, fabulously stylish as ever. His burgundy sleeves are rolled up to his elbows and buttoned in place, his hands in the pockets of pants that look like some weird hybrid between jeans and designer dress slacks in dark grey.

Nora immediately brightens.

She's married with kids, but the second she sees Ulysses, her cheeks flush. "Ulysses, hi! Speaking of devils we don't usually see in town..."

"Too flattering," he answers mildly, his emerald eyes glittering with humor. "Come now, I'm just making sure our darling new schoolteacher is settling in well."

Suddenly his gaze snaps to me and I can't look away.

Oof.

He's so *intense* under that layer of superficial playboy charm, and I wonder why.

"Are you, Miss Clarendon?" he rasps.

"Am I what?" I ask dumbly, which gets me a lazy, warm smile.

"Settling in. Or are we overwhelming you with our small-town affections?"

"Only a little," I joke, trying not to flush, but I don't have much control over my capillaries.

I can't help being embarrassed that things just aren't clicking for me right now.

There's too much going on at once and it's throwing me off-kilter.

"But I'm settling in fine, thank you," I say.

"Just out shopping then?" He glances at the store window we've all stopped in front of. "That's a lovely piece. Planning to buy it for your classroom or for home?"

"Neither! Unless, um, you're planning to give me a giant raise before I even start," I say wryly.

He grins. "I'm afraid that's not on the books yet, but perhaps we could discuss it over coffee."

"Oh, I—no, Ulysses, I couldn't possibly ask that. Plus, I'm out with Nora and—"

"And Nora needs to go home and pull her sons out of the mud pit they started in the backyard this morning," Nora replies warmly. "So we won't be out much longer. She's all yours, Ulysses."

I flash her a dirty look.

She just grins, knowing I'm outmaneuvered again.

I hold in a groan.

"Fiiine," I say. "Let me just get my bags in the car."

"Of course," Ulysses says, offering his arm. "Here, let me carry that for you. You too, Nora."

It's easier to let him than to argue at this point. He's so persistent, and we both end up transferring half our bags to Ulysses.

Rich boy or not, the man holds his own with heavy things. I noticed it when he helped with the moving. Now he carries them like they don't weigh a thing.

But as we turn to lead him to where we parked our cars, I can't help glancing back where the Jacobins were standing.

They're gone.

The sidewalk totally empty.

Nothing but an eerie memory like they were never there at all.

* * *

BY THE TIME I'm settled in at the café with Ulysses, I'm wishing I could pull the same kind of disappearing act.

He's not bad company.

He's handsome and overly flirty, sure, but he's not too pushy and doesn't keep pressing when I deflect. Mostly, he keeps asking me about work.

If the starting stipend was enough for school supplies, if I've started meeting any of the parents and kids yet, if I've had any trouble with the principal over lesson plans.

He tells me his parents, who he calls the Iron King and Iron Queen, personally review the lesson plans every year to ensure what's being taught 'fits the spirit of Redhaven.' Whatever that means.

All it tells me is they're control freaks, and I'd better get used to them having their thumbs in all my pies.

"Are they that controlling with you, too?" I ask, taking a sip of my latte frappe. "And your brothers? I heard you had brothers."

Ulysses lifts both blond brows. He's never looked away from me once, his piercing green stare unblinking, and now it sharpens with interest. "Have you been asking around about me, Miss Clarendon?"

"Not exactly, but you're all anyone wants to talk about," I retort with a smirk. "Seems like your family are pretty much the town celebrities."

"Only because we cultivate that image very carefully. It's easy to be famous when you're the only game in town." He winks. "To answer your questions, when I was home, they were very particular about bringing me up with Arrendell family values. Being shipped off to boarding school was almost a relief. Now, though, they mostly leave me to my wicked ways as long as I do my administrative duties. I'm not an elected official, of course, but..." He pauses and lets out a long-suffering sigh. "They delegate."

"Do they?" I can't help being amused. "I've heard some rumors about those wicked ways, and that your parents weren't always such sticklers. Wild parties with supermodels? Is it true?"

He snorts. "My reputation does precede me." His eyes darken, though, and his smile is almost sad. "I hope you don't believe all that bullshit. I'm not so awful. With money comes the obligation to entertain other wealthy people, but I'm not the bodice-ripping playboy everyone imagines."

He watches me giggle.

If only he knew I'm a fan of those books.

"Most of those so-called 'parties' are actually courting other folks for contributions to philanthropic causes. World hunger, poverty, that sort of thing. It's rather sad, really, that one must bribe so many egos in order for them to give a damn," he continues.

He has a point.

There's something pensive in his eyes that seems more human than his flirting that smacks of desperation to be liked. Maybe that's what's behind that look.

Ulysses Arrendell has one face he shows the world—playboy son of a powerful family—but underneath it, he just wants to be liked for *himself*.

"I'm sorry if my teasing was a bit much." I offer a smile. "It's probably pretty inappropriate right now, anyway."

Ulysses sobers. "Because of the dead girl, you mean."

I wince and look away.

The easy air between us immediately evaporates.

"Yes," I force out.

"I suppose the usual rumors are flying, aren't they? Rich single man, beautiful young girl, a reputation for extravagant parties and dirty affairs. Tell me, am I a murderer now, too, Miss Clarendon?"

"No!" I say quickly, shaking my head. "She died of a drug overdose, I think. How could you have murdered her?"

He looks relieved. Almost pleased, really.

"I know I shouldn't ask where you get your information from," Ulysses says softly. "But it calms my heart to know you have some faith in my innocence. In *me*."

Whoa.

I don't know what to say to that or to the heavy look he beams over.

So I look down, avoiding his searching green gaze, swirling my straw in the last slushy remnants of my drink.

"I should probably get going. I'm still not done unpacking, and I need to get used to waking up early. Especially since there's a staff meeting tomorrow. I think I get to meet the PTA."

"Don't forget to cover that tattoo. The Stepford Army will *not* approve," he warns gently. Then he stands, offering me his arm.

"Let me walk you to your car. It's late, and you never know who's around."

God help me, I almost say *no*.

But then I look out at the last orange light fading into evening gloom.

I remember the Jacobins just *staring*, like they had a terrible reason to.

That hideous red X under the window of The Rookery pokes me in the brain again.

Okay, fine.

Maybe just this once.

Nodding, I drain the last of my drink and stand to throw it away before slipping my hand into his arm. "It's not far. I appreciate it."

"Miss Clarendon, I would escort you every night—if you'd allow me."

My face heats.

I *really* don't know what to say to that.

Is he asking me on a date?

Was *this* a freaking date to him?

Sweet Jesus, I'm confused.

That's definitely not a minefield I want to walk into tonight, and Ulysses shares blood with the people signing my paychecks.

I just force on a polite smile as we step out into the twilight. On the way to my car, we pass that furniture store again.

I can't help how my steps slow, how I cast one last longing look at that gorgeous desk.

I must be pretty obvious.

Ulysses stops, looking at the display window with its soft lights bringing out the wood's finish.

"Striking, isn't it?" he says. "I always admire what you can make when you put in the time and dedication. I suppose that's how my family has always felt about Redhaven."

I let go of his arm and push my hands into my pockets,

studying the desk—but also our reflections, thin and pale in the window.

Me, short and dark; him, tall and bright.

We're two different worlds that shouldn't be seen together.

"Is that how you see yourselves?" I ask. "Like small-town caretakers?"

"We've been here longer than everyone, aside from the Jacobins, maybe. I suspect we'll outlast them by generations," he whispers. "An Arrendell was the first artisan to cut this fine furniture from the poplar and cherrywood here, long before it started attracting some of the finest craftsmen in the world. We help import a great deal of exotic lumber now. It's part of what we do to help the town thrive—broker those sorts of deals, handle shipping, manage the tree farms we own around town. I suppose it's hard *not* to think of ourselves as caretakers, yes, when the town relies on us for damned near everything."

I'm supposed to be impressed, I guess.

But actually, it just rings a little hollow and arrogant.

Then again, it can't be easy when your whole identity is built on a savior complex and nothing else.

I wonder if he senses my discomfort.

Ulysses suddenly glances at me with a self-deprecating smile. "You'll be wanting to get home soon, won't you?"

I wince guiltily. "It's not you, Ulysses. I promise."

"Did I *say* it was?" he asks sharply.

"No, but..."

But what? I swallow thickly.

"But you're painfully aware that you're trying to escape me," he finishes. This time, his smile is bitter, but it seems more directed at himself than me. "Lucky you, Miss Clarendon, living all the way out there by yourself, where no one ever bothers you."

...okay.

So I think I've upset him.

That's the only explanation for this odd mood change.

I'm not even sure how to apologize.

So I let the silence linger as we make our way back to my car. Even though he's quiet and seems locked up in his own head, he's still almost courtly as he opens my car door for me and bows his head, watching me from under his brows with mournful eyes.

"Good night, Miss Clarendon," he mutters. "See you again soon."

He really is a little boy, I think.

All that money and he's never learned how to handle rejection well.

It confuses him, hurts him, and I think he's stuck on that. But at least he's not being totally ugly about it.

On the scale of *don't care* to *raging mantrum*, this is pretty light.

I smile. Just because I'm not that interested in hooking up doesn't mean we can't be friendly, and I want him to know it.

"I promise," I say. "If anything comes up with the school, I'll call you first thing."

"You better," he says darkly.

Before I can react to that, another voice speaks up.

"If Ulysses cannot handle it," the new voice says, rich with its strange old-world accent, "you can always call on me."

If I thought of Ulysses as immature before, it's nothing compared to the guilty flinch that makes his eyes widen as his father's voice rolls over us.

Montero Arrendell.

We both turn simultaneously.

Montero stands just a few feet behind us, a dramatic figure under a streetlamp that makes him look like he just stepped out of an old noir film. He's all stern shadows and reflections with his ivory skin, black hair, and neatly pressed black suit.

The only hints of color are the tints of amber from the light and those jade eyes so much like his son's. They watch me with the same intensity that makes me feel like he can see right through me.

"Mr. Arrendell," I greet him uncertainly.

A smile instantly softens the saber-sharp lines of his features. His eyes gentle as he tucks his hands into the pockets of his slacks.

"Miss Clarendon," he says. "I hope I didn't startle you. I saw you two walking, and I couldn't help but stop and say hello."

"Father," Ulysses retorts. I have to try not to smile. He really looks like an awkward boy playing at being a grown-up in front of his dad. "What are you doing in town today?"

"Budget meetings with the police chief," Montero answers. "It ran a touch long. I was just on my way up to the house for dinner, if you'd like to ride back with me. You know how much your mother fusses when you don't get a proper meal." Montero arches his brows, shifting his attention back to me. "Would you care to join us, Miss Clarendon? I feel so dreadful, thinking of you dining all alone in that little house."

"Oh—no, I'll be fine." I shake my head quickly.

Holy hell, what is happening?

I'm *so* not cut out for eating with small-town royalty.

"I'm so tired I'd probably embarrass myself by passing out on my plate in front of you. But thanks for the offer!"

What else can I say?

"Another time then," Montero says. "You are always welcome in our home."

I'm spinning.

This weird request, however kind, just doesn't compute in my brain.

I'm the newly hired schoolteacher. These people don't even have young kids.

Why is he talking to me like I'm some long-lost family friend, or even his next pet project?

That's probably all it is, though.

Rich people posturing or looking to feel good about themselves by slumming it with the poor city girl, treating her like Cinderella.

Ulysses saves me from saying anything by gesturing to my open car door. "She was just on her way home, Father."

More weirdness.

I'd almost feel like he's dismissing me—trying to get rid of me—if he wasn't giving me an easy out from this awkward situation. But there's something about how he looks at his father that makes me feel more, too.

Almost like Ulysses is *guarding* me.

Didn't Nora say Montero Arrendell had a roaming eye?

I wonder if Ulysses is worried about me becoming another one of his father's conquests.

If he's anything like the little boys I've seen who know their fathers are womanizing cheaters, then he's also trying to protect his mother's feelings, too.

My heart aches.

Seriously, I'm not someone Lucia Arrendell ever needs to worry about.

It's time for me to make myself scarce before the tension chokes me, anyway.

"I really do need to go," I say hastily and smile, sliding behind the wheel of my car. "But it was nice seeing you guys. Have a good night."

I close my car door just as Ulysses steps out of the way, backing onto the sidewalk.

There it is again—that heavy feeling of eyes everywhere, of someone watching me.

Only this time, it's not just Ulysses and Montero standing on the curb.

It's different. Warmer.

Just a hot prickle of awareness.

It doesn't fully hit me until I look through my windshield at another vehicle.

Lucas' patrol car, parked across the street.

My heart leaps up my throat.

He's behind the wheel, his head bowed.

He's not looking right at me, though. I just glimpse a paperback in his hands, peeking up over the steering wheel... but I get the feeling he *was* watching a minute ago.

There's always a certain quiet tension to him, the way his brows draw together, overshadowing his stark, handsome face.

I can't see his eyes in the darkness.

But I wonder how I'd feel looking into his green eyes again, without the strangeness of Ulysses and Montero. They stare at me like I'm something they want to buy in a shop window.

That's what makes me so uncomfortable, I realize.

Ulysses looks at me the same way I was admiring that desk in the shop.

His father, the same.

In their world, everything has its price.

But Lucas, he looks at me like he sees me—and I hope he likes what he sees.

There's a wild magnetism in my blood, this urge to climb out of my car and walk over to his. This urge to tap on his window and see how his eyes ignite when he drawls, *Well, well, Miss New York.*

Shame I still feel the Arrendells eyeballing me, even if Lucas isn't.

Something tells me it would be a bad, bad idea.

So, no, I don't give in.

I don't have the stomach for more trouble or awkwardness tonight.

I just start the engine and pull away.

When my eyes flick to the rearview mirror a second later, I gasp.

Just like the Jacobins, the Arrendells are gone.

Is everyone a human jump scare around here?

* * *

I'M NOT SCARED.

I'm *not*.

I've been fine on my own in this house so far. Sure, the silence makes me listen harder sometimes, waiting for the snap of a footstep on a twig or the sudden creak of a porch board.

But I have the fireflies for company, this constant lovely swarm of living string lights right outside my window.

The alarm system Lucas installed definitely helps, too.

As long as it's not going off, I know I'm really alone—or at least Roger or anyone else won't dare get too close.

But there's something different in the air tonight.

I curl up on my air mattress for another lonely night in the house. I'm scrolling this local secondhand store's website, smiling at a nice-looking bed that's in my budget. If I order tonight, I could have it by tomorrow afternoon and spare myself a week-long backache.

There's wind out there, whistling through the trees.

It tells me where the chinks in the weathered wood are, little gusts slipping in around the windows and the eaves to tickle the fine hairs along the backs of my arms.

Why does it feel like ghostly fingers walking over my skin?

I swear, it's even messing with my internet connection.

I'm still using my phone's mobile hotspot for my laptop. I guess the cell tower it's using isn't doing so well in speeding gusts that bend the trees like sad mourners.

But it holds on long enough for me to place my furniture order, plus a few other odds and ends.

I should shut it down and sleep, but I'm too restless.

I need a distraction, something to get my mind off Redhaven's unease and weirdness.

I can't help glancing out the window, trying to fight down that feeling of being *watched*—it has to be my imagination this time—and I sneak a hand into the little organizer basket next to my air mattress that's filling in for a nightstand.

Underneath my Kindle is a long, slender unmarked box.

These things always are.

And if it wasn't for butterfingers the other day, Lucas Graves never would've seen the secret it holds.

I thumb the box open and slip the little purple vibrator bullet into my palm. A plastic-wrapped duo of AAA batteries comes tumbling out after.

Convenient.

I'm already blushing as I pop the batteries in.

It's the mundaneness of bringing this thing to life that makes it a little embarrassing, but it's also memories of growing up.

I never had much privacy.

My foster parents always suspected me of horrible things and would come whipping into my bedroom in the middle of the night to catch me in the middle of—I never knew what they expected me to be doing.

Drugs? Prostitution? Summoning demons?

Who knows.

But it only took one instance of Foster Mom #4 catching me with my fingers inside my panties to make sure I never did *that* again.

Not until my college dorm and long nights when my room-mates were out.

Nights when I started feeling like it was okay to explore, the desperation of hormones on fire when I was too nervous with boys.

Even back then I was secretive.

But I need this now.

I need this after a freaky, long-ass day and what's shaping up to be a long night haunted by a green-eyed beast stuffed in a police uniform who knows my dirty little secret.

So I slide on my back, tracing the cool kiss of the bullet down across my stomach, teasing it against my pussy.

I close my eyes and touch.

Touch.

I think about him without actively trying.

My body jolts like lightning and I hiss through my teeth, lifting my hips off the bed.

Oh—oh, it's *strong*, and I'm already so hot.

Teasing myself with sizzling circles around my clit, pleasure darting up my spine until my nipples peak.

With a whimper caught in my teeth, I arch my back, rubbing my nipple with my free hand.

God, there's a good rhythm, working up an itch between my legs I desperately need scratched.

I like to draw it out, though.

It's so nice to sink into a fantasy that comes this easy—a hard body over me, rough hands parting my legs, commanding my flesh.

His lips and tongue roaming, turning fevered breaths into whimpers until I'm trembling all over.

I don't feel the metal anymore.

I just feel how wet I am, how I'm trying to hold back the name on my lips, digging my teeth into my bottom lip until I taste metal.

"Lucas! God," I whisper, holding the bullet over my clit.

I squeeze my eyes shut, gasping as I rock my hips again and again, wondering how sweet it would be to meet his rock-hard body, to feel him thrusting, to have his teeth sink into my skin.

Yes, fuck.

Mark me.

My pussy spills all over my hands, the rhythm building to an angry tempo.

I can't help myself.

I want this and I want so much *more.*

And I finally give in, focusing on my clit, shocking myself so fiercely my entire body arches off the bed in a sharp, gasping jerk.

I see my whole ideal sex life flash before my eyes.

Green eyes.

Corded muscle.

Skilled, rough hands.

Muscular hips that strike hard, strike deep, and always without mercy.

Dark stubble raking my throat, whispers in my ears, louder and growling with every thrust.

"You think you can hide shit from me, New York? Come for me. Come your little pink pussy sore on my cock, Lilah."

I'm so gone.

I come so hard my vision turns red with the violent blur of pleasure slicing through me.

There's nothing here but him.

Nothing but Lucas and his heated expression, his flashing eyes fixed on me, sweat dripping off his hard-toned jaw.

He's all rippling muscle as his cock claims me in rough, deep, intimate thrusts.

The vision shocks me almost as hard as my orgasm.

My body wrings itself dry and then drops me back on the mattress in a gasping mess.

Suddenly, the vibrator feels like too much.

I toss it aside before rolling my face into the pillow with a moan.

...what the sexy repressed hell was *that*?

Okay.

So, he's hot.

But I'm not—I don't really—

Stop worrying about it, I warn.

It's not that important.

Just a dirty little fantasy about a big man who's been around me a lot lately. It's easy for your lusty subconscious to fill in the blanks.

That's it.

That's all it is.

I don't really want to jump Lucas Graves' bones, I lie to myself.

I open one eye, peeking out with a groan.

"Emma?" I mumble into the pillow. "You there? Got any idea why my brain did that?"

There's no answer, of course.

Ghosts don't run advice columns and I guess they don't like watching me treating my body like an amusement park.

So I push it out of mind and curl up as the wind growls through the trees like a rabid animal.

Dang.

So much for relaxing.

Now I'm just a hot mess of endorphins and confusion.

Sighing, I stare up at the ceiling, my mind running circles, trying not to think of Lucas.

Yeah, good luck with that.

I'd have an easier time not thinking of a pink elephant when someone challenges me.

Eventually, with the wind still roaring, my brain pings on Emma again.

What were her last hours like?

Did she even realize she was dying before she was gone?

I keep going back to Ulysses, too.

That mood change, the weird look on his face when he thought people actually suspected him of murder.

He looked so hurt, almost like he's faced this kind of thing before.

I don't actually know that much about his evil reputation, do I?

But it can't be that atrocious.

Nora laughs and teases about him being a philanthropist player. Kind of clashes with Lucas' dire warnings that the whole family is rotten to the core. But if they're so wealthy, they're easy tabloid fodder.

Oh, to hell with it.

I grab my phone and pull up Google.

Searching "Ulysses Arrendell" immediately gets hits.

A few puff pieces in national travel magazines about the

illustrious history of the town come up first. They rave about how the Arrendells are such grand hosts of their own tiny kingdom.

There are also several AP News hits with a dizzying list of charities and causes and contributions.

The Arrendells are seemingly responsible for curing diseases, bringing several small countries back from the brink of poverty, and revitalizing a slice of the US economy from Davenport to El Paso to Key West.

There are only a few bits here and there in the gossip rags, feasting on the juicy news of whatever hot celebrity just dumped one of the brothers, with no real reason ever given.

One starlet says Ulysses was always too busy for a real relationship. He cared about his nonprofits and NGOs more than he cared about her.

It's a little crazy, realizing just how far their reach extends outside this little town.

I get a glimpse of the other brothers, too. They're older than Ulysses.

All of them have the same translucent green eyes and expertly styled hair.

Weirdly, there's not much about the eldest son, Vaughn—just a few hints at scandal and him separating from his family. He's a dignified-looking Silicon Valley billionaire, large and imposing, not built like his trim, elegant brothers.

The next, Xavier, apparently works in overseas agriculture focused on making palm and coconut cultivation more sustainable. At a glance, he's dashing with hollow cheekbones and haunted eyes.

Then Aleksander. I'm not surprised he works in fashion, as lithe and pretty as he is. A little more surprised he's got a rotten reputation for hooking up with everything in a skirt, usually supermodels and—

Wait.

Didn't Lucas say Emma Santos was an Instagram model?

But that wouldn't line up, would it?

Unless Aleksander Arrendell snuck into Redhaven with her, then skipped town the night before I arrived, leaving her body behind. I wonder if there's any way I can ask Ulysses without being obvious.

But *do* I really think his brother committed a murder? I've never even met the man.

That's a hell of a leap and probably wildly wrong.

Still, I can't get over it.

I can't let it go when I'm haunted.

Every part of me wants answers when the drug overdose story feels too neat, too easily wrapped up. I'm obsessing over what really goes on in that big old house on the hill behind its perfect façade of fairy-tale royalty.

Especially when I remember what Lucas said about Montero Arrendell.

The patriarch and his *tastes.*

I shudder.

Do those tastes include murdering dark-haired young women in cold blood?

I know what it's like, Lucas said. *Feeling a bond with family you haven't seen in years.*

What did he really mean?

Sad, restless thoughts drag me deeper.

I guess it comes with the territory when you bring yourself off to a strange, handsome man who's on your mind constantly.

Okay, Lucas.

Who haven't you seen in years?

And is that why you hate the Arrendells so much?

Google can't give me any answers to that.

But I wonder if this idyllic little town is just like everything else that's too good to be true.

How big and nasty and deep is Redhaven's dark side?

X: RED FLAGS (LUCAS)

*S*hit.

I think I might be in the running for biggest creep on the face of the planet.

Here's Delilah, fresh off dealing with a stalker asshole ex who may have followed her to Redhaven.

And here I am, following her around like another obsessive weirdo who's too fucked in the head to quit.

I can tell myself I'm not a threat to her.

That it's for her own protection, when there's just some deep-seated instinct that says she's in *danger*, and besides—it's a small town. I'm a cop, so I'm gonna patrol and I'm gonna run across her.

That doesn't change the fact that she's probably sick of catching me out of the corner of her eye every time she turns around.

This isn't Celeste again, I tell myself.

It's not another dark-haired, starry-eyed, pretty young woman getting pulled into the Arrendells' orbit, seduced by their wealth and flashy bullshit. She's not falling under Montero Arrendells' black magic spell.

I have good reason to worry. As he's gotten older, Montero's had to be more subtle.

More cautious.

He lets others do more of his dirty work.

If you didn't know better, you'd think he was a saint with how squeaky clean he's been the last ten years or so.

That doesn't mean he ain't doing shit.

Just means he's gotten sneakier, better at keeping the blood off his hands, throwing up a dozen proxies who'll take the fall for him if there's ever a little slip.

It fits right in with his pattern, considering how many people believe Ethan Sanderson had something to do with my sister's disappearance. Ethan was just a local boy who was in love with Celeste, and once Captain Faircross' best friend.

I know the rumors.

I still hear 'em being whispered around town, every time I walk past and people think I don't hear them mention 'that poor Graves girl.'

And I know they're dead wrong.

Old Ethan wouldn't whack a mosquito, wherever he's gone.

I kick the heel of my boot against the leg of the captain's desk as I flip through a folder. Technically, it isn't a case file, even though I store it among the files when I'm not using it.

It's just a mess of old newspaper clippings.

Mostly stuff from the tabloids and a few old internet rumors printed out, shit you can't really trust. Though sometimes the best way to hide the most outlandish truth is to put it out there and let people laugh it off as sordid rumors from the lunatic fringe. Whatever feeds people's hunger for scandal and intrigue.

There's sure as hell plenty of scandal swirling around the Arrendells, going back years.

All old, though. Montero's era and before.

In the age of social media, they've been scrubbed squeaky clean and polished by reputation managers till they're damn near sporting halos.

But there's still the old stuff, if you know where to dig.

Ugly rumors about sleeping with other people's wives.

Husbands. Politicians. Celebrities. The works.

For small-town kingpins, they get around like humming-birds. There are whole albums stuffed with photos of them dining with billionaire oil sheikhs, former presidents, corporate titans, wealthy global arms dealers.

No one ever seems to know what they're doing there, of course, besides rubbing elbows and having a little fun gliding around yet *another* party. Charity might be the cover story, but there's always something darker behind the scenes.

Those parties are never *just* parties.

How damned deep does their influence really run in certain circles?

What kind of power do they have to make a real scandal disappear?

1992. A male movie star found floating dead in his own swimming pool after an all-night party at his Hollywood mansion. The list of drunken attendees was a who's who of the nineties—and Montero was a guest of honor.

Lucia, his wife, was totally absent. The implication in the headline was that before the actor was found *accidentally* drowned, he and Montero were fighting over a certain dark-eyed, dark-haired Latina music star.

1995. A younger Montero brooding in the background of a drug bust that put several dozen young stars in jail. Sure, they got out on bail in a day, and house arrest was the worst of their rich-people punishment, but Montero wasn't even hauled in for questioning.

Did I mention the bust was at that damn house up the hill?

It just keeps coming, year by year, sin by sin.

More accidents.

More overdoses.

More unfortunate slip and falls and accidental gun discharges and drownings and unexplained disappearances, always with one thing in common.

Somehow, there was always Montero and a dark-haired woman involved. Most of the time she was just a passing interest, hanging on his arm instead of his wife.

But sometimes, she was the one who disappeared.

A rising actress named Carla Oneida, 1996. A party on a yacht in Boston Harbor. Over two hundred people on the boat, yet somehow, no one was around when she and Montero went strolling on the deck. She slipped and fell overboard. Her body was never recovered.

A singer named Marjorie Denton in 2001—supposedly vanished hiking, but she'd never been known for hiking trips. She *was* known for getting her way with rich men to pay for her every need, and her latest sugar daddy? Take a good guess.

So many more.

And even though his name comes up again and again as someone connected to the dead and missing women, the man was never implicated.

Never accused.

Only by yours truly, and maybe the *one* person I might be able to get on my side—Captain Grant—if he'd man up and stop running away from his past.

My sister didn't just walk off and leave me at seventeen, all alone, our parents dead.

Celeste never would.

Not even if Ethan Sanderson tried to run off with her and elope under new names.

Not even if Montero promised her a billion dollars if she'd just up and *run*.

Celeste didn't leave me.

She was taken.

First by the world he seduced her into, lavishing her with expensive gifts and attention, making her feel special.

Then by whatever the hell he did to her next.

I almost don't want to know.

But I *need* to.

I need to know my sister's fate.

Just like I need to make sure it doesn't happen again, when I don't trust for a second that Montero Arrendell ever stopped his debauched ways.

He's just adapted with age and the times.

A trio of handsome, charming young sons makes for perfect bait.

Think of the Arrendell brothers as talent scouts, luring his prey to him.

That's why I don't like the way Ulysses has been eyeing Delilah lately one damn bit.

Another dark-haired, beautiful young woman with stars in her eyes.

For all her Big Apple worldliness, there's an innocence there that would make her the perfect prize for a warped fuck like Montero.

I won't let that happen.

I also can't concentrate with a trio of jackasses talking over my head, not that it's ever stopped them before.

"Do you guys mind?" I snap.

"I do," Captain Grant Faircross says, stroking his thick, silver-peppered brown beard. He's a bear of a man, taking up so much space in our tiny dispatch area. "Remind me again why we're not telling this girl's parents she's dead? She was only twenty-two. Barely out of the damn nest. If that were my daughter, I'd be hysterical. She's been missing for God knows how long, and we're just sitting on it?"

"You, hysterical?" Micah says dryly. "Very funny."

Next to Grant, Junior Sergeant Micah Ainsley is a ghost—pale blond-white hair, white skin, you'd almost expect his eyes to be white too, but they're kind of an icy blue-grey. He's stronger than he looks, too. I've seen him push a stalled truck up a hill, but that's just what Micah does.

Always doing too much, pushing too far, and right now he's trying to push Captain Grant's buttons as he says, "Think that

GED failed you, Captain. I don't think you know what hysterical means."

"I know what 'beat your albino ass' means," Grant mutters.

"Hey." Henri Fontenot's lazy Cajun drawl cuts in. He glances between us, pushing the not-regulation mess of his long brown hair out of his eyes as he gives us one of the broody looks that doe-eyed Louisiana boy's known for. "Not one of us is givin' Lucas a chance to get a word in edgewise."

"See? You know you guys suck when the new guy has to play the peacemaker," I point out, dropping the stack of newspaper clippings I've been holding on top of the ever-growing pile in the folder. "Look, guys, call it a hunch. There's more to this than an overdose. I want to be able to tell her family the truth—the real truth—and if there's justice to be had, I want it settled before they have to deal with something so painful."

"What you mean," Grant growls, "is you don't want her family publicizing this and fucking up your solo investigation."

"You know me too well." I lean back in the chair till it creaks and Grant gives me a dirty look.

I spread my hands innocently.

Hell, if anyone broke the springs on this thing, it's him. His desk, after all, and he's a human moose when I'm just big.

"Look," I continue. "If there was foul play involved, right now, the person who did it—whether it was an accident or intentional, planned or a crime of passion—is probably feeling pretty damn smug. Thinking he got away with it. So they're gonna get careless. But if the family makes it known it was a murder, especially if the murderer's keeping tabs, they'll work even harder to cover their tracks. Go to ground. Then we'll never find them."

There's a long silence.

I give my boys time to think.

I've been working with Grant for a good long while now, and Micah for a few solid years. Henri's the new guy, just hired on under a year ago, but he's a decent type and he blends in well.

We're all long thinkers and slow talkers. Maybe a hazard of being cops.

But after a while, Grant nods, scruffing his beard a bit.

"I'll give you a week, maybe two tops. Any longer than that and the trail's cold anyway. At that point, it's just cruel to the family."

I let out the breath I've been holding in.

I figured it'd go my way, especially since Grant, of all the people here, knows what happened with my sister, and what I suspect.

I'm not the only one who's lost someone to mystery disappearances when his best friend Ethan has been missing forever.

Ethan Sanderson disappeared the same night Celeste did. Rumor is they ran off together, or he killed her and fled town, but I don't believe it—and neither does Grant, even if he won't admit it.

He's always had questions, suspicions, shit we don't talk about but we both know in our bones. That's why he's usually softer on me than anyone else when I start talking crazy.

And this could've been the one time he went against me.

He *does* give me the stink eye, though, his blue eyes stern. He's only like a year or two older than me, but he acts like my damn father.

"Just don't go starting any shit you can't finish, Graves," he rumbles.

I know what that means.

Don't go fucking with the Arrendells unless you've got hard proof.

Good advice. I may or may not have had Lucia Arrendell demanding my head on a silver platter once, during my first rookie year when I got a little overzealous trying to go after Montero.

Since then, I've learned to be careful.

That doesn't mean I've let it go.

Just that I've learned to play the long game.

I smirk as I snap off a salute. "I will finish all my shits, Captain. Rest assured."

"You and that fuckin' mouth," Grant groans.

"Got one just like everybody else here, Cap."

"...you *trying* to get fired today?" He shakes his head slowly, then glances toward the chief's closed office door. Not that Bowden's likely in there; who the hell knows where he takes off to these days. Gone with a pile of nail clippings left on his desk sometimes. Grant glances back at us. "What about the new teacher? We sure we're all okay letting her move back into a possible murder scene?"

"Nothing there," Micah says. "Henri and I gave it a triple-check, and Lucas looked again. The only evidence was that girl's body, plus a little crushed grass that could've been from Miss Clarendon herself. No point in taping it off forever. We took our photos and it's too late now anyway. She's already in."

"The house isn't the problem," I grumble.

"Yeah?" Henri looks up with a cutting glance. "So you're saying the teacher is. Miss Clarendon, was it?" He whistles. "Girl's got some legs on her, *mon ami*."

I glower at him. "The fuck you doing, looking at her legs, Frenchie?"

That gets me a shit-eating grin. "Gettin' you riled up, for starters. You been spendin' a lot of time out there, my friend."

"She's new in town. Fresh meat. I'm just being neighborly, helping her get settled in. *Just* helping her," I emphasize, jabbing a finger at all three of them.

Micah's mouth is a mess, clearly trying not to smirk.

Henri's still giving me that grin.

Grant just eyeballs me skeptically.

"Can we move the fuck on?" I flare. "Don't we got anything better to worry about?"

At least they take the hint.

Henri sighs. "We got six calls the last few days about the

Jacobins. Been moving distilleries again, I think, and people are complaining about all the clanking and grinding in the hills."

"By the time we go looking for their still, it's always too late. Damn thing disappears like a ghost," Grant points out. "And triangulating by sound doesn't help much with the way noise carries over the trees."

"They'll settle down eventually. People will forget they exist again in a day or two," I say. "I mean, unless you want to arrest them over some rotgut whiskey."

Grant shrugs. "We'd just be chasing our tails while they laugh from the shadows. They move on to exporting cocaine, then we'll worry about a sting. But right now, we've got other things to worry about."

"Like what?" Micah asks.

"Like working out the shifts for crossing guard duty," Grant snarls.

We all groan.

Life as a small-town cop sure is wild.

* * *

BY THE TIME we're done sorting rotations for the first semester of the school year, it's time for me to head out on patrol.

Not that there's much to patrol. Most of our crime happens during tourist seasons, first in high summer, then in mid-fall. Summer's when the vacationers and shoppers come through.

There's always somebody who wants to shoplift or people getting into fights with their significant others in the middle of the town square—sometimes pretty violently, too.

Then there's the kids they bring along, little brats defacing public property.

Autumn's when shit gets weirder.

The hikers come out to see the trails and the exploding fall foliage.

Those are the folks who get arrested for flashing 'cause they got caught fucking in the woods, and some of them do it deliberately, getting off on exhibitionism.

Then there are the folks who didn't mean it, didn't realize their midnight skinny-dip in Still Lake was too visible. Poor humiliated bastards.

We've had to break up a few altercations when people stumbled on the Jacobins, too, though mostly the hillfolk take care of themselves. They've been known to run people off their property with a sawed-off shotgun, meaning me or the captain have to go up to their farm and have a stern talk with them about not shooting our goddamned economic backbone.

Mostly, though, it's the kinky shit in autumn.

It's *always* the kinky shit in autumn.

Being out in the woods does strange stuff to people.

Right now, it's just a few of our local kids trying to sneak a little shoplifting. Half of them feel so guilty they confess and return the stolen shit before they get caught. Plus, a few drunken brawlers.

Which means all I have to do is park my car and read.

Instead of a book, though, I've brought along my thick file on Montero Arrendell and his sons.

I wonder about Vaughn, too, something with him that doesn't sit quite right. The way he just packed up and left, cut all ties with his family.

What drove him away?

Did he learn something about his old man, about his family, that he couldn't stomach?

Or did he do something so monstrous that even they couldn't stand the sight of him?

Face it.

You're wondering if something really did drive Celeste away.

If she's still alive out there somewhere, better off than when she was stuck with your dumbass. Living happily ever after with Ethan, both of them running away from everything that hurt them.

Part of me wishes it was true.

I'd rather find out my sister hated me—we sure as hell fought enough—and ran off. That we didn't have the bond I thought we did. That beats knowing for sure that she's truly dead and gone.

Celeste and I were oil and water.

We tore each other's egos up and down all the time, but we were all each other had, and underneath all that bickering, there was always a hell of a lot of love.

I'm smiling when I think of the way Delilah and I claw at each other, snipping and snarling and pushing each other's buttons.

Like every barb is just a little warmer, the venom in the sting a bit sweeter.

Nothing like that last fight between me and Celeste.

Nothing like that last fight at all.

* * *

Years Ago

"WHAT THE HELL do you mean, you enlisted?"

Celeste glares at me, clutching my enlistment papers in her shaking fingers. I won't lie, her posture is a little intimidating.

Normally, I don't blink when we start shouting at each other, but tonight Celeste doesn't look like Celeste.

She looks like someone else.

Someone fake, all dolled up in that expensive red dress that costs more than our house, wearing it just because that man gave it to her. Her hair's tied up in this weird twist of knots, and she's wearing stark red lipstick that makes her mouth look cruel and angry. The thick mascara and eyeliner make her eyes look less green and more white, more cold and furious.

That's not my sister—my earthy, messy, scatterbrained sister.

That's a doll created by Montero Arrendell.

Not a real person at all.

But the anger in her voice is very real as she snaps, "You're only seventeen! You're too young for the Navy, dammit."

"Jesus, Cel, it's preliminary." I scowl. "Can't go till I'm eighteen, anyway—and they want me to finish high school first. Hell, after I serve my first tour, they'll pay for college. How the hell else we gonna pay for it?"

"I don't know!" she flares. "Look, this—this whole stupid thing, it didn't come with an instruction manual, Lucas. Mom and Dad didn't leave me a step-by-step guide to raising you, but we could—we could sell the house—"

"No way. We're not selling this place. It's all we've got left of them," I spit back. "Screw it. I'm not going to college at all if that's what it takes!"

"You have to go." She shakes her head sharply, her fingers tightening until the papers she's clutching crumple. "They would've wanted it. But not like this. The military... Jesus Christ. You won't even survive to take your first classes. Do you know how dangerous it is over there? We're at war."

"Iraq? Afghanistan? Those are brush fires, not World War Two," I throw back in all my youthful ignorance. "I just gotta make it through a full tour or two, and half the time I'll be polishing ship decks. It's not that scary, Cel."

"You don't know that. You—"

An impatient honk from a horn outside stops her.

There's a limo waiting, black and gleaming as a snake.

Her face transforms and it scares me.

This desperation I've never seen before, this hope, almost like she's in thrall to some horrible beast she can't resist even as it drains the life from her.

And is that fear underneath it?

It's funny how terror and longing look the same sometimes.

Her hands go lax and my papers drop to the floor.

"I don't have time for this. We'll talk more when I get home," she says hollowly. She won't even look at me now. "You're not enlisting, and that's final."

She gathers up her skirts, the bracelet on her wrist jingling and flashing.

Then she's gone.

Right off to *him* again, so he can parade her around on his arm in front of all his rich friends, in front of his wife. Showing my sister off like a toy he'll throw away tomorrow.

I fucking hate it.

I hate him.

I hate the way she is when she's around him.

I hate everything.

Hate waking up in the morning and hate realizing my sister hasn't come home.

Hate that no one's seen her since yesterday.

But more than anything, I hate the fake-ass look on Montero Arrendell's face when I go storming up to the big house and fling myself past his fancy butlers and doormen to roar in his face, to demand he give my sister back.

"Poor boy," he says, smiling, wearing the cold eyes of a man asking *What are you going to do? What* can *you do?* "Your sister told me she was done with me long before my invitation to last night's soiree. I'd asked her to attend in the hopes of making amends and restoring our—friendship—but when she never arrived, I assumed I'd been soundly rejected. You're looking in the wrong place, son. Perhaps a flighty girl like her just couldn't handle the pressure of raising a teenager all on her lonesome."

It's a goddamned lie and I know it.

A hurtful, hateful lie that hits my deepest fears.

I want to hurl myself at him and claw his eyes out.

I don't even realize I'm dangerously close to doing it, his cold green eyes blurring into mist with the furious tears streaming down my face. Not until hands are on me, pulling me back.

Those butlers and doormen I dodged before are dragging me now and I'm kicking and shouting and blind with rage.

They chuck me out of the house with lots of threats about calling the cops.

When my senses come back, I'm down the hill, left in the dirt in a sobbing heap.

All I can do is make a vow.

I'll never fucking stop.

Not till I know the truth about where my sister's gone.

* * *

Present

ALL THOSE YEARS.

All those years, multiple tours of duty with the Navy, coming back home to Redhaven to sign on with the police, and I still haven't found my answers.

I still haven't found my sister.

But I know she didn't leave me that night.

If she meant to run away, she'd have taken *something*. She would've packed her bags in advance, tucked away a few mementos and keepsakes. There would've been things missing from the house, things she needed, money missing from her bank account or signs of her using it somewhere else.

Instead, there's an abyss.

Celeste ran out with nothing but that dress on her back, her little clutch purse with her phone and ID, and that ugly goddamned bracelet.

She expected to come back.

I linger on Montero's cold face in the photo, his sleazy old-world charm, then glance up as a familiar splash of color goes cruising past where I'm parked on the edge of the town square.

Delilah's Kia, winding around the central roundabout onto the street leading down to the school.

Maybe it's that I'm still caught up in bad memories or maybe it's just this *pull* Delilah has on me.

Or maybe I'm just a nosy bastard.

I can't help myself today.

I start my patrol car and pull out after her.

By the time I arrive at the school, she's already out of her car, looking trim and sleek today in a loose shirt, capri jeans, and sandals so worn they've got to be devilishly comfy.

She's got a huge shoulder bag today, bulging with school supplies and massive rolls of poster board, making her clumsy as she tries to jiggle the door the way I showed her.

I slip out of my car and walk up behind her.

"Let me," I say, nudging her aside gently and reaching for the handle.

Delilah gasps. She flinches away, looking up at me without recognition, but with a look I know too well.

That flash of fear.

What I'm not expecting is the relief on her face when it clicks that it's me. Then she smiles, stepping back and letting me have the door and the key.

"Just like Superman," she says. "Always showing up where you're needed. Superman was a stalker too." Her lips curve into a teasing grin. "He just used his superhuman hearing to do it. What's your excuse?"

"Good timing, luck, and the fact that my patrol shifts overlap the hours you're out and about." I hitch the door handle up just right and push it open, holding it for her. "After you."

"Thanks. I didn't have any trouble with it when I came in for the faculty meeting this morning, but I wasn't carrying half a craft store, either."

She ducks under my arm, and as she passes, I catch a whiff of that soft floral fragrance rising off her hair.

That scent practically kisses me, reaches down deep, and strokes me rock hard.

Goddamn.

In the hall, Delilah turns, watching me with her lips quirked. "You coming, or did you just stop by to help with the door?"

I hesitate.

There's no good reason to be here. I should be watching my beat just in case this is the one day something serious happens in town while I'm fucking off doing other things.

Too bad it sticks with me.

That flicker of fear in her eyes, and not for me.

Who are you afraid of, Lilah?

I want to ask, but I know this little cactus woman. If I prod her now, she'll just gore me with her spines.

Yeah, I'll stick around a little. See if she'll volunteer a little information, or at least give me an opening to ask without getting stabbed.

Hell, and maybe I want to stay close by.

Wherever I can guard her and make her feel safer.

"I'm not doing much right now," I say.

Her gaze flicks to my badge, my uniform, her mouth quirking, telling me she doesn't believe me.

"Could help you with that, if you like." I nod at her bag.

"So arts and crafts are among your many other talents?" Delilah's brows rise, her voice mocking me gently. "You install alarm systems, you repair steps, you cut glass, you jiggle doors... is there anything you don't do?"

That pings me for a second. It's a familiar line from a movie, and when I remember why, I grin.

"Fly," I grind out.

She blinks, flushing faintly.

"What? You've seen Ever After?"

"I'm a man of varied tastes, New York."

Delilah laughs. "You're definitely no Danielle."

"And you're damn sure no Prince Henry." I duck into the hall, stepping closer to her. "Guess I can toss you over my shoulder to rescue you, if you'd like."

Her eyes widen and she stares at me incredulously.

"You wouldn't dare."

"Wanna bet?" I crouch down like I'm about to spring, prowling closer.

She takes a step back with a sharp breath, then turns with a high laugh and takes off running, her sandals pelting the tiles. "Don't even try it, Graves!"

It's fucking on.

I don't think I could stop myself from chasing her if my whole life depended on it.

That fluttering black hair pulls on me like a leash, draws me like a will-o'-the-wisp, luring me deeper and deeper into her.

I take off after her, sprinting, a rough laugh slowing my stride. Or maybe I'm just letting her win because I don't quite trust what I'll do if I catch her.

Pull her into my arms.

Pin her against the wall.

Take that bratty strawberry mouth with my teeth and show her who's in charge.

Find out if that little tongue tastes as sharp as it sounds.

Those thoughts make my heart pump harder, leaving me breathless after only a light jog. My chest aches by the time I round the corner and find her frozen in the doorway of her classroom, her fingers digging into the strap of her bag.

Playtime's over.

Her tension draws me up short.

I stop behind her, frowning. "Delilah, what's wrong?"

"I... I don't..."

She makes a clicking sound, then gestures to the room.

I look over her head.

The classroom's exactly what I expect: a normal classroom, kid-sized desks all lined up neatly, activity tables, bookshelves, wall displays, cubbies.

But at the front of the room, there's something out of place.

The fanciest teacher's desk I've ever seen.

It's brand new and varnished with delicately carved cherrywood. I recognize it as the signature piece from A Touch of Grey, one of our best local furniture shops. It's been in the display window for a while.

Now it's parked at the head of Delilah's classroom, pretty as a picture—and wrapped up in a giant satiny red bow. There's a jewelry box sitting right in the center of it, the same shade of red, and something about that turns my blood into needles.

"Been doing a little shopping lately?" I ask lightly. *I try.*

"What? No! Are you crazy? I could never afford this." Delilah shakes her head, walking deeper into the room. She drops her bag to let it lean against the desk's smooth varnish, and she picks up the jewelry box—but instead of opening it, she sets it aside, revealing the folded bit of parchment paper underneath. "Oh. There's a note."

My gut sours, bile churning like lava.

I have a bad fucking feeling about this.

That feeling gets worse when she reads the note and her brows knit together.

"I don't understand," she whispers.

And I can't stay silent for a second longer.

I cross the threshold, moving by her side. "Let me see."

Without a word, she hands me the note—and it's as bad as I expect. All handwritten in fine, scrawling script, loops of old ink shitting up the page.

DON'T THINK *you can't ask for things for your classroom. There's a budget for furniture expenses, and you shouldn't have to gaze so long-ingly at a treasure that's well within your reach.*

Don't worry.

My father insisted. He said you should have anything your heart desires and he doesn't count little things like desks as a strike.

—*U*

. . .

U.

Ulysses goddamned Arrendell.

Worse, Montero, using his son as a pawn to deliver the bait.

Nope, I *definitely* don't like this shit.

I barely stop myself from ripping the note up and crushing it into an unreadable ball in my fist.

"Ain't that generous?" I snarl.

Delilah does a double take.

"If it's in the school budget, I guess, but..." She stops and shakes her head, trailing her fingertips lightly over the wood. "I feel weird about this. Do they do this sort of thing for all the teachers?"

One hard look from me says *hell no.*

"It's damn strange. Don't know what to make of that wording about strikes, neither." I drop the note on the desk. "You gonna keep it, or what?"

"I mean, do I have a choice?" She looks up at me, her dark-blue eyes glimmering with uncertainty. I wonder how often she's ever let anyone see this side of her—the hesitation, the nerves. "If they just bought it for the school, and not for me, I suppose I can live with it."

I hold in a litany of curses.

Woman, if you think that for a second, you're a hell of a lot more innocent than your badass big-city exterior.

"If it makes you uncomfortable, I think it's fair to say no," I point out, jerking my chin at the jewelry box. "Especially since I doubt that's for the school."

Delilah stares down at the box like she thinks it might bite.

Me, I want to chuck it out the fucking window like I'm going for a no-hitter on the diamond. Especially when she looks *pained*, like the desk is a radioactive hunk of metal poisoning her.

Did something else happen? Is that what has her so on edge?

I haven't missed that she's been spending a lot of time with Ulysses lately. Or that he's the one who keeps crowding into her life.

"Delilah," I say softly. Fuck, I'm probably gonna get a cactus stabbing for this, but I have to ask. "Has Ulysses been making any moves on you?"

Just heaving up those words makes my throat raw with rage.

Her shoulders stiffen. "No, I... I don't think so? He's a flirt, and sometimes he comes off as a little desperate, I guess. Which is weird, considering who he is. He shouldn't have any trouble with women. But he doesn't get too crazy. He's never tried to force anything. Nora told me he's like that with everyone."

Like hell.

But I keep my mouth shut while Delilah reluctantly picks up the box and flips it open—only to gasp. Her color goes pale.

"Um. What the hell is this?"

I lean over to see what's in the box.

Then my vision goes almost as red as the velvet inside.

That bracelet.

I know that *fucking bracelet.*

It's a bar of rose gold. Its simplicity disguises just how exquisite the craftsmanship is.

A slender chain of rose gold loops around from the bar, turning it from an ornamental piece into a bracelet.

The last time I saw that bracelet, it was on my sister's wrist.

And it was plain. *Unmarked.*

Now, it's been engraved.

Seven Xs, starting from left to right, off-center, with more room on the right, like someone made space to add more.

"Strikes," Delilah whispers, touching the bracelet with trembling fingertips. "Xs." Then she jerks her head up, staring at me. "Was that what the red X was? A strike?"

Fury knifes through me as I stagger back a step before I stiffen, straight as an arrow. "You think Ulysses left that? That he was marking you somehow, and not your ex?"

"No clue." She shakes her head too quickly, dropping her gaze back to the box. "That sounds a little crazy. It doesn't make sense. Ulysses isn't a bad guy. Maybe he's just awkward and this is a really, really bad joke. Probably trying to make me feel better about all the weird stuff happening since I came to town."

I gawk at her.

Jesus, if that's what she thinks this is...

"Bullshit," I snarl. I can't stop myself—I reach for the box, but Delilah jerks it away, twisting to guard it from me. "Damn it, Lilah. I told you those Arrendells are bad business you don't want to get tangled up in."

"You *told* me that, but I haven't seen it," she snaps. "Ulysses has done everything he can to help me get settled in. And he's actually been trying to find out who killed Emma. Did you even follow up on the lead about the cleaning crew, or were you too busy following *me?*"

I recoil, shaking my head. "What cleaning crew? What shit has he been feeding you?"

Delilah's eyes narrow suspiciously.

"He didn't report it? He hired a cleaning crew the day before, and they were the last ones in the house before I showed up and found Emma's body."

I feel like I've taken a bullet right between the eyes.

"Fuck no. He didn't say one word about that, and I'm the first one he should've told," I growl. "It's a little convenient, don't you think?"

"Lucas, what are you implying?"

That you've been marked, New York.

That it's happening all over again.

That I can't stand to see another woman fall down the murder pit of that fucked up freakshow masquerading as a family.

Next Montero will be wanting to meet you in private, and then—

Fuck!

I'll be watching you run away from me in a red dress.

Right into the arms of a devil.

The words won't exit my mouth, though.

They're lodged in my throat like gnarled-up barbed wire.

I can't tell her I'm afraid for her, that I need to protect her, but not when all the emotions bottled up inside me for years are choking me to death.

"Listen, Lilah, I'm not implying shit," I snap. "I'm *saying* you shouldn't believe a goddamned word Ulysses Arrendell ever tells you."

She cocks her head, her eyes wide with worry.

"So, what? I should just believe you instead?" Her eyes crackle, all hot blue witchfire as she glares up at me. "Let me tell you something, Lieutenant Graves. I've known you exactly five minutes longer than I've known him, and *neither* of you gets to tell me what to think or who to believe. I'm a grown woman with two degrees. All you've told me is that you've got some weird grudge against them, so I should hate them because you do." She drops the jewelry box on the desk, her fists curling up as she slams one sandaled foot to the floor. "So take your attitude and your grudges and your paranoia and your *stalking* and fuck right off, Lucas. Because my life has been crazy enough since I got here, since Redhaven decided it wants to drive me crazy, and you're just making things *worse*."

So fucking much for warning her.

I'm not getting through.

I'm not getting through to her and it's my own fault. I'm too smothered in this mess of scar tissue to tell her the truth, even if it means keeping her safe.

I learned too hard, too long ago, to keep my mouth shut about things with Celeste. A man can't undo years of getting that beat into him in one screaming instant.

Not even for this little wildfire burning me down with her get-fucked glare.

"Goddammit, Delilah, if you don't think it means anything, that bracelet coming after that nasty fucking red X under your window—"

177

"Don't. You're starting to sound like some conspiracy crank, you know that?" she bites off. "Everything comes back to the Arrendells. Everything is their fault. Just what did they *do* to you, mister? What the hell did they—"

They slaughtered my sister! I want to roar, but what comes out isn't that.

What comes out instead is impulse, torn emotion, blood boiling frustration, and—fuck.

Yes, sheer desire.

I give in to the urge to make that sharp, biting mouth of hers *stop* for just one minute.

That's why I grab her.

That's why I pull her in.

That's why I kiss Miss New York till she turns into a stunned, whimpering icicle, and then slowly melts in my arms.

XI: RED HOT (DELILAH)

*M*y life has been one big ball of confusion ever since I set foot in this weird little town.

But there's nothing on Earth more bewildering than Lucas effing Graves pulling me into the hard slab of his body, tilting my chin, and crushing his mouth down on mine like the rest of his life depends on kissing me breathless.

Oh. My. God.

Two seconds ago, I was one sharp word away from straight-up slugging him in the face, even if he has an iron jaw that would break my fist.

Now, I'm so—

I don't even know.

I can't think.

I can't wonder.

I can't count the myriad ways my new life in Redhaven explodes in the delicious sting of his teeth.

He won't let me do anything but *feel.*

And what I feel most is Lucas in all his bossy, infuriating glory.

His lips scorch me from the inside out until I'm ash from my fingers to the tips of my toes.

I just clutch at his arms, hanging off him in midair, pressing so, so hard to him as my mouth goes magnetic against my will.

I'm supposed to hate this man.

But why does he kiss like *that?*

Resistance? Ha.

It's so pathetically futile my body betrays me in a moan.

His lips are so hot, so firm, and *God*—Lucas may talk slow, but he moves like lightning, all swift sizzle and a hint of growling thunder.

All *man,* claiming and teasing and making me shiver so deeply as his stubble rubs my mouth, my skin, all of me raw.

His kiss caresses with a dominating promise that leaves me boneless.

Boneless, tingling, and fighting back.

When he bites me, his teeth dipping firmly into my bottom lip, I give back as good as I get.

And it makes him groan like the beast he is.

His hold on me shifts until his hands slide down to the small of my back, burning hot and dragging me in, jerking me hard against the hard, honed machine of his body.

Then he delves into me.

His tongue plunges into my mouth.

I'm blinded from the heat, arching with a loud gasp, feeling like he's just thrust his devious tongue between my thighs.

It's beyond sinful.

And my knees clamp together like they can keep that feeling inside me—but it won't hold when it's just as disobedient as the rest of me.

Liquid fire races through me and electrifies every inch of my skin.

Napalm fills my veins.

Every inch of my skin feels incandescent, awakened by this man who messes me up in all the myriad ways.

My knees go so weak the longer we kiss.

I cling to him as his growl vibrates through me.

God, I can't even stand without him supporting me.

My fingers claw his arms and those broad hands keep me pinned so close.

The rock-hard muscle under his uniform makes a lie of the neat, crisp shirt. The promise of the brute behind the stern gentleman.

Rough sensations come in ruthless waves like the ocean tide slapping the shore.

And those punishing waves are all Lucas Graves.

"New York, fuck," he grinds out when he breaks away for breath.

I moan a reply, already too worn for words.

Too awestruck.

How coarse his fingers are, scraping through my thin shirt.

His heat—God, his *heat*—it soaks me until I melt against him, my breasts tingling against his chest, peaking my nipples.

The hardness between his thighs, pushing against me with a needy insistence, dragging against my stomach and my hips.

I want it.

I want *him*.

And I'm utterly shameless when I move, twining my tongue with his when he kisses me more greedily than ever.

I push my fingers against his shirt and skim down his chest.

I'm rewarded with the taste of more hot desire growling up his throat, filling me with fire in every kiss.

We're rampant.

Unthinking.

Explosive.

There's no flipping stopping now, not before I find the waist of his slacks, his belt. My fingers work clumsily on the buckle.

More thunder booms up his throat as the backs of my knuckles brush his cock through the material.

He grinds into my fingers, showing me the power in his hips.

"Delilah," he rasps against my mouth, fierce and animalistic and needy.

"*Yes,*" I whisper, dragging his belt buckle open.

I don't know what the hell is happening right now, this imminent chaos.

I just know this feeling, right here, is the one thing I didn't know I've been looking for.

Every kiss feels so *certain* when everything else in my life is a total vacuum.

Lucas stills for just a moment.

He breaks that last slick kiss, his mouth red and wet, his eyes lit with hunger as he stares down at me.

That flinty green in his eyes is blazing, so intense, so captivating against the stark blackness of his hair framing his face.

One look flays me open and I finally understand exactly how he makes me feel.

Naked.

With one sharp glance, he strips me down before he's even taken any of my clothes off—and I know that's coming.

He bends, brushing his lips over mine, more questioning than before.

Last chance. Last fucking chance to turn back, Delilah, I feel him asking.

He's giving me a choice and it's like he doesn't know I've already decided.

I'm trembling with the unexpected softness, the slow, careful way he traces the corner of my mouth.

When he turns wild, the whole world spins with one quick movement.

Before I can blink, I'm slammed against that brand-new desk like we mean to defile it.

Only for a second before he flips me around, bends me *over* it, pressing me down with my breasts against the cool cherrywood and my ass thrust up and waiting.

His hands are so deliciously cruel now.

I shudder.

"Peach fucking perfect," he whispers. I don't know what he means until his hands move lower.

His bestial strength drags my jeans down, baring my thighs, my ass in my little lace panties.

My ears bristle when I hear him inhale with furious approval. He inhales deeply like he's caught my scent, a lion set to devour.

Oh, God.

His hand splays between my shoulder blades, and—oh *fuck*, I feel it coming like he's radiating static force. But I'm still not ready for the exact moment when his fingers trace my panties, sliding lace against my skin, teasing my opening.

I'm so dead.

My already soaked skin becomes so slick, so sensitive.

With a soft moan, I'm squirming, trying to push back toward him.

I'm already *begging*, dragging my body against the desk like this. The cool wood teases me through my clothes and Lucas only makes it worse.

He strokes me slowly, hypnotically, with a slow insistence, each time working the fabric of my panties deeper against my flesh, into my folds, making me pulse and clench.

I couldn't hold it in for a billion dollars.

I cry out, terribly aware that we're still at school, and the door is hanging open.

This is absolutely *not* how I imagined starting this job.

Anyone could walk by right now and I don't *care*.

Because when his thumb brushes my clit, desire erupts in a wild burst, a monster that grabs me by the throat and won't let go.

"Lucas," I hiss out, clawing the desk.

But I can't get free, not before he's good and done with me.

Not when he plays me like a fiddle, the pad of his thumb toying with my clit until it's swollen, throbbing, starving.

I'm so wet for him it's killing me, spilling down my inner thighs, making a mess of myself for this man I hardly know and yet who seems to know my body like he's already memorized it from a map.

I throw my head back and whimper, squirming with shame.

"Lucas, we have to—"

"Hush, Miss Lilah. Just breathe," he whispers.

I obey.

It isn't even a choice.

His hands move quickly, pelting me with rough pleasure.

His fingers work faster, pushing me to soaring pleasure in a few blinding seconds.

The relentless assault on my senses melts my worries into a mess of hot gasps and countless firm kisses on the back of my neck.

Every flick, every tease hits like an earthquake, tremors building and building until I'm biting the back of my hand for dear life.

His breathing grows more ragged, and mine becomes a mess of moans.

"Holy hell, don't stop. *Don't stop,* Lucas, I'm—"

The way his rhythm quickens on my clit tells me he knows.

He knows I'm right on the edge, and he's about to throw me over.

When the tidal wave hits, it brings me down with a thousand tiny convulsions.

One fierce eruption of pleasure.

I come so hard I see stars and they're all bright green.

It breaks me, and his fingers slow, pressing lightly against my panties while I ride his hand through the storm.

When the wave passes, I slump down on the desk in a panting mess—only to flinch as he touches me again.

It's not that I don't want him now.

I just don't expect his touch so soon.

He's barely said a word since we collided, but there's a word-less language of Lucas Graves telling me how it is.

His low rumble whispers appreciation for the way I gasp, the way I shudder, the way I completely surrender.

His fingertips brush me so gently, sparking my nerves all over again.

A single fingertip hooks the fabric of my panties and sweeps them aside. Cool air kisses my wet flesh and I arch against his hand with a low whimper.

"Hotter than July, woman. Tell me you needed that, Lilah. Do not bullshit me."

I don't dare.

I just release a satisfied whimper and collapse against the desk into a pile of sex-wrecked jelly.

Then he lets me go.

I don't have the strength to get up, to even look back at him. Not when that orgasm obliterated me and still somehow left me wanting more.

And I realize he's about to bring it—that's why he let me go— when I hear a familiar crinkling sound. A condom wrapper ripping open.

Okay, now I *have* to look, have to watch him.

I twist to glance over my shoulder.

I need to see it.

Just like I need to see the feral glint in his eyes.

I need to see the heat darkening his face, relaxing into slack pleasure as he frees his thick cock from his slacks, from the boxers underneath, and smooths his hand over its full length as he slides the condom on.

Anaconda.

That's the only word that comes to mind.

His cock is a battering ram, pulsing with hunger and so thick I wonder if I could even close my fingers around it.

Holy hell, this might hurt—but if it does, it's the kind of pain that's worth it.

My core burns, wanting him to stretch me, to claim me, to really make me *his*.

His eyes lock on mine.

"The hell you looking at, darlin'? You like what you see?"

The way I bite my lip gives away my answer.

He's so close, heat radiating off him, burning my bare flesh.

It's like we're on our own private wavelength, where my body can already *feel* him inside me, and it pulses with the emptiness of knowing he's not there yet.

But I think he's waiting.

For me to say the final words that will let him off his leash.

It's heavy, knowing a man like this will hold himself back for you when it's got to be killing him.

Underneath his brooding and slow-talking stillness, there's a savage, and he's holding back until I say *ravage me.*

"Lucas," I whisper, stretching my arms across the desk and curling my fingers against the edge, bracing and ready as I spread my legs as far as the snare of my jeans around my thighs will let me. "Lucas, please."

His only answer is a rumbling hot snarl.

Then I feel it.

The head of his cock, pulsing against me, spreading me open one slow, rough push, so close to—

His hand curls against my shoulder, thick and possessive.

I brace myself, holding in a breath.

I don't even try to force back my raw, needy cry as he slams into me in a single gliding thrust, his hips crashing against my ass as he sinks in deep.

So *deep.*

God, I don't think I've ever felt anyone else bottom out like Lucas.

He strokes unclaimed places, filling me with this heavy warmth that drains my strength, leaving me helpless to the burning friction, the scorching thrust, the pure unrestrained power radiating off him.

Guttural delight torches the air as he growls his pleasure.

He grinds into me hard, yet his thrusts are so controlled.

Like he knows exactly what drives me crazy with every precisely timed, measured drive of thick, teasing flesh.

I feel him so deep it's almost shameful.

Wave after wave of screaming pleasure picks me up and slams me down again as he fucks me against the desk, open and begging.

I'm not sure anymore if I'm screaming or moaning or sobbing.

Holy hell, what is this?

I didn't know sex with this much violent emotion existed.

I'm too sensitive, I almost can't stand it—but I'm already hooked.

And he gives me *more*, his hulking body arched over me, intensifying every thrust when his hips swing forward like a hammer made flesh.

His mouth pelts my shoulders with kisses, with bites, with fire.

His hand slips under me, taking my breast in his palm.

His thumb and forefinger find my nipple, teasing me with rough tugs, twisting.

The friction alone is enough to rob my voice away in broken gasps.

Every thrust only kindles me hotter like he's setting me on fire with pure friction.

And I'm gone in the crash and flow and rhythmic scrape of the legs of the desk, tossing my head back against his shoulder as I—

Oh, *shit*.

There—right there, where he fits against me and touches something that ignites like dynamite.

I toss my head back against his shoulder, losing his rhythm as my body finds its own, spasming and rocking and writhing under him.

This sweet tension bolts through me so hard it locks me

around him, making it worse as I imprint him on me from the inside out.

And he's trying to move again but I won't let him.

I can't, not with the convulsions ripping through me, turning me into a vessel for Lucas Graves.

"Fuck, Delilah, you're killing me," he grinds out. "Make it fucking hurt, Lilah. This is all for you."

It's only when our collision peaks that I realize he's stopped moving, staying buried deep inside me to the hilt.

He's whispering my name now, his senses just as frayed as mine.

"Lilah, Lilah, Lilah." It sounds husky, almost reverent, and he jerks my body closer to his every time.

Then comes the throbbing, the shudder, the swell.

A tortured groan claws its way out of him as his face screws up, his hips grinding, stirring his cock inside me as he comes.

He orgasms the same way he does everything else.

Quietly but so intensely he could split you open with one look.

There's a part of me that wishes the condom wasn't in the way so I could *feel* it as his cock heaves.

One fist tangles my hair and pulls as he empties himself, growling with every pulse, a human storm that won't let go until we're so spent I'm not sure either of us are still breathing.

When I'm able to think, we're both slumped against the desk.

Of course, I'm a mess.

Weak, trembling, satisfied, and slick with sweat and God only knows what else.

Then my brain starts to work again through the fog of the best sex I've ever had. My jaw drops.

Oh, Christ.

What did we just *do?*

Fear bolts through me, almost as powerful as that orgasm to end all orgasms moments ago.

No, I'm not blaming him.

Lucas kissed me first, but I practically threw myself at him.

"Oh, shit. Shit, shit, shit," I whisper, my throat dry and my voice cracking. "Lucas, the *door!*"

His weight slides off me as he jerks back.

He was still inside me, rooted so deep it's jarring when he's gone, making me feel like I've been hollowed out.

Lucas rests his soothing hand on the small of my back.

"Hold still," he murmurs. "Keep breathing."

I can't do anything else as he pulls away, leaving me sore and aching with his absence.

So I bite the sound rising up my throat behind my teeth, holding it in as he separates before I'm scrambling upright, pulling my panties back into place, yanking my jeans up over my hips with a desperate look toward the *open freaking door.*

I can't quite bring myself to look at Lucas.

Not yet.

It's just too real.

But I hear his zipper closing and then the wet *thunk* of —oh *no.*

The condom hits the little wire wastebasket next to the desk.

I dart for it, refusing to look at it as I close up the bag with only one thing inside that definitely doesn't belong here.

Behind me, there's a creak, then the sound of the door latching shut.

"There. Crisis averted," Lucas rumbles. His voice sounds like he's blown his throat out with growling whispers, the way he made my name a mantra of pure lust. "Don't think anyone saw. We're the only folks here."

"I sure hope you're right! If anybody heard that..." I don't finish. I just try to gulp down the rock in my throat and what's left of my shattered dignity.

It's too late for whispers and regrets, anyway.

I stare down at the little white bag crumpled in my fists.

What the hell was that?

What came over me?

189

Rutting like animals bent over this brand-new desk from the Arrendells, a classroom door open, blinds up, screaming like a banshee for anyone to hear in this supposedly empty school.

Holy hell, what's wrong with me?

"Delilah." His eyes glow softly, almost apologetic. "The lot was empty when I pulled up, I swear. We're the only ones here. Even if we're not, no one would ever guess it was you."

"I... yeah." I press the back of my hand to my mouth and lift my head slowly, forcing a smile past the knot in my throat. "Listen, um, can we talk about this later? I still need to tidy up and take care of some things before I lock up and leave."

For the briefest second, hurt flashes across his face, darkening those soulful green eyes.

I know.

I know what I'm doing.

Trust me.

But I'm also avoiding, deflecting, struggling.

Honestly, I need a hot minute alone to process this.

Maybe a few hot hours.

I need to figure myself out, everything I've been denying about why I bristle and snarl and get so defensive around Lucas Graves.

Every reason why he was the one dominating my mind when I broke out my battery-operated boyfriend the other night.

But I can't do that while he's standing there, staring like a whole season of spring greenery distilled into a man, his lips parted like he wants to say something but he *can't.*

I don't blame him.

Lord knows I don't know the words, either.

And I don't know what to say. I don't know if what we just did was a casual impulse we'll pretend never happened, two consenting adults letting off a little steam, or something wilder.

If it's something else, if it's—

No.

I can't say it.

I just silently beg Lucas not to press me right now, even if I hate rejecting him like this, leaving him wondering.

There's a silence hanging around us that's too loud, devoid of that peaceful stillness he normally brings that makes it so easy to just be around him.

His hands hang helplessly at his sides.

"You'll call if you need anything?" Lucas nods slowly, heaving a deep breath.

There's an implication there.

A promise.

He doesn't just mean if my crazy ex shows up, or someone new comes creeping around my house, or my alarm goes off, or I discover something shocking about Emma Santos.

He means *me*.

If *I* need anything.

If I need *him*.

I'm not sure what to do with that.

I hardly know anything about him except that he's kind underneath his snarls and smart-assery. Ever since I've shown up here, he's done everything humanly possible to help me feel safe and like someone in this town gives a damn.

And I know that he knows how it feels to miss someone.

But the rest is as mysterious as that look anchored in the second-guesses flashing in his eyes.

I smile unevenly. I can't help it.

"I will," I tell him. "I promise."

Lucas just looks at me a minute longer.

He always seems on the verge of saying something, only to reel it back in at the last second.

He bows his head, raking a hand through his thick black hair, a slow gesture that's weariness and confusion.

Then he pulls the door open and walks out, leaving me alone with a deafening *click* of the latch.

I slump back against the desk, still trembling—then jerk away from it.

I need to clean this place ASAP. I'm not leaving sloppy seconds for some poor janitor.

But I almost don't want to touch it.

I don't want to touch this desk after we just *fucked* on it.

Maybe it's just in my head, but there's this weird feeling like it's the same as touching Ulysses, touching Montero...

That's something so complicated and weird I can't even think about it right now.

I still don't understand them, or why they want to shower me with insane gifts.

But as I move, something flutters against my ankle.

The note.

It must have fallen to the floor while we were busy.

The jewelry box, too, still holding the bracelet with those weird Xs in rose gold coiled on the floor.

I bend down to pick up the box, the bracelet, and the slip of parchment paper—only to realize there's something written on the back I hadn't noticed before.

A phone number.

Frowning, my brows pull together.

I wonder.

* * *

I GUESSED IT MIGHT BE ULYSSES' number—his personal cell, not the extension for the town council that goes directly to his rarely occupied desk.

I wish I knew how to feel about being right. But I have questions, and only answers will put my mind at ease.

So I curl up in my brand-new bed topped with fresh sheets and give him a call.

"Miss Clarendon." He sounds delighted when he picks up. "How are you today?"

Deliciously sore and well used, I think, but of course I don't say that out loud.

I doubt he'd think of me as harmless Miss Clarendon then.

Funny how I'm *Miss* something to everyone here, even to the man who bent me over a desk and made me scream.

I needed time to myself after Lucas left. So after a good deep cleaning, I spent all day putting up maps and colorful alphabet posters and bright cartoons of historic figures designed to engage young learners.

All soothing, repetitive tasks that kept me focused on why I was really here instead of turning myself in circles over Lucas and the fact that every time I moved, I still *felt* him.

My mind is stuck in that moment and it doesn't want to move on, no matter how I try to rip myself away.

And I realize I'm doing it again, lying there drifting off and thinking of that hurt, haunted look in his eyes, all the things he wouldn't say.

"Miss Clarendon? Are you there? Is something wrong?" Ulysses asks.

"Oh!" I snap back into myself, startled and clearing my throat. I press my palm to my overheated cheek. "Sorry, it's just been a long day. I called to thank you."

"Ah. I take it you found my gift? Even if it was technically a gift from the town and my father." Ulysses sounds too smug.

"Yes, I'm over the moon with it, really... but that desk is so expensive. Are you *sure* it's okay and it isn't a little too much?"

"Consider it our sincerest thank you," he says confidently. "When the last elementary teacher quit, we were left holding the bag, you know. So a nice welcome gift to show our appreciation is nothing. We want you to feel at home, Miss Clarendon. Ideally, we'd like to keep you."

The way he says *we* is a little odd, but I guess he means the town.

"Why did the last teacher quit?" I ask.

"She wasn't cut out for Redhaven. Not a good fit for the pace here. She complained her online deliveries took more than a week to arrive," he says dryly. "I do hope you're more adaptable to the rigors of small-town life."

I snort. "Usually when people say 'rigors,' they mean dilapidated outhouses and no hot water. I'll manage. I don't shop online that much anyway."

"I hope that's a promise," he says cryptically.

I pause.

I don't want to say it is.

Because there's a lot more about this town that's off than a few boring days and slow deliveries.

I push myself to ask, firming my voice, "I'll think about it. But about the bracelet—"

"Did you like it?" he cuts in abruptly. "I thought rose gold might complement your olive skin."

Holy hell.

My skin? What do I even say to that?

"Sure," I manage, wrapping my arms up tight as I look outside and watch how the leaves shiver in the evening breeze. The soft twilight gloom turns everything a gentle blue. "I'm just kind of curious, why the Xs, after what happened at The Rookery?"

"What happened at The Rookery?" Ulysses sounds genuinely puzzled.

"You didn't hear?"

"Believe it or not, sometimes our gossip mill has a limited altitude, lady. It occasionally loses steam without making it to the top of the hill." He chuckles.

"Oh. Oh, right." I chew the inside of my lower lip. "Well, when I was staying there, I saw someone outside my window. They spray-painted this huge red X just below it, then disappeared. It's possible it's my stalker ex from New York, but I... it almost felt like someone sending me a message. You really didn't know?"

He inhales sharply.

"I wish like hell I had. Besides being insensitive and threatening, it's downright *tacky*." Ulysses growls with this rushed sincerity. "My deepest apologies, Miss Clarendon. I promise you I knew nothing, and I'm deeply sorry Redhaven has done its damnedest to make you feel uncomfortable. If you'd like, throw that nasty thing into a shredder and be done with it."

"What? No!" I say quickly—*but why?* Why am I reluctant to get rid of it? I glance at the nightstand, where the little red box sits with the bracelet safely tucked inside. "Sorry, I just... I hate wasting things, Ulysses. I guess it's a hazard of growing up without much stuff. So if you really didn't mean anything by it—"

"Hand to God, I did not. Besides taking a clumsy stab at flirting, I guess." He pauses. "The Xs were kisses, Miss Clarendon. You know, the X in XO, kisses and hugs?"

My face flames. "O-oh."

"See? Clumsy as hell. Now I've gone and made you feel like shit." Ulysses makes a self-deprecating sound. "Forgive me. I suppose I'm the stereotypical rich eccentric. Kisses aren't meant to be so heavy. Hell, I still kiss my own mother on the cheek."

"How European," I point out.

"Exactly. We brought over some odd habits generations ago, and I suppose our international upbringing only makes it stick." With a rattling chuckle, Ulysses sighs. "You should meet my brothers one day. They and my old man tease me constantly for talking about nothing but you. My father was happy to meet with you anyway, and my brothers will be home soon. There'll be a big reunion party of sorts, as always when the family reunites. Why don't you stop by then? Dress code optional. No one will judge you if you aren't dripping Vera Wang."

I smile crookedly.

"Pretty sure they'd judge me if I showed up in a ripped tank top and jeans. I really doubt I'd fit in with that crowd. Limousines and rich people? No way."

"You can fit in wherever you desire. Status is so artificial," he says flippantly.

Hmm.

"Maybe," I bite off.

Truthfully, I've never liked getting dolled up and going fancy places like that, squeezed into a dress that's cutting off my circulation and with my face feeling like a plaster mask. "Let me think about it, okay? I still have a mountain of work to do before the school year starts, and I don't know what my workload will look like then. I might end up pulling an all-nighter cutting out cardboard stars."

"No better way to spend an evening," he mocks gently. "I'll text you the details just in case you can grace us with your presence."

"Oh, no. My presence is hardly a gift. But thanks for your gift, Ulysses. The desk, I mean. It makes me feel very... official."

"So *stern*, Miss Clarendon. Will you take me across the knee with your ruler, next?"

"*Ulysses!*" I almost choke.

I was so not expecting that.

A wicked, husky laugh drifts over the phone. "No worries. I'll be a perfect gentleman from here on out. Enjoy your evening, Miss Clarendon. Hope to hear from you soon!"

"Yeah," I say faintly.

I'm a little surprised he's the one to hang up first.

I'm also surprised by how fidgety I feel after that call.

Hugging my knees to my chest, I glance down at my toes and scrunch them against the coverlet.

I can't stop frowning.

He talks to me like we're old friends, and always with that superficial gloss of politeness.

It's just odd, like he's treading all over my personal space while still standing so far away.

I might still be feeling off-kilter after getting myself so messed up with Lucas. Or maybe I'm having trouble adapting to small-town hospitality.

I should be less judgy. If I could actually relax, then maybe—

A scraping noise just outside my window stops me mid-thought.

It's faint, just a scuffing sound like a foot dragging through fresh-cut grass.

My heart compacts into a withered pea.

Only to explode up my throat in a throat-ripping scream the second I glance up.

There's someone in my window!

The same silhouette from the night at The Rookery.

Tall, lean, hunched, shadowed, his features indistinguishable.

Sweat beads like ice all over my body. I clutch at my calves, staring at that dark, unmoving shape.

He stays where he is for several halting seconds.

He must *know* I can see him—he has to be looking right back at me—making sure I know he's there, making me feel the threat.

Then he turns and walks away, heading toward the back of the house, moving in that same shuffling, slouched lope like he's trying to mask his stride.

Trying to make sure I don't recognize him.

Roger?

Anger surges through my fear, unlocking my limbs.

I rocket off the bed, nearly tripping over my bare feet as I tumble to the floor.

I race out of the bedroom, down the hall, toward the back door.

The muted chirp of crickets turns from a whisper to a shrill cry as I fling the back door open on my tiny deck, banging it against the wall.

Desperate, panting, I scan around, searching the darkness.

My feet move faster than my brain, tumbling me down through the grass. The blades tickle the soles of my feet as I dart around the side of the house and find—

You guessed it.

Nothing.

No one.

Not even a whisper of the trees beyond the fence this time.

I'm flipping alone.

Except for one thing that numbs me like frostbite.

A very fresh, very bright, very wet red X painted on the blue siding below my window.

And this time, I don't think that crimson is paint at all.

XII: SEEING RED (LUCAS)

*E*very time my phone lights up with Delilah's number, she's already on my mind.

I've been a goddamned wreck all day.

Completely spaced, zoning out on my patrol, unfocused during meetings with my crew, during everything.

I just can't stop flashing back to that wildfire—reliving that sweet, sweet moment when this bristling thing between us went off like an armed grenade.

Fuck me, when did I turn into nothing but a horny-ass goat?

I drop my face into my hand, then think better of it and replace my hand with my beer, slouching deep into the rocking chair on my front porch.

The late summer heat is baking today.

I was supposed to pick up an extra shift tonight—we still like to have at least one officer on night duty even if things are quiet. It's usually peaceful enough, staying camped out with dispatch and trying not to fall asleep over a book or three.

But the captain took one look at me after I dragged myself in from a shift posted in the town square and told me in no uncertain terms to go the fuck home and get some rest.

No argument there.

Grant was right.

Uneventful night or not, I'd be fucking useless if something *did* crop up.

Hell, I'm useless as a knitted condom right now, spinning around in too many circles. Whacked out of my gourd with those buttery moans I forced out of her with every thrust.

Also, I'm still damn worried about Delilah.

I don't think I hurt her.

I'm pretty sure we were on the same page, and she was right there with me in the storm, begging for it as much as I did in the heat of the moment. But there's always that horrible instant when your body speaks louder than your brain, and after, when what you did truly sinks in.

When it hits, I can't deny shit.

Not that I'd been trying all that hard, mostly just keeping it to myself. But there's no hiding it any longer.

I'm tripping all over myself, falling face-first into that New York cactus.

I'd like to tell her that in person. Wish like hell I'd had the stones to ask her out on a real date, making sure she's comfortable with me before we boned.

Making sure she truly felt the same way before I slammed her sweet ass over a desk in the wildest, hardest romp of my life.

That's on me.

No ifs, ands, or buts.

I was the asshole who thought kissing her to stop her from jabbing me with those spikes was the most brilliant idea in the world.

Now, I'm wondering if it's the dumbest fool thing I've ever done in my life.

Yes, she kissed me right back, nearly tore my frigging pants off.

But the look on her face, when she asked me to leave, that was something else.

Fuck.

The shock. The regret. The embarrassment. The questions etched into her face.

What have I done?

Is she sitting in that little blue cottage right now after working herself silly all day, still mulling over how stupid and crazy one man can be?

I can see her there alone with a beer—just like I am now—thinking about me as much as I'm thinking about her till she ponders herself into a blinding headache.

I need her to be okay.

That's all I care about.

That whatever reckless bastard thing we just did, slamming our way into passion, she's not upset with herself in the end.

Let her be upset with me, sure.

I'll take that in a heartbeat.

I'm starting to develop a pretty thick skin for cactus spikes.

Also, I've definitely got a thing for the way she pushed against me, clenched around me, begging my hips to give her more, more, *more*.

My cock twitches, drunk on what my brain can't forget, when my phone lights up next to what's left of a six-pack of Redhaven's finest pilsner.

I don't even let the ringtone blare for two seconds before I swipe it up and answer.

"Lilah, you okay?"

"Lucas! N-no," she gasps out—and fuck me if I don't notice this strong, proud, stubborn woman sounds like she's crying. "Lucas... Lucas, you have to come now. There was someone outside my window. There's another X and, and... and this time there's blood."

* * *

ASK me how I got to Delilah's house and I couldn't fucking tell you.

One second I'm at home, lounging on my porch with my blood turning to smoke as her trembling words echo in my ears.

Not quite processing anything when all I hear is *Delilah's in danger*.

Next thing I know, I'm fishtailing my truck—my patrol car's at the station—onto the curb outside her fence, just inches from tearing over the sidewalk.

My heart thunders. Icy beads of sweat form on my skin as I go tearing out of the truck and charge up her front steps.

She's got all the lights on in the house.

I'm hoping she did what I remember telling her to—to lock all the doors and windows and arm the alarm system.

"Delilah!" I call, banging on the door. "It's Lucas. Let me in."

Soft, hesitant footsteps pad from inside, and then the faint beep of the alarm console, the click of the lock.

Then this fragile creature flies into my arms.

For such a small woman, she's got power behind her.

I rock back as I catch her, then right myself and wrap her up tight in my arms.

"Shhh. Not one word," I whisper, stroking her back. "I'm here now. You're safe."

"Am I?" She sobs against my chest. Her shoulders are shaking. "Lucas, I—I feel like I'm going *insane*. Why? Why would anyone do this?"

"Don't know, Lilah, but I'm thinking they're trying to scare you." And the fact that it worked makes me furious. I keep my voice gentle, though, holding her so close, breathing her in like I need to convince myself she's truly okay. "Nothing's gonna happen to you, woman. I promise on my life."

"You don't know that," she whispers. "I just... I feel like I'm being watched *all the time*, even when I'm alone and there can't possibly be anyone around. I thought I was being paranoid and imagining it, but now..."

"That's how stalkers work. They rattle you, make you think you're nuts, and a lot of times it's someone who knows you so well that they can do bullshit no one but you would notice." Slowly, I weave my fingers through her hair, cradling the back of her head. "You're not crazy, Delilah. Not at fucking all."

Sniffling, she tilts her head back, looking up at me with her starry eyes brimming with tears, her fingers clenched hard in the front of my shirt.

"Someone who knows me personally," she gulps. "Like Roger?"

"Definitely a prime suspect." I brush back a lock of her hair clinging to the dampness of tears on her cheeks, tucking the dark strand behind her ear. "Can you show me the X?"

"Y-yeah."

But she's so reluctant when she pulls away—and damn, I can't stop myself.

I catch her hand in a bracing squeeze.

I let her know I'm *here*, dammit.

Right here beside her with every breath, every second, every step.

Delilah pulls up short, her gleaming eyes darting to me and her lips parted.

Then her hand curls against mine, gripping so tight as she leads me off the porch, around the side of the house.

There it is.

A slashing X formed in menacing hell-red.

I'm no expert in forensics, but I'd say it was drawn by the same fuck who painted the X on The Rookery.

Same nasty, domineering strokes, all done from the same height.

Same dramatic swoop and flourish.

Same angle, I think, done by some asshole about six foot one, standing roughly two and a half feet away.

Damn.

Six foot one.

Just like Roger Strunk, judging by the info I dredged up from his public records.

The wet gleam of it has dried, but even in the evening gloom I can tell it's darker, more rusty and organic than the last X. Not the same bright artificial crimson of spray paint.

I squeeze Delilah's hand firmly, then let go and hunker down into a crouch, leaning in to breathe, though I keep my distance so I don't step on the crushed grass in front of the X.

Still close enough to get a good whiff.

It's coppery, all right.

Kind of tinny, thin, *meaty*.

"Shit." I drape an arm over my knee. "Yeah, I'd say that smells like blood. Doesn't mean it's human, though. Little chickenshit cowards who do stuff like this usually go for animals. Might even be something from the butcher shop, squeezed out of a fresh cut."

"I tried not to touch anything so I wouldn't disturb the crime scene," she whispers. "But you're sure it's not human?"

"Can't be one hundred percent positive till we run it through forensics." I fish my phone out of my back pocket and line it up to start taking photos, snapping them between words with the flash on my camera bright. "But if it was human blood, whose blood would it be? We got no recent missing persons reports, nobody reporting any assaults. So it'd have to be the perp's blood—or an out-of-towner we don't know about. Factor in the psychology, too. Most stalkers are too coward to be murderers. So an animal's more likely."

Delilah releases a miserable, sad sound.

When I look up, she's clutching her hand over her mouth. "God, that's awful. Who kills animals just to threaten someone?"

I have a few ideas.

Right now, though, the asshole ex is looking pretty likely.

Ex.

X?

Huh.

I push myself up, throwing an arm around Delilah's shoulders. "Let me call this in so we can get an official report and get started investigating. Then if you want me to, I'll stay with you tonight."

For a moment she goes stiff against my side—but then she relaxes, melting against me, turning her face to me till she's practically hiding against my rib cage.

"Okay. Yeah, I think I'd like that. I think I'd like that a lot."

* * *

It takes me five minutes on the phone with the captain to explain the situation.

Ten more minutes and Grant pulls up with Henri like I didn't just drag both of them out of bed. We probably should've called in Bowden, but he'd just make some excuse about taking a look in the morning.

He's feeling his age, and if it's after nine, the odds of getting him out to a crime scene are pretty slim.

The whole time, I keep Delilah glued to my side—and she doesn't protest.

The captain and Henri take more photos. Henri throws up some crime scene tape in a neat square around the X and the crushed grass before swabbing the blood and sealing it away in a sample bottle.

I make sure they're up to speed on Roger Strunk, including the NYC DMV photos we pulled along with the photos Delilah turned over, plus vehicle registration and plates.

Tall man, light-sandy-brown hair, a narrow face, shallow blue eyes. Drives a midnight-blue Mazda Miata, fairly new.

Right now, he's our best suspect.

And the fact that it's likely blood elevates it from a petty crime to stalking and harassment with intent to harm.

For a moment, I'm separated from Delilah as Grant pulls me aside, and we put our heads together for a low, muttered conversation.

"Should she be staying here tonight?" he asks. "I don't feel good about it. At least not until we get the samples back from the lab and confirm if it's blood or not."

"If she wants to stay, I'll stay with her," I answer. "But I'll see if I can talk her into crashing at my place or The Rookery."

"Might be for the best." He shakes his head, tugging at his beard, this little thing he does when he's agitated. He wasn't promoted to captain that long ago, but Grant doesn't like this kind of disquiet in his town. "Been real damn busy in Redhaven lately. Ever since she showed up."

I can't help how I bristle. "She's the victim here, Cap. Not the problem."

"Not what I'm saying. Stand down, Lucas." Grant gives me a grave look. "You know that old saying, trouble comes in threes? We've got a dead girl with an overdose, a new teacher being stalked by her ex... I just wonder what's coming next."

"Nothing, if I have my say," I growl.

What if he's right, though?

Right now, I'm thinking of another old saying.

The simplest solution is usually the right one.

The fact that all of this is happening now, after Delilah blew into town, can't be unconnected.

We're not looking at separate incidents.

Somehow, the fucking creepy crawler stalking Delilah is tied to Emma Santos. That could still make her ex a suspect.

If Strunk is deranged enough to use blood for a threat, he might just be deranged enough to kill a girl in cold blood and plant her body to scare Delilah into running back to NYC, where he has more access to her.

It's not real likely when the criminal profiles between *stalker* and *murderer* normally don't overlap. Especially when he's doing this petty shit, but if he keeps escalating, that's where that Venn diagram starts looking more like a circle.

Still, I can't help thinking Delilah is dangerously close to being Montero's type.

Dark hair, slender, curves for miles, long legs on a short frame made for sin.

Eyes full of stars, bursting with dreams.

Celeste was like that, too.

My sister wanted to be a singer, a Swiftie from the start, and always hoping to wind up on the big stage with pop stars like Milah Holly and Easterly Ribbon.

Montero promised to hook her up in the music industry.

What would he promise Delilah, to lure this butterfly into his spiderweb of unspeakable fuckery?

It's already started.

That desk, the bracelet, the compliments.

Using that smarmy fuck Ulysses as bait to draw Delilah into the fold.

Ollie might be the one who gifted that desk, but I don't doubt for a second that Montero magically made room in the school's budget for it.

"Lucas." Grant waves a hand in front of my face. "You still here?"

"Yeah," I mutter grimly. "Tell you what, I want to get Montero Arrendell into interrogation and ask him some questions."

Grant stares at me, his jaw clenched. "That's unwise and you know it. Not unless you're packing enough evidence for a warrant —*real* evidence. One word in Bowden's ear and he'll have you fired."

"Don't care, Cap." Past Grant's broad bulk, I watch Delilah lingering by her gate, staring blankly at the patrol car Grant and Henri arrived in. "I care about making sure no one hurts her."

Grant snorts. "What? And you think Montero Arrendell is sneaking around in the middle of the night, peeping in girls' windows and painting bloody warnings on their walls? Come on, man."

"Not him," I mutter. "But there are plenty of folks in this town that they own, and you know it."

"Like our boss, you mean." Grant gives me a long, measured look. "Just be careful, Graves. I know you've caught feelings for this girl, but don't let any personal shit cloud your judgment. We can't haul in Montero Arrendell on vapor. Only gonna say this once—find something ironclad or drop it."

"Got it," I snap.

He's being fair, but the trouble is it might be too late for that.

Slowly, Henri and Grant clear out.

Henri promises he'll stay on night patrol and do a few swings through the town until morning, just in case he catches anyone creeping around.

There've been a few neighbors peeping out their windows by now. The gossip factory's going to be in overdrive by morning with crime tape roping off a square of Delilah's lawn and flashing patrol cars rumbling up the street.

That's a tomorrow problem, though.

Tonight, there's just me and Delilah, and she's locked up inside herself in this nervous little knot that makes me worry like hell.

"Hey." I approach her slowly, no sudden moves, offering my hand. "Let's get you inside. I'll make some tea to settle your nerves."

She chokes back a sound that's almost a sob, scrubbing at one eye as she gives back a weak, tired smile. "It's my house. I should be making you tea, mister."

But she slips her hand into mine.

Her fingers are so cold.

I hold them tight—goddamned reverently—as I coax her to the porch and up inside the house. It's looking neater than the last time I saw it with her stuff unpacked.

She's chosen a minimalist style that makes the most of small spaces, turning the place homey.

"I ain't the one who's upset," I point out, closing the door behind us and waiting for her to rearm the security system. "I'm just pissed."

"But why?"

"Because some shithead's trying to scare you. If I catch 'em, I'm afraid of what I might do, Miss Delilah." I squeeze her hand again, guiding her over to her new sofa, this deep cushy thing in off-white linen. "Can't say I like that too much."

She drops down on the couch, staring at our clasped hands.

I sink down on one knee in front of her, searching her pale face.

"Do you fuss this much over every new girl in town? Or is it just the ones who show up with dead bodies and stalker exes?" she asks.

"Nah, just you." I don't even hesitate. Fuck, I'm smiling as my thumb grazes her knuckles. "Let me make you that tea. Then we'll talk."

She winces, her eyes darkening. "...oh, yeah. Right."

"Not about *that*," I snap off. "Well, hell, come to think of it, we *should* talk about that eventually, but only when you're feeling better." I give her hand another reassuring squeeze before I stand. "Be right back."

Her eyes follow me almost desperately into the kitchen.

The kettle's already on the stove. I get the water going and check cabinets till I find a pack of herbal chamomile tea bags and a couple mugs.

"Sugar?" I call.

"Just one teaspoon. Or some honey. They're both in the pantry."

"Got it."

I don't like how her voice sounds, small and thin, her usual fire gone.

It leaves her sounding gone, like she's left her body and gone someplace where the real world can't touch her. That makes me move faster, this desperate need to get back to her, even if there's only a few feet and a wall between us.

I load up my own cup with sugar, drop one teaspoon in hers, pop in tea bags, and grab the kettle before it squeaks. No point in scaring her with that thing screeching like an angry cat.

Steaming tea in hand, I step back into the living room, passing her a mug before I set my own down on the table.

"Breathe it in."

"Y-yeah." She bows her head to the mug blankly, inhaling the steam, her shaky fingers cradling the blue-glazed ceramic so tight. When she looks up, her gaze is so vulnerable. "What did you want to talk about? I think I already told you everything about Roger, but I can try to remember more..."

"Not that. Fuck Roger," I snarl, shaking my head. I settle on the couch and stretch, propping my arm on the back—offering her a place at my side. "Before we talk, I gotta ask—do you want to stay here tonight? Or do you want me to take you to The Rookery? Or even my place?" I half smile. "I'll sleep on the couch. No charge for pillows this time."

A tired smile flickers across her lips.

She looks at me slowly before she collapses against my side, kicking off her sandals and pulling her legs up against her side.

I try like hell not to notice the thin shorts they're clad in tonight.

She's a warm, soft bundle against me, so short she can't pillow her head on my shoulder. Instead, she rests her temple to my chest, her dark hair spilling over her shoulder on my side.

"I'm a little scared to be here," she whispers. "But not if you stay. Going anywhere else feels wrong, even if it might be the smart thing to do. It feels like running."

"No shame in running sometimes. It's survival instinct." I hold in a sigh, letting my arm cradle her shoulders. "Hell, I wish my sister had cut and run. Maybe she'd still be here."

Delilah's brows knit together. She looks up at me from under her long lashes.

"Your sister? Is that who you were talking about, that thing about missing someone?"

"Yeah." I hesitate. "You remember that?"

There's that shaky smile again, there and gone in an instant. I wish I could make it stay.

"I listen to you more than you think, you lunk. Except when you're pissing me off."

"Will you listen to me now without getting pissed?"

She snorts softly. "You're in luck. I don't have the mental energy to lift my middle finger tonight."

I chuckle, but damn my throat feels like I've got a noose *inside*, closing up my airways and choking off my voice.

Goddamn.

It's been so many years, and it still rips me up inside to even think about talking through this.

Guess it's a little easier with Delilah's warmth curling into me.

"This is gonna sound crazy," I force out. "But after I've said my piece, I think you'll understand why I get such a goddamned stick up my ass about Ulysses Arrendell. Yeah, he's a nice guy—a little *too nice*. I don't know what the hell he knows or how complicit he is in the shit they do up in that house on the hill. That whole family's rotten to the core. Trouble is, their roots in the town go so deep it's almost impossible to cut them out. They own everything—and everyone."

Delilah bites her lip, tapping her fingers against her mug as she takes a slow sip.

"So, what? It's some toxic family thing where Ulysses is just caught up in the generational cycle? I've met a few people like that. Lived with a few like that. Most of my foster families were in the game for the social clout, bragging about how much they loved themselves for being so generous to a useless brat like me."

My frown drags down my face.

I sure as hell hate hearing her talk about herself like that.

Makes me want to bust a few faces belonging to any assholes who made her feel that way once. Probably not my place to say it, though, so I just squeeze her shoulders tighter, curling my hand against her arm, taking pleasure in the quiet way she snuggles into my side.

"You're not useless," I say, sinking deeper into the sofa. "And it's a little deeper than that whole family acting like they're straight from a goddamned V.C. Andrews novel. It's..." I pause, blowing out a sharp breath. "I don't know where to fucking start."

I'm surprised by the soft fingers in my hair at my temple—threading in, brushing it off my brow.

"How about at the beginning?" she says gently. "This is something that really hurts, isn't it?"

"Am I that obvious?"

"It's your eyes." She looks up at me now, searching my eyes, her own blue gaze brimming with emotion. "It's funny... you and Ulysses have almost the same eyes. This green like spring, like emerald. But where his green says nothing, yours says everything. Even the things *you* won't say."

Fuck me.

I suddenly get the urge to kiss her so bad it aches.

Suddenly I want to ask her what this thing is between us.

Shit, I know I might just ask her, might just kiss her into ashes, if only I didn't feel Celeste's ghost sitting here between us, hand in hand with Emma Santos.

Still, I catch Delilah's hand and draw it down to kiss her palm with a smile.

"Feels nice to hear you say that. I'm not real good at talking most of the time. I either get mad, or just clam up and can't get the words out."

"Sometimes that's just how people are when they don't feel safe," she whispers softly. "But I promise whatever you're about to tell me... it's safe, Lucas. I won't get mad. I won't think you're crazy."

"Okay." I'm gonna have to trust her word on that.

Still takes me another minute and her coaxing hand to unglue my lips.

"My folks died when I was twelve, and my sister Celeste was eighteen. Awful car accident. We didn't have anyone else—no surviving family—and since she was legally an adult, she wound up being my guardian. Stuck raising me all by herself, me this furious punk-ass preteen, mad at the world for taking his family away. If the family house wasn't bought and paid for, we'd have been out on the street, but at least we had a home. She did cashier work to pay the bills, and I picked up a little under the table work at the lumberyard, hauling scrap."

"Little Lucas the lumberjack." Delilah smiles, tucking her head against my side again.

"Wasn't so little, even back then. Big old rangy thing like a colt with all his bones poking out everywhere while he tries to figure out what to do with legs too long for his body." I chuckle, then trail into a sigh. "It was rough, but even when we fought, we were good to each other, me and Celeste. We were all we ever had. I was looking forward to when *I* turned eighteen, 'cause I guess I—well, I was hoping to set her free. She wanted to go off to make music. She wanted to *sing*. She had this gorgeous voice like a nightingale. I really think she would've made it big, and even if she didn't, she would've had an honest *shot*. She'd have made people happy and done right by herself. But Celeste couldn't go anywhere with it. Not when she was tied down being stand-in mama to her bratty little brother."

"I doubt she felt that way," Delilah says. "Not if she loved you as much as it sounds like you loved her."

"Maybe. Who knows. Just know that one day she started changing." I stop and steel my voice. "She was always a bit of a daydream believer, sort of flighty, but suddenly her head was in the clouds all the time. I figured out fast my sister was in love. But I didn't figure out who it was till it was too late. She..."

I stop.

Fuck, this tastes so bitter.

Every word scratches my tongue like pitch-black venom.

"Lucas," Delilah whispers, squeezing my arm to urge me on.

"I think she was having a fling with Montero Arrendell. Think he promised to use his money and his connections to get her into the music industry. Suddenly, Celeste was wearing expensive dresses we couldn't afford, nice jewelry, going up to that house at all hours of the night." I press my teeth against my lips, chewing on ugly words, struggling to breathe. "Then one night, we had the mother of all fights. I told her I'd pre-enlisted in the Navy for when I finished high school so she wouldn't have to keep working to put me through college. She really thought she was gonna pay my tuition, when she never even went herself because she had me to raise. But she was so pissed, talking about how I'd go and get myself killed. And, of course, she was all dolled up that night. Montero sent a car to pick her up, and she left in a huff right in the middle of our fight."

Deep, hoarse breaths rattle my lungs.

There's an invisible fist of pure grief slamming into my gut, over and over, robbing away my words.

Fuck, I'm hollowed out from head to toe.

"What happened?" Delilah whispers.

"About what you'd think. Celeste never came home," I rasp out. "Just gone. Disappeared. This pretty young woman in a red dress—just like Emma Santos—and everyone saying she got sick of having to be my guardian and ran off to start a new life as somebody else. Another local boy, Grant's best friend, Ethan Sanderson... he disappeared the same night. You can imagine the story everybody told, when Ethan didn't make any secret that he was head over heels for my sister. The police didn't fucking bother with a missing persons report. Still, I know the truth." My jaw sets. "Montero Arrendell used her. Then he got rid of her when he got bored. Probably found a way to shut Ethan up, too."

There's a dead, awful silence when I finish.

I can practically hear the *click* going off for Delilah with a shuddering breath, the grim realization.

"Holy shit. So you think Montero killed her? Killed them *both?*"

"It's the only explanation," I say. "I knew Celeste, goddammit. Maybe we fought like wildcats, but she wouldn't leave me like that, seventeen and fending for myself."

"And Emma..."

"She fits the same profile, yeah," I point out. I can't look at her, staring instead at the dark-shaded front window as I hold Delilah tight. "Nice dark eyes, silky black hair. Young and full of promise. Montero's got a type. Just like the girls who show up on Ulysses' arm before disappearing, never to be seen in Redhaven again. Hell, not just Ulysses, but all the Arrendell boys. It's like they're his personal shoppers. Scouting him women who'll play around to distract him from a wife he clearly hates. It's gone on for a long-ass time. I've got newspaper clippings going back decades. Girl after girl after girl."

There's a long, dead silence when I stop.

One where I don't think either of us has to point out that Delilah meets that description, too.

I feel the shudder that rolls through her as she presses against me.

"I'm so sorry," she whispers hoarsely. "I'm sad you lost your sister that way, and with no answers, either."

The feeling that hits rings me like a bell.

I turn my head, looking down at her, my chest seizing up.

"You saying you believe me?"

Delilah's brows draw together.

She tilts her head back, puzzled, and suddenly I don't want anyone looking into those starry blue-indigo eyes but me.

Not ever again.

Especially not Montero goddamned Arrendell, or any of those twisted pukes he calls sons.

"Why would you lie about anything?" she asks. Her fingers toy with my shirt, plucking at it thoughtfully. "You don't fake that kind of hurt, Lucas. I can tell it's cut deep. And if you say

215

your sister wouldn't have left you like that, you'd know better than anyone. So maybe the Arrendells had something to do with it. And maybe—"

"Maybe what?" I cut in because I can't wait.

"Maybe they had something to do with Emma, too," she finishes in a whisper. "It makes sense, doesn't it? You said she fits the bill. Another beautiful young woman in a red dress. Maybe she was supposed to disappear, but something went wrong and I found her body. Or maybe she was just there to scare me and—"

"Drive you into Ulysses' arms. Your knight in shining armor, conveniently standing by," I finish. "All so he can deliver you up to that fuck, Montero."

My lip curls with rage.

Biting her own lip, Delilah says, "He did invite me over for a party. Ulysses, I mean. He said his brothers are coming back soon and there'll be some big shindig to welcome them home. He said they and their father would be delighted to see me there."

"Damn. Doesn't make sense, does it?" I point out. "Inviting the local schoolteacher to a family function."

She smiles weakly. "Ulysses *is* acting like a boy with a bad crush. Giving me stuff I never asked for. He said the Xs on the bracelet were like the Xs in XOXO. Hugs and kisses. He claimed he didn't even know about the X-marks."

"About that," I growl. "The reason I got so pissed when I saw that bracelet is because I've seen it before. Only that time it didn't have any X-marks. Last time I saw it around, it was a plain rose gold bar—and it was on my sister's wrist the night she disappeared."

Delilah's sweet face goes white.

"Oh my *God*."

She twists to look over her shoulder. I follow her line of sight and realize she's staring at a shelf against the living room wall, at the threshold to the hall.

The little red box sits on the third shelf, perched there like a silent curse.

My heart drums hard against my ribs.

Delilah just stares at me, her eyes too wide now.

"Jesus. It is..." she swallows. "Is it really the same one?"

"If it's not, it's one just like it," I clip.

"Then the Xs... oh my God. What if they're not strikes, Lucas? What if they're..." She can't finish.

"The number of women Montero has crossed off since my sister," I finish for her, choking back bile.

"Then that bracelet means he's marked *me*. And he's the one leaving those X-marks and Roger's got nothing to do with it. He probably doesn't even know where I am!"

"Possible," I say. "Though I don't think he or Ulysses is the one painting them. The Arrendells never get their hands dirty when they could get caught. They have an accomplice. Probably some dick in town they're paying, thinking it's a harmless prank."

Or not so harmless.

A million gut-wrenching blackmail scenarios come to mind. With great wealth and deep roots comes overwhelming power, and this family has half of Redhaven on a tight leash.

Delilah leans forward to drink her tea and sets the mug back down on the square wood coffee table with a sharp *thunk!*

Then she lurches up, this tiny ball of vibrating energy. "I'm going to kill them. *Kill them both.*"

"Delilah," I bite off.

Her eyes whip to me, bright and spinning.

I can't help myself.

I laugh warmly, breaking this bubble of misery. Wrapping both arms around her waist, I drag her back before she can make it more than a step, pulling her curvy body against me, hauling her into my lap.

"Lucas, I'm not joking. I really mean it," she hisses.

"Stop." I bury my face in her sweet-smelling hair. "Woman,

you can't just go charging up to that mansion in the middle of the night making threats. Also, you probably shouldn't be confessing intent to murder right in front of a cop."

God, she overloads me with so much *feeling*, this pint-sized dynamo of raw energy.

Five minutes ago, she was shaking with fear. Now she's revved up to slay dragons.

My brave little cactus.

Only, she isn't really mine yet, and that bothers me a hell of a lot.

Also sobers my dumb ass up.

I hold her tighter as she settles against me.

"You wouldn't rat me out," she throws back with a huff. I like the way her body fits against mine, compact and warm and close. "So what do we do then? If we can figure out who's helping Montero, wouldn't that give us evidence that he's responsible for Emma Santos? And targeting me next?"

"*We* don't do anything," I say firmly, bracing for a fight. "Look, I've been working this case for a long time on the down-low, Lilah. What I need you to do is stay safe. Don't go to that party. Don't let them pull you in, no matter what, even if you're just trying to help. I won't be solving your murder next."

"But..." Groaning, Delilah slumps against me, then turns herself sideways, curling up in my lap with her head pillowed against my chest. Her legs are stretched out on the couch, bare and tanned and too tempting for life in those tiny cutoff shorts. "I just want to do something for Emma."

"Emma would want you to be safe." I rumble, running my hand down her thigh, her warmth melting into me.

When she doesn't pull away, I let my hand settle, keeping my other arm wrapped around her. "Trust me, the best thing you can do for her is to not wind up just like her."

"I just feel like she's haunting me, you know?"

"Maybe she is," I answer. "Not begging you for justice. More like she's watching over you."

Delilah smiles faintly, and there's a sadness to it.

"That's a sweet thought," she whispers. "But it still means Montero Arrendell got away with murder."

"Only for now. I *promise* you I'm looking for a way to expose him without them being able to use their money and connections to wiggle out of it." I kiss the top of her head, closing my eyes, breathing her in. "For Emma. For Celeste. For every woman he's ever hurt. For you, darlin'."

With a soft purr, Delilah snuggles in closer.

It's a nice feeling, basking in her warmth with the quiet night all around us. Feels like we're curled up in the eye of a storm.

Nothing but me and her and the scent of tea filling the room, a refuge from the chaos outside.

Her body heat bleeds through me in this soft swell.

Fuck, I want to ask her so much if the fact that she's letting me hold her like this means what I hope it does.

That maybe, just maybe, she feels something more serious than a hankering for another one-off fuck, too.

But this isn't the time or place for feelings.

Not tonight.

Not when I could just be misreading her needing comfort, her fear, and the physicality of someone close by grounding her and keeping her safe.

I can be her rock, without any expectations.

Still, I can't stop thinking that right on the other side of that wall there's a yellow ribbon of crime scene tape and a splash of blood against Delilah's wall.

Resting my chin on top of her head, I break the silence between us and say, "If you're set on staying here, let me put some motion sensor lights in the yard. The prick who's been creeping on you, peeking in your windows, he's using the shadows to slink around and hide. He won't expect a floodlight to the face. We can try to ID him that way, whoever the hell he is." I stop and consider, then add, "And maybe you ought to get a dog."

"A *dog?*" Delilah's shoulders shake with laughter.

"Sure. A nice pup might help, having someone here to protect you who doesn't piss you off so much."

"You only piss me off a little. Lately." She beams me a saucy smile, then touches her fingers to my nose. "You remind me of a dog, anyway. One of those big ones. Maybe a Norwegian Elkhound. Or a husky."

Leaning in closer, pressing into that light touch of her finger, I drop my voice to a growl and look at her very seriously, letting a one-word growl build in my throat.

"*Woof.*"

She doubles over laughing when I let it out.

"See? Right now you're not annoying at all. You're actually kind of cute." Her fingers slip down to rest over my lips.

I never knew how sensitive a pair of lips could be till her touch ignited every last one of my nerve endings, electrifying my skin.

Her smile turns sly as she leans in closer and purrs, "*Meow.*"

Goddammit, I laugh, inadvertently kissing her skin.

"So are you saying we bicker like cats and dogs?"

"Something like that," she teases softly—and the way she's looking at me right now grabs me and holds on.

She's a prickly one, all right.

All fire, but there's a difference between *heat* and *warmth.*

That difference is in her eyes right now, turning those glimmering stars into constellations that feel like if I knew how to read them, they could point me straight to her heart like a navigator's charts.

There's a gravity between us.

No denying it.

If you'd asked me this morning, I'd have thought maybe it was just lust. Denied attraction exploding in charged arguments, then in that wildness that turned us into rutting animals giving in to our primal instincts.

You ask me now, with the air crackling and her fingers

tracing the corner of my mouth and those starlit eyes watching me so intently, fuck.

No.

The way my heart thrums right now sure as hell isn't lust.

It's the biting urge to kiss her so goddamned bad I could die.

Hilariously, she beats me to it.

That little hand drifts up, curling against my cheek, her thumb stroking the corner of my mouth, her eyes searching mine.

"You confuse me so much," she whispers.

Then she stretches herself up and presses her lips to mine.

You'd never think a little whirlwind could kiss so softly, so sweetly.

I hold still, letting her do whatever she pleases, her lips moving against mine, her tongue searching as it teases me like mad.

It's like she's asking me not to fight with her tonight.

She's telling me she doesn't want to be alone.

Gently, I draw her closer, gathering up her hair against her sleek back, and slowly leaning into her kiss. Meeting her energy instead of clashing with it.

Fitting my mouth to hers, our lips part in this burning intimacy.

Fuck me, she's like nectar.

Before, I had no time to savor her sweetness.

Now, I drink her in.

Now, I let myself *feel* everything that blew past me like lightning before.

She's got a mouth like sinking into rich cream when I kiss her.

Her tongue is slow and shy, stroking mine, and when I twine my tongue with hers and tease her, flick her, she gives back a soft sound in the back of her throat, arching against me until her tits press against my chest.

Goddamn, woman.

Her body is all lush curves on the outside, but toned underneath.

I rake my fingers down her back, still tangled up in the silky wisps of her hair.

She really is a wildcat through and through.

Sinuous.

Sleek.

Grace and sensuality in one firecracker package.

Her delicate weight in my lap is a goddamned torment.

Every time she moves against me, twisting to the rhythm of our slow kisses, she churns my blood.

In no time, there's a hell of a lot more pressure between my lap and the undersides of her thighs.

Slowly, I curve one hand over her hip, spreading my fingers across the heavy swell of her ass.

I sink my fingers in till firm flesh gives in a way that makes me groan, that makes my cock jerk *hard* against my jeans.

Delilah responds with a moan, lifting herself against me.

Her hot, thick thighs quiver.

Just enough warning before she pushes herself up, moving over me, spreading those luscious thighs to straddle me without ever breaking our kiss.

"*Fuck,*" I rasp against her mouth—and I can't help grinding up, thrusting against that hot place between her thighs. She's already spread open for me, waiting, nothing but this damn fabric in my way. "You're gonna drive me crazy, Lilah."

"So go. Go crazy," she breathes, curling her fingers in my hair, sinking down and rocking against me.

Her soft, husky cries come in waves as she tortures us both, grinding against my cock.

Fucking hell, I can smell her wetness. The scent grows every time she writhes her hips, using me to tease herself and I sure as hell don't mind.

"Go crazy, Lucas. Don't hold back tonight."

This girl.

This girl's gonna rip my heart out and shred it right in front of me.

She's already left my self-control in tatters, but I can't fuck her in here.

Not in the living room, not feeling so exposed.

Stealing one last taste of her mouth, I bite her lower lip before I say, "Hold on to me."

Before I stand, I haul her up in my arms.

Just getting up fucking *hurts*, dragging my jeans against my straining cock. I ignore it as I turn to carry her down the hall. Delilah stares up at me breathlessly, her eyes dark and dilated.

"Really? Carrying the damsel off to bed?"

"Just being efficient," I tease, bending to press my lips to her brow. "If you'll let me stay tonight, I'd rather not have to get up after."

There's something almost beautiful about how this bold, fearless woman turns soft and shy as she presses her face to my shoulder like she wants me to hide her from the world.

It makes my heart swell, knowing she finds me that safe.

Not nearly so much as it swells when she whispers, "Stay. Stay until morning. Please."

No words.

I have no fucking words for the way she makes me feel, so I don't say a damn thing.

Instead, I show her.

One more step into her bedroom.

One plodding step, and then I'm tumbling her down against the tangled sheets, her hair spilling everywhere like ink.

Underneath me like this, it's impossible to escape how *tiny* she is.

She's the sort of doll you'd expect to be breakable, wispy and sweet instead of the little cherry bomb she really is.

That fire lashes in her eyes as I devour her with a glance.

"Stop staring," she whispers, her cheeks turning a furious red.

I smirk.

"Can't help it, darlin'." I smooth my hand over the taut curve of her stomach—a real woman's belly, not model thin, soft and supple and ready for a man to put a baby in her someday—the thin layer of her tank top isn't nearly enough to stop me from feeling her heat. "You're too damn beautiful to do anything else, and I appreciate beautiful things."

Her lips turn up in a losing battle.

Delilah presses her bare foot to my chest and pushes. "Don't start with cheesy pickup lines or you'll turn a sure thing into a maybe."

"Well, hell, since I'd hate to ruin my odds..." I set to work, giving this bossy girl what she wants, using my mouth for better things.

I catch her foot, lifting it up to press my lips to its arch.

Her breaths catch softly, her chest rising and falling in a swell that makes her breasts strain against her top.

She's a vision.

Every little reaction captivates me as I kiss up her inner calf, my fingers following my lips, gliding over her skin in slow caresses higher and higher.

The closer I get to the sweetness waiting between her thighs in blushing pink, the more she shudders. I bite down gently on her inner thigh.

She whimpers real sweet for me.

Then she claps a hand over her mouth, her eyes widening in embarrassment.

I grin like mad as I stamp a kiss to the button of her shorts, skirting around those tempting hips to the slip of skin above the waist of her cutoffs.

Then the dip of her navel just under the fabric of her tank top.

Then the apex of her ribs.

Mine, mine.

Fucking all of her.

"Don't hold it in," I demand as my lips graze her naked,

smooth skin between the round swells of her tits. "Let me hear you, woman."

Seizing her nipple with my teeth, I draw it out through the layers of her shirt and bra, letting the fabric go hot in my mouth.

I tease her, flicking my tongue over that pink bud, pulling more pleasure out of her.

She answers me brilliantly with her back arched, her chest thrusting toward my mouth, her fingers digging in my hair.

The longer I suck, the harder she gasps.

A charging bull couldn't rip my eyes off her.

Can't stop myself from taking *more*, claiming new inches of her with my mouth.

Every sound she makes drugs me till all I want is the high of the next moan.

This inescapable craving burns me down, igniting my blood, thrilling my cock with the sensual pain of a hard-on pulsing with one raging heartbeat at a time.

The way I want Delilah hurts me wonderfully.

Each jolt leaves my jeans tighter, turning my cock to pure steel.

With the gentlest pinch of my teeth, she shudders again, squirming restlessly under me.

Catching her under the knees, I spread her open slowly, then lower my body to rest on hers till there's no escaping just how much I eclipse her with the way she fits so snug against me.

It's a fucking heady feeling, this closeness, teeming with desire.

Pleasure boils up my throat as I slide along the length of her, bringing us together in a mutual rush of gasping friction.

Goddamn.

God fucking damn.

I could overpower her so easily.

Break her without a second thought.

Which makes it that much sweeter that she's letting me, trusting me with every bit of her.

225

Soft thighs clenching against my waist.

Nimble, pleading fingers drag through my hair.

A stifled moan pours out when I switch to her other nipple, sucking hard, scratching her skin with my stubble, cupping her other breast until its fullness spills over my hand.

Not enough.

I need skin.

Growling, I drag the front of her tank top down, taking the cups of her bra with it. Her tits spill out in a ripple of full, swaying flesh that makes my mouth water with hunger.

A carnivorous hunger I satisfy by taking one dark-pink nipple back in my mouth, flicking and twisting and sucking and teething till she writhes against me helplessly.

I sate myself by sinking my fingers deep into the plush globe of her breast.

This woman's a sensory feast, overwhelming me with the way it feels to touch her, to feel her against me, to hear her gasping my name and—fuck.

Fuck.

That scent, that soft mix of fruit and florals mingle with something musky and creamy and tart that just screams desire.

It's a level of sexy that must be illegal in forty states.

"*Lucas,*" she whispers, her small nails biting into my scalp. "Stop. Stop teasing me."

"You telling me this doesn't feel good?" I drag my tongue over her nipple.

Delilah tosses her head to the side, her lips parted and gleaming.

"Or this?" I growl.

While she curses my name, I flick the button of her cutoffs open and flatten my hand against her belly.

Then I slide down, into the secret space between layers of fabric, molding over the lace of her panties as I skim down between her thighs.

When I press two fingers up, she curls forward, almost

hugging me to her breast as she whimpers in my ear, giving me her answer with every breath.

I'm gonna love this woman even more when she begs.

She's absolutely soaked, dripping all over my fingers as I rub slow, taunting circles over her drenched panties.

I press my lips in hot, open-mouthed kisses over her jaw and throat, adding teeth as I play with her flesh until her voice breaks.

Until she tenses.

Until her thighs clench against my sides and her hips buck up and my fingers are so fucking coated in her that I can feel it running over my skin.

I slow down, my fingers just barely resting against her.

"Still want me to stop?" I whisper.

She whimpers against my shoulder.

"No! I'm—I'm going fucking crazy," she breathes. "Lucas, *please.*"

Damn her, I smile.

"Lucky you, darlin'. Won't make you beg tonight—not much. I want this just as much as you do."

It almost hurts to pull away from her, lifting myself off her and tugging my hand out of her shorts.

Only for a second.

Only long enough to fish around in my back pocket for my wallet, fumbling till I snag the condom tucked inside and drop the leather wallet on the bed.

In a flash, her shorts are gone, tossed on the floor.

She watches me with smoky eyes as I unzip my jeans, reaching up to touch my lips as a slow, mocking smile spreads over her lips.

"...so you keep condoms in your wallet all the time?" she teases.

"A good cop is always prepared," I answer.

Then it's too hard to form words as I roll the condom over my cock, my mind centered on one thing.

The pressure torments my blood.

She's got me so ready.

Hell, she's got me on a string.

Just the slightest tug and I'm hers.

Don't know how this prickly, wild woman got under my skin so deep, so fast, but I'll be damned if I know how to fight it.

There's no question she wants it just as bad, lying under me with her breasts bared and her legs spread with the blue lace of her panties soaked dark against her pussy.

Her fingers lace with mine as they curl around my cock.

A ragged, tortured growl rips out of me as she draws our laced hands fully down my shaft.

Shit.

I didn't know a man could get any harder than this.

My dick jerks in our grasp, pulsing like a second heart.

"Lucas," she whispers again, longing and sweet, and I'm so fucking done for.

I sink down over her, capturing that pleading mouth with mine, taking over her mouth like I can mark her from the inside and leave my brand.

We're already moving together, both of us shivering in perfect chaos.

Her mouth opens for my tongue, taking me in, surrendering so deliciously as I fill her.

"Lilah." I grind out her name against the slickness of her lips as I shift my hips just between her thighs, one hand drifting down to catch her panties and tug them aside.

I don't know why that gets me so fucking hot, leaving her in soaking wet lace and just pulling them aside to fuck her, but it's the last straw.

I need her.

Right the fuck now.

With one more kiss that burns my mind blank, I grip her hips, lift her up, and take her.

Last time was so raw, wild and swift, an explosion of sensations.

It was over before I ever had time to process more than the pleasure storming my nerves.

Now, I take my sweet time, savoring every last sensation of her tight flesh wrapped around me in a luscious grip.

She envelops every inch of me in her burn and it urges me on, deeper and deeper in her hot wetness.

Fuck, she feels good.

I have to stop myself barely an inch in, and then again—one inch at a time, as far as I can make it before I'm wrecked.

Every time I pause in little jolts she jerks and clenches around me with buttery moans, little ripples inside her caressing the length of my cock like she's trying to pull me in deeper.

Deeper.

Goddamn, deeper.

I bury myself inside her a little more with every stroke till we're locked together.

I can hardly breathe from the intensity.

From being joined to my Lilah.

I just kiss her harder, thrusting into her mouth, meeting the dueling spear of her tongue.

I fight the urge to kiss her into oblivion and the desperate need to keep moving, to take more of her with every thrust.

When she bites my bottom lip, when she wraps her legs around my waist, when she tightens her body around me and writhes in a sinful little twist, I don't know who or what the fuck I am.

I lose anything that resembles control.

I lose my mind.

I lose a piece of my sex-cursed soul.

Snarling, I dig my hands into the bed on each side of her, bracing as I rock my hips *hard*, dragging in and out of her with a surge so fierce it steals our breath away.

I don't know what we're doing.

Kissing, fucking, fighting, worshiping, or maybe all four at once.

I just know we're tangled up together now.

And it feels so fucking divine I can't imagine ever feeling it with anyone but her.

My hips drive on, one hand pulling at her hair, urging her up into a biting kiss that devours her as much as she's consuming me.

My mouth hurts with the fierceness.

My whole being throbs with the pleasure as we flow, two crashing symbols of flesh and desperation.

Every second I'm buried inside her ignites me till it's unbearable.

We're too wild.

Too perfect.

I pinch my eyes shut, losing myself in this, and then open them again because I can't bear to miss even a single second of her face, her body, the beauty in every tensed, straining line of her.

And I see it when she comes.

Ecstasy crisscrosses her face, an agonized bliss that leaves her lips slack under mine.

Her eyes dilate, exploding with stars like the night sky.

Then it hits me, too.

This crushing impact, this force, everything that brings her off in a piercing cry, clutching at me desperately, losing our rhythm with her legs thrashing around me.

It's the last ounce of pressure I can take, building up inside me to a bursting point.

When she locks around my cock, when her tightness wraps me up and pulls me so *deep* into those fluxing shudders, when I feel the wetness coursing between us as she comes, making my every stroke slick and smooth, I can't hold back.

I'm gone in growling fuckery.

Dissolved into our beautiful mess, coming so hard it turns me inside fucking out.

My cock plunges deep, swells, and unloads.

My spine goes electric.

I become one long pulse, fusing my release to hers.

I'm wrung dry from head to toe and spent like I'm being crushed by the hand of God—and I adore every manic white-hot second.

I can hardly breathe as we fall down in a tangle of sweat.

My body doesn't want to move.

But that doesn't stop me from holding her close, from pouring everything I have into cradling her against me.

Even now, it's like my body is hardwired to protect her.

To guard her at all costs.

To shelter Delilah Clarendon, including her poor beat-up heart.

Hell, *especially* her heart.

God help me, I will, for as long as she'll let me.

XIII: RED MEAT, DEAD MEAT
(DELILAH)

I don't remember falling asleep.

Lucas left me *that* worn out.

By the time I came down from my high in a boneless mess, I barely had enough sense to snuggle up to him and pass out.

But God do I remember how he felt.

All wrapped around this big protective beast until he formed a wall between me and a world that's just getting scarier.

His warmth stays with me, the memory of his powerful arms cradling me while he sprawled out with ease, sheltering me.

Sheltering us both.

It was like an unspoken message.

Like he was telling me, *hush and sleep easy, Miss Lilah. Long as I'm around, nothing's gonna get you.*

Every last fiber of my soul believed him.

There's just one drawback to having a bear of a cop as your personal protector.

When I wake up in the pale pink-gold light of dawn still draped over him, the late summer swelter just about smothers me in a sweaty layer doubled by his body heat.

I shove lightly at the massive sleeping lump in my bed.

He doesn't even twitch, just snorts and holds me even tighter.

If the heat wasn't killing me, I'd laugh.

I might as well be a squirming kitten shoving at a bulldog.

After a few more lame attempts to jostle him awake, I reach up and pat his face, loving the sharp scratch of his morning stubble against my fingers.

"Rise and shine, dude. Wake up. *Lucas.*" Snickering, I smack his face harder. "You're going to give me heatstroke."

A drowsy groan rumbles out of him, and though he never opens his eyes, a slurred, half-asleep mumble comes out.

"Then how're you talking..."

"Magic. Now let go, big boy. I'm sweating half to death."

His grip finally relaxes and he cracks one green eye open.

"Do I have to?" he whispers. "You feel damn good."

Oh, God.

That shouldn't melt me so much.

But I can't pretend he doesn't feel amazing, too.

I wouldn't have been able to stay here last night without him, much less sleep through the night. With Lucas still curled around me, the danger feels more abstract, less real.

I soften, curling my hands against his chest.

"At least let me get the covers off. I'm about to pass out."

"Mmph." Lucas shifts his weight.

My breath catches as his lips graze my throat, finding my pulse. He traces the tender marks where he bit me last night—until suddenly he blows a raspberry against my neck.

"Hey!" I burst out laughing, squirming and shoving him again. "You overgrown *baby!*"

"Don't think a baby could do the shit I did to you last night," he teases, loosening his grip on me and shoving the covers back, letting air rush over us, the taste of morning on every breath.

It's a crazy thing.

The minute I'm free, I *want* his suffocating warmth back. It's the perfect counterpoint to the cooling wetness misting my skin.

We're both naked now, shimmying out of our clothes after our first round.

We settle against each other, enjoying the morning stillness and a few happy birds chirping outside.

I lay my head on his shoulder, cheek on his chest, just listening to his heartbeat drumming away.

It's so steady, this calming thing that makes me think of all the times we've been *quiet* together, how easy and simple and peaceful it was.

Lucas Graves makes me feel at ease even in the total chaos.

He soothes my jagged edges and blunts my thorns.

Even when I'm ready to take his head off, there's just something about him that makes it easier to breathe.

God.

I think I'm even starting to *like* him.

I don't just mean the sex.

Him him, the man behind the badge and grumping snark.

...honestly, maybe even more than *like*.

There's a sweetness fluttering inside me when I feel how he holds me, turning me to soft, warm putty inside.

But I hardly know anything about him.

His parents died when he was young and his poor sister was next. Then he eventually became a cop.

He's a kind, caring, loyal man who lives out the whole *serve and protect* oath cops take.

I think he can fix almost anything, from the broken glass in a picture frame to busted steps to wiring up an alarm system.

And he's lost so much—possibly due to the Arrendells—and he carries that heartbreak with so much dignity and strength in a town just full of people who'd never guess what their benefactors are really capable of and probably wouldn't believe him if he spoke up.

I get it.

I really do.

Even if Ulysses is overly attentive and weird, even if I've heard the rumors about what *really* goes on at their glam parties where half the guys are snorting coke off supermodels' asses, even if I've seen the Twitter exchanges wondering if they're somewhere between Armie Hammer's nightmare family and Epstein island on the creep-o-meter...

All I've seen for myself since I moved here is what they claim to be. Rich folks free with their influence and money, seemingly for the good of Redhaven. Eccentric, yes, but welcoming and kind. That's the face they show the world, and the only world they've shown me.

So why do I want to believe Lucas so badly?

Easy.

Because I can't fathom why he'd lie.

And I can't imagine that so much raw hurt spilling out of him could ever be delusion and nothing else.

That's the thing.

When people tell big lies, they're either crazy or doing it for some selfish benefit. They wouldn't tell lies that could mean ridicule or exile.

Sometimes when people tell you things that are hard to believe, *knowing* they'll get serious backlash for it, they're telling the truth. Or at least telling you what they truly believe, damn the consequences.

If nothing else, Lucas believes what he's told me—sincerely and honestly, with absolute faith. He's not lying to me.

As for whether it's true...

I hate that I'm leaning toward *yes.*

It sucks when the Arrendells have been nothing but kind to me.

But there's being eccentric.

Then there's the kind of scary weirdness that sets off my senses until my skin crawls.

Suddenly I remember Ulysses standing between me and his father. Montero looking at me with cold, possessive eyes, and Ulysses blocking me with his body like he was quietly signaling to his father.

No.

Not this one, old man.

You can't have her.

Even with Lucas' body heat, I suppress the chill sweeping up my spine.

Something's not right with that family.

I don't think it's just my infatuation with Lucas talking, either.

I nuzzle his shoulder, skimming my fingers down his arm, following the thick, hard shape of his biceps.

His muscles are so sharply defined, all harsh angles softened by veins like rivers branching over his flesh.

He lets out a lazy growl, the only sound between us save for our breath and the chattering birds outside.

His lips press into my hair, his arms tightening around me again.

"Lilah, fuck. What are we doing?" he growls. "Just a few days ago, I could've sworn you hated me."

"A few days ago, I could've sworn I hated you, too." I smile. "I don't know, Lucas. I don't know what this is. But you make me feel good, and that's no easy accomplishment."

He smiles.

"I want you feeling safe with me constantly, woman," he answers softly. "I want you knowing I'll never let anything happen to you. I know a damn hell of a lot has been stalking you around ever since you got here, but I swear—I *swear* I'll get to the bottom of this, Lilah. No one's threatening you again."

"Lucas." I touch his cheek, grazing his dark stubble that tickles me so deliciously. "You don't have to make that your responsibility."

Honestly, I don't want to be just his responsibility.

I don't want him to be here in my bed purely because he feels like he has to guard me, to stop what happened to Celeste Graves from happening to me.

But I don't know how to say that when the words knot up inside me.

I hate that it's so hard for me to admit something vulnerable, to squeeze emotion past my pride.

There must be something on my face, in my voice, though.

Lucas pulls back, looking down at me with his green eyes set like shining emerald.

"It's not responsibility to protect someone you care about," he rumbles. "It's what any man would do."

"Oh?" I raise both brows with an amused sound, failing to hide the red flush that goes through me. "So you don't think a woman would, too? Let me tell you something, Lucas Graves." I press a fingertip lightly against his chest. "I'd gladly bash someone over the head with a frying pan if they were trying to hurt you. Possibly a coffeepot. A blender. Whatever appliances hurt most, really."

"Yeah?" With a husky chuckle, he captures my hand and kisses my fingertips. "So you're saying you care about me enough to crack some heads?"

"Hey now. Don't get carried awa—"

My alarm clock cuts me off, flashing *6:00 a.m.* from the nightstand with a shrill beeping.

My heart turns over sharply—not with surprise, but with the stark realization of what day it is.

Oh, no.

I start pushing at Lucas again, this time in earnest.

"Oh crap, *crap,*" I gasp, wriggling out of his arms. "I gotta go! It's the first day of school and I can't be late."

Lucas sprawls there lazily—and for a heady second I can't help but soak in his animal charm.

There's too much grace to call him bulky, those broad shoulders tapering down to narrow hips and long, well-toned legs.

Still sleepy, his spring-colored eyes glow beneath thick, decisive, arrogant brows, just as cocky as the curve of his full mouth.

There's just something about the way he looks with his black hair still tangled from sleep, wild and loose instead of neatly combed like it is while he's on duty.

Sweet Jesus.

A terrible part of me wants to crawl right back into bed with him. But the rest of me buzzes with adrenaline until I feel like a hummingbird.

I can't wait to meet my kids.

After drinking in one more look while he watches me with heated eyes like he *knows* what I'm thinking, I tumble out of bed.

"I need to get ready," I call back as I sprint for the bathroom, nearly tripping over his tangled jeans on the other side of the bed. "If you want coffee, you've got to make it yourself, sorry!"

"Better get a move on, teacher," he calls after me.

I laugh before I duck into the bathroom and crank the shower on.

I scrub myself down in a whirlwind.

By the time I walk back into the bedroom wrapped in a towel, his clothes are gone and so is he.

The smell of brewing coffee and eggs frying floats back from the kitchen.

I stuff myself into a pair of nice black pants, demure but cute brown boots, a lace-edged white camisole with a high neckline, and a close-fitting pale-blue cardigan. I finish with a quick dusting of makeup.

When I'm done, I follow the smell of coffee into the kitchen —only to find Lucas standing barefoot in front of the stove, his shirt draped over the back of one of the kitchen chairs.

My breath sticks in my throat.

His jeans nearly fall off the stark angles of his hips, making me think of handles. Something to grab him by and cling to and not let go.

I'm distracted from watching how the rising sun from the kitchen window plays over his bare chest by the sudden realization that he's raided my fridge and pantry.

There are cheesy scrambled eggs, sizzling bacon, grated potatoes forming crispy hash browns, and the smell of toast. It's only taken me twenty minutes to get ready.

Damn, he's good.

He glances up at me lazily and lets his eyes drift over me with a growing smile as he shuts the burners off and starts piling the eggs on two of my new blue ceramic plates.

"Look at you," he drawls. "Think I'm gonna start calling you Miss Rockwell, not Miss New York. You're straight out of a pretty painting."

"I could also start kicking you out." I smile sweetly.

"You wouldn't dare, darlin'. I made you one hell of a breakfast," he says with mock-innocence.

He's quick to arrange both plates, flipping bacon and hash browns next to the eggs, plucking out the toast the second it pops up and slathering the slices in strawberry jam.

For a second, it's familiar. I know those movements.

Someone who's done diner work.

That's where I learned to cook, too, and how to put together plates in under thirty seconds.

He's just as quick to balance the plates with one arm, two mugs of coffee in the fingers of his other hand, bringing them to the table.

"You look like the type who'd run out the door without breakfast on her first day." The look he gives me is less teasing and more affectionate. "Eat, Miss Lilah. You need food to handle all those munchkins."

I don't quite know what to do with myself as I settle down at my little kitchen table. He arranges forks and knives on napkins for both of us while I watch, way too amused.

"Thank you," I say a bit hesitantly, picking up a fork. "Diner job, huh?"

"What?" He gives me a puzzled look as he sits in the chair opposite me. He apparently eats like a heathen, shirtless and barefoot, but I can't say I mind the view.

"The way you were slinging those plates. It reminds me of when I worked at my mom's diner. I guess I was just wondering if you've done that, too."

"Oh." With a low chuckle, he scoops up a bite of eggs. "Nah, but galley work on a Navy ship isn't much different. The new recruits get to be everyone's waiters."

"So you *did* join the Navy." I scoop up my own eggs, taking a tentative taste—and I can't help purring my appreciation.

He made these with *butter*. They're melt-in-your-mouth good.

Lucas goes quiet, though, pushing his eggs and bacon around his plate with his fork, looking down at them.

"Yeah. I did. Celeste didn't want it, but with her gone, it was the best way to find my footing. Got my GED and a special dispensation to enlist before I was eighteen. Easier than making me a ward of the state."

"Yeah," I say softly. "If I could've avoided that... I would have."

It's a strange thing to have in common.

We both lost the people who mattered most before we were eighteen, and someone else got to decide what to do with us.

I'm glad for him, in a way.

He had a chance to choose his own destiny before someone snatched it away from him like they did with Mom and me.

But he's quiet, his eyes downcast.

I'm not sure what to say, so I just set my fork down and reach across the table, curling my fingers lightly against his wrist.

He glances up at me, his eyes guarded, offering a smile that doesn't mirror that sad green gaze.

"I didn't stay real long," he says. "Just a few tours. Saw some interesting places. Japan, South Korea, Bahrain, Oman, Djibouti. But y'know, as messed up as this place is sometimes..." He looks away from me, holding a piece of toast to his lips, his gaze fixed distantly out the window. "I just couldn't stay away from home. It's like Celeste kept calling me back to Redhaven."

"You still need to know what happened," I say firmly. "And you can't turn your back on this place until you have your answers."

"Somethin' like that." Another faint smile flicks across his lips before he looks back at me. "Anyway." He jerks his chin toward my shoulder. "Don't think I don't see you hiding that tattoo."

It's not hard to tell he's changing the subject.

Fine.

I let it go with a smile, squeezing his wrist before I pick up my fork again.

"I don't want to have to explain it to any upset parents," I say dryly. "Even if the whole point of getting it was, uh, to upset some parents."

Lucas arches a brow—but there's a warmth in his eyes, like he appreciates me accepting the change. He takes a bite of his toast, swallows, and says, "Any parents in particular, or you mean all of 'em?"

"My foster parents. Well, one set in particular, before they sent me back. I was seventeen." I clear my throat. Now it's my turn to rearrange my plate, shoving food around with my fork and ducking my head, my cheeks flaring hot. "That foster mother *hated* me. The way I talked, my temper... and maybe I had a sharp tongue. Maybe I did a few other things, too. She called me a vicious little dragon. I saved up my allowance for weeks and found a tattoo artist who didn't check IDs and got it just to spite her."

Lucas barks out laughter. Just like that the tension bleeds out of him, leaving him easy and relaxed again. His eyes glitter.

"I'm curious about those other things."

"Oh, the usual." I try to keep a straight face. "Turning in homework late, staying out too late, a little shoplifting once or twice—don't worry, I felt so bad I gave the stuff back right away. Before I even got caught. Just the usual troubled teenager crap you shouldn't talk about with the hot cop you just had wild sex with all night."

His proud grin drips with filthy thoughts brimming in his eyes.

"No worries. I'll cuff you for your misdemeanors later, after you're done with the kids. For now, eat your breakfast, New York."

"You," I say, pointing my fork at him and very *firmly* ignoring how my stomach quivers at that subtle promise, "need to stop filling my head with terrible thoughts."

"Just being polite, Lilah."

"Lilah. Delilah. Say it. One or the other."

"Lilah. Miss Delilah." He smirks. "There. I said 'em both. You just didn't tell me not to say anything else."

"You—"

Fighting back my laughter—and failing—I snag the folded paper towel under my cutlery, ball it up, and throw it in his face.

It bounces off his head and he gives me a deadpan look.

"That does it," he snarls.

Next thing I know, he launches out of his chair with a playful growl and comes diving at me.

Shrieking, I fly out of my chair, darting for the kitchen door —but he catches me around the waist, swinging me around, leaving me laughing wildly as I kick my feet.

How did life get this weird?

Here I am, first day on the job and surrounded by creepy threats.

There's dried blood splashed on my house. Either from my psycho ex or one of the effing Arrendells or one of their freaky minions.

A girl *died* in this house, not ten feet from where I'm squirming in Lucas' arms.

Yet somehow, I'm *happy*.

Happier than I've been since the day I first met Mitsi Clarendon and she pulled me into her arms and burst into tears of joy only a mother denied can have.

Maybe Emma Santos has a hand in this, wanting me to be happy because her life was cut short.

"Let go!" I hiss.

"Brat." Mock-snarling, Lucas playfully pulls my hair, then

sets me down next to my chair, nuzzling at my ear. "Eat your breakfast, I said." The way he slaps my butt makes me squeak. "Finish your food or you're gonna be late, brat."

So I do, giving him an irritable look before I plop back down in my chair. "You're lucky you're such a good cook."

"Y'know," he says, sliding lithely back into his chair and diving back into his hash browns, "you better go easy on the backhanded compliments. I'm starting to figure out your game, and if you're not careful, I might start thinking you like me."

"Really?" I snort. "Then you're not as good a cop as I thought you were, if that's the conclusion."

"See?" That just wins me another sexy smirk. "You went and did it again. Nice knowing you have such faith in my skills."

"Lucas Graves. There's an entire roll of paper towels not three feet away from me, and as far as I'm concerned that counts as artillery."

"Cease fire. I surrender." He sets his fork down and holds up both hands.

I just laugh, shaking my head, and finish the food while it's still warm.

He's right about the clock ticking.

There's just enough time to eat if I want to make it in time to get settled before the kids roll in. I shovel it in, barely remembering my manners, even if he's eating just as ravenously next to me.

No surprise, the man has an appetite to match his lion build.

I'm starting to wonder if he meant to eat all of this himself and only shared it with me when he realized he'd co-opted my kitchen.

It makes me smile.

And I'm still smiling like a lovestruck fool as I load everything into the sink to soak, then snag my messenger bag and dart for the door.

"You on duty today?" I ask, stopping on the porch and looking back at him.

Lucas hovers in the doorway, his arms stretched lazily over his head to grip the frame, drawing the stark lines of his chest into sleek relief. There's raw power in every muscle that flexes with his breath.

"Not till afternoon." He gives me a lopsided grin. "I drew crossing guard duty this month. Swear it was random. We drew straws and I came up short. I ain't stalking you."

"Sure you aren't. Also..." I bite my lip. "You know the alarm code, right? When you leave, just set it and the door lock engages after thirty seconds."

"I know how it works. I put it in, remember?" he teases. "I'll also clean up and get those motion sensor lights put in today, then close everything up nice and safe for you."

I flush. "Lucas, you don't have to—"

He silences me by catching my chin.

And I'm breathless as he tilts my face up for a kiss, capturing my lips in this slow, soft movement that makes me remember the feverish way he kissed me last night.

That warmth rocks through me as he plies my lips in lazy caresses I feel all the way down to the tips of my toes.

When he draws back, I'm dazed, still looking up at him.

"I want to," he whispers. "Have a good first day of class, Miss Clarendon."

"Y-yeah. Okay. Sure."

I'm walking on sunshine as I head to my car.

I'm amused that this is the first time I can actually see out of my rearview mirror since I moved here, without a gazillion boxes piled in the back.

But as I fit my keys in the ignition, I stop, glancing back at Lucas. He's still watching me from the doorway with one hand up in a wave.

I also can't help noticing the yellow crime scene tape peeking around the side of the house.

What am I doing?

Everything's such a mess.

Whatever's really going on with those Xs, my feelings, my everything.

Still, right now, I just want to bask in the moment.

I want to be happy.

I'm off to my very first day as a real teacher.

Not a teaching assistant, not a sub.

A bona fide honest-to-God *teacher*, with my very own classroom.

With one last look at Lucas and a fluttering wave, I smile and head off to work.

* * *

THE WORLD just glows brighter as I drive through town.

I feel like I'm in my own freaky Disney movie, everything hyper-saturated with color and twittering with birdsongs.

Only to have it all go grey the instant I turn onto the wider road leading to the town square.

There they are.

Standing on the corner like grim reapers.

Tall thin lampposts of men—Ephraim and Culver Jacobin—both of them smiling the same empty grins.

As I drive past, their heads turn slowly, tracking me, flash-freezing the warm, sunny morning.

My fingers go numb on the steering wheel.

I can't help thinking Roger's not the only one in town with a skinny, tall build—and a horrible talent for not being seen until he's good and ready.

I don't stop watching the Jacobins in my mirror until I turn into the roundabout and they vanish from my sight.

I don't breathe until they're gone.

I'm sure they never stop watching me until they can't.

* * *

I WON'T LET any weirdo scarecrow-men ruin my whole day.

Also, I thought I was prepared for how rambunctious my students would be.

I was very wrong.

I'm the only main teacher for K-4, aside from arts, PE, and elective teachers who only get them for an hour or two at a time. They're with me almost all day, thirty-three total between all the age groups.

I've never managed a blended class like this before.

It's a challenge to keep them all engaged, entertained, and actually learning. I only let certain grades out for an hour at a time to attend their rotating electives.

I'm basically doing the work of five teachers, even if my class is pretty small for spanning kindergarten through fourth grade.

Go figure.

I'm lucky the older students are eager to pitch in.

It doesn't take long to figure out that I can make this work by covering each subject one at a time, and asking the older kids to help the younger ones.

The strategy lets them sharpen their own social skills by assisting, letting them feel helpful. I'm actually pretty proud of the strategy.

One especially bright, precocious nine-year-old keeps me on my toes, though.

Nell Faircross.

She's in fourth grade, but well ahead of her peers, this restless little butterfly. The younger kids can barely keep up with her, and she's my little helper all day.

I find out fast that she's also a little gossip.

Every time I forget a name in the sea of new faces, she whispers in my ear, *That's Billy Compton* or *She's Sarah with an H, remember the blonde one is Sara without an H* but also with a little giggle of *Billy pinches girls' skirts and tries to peek* or *Mary steals pencils, watch out or she'll take yours too.*

I appreciate the little warnings.

But I also feel like I should keep an eye on Nell.

She forces me to cover a loud laugh more than once, but that kind of behavior could quickly turn from helpful to malicious gossip. I don't want people picking on her for helping the teacher or ratting them out.

Trust me.

Snitches get stitches applies on the playground more than the streets.

Hell, *especially* on the playground.

By lunch, they've worn me out. I get five minutes to stuff my face with Nora.

Of course, she teases me about looking like an exhausted soldier in the trenches before I'm back at it with the kids.

Don't get me wrong.

I'm enjoying myself like mad, but the burnout hits hardcore.

I'm relieved that a little recess and full bellies seem to dampen their energy, too.

By afternoon, I've put the little ones down for their nap. The older kids are quiet and content with reading time, diving into classics by Roald Dahl and C.S. Lewis.

Then Nell wants a story about an hour later.

I smile at her and ask, "What kind of story?"

She perks up, her brown hair bouncing around her face.

"Can you tell us a story about the people who live in the hills, Miss Clarendon?" she whispers, drawing it out dramatically. Her eyes widen. "Y'know, the ones in the scary house with the windows like eyes. The ones who *eat* people. My uncle says if you go too deep in the woods, they'll chop you right up and put you in their stew pot."

Gasps rise around the room, hushed and excited.

Many of the students stir restlessly.

"Nell, your uncle shouldn't tell you stories like that," I say. "And you're going to wake the little ones. Be good now. Hearsay isn't always the truth. I'm sure the hillfolk are perfectly nice people—" I stop. Yes, perfectly nice people, with their terrifying habit of *standing by the side of the road and glaring at me like they really do want me for stew meat.* But I can't let my own goofy bias infect my kids.

"They just live a little differently than we do," I tell her, choosing my words slowly.

Nell pouts, folding her chubby little arms. "But why would Uncle Grant tell me that if it's not true?"

"Because," I tease gently, "you're a fearless little adventurer. I bet if he didn't tell you fun stories to keep you from going out looking for the hillfolk, you'd wander all over the place to find out what it's like for yourself. If you got lost in the woods, you'd wind up in a really scary situation. Your Uncle Grant would worry himself sick. So, I think you'd better listen to him and not mess around in the forest, but don't pay any attention to silly stories about the hillfolk. He's just teasing you."

I hope.

After everything I've seen in this town, I honestly wouldn't write off living in a bad remake of *The Hills Have Eyes.*

Nell lets out a long, dramatic sigh.

"Oo-kaaaaay," she drags out.

"I appreciate that, Nell." I smile. Even if I had to chide her, I prefer teaching through positive reinforcement, and I don't want to embarrass her. "Now, does anyone want to hear any other stories? What else do you know about the history of Redhaven?"

A few kids chime in, talking about how they have a dad or a grandfather in Sons of the American Revolution because their sixth generation grandfather did something or other in the Revolutionary War.

Then Sarah With an H raises her little hand. "Can you tell us a story about living in New York, ma'am? That's where you're from, right? My mama told me."

I'm not surprised their parents have been talking, wondering what kind of person I am and how I'll be with their kids.

I just smile wider. "Sure! Buckle in, guys, because I'm going to tell you all about the Cinderella of New York City."

Okay.

So I'm making up a fictionalized version of my life on the fly.

In the story, I'm a princess, stolen away from my mother by evil fairies. The evil fairies leave me with a cruel royal family who may be rich and rulers of a bigger country, but they don't love me.

They keep trying to change me.

They make me a servant girl who just does backbreaking chores instead of the little princess I was born to be.

But one day, a prince with flashing green eyes and dark hair from another kingdom arrives. He's a prince, but he's also the sheriff.

I know, I know.

Don't judge me. You work with what you've got when you're not a bestselling author.

Prince Gravely recognizes me as the missing princess I've been searching for my whole life. He falls in love with me instantly and enlists the good fairies who work with my mom to spirit me away.

They restore my family and my crown before he proposes.

I become queen while my mother resigns to enjoy her retirement.

We all live happily ever after as beloved rulers over a small, but happy kingdom of kind, gentle people.

The end.

Yes, it's a little far-fetched.

But I think they're too spellbound to notice. Though Nell gives me a little smirk that says maybe, just maybe her clever little mind has put two and two together.

Hush, girl.

I might be a bit spellbound myself.

When I was a little girl, I never got many fairy tales.

I had to grow up fast, grow up hard, and learn quickly to

keep my dreams and fragile feelings to myself, hidden behind sarcasm and defensive sharpness.

So it's nice to daydream for a minute or two along with the little ones.

It's nice to be young again with kids who are too innocent to judge you, or dismiss fairy tales as ridiculous, or do anything besides smile and sigh with satisfaction when the happy ending comes.

Before I know it, the kids are waking up, and I've got to wrap up for the day.

Later, when their parents come to pick them up, there are a lot of smiling new faces.

I stick around on the front walk so I can shake hands with people whose faces are becoming more familiar.

Of course, little Nell manages to embarrass me when her uncle shows up.

Grant Faircross, the police captain.

How could I forget him after the last crisis?

He gives me a somber look as he offers his hand to shake while Nell crowds behind his legs and hugs them, clinging like a happy little burr and looking up at him with adoring eyes.

"Miss Clarendon," he says gruffly.

If an ancient oak tree could talk, it would sound like this guy, and he's built like a tank—just a wall of bull muscle, nearly as tall as Lucas but almost twice as wide.

His eyes are grave, but kind, set above a thick brown beard shot with silver.

"Sorry I didn't get a chance to introduce myself properly before. Call me Grant."

I shake his hand quickly with a smile. "It's nice to officially meet you—and don't worry, Captain. I just appreciate you and Officer Fontenot coming out so late to help Lucas."

"It's what we do, ma'am."

"Hey!" Nell pipes up pointedly, her smile just a little too wide and innocent. "Did you know Uncle Grant's never had a girlfriend?"

Holy shit!

I sputter, fire igniting from my neck to my scalp.

Grant's expression doesn't change in the slightest, though his entire face goes red. What little I can see of it above the beard, anyway.

He dips his head to me with almost formal politeness. "Have a good day, ma'am."

Then he turns around and firmly but gently marches Nell away, his shoulders stiff with embarrassment while I fight not to laugh.

He obviously dotes on that munchkin, and they're sweet together.

My God, though.

I hope she doesn't try playing cupid.

There's only *one* hot cop in Redhaven I'm interested in.

Silly little matchmakers aside, all in all, it's been a great first day.

I can't wait to finish grading pop quizzes, take down some notes for tomorrow, and head home to bask in the afterglow of a job well done.

* * *

My afterglow vanishes when I get back to my house and find a pickup truck I don't recognize parked on the curb.

It's the most beat-up thing I've ever seen in my life, and I drive an actual shitbox. So caked with dirt I can't even tell if it's supposed to be blue or grey.

What paint I can see is scratched and rusted, and there's a huge dent in the passenger side door.

Tall wooden slats form a makeshift fence line around the truck bed. Repurposed stock pallets, I think, creating a rickety enclosure the way people who haul trash or livestock do.

Probably livestock, considering the hay scattered along the metal bottom, along with a few crates of tools and—

Bottles?

Yep.

Lots and lots of empty bottles, mostly crusted with mud.

I park a few feet behind the monstrosity. Through the back window I can just make out a shadow behind the wheel.

My heart thumps nervously.

My hands go clammy on the steering wheel.

I don't like this when I've had way too many weird shadows haunting me lately.

Drawing in a deep breath for courage, I step out and warily approach the driver's side door.

I rap on a window so greasy I can barely see inside—until I realize who I'm looking at.

My heart stops, weird prickles shooting through the tips of my fingers like arcing electricity.

Culver Jacobin.

The younger of the two creepers who stare at me every time we cross paths in town.

I've never spoken to them once. I only know their names thanks to Nora.

He's slouched in the front seat, wearing a pair of muddy overalls, and—is he playing Bejeweled on his phone?

Oof.

Well, there goes the image of the scary crazy hillbilly who wouldn't know what to do with a smartphone if it fell out of the sky and popped him on the head.

I flush guiltily.

You can't tell the kids to stop making assumptions if you don't.

So I muster up a smile and knock gently again, this time a tad louder.

"Hey," I call. "Is there something I can help you with?"

He looks up with a surprised jolt and grins, showing off a

mouth full of very large, very white teeth. Apparently these hill-folk keep up with their dentistry, too.

Then he rolls down the window.

"Hey there! I was waiting for you, wasn't sure if I had the right address," he says with a friendly twang. His eyes crease. "Miss Clarendon, right? Three p.m. appointment?"

"Huh?" I shake my head. "I don't think I made an appointment for anything with you, Mr. Jacobin?"

"Not with me, no." He reaches over and thumps the toolkit in the passenger seat with one dirt-smeared hand, grins wider and —oh, *crap*, he's doing it again.

Staring at me.

Not just holding eye contact, but gawking with this fixed, unblinking stare boring through me. "Cable company sent me over to wire up your internet and TV. Tried to wave at you this morning, just to let you know I'd be seeing you later, but you sped by like a bullet."

"*Oh!*" Now my guilt turns into shame. "I'm so sorry. I'm such an idiot. I must've accidentally scheduled it for my first day at work. How long have you been waiting?"

"Oh, not much more'n an hour or two. Wasn't no problem. Thought I might have the wrong address, but it's real hard to have the wrong address around here." He unlatches the door and I step back, giving him room to swing it open. "Guess I don't need to introduce myself, huh?"

Now *I* feel like the creep.

I smile sheepishly.

"Sorry," I say. "I've seen you around town, and Nora and Mr. Arrendell—Ulysses, I mean—told me your name."

"Ain't no worry at all, ma'am, I know how Redhaven is. It's like that song in *Cheers*, y'know?" He hefts himself out, pulling his toolbox with him and pockets his phone in front of his over-alls with a sad little *bloop-bloop* sound of the game ending. "Sometimes you wanna go where everybody knows your name."

I fidget awkwardly for a second, then force another smile.

"Yeah, I guess so. Um, if you still have time to do the job, I think the cable hookup is out back."

"Sure! I'm not too busy today. Just do this stuff part-time for a little extra coin to pay for things around the farm." Culver slams the door of the pickup shut and follows me as I head toward the gate.

But as I unlatch it and step inside, leading him around the side of the house opposite from the one with the police tape, he stops, craning his head toward the glimpses of yellow and black visible around the other side.

"Hey, what happened there?" he says.

"I don't know, don't—"

Before I can stop him, he's traipsing through the grass, disappearing around the corner.

Crap.

I dash after him, dropping my messenger bag on the porch.

"Wait! I think that's still a crime scene!" I rush out quickly. "You shouldn't—"

Too late.

He's crouched in front of the yellow tape, reaching right under it to touch the bloody red X on the paint. Even though it's long dried, a few flakes still smear his fingers.

He brings them to his face, sniffs them, and then—

No.

No, no, no.

He *licks* them as I watch in abject horror.

"Oh my God, why would you—there could be diseases, I—"

"Nah," he says. "Blood this dry, out this long? Anything in it's dead. Can't make a man sick. 'Sides. Unless this fella had swine flu, nothing in it that can jump to a human. It's pig's blood, ma'am."

I swallow hard.

I feel sick, my mouth flooding with saliva.

"How... how c-can you tell?"

"Tastes a little sweeter, a little grassier. Our pigs eat sweet corn, mostly, so it changes the taste of their blood. Humans taste kinda gamier, more metallic, y'know? Since we're meat-eaters," he adds, almost as an afterthought.

I just stare at him, my pulse tracking every horrified second that seems to last way too long.

Culver blinks and gives me a wry smile, full of self-mocking humor.

"You can relax. I never ate no one before. When we slaughter our hogs for the meat, we collect the blood and sell it in the butcher's shop down in the square. People use it for cooking, making sausage, all that good stuff. Sometimes if a pig seems like it might've been sick, we taste the blood to make sure it's clean before we sell it. Test it, too. Hell, we practically got our own lab up at the house like big nerds." He grins. "Now ask me how I know how human blood tastes."

I'm about to die.

"...okay. I'll bite. *No puns.*" I point at him, although now I feel a bit silly. "How do you know?"

"'Cause my younger brother's an asshole and he punches me in the mouth enough that I know damn well what my own blood tastes like, ma'am."

I burst into laughter.

Well, that's a relief.

Culver laughs, too. Just a quick awkward thing, almost a giggle, high-pitched and startling enough to silence my laughter instantly.

But I hold on to my smile better than before and shake my head.

"You really shouldn't mess with that, though. The cops are still trying to figure out who did it."

"Seems like a real mean thing to do to a new lady in town." He claps his hands against his thighs and stands, then hefts his toolbox again. "Why the X, though? What's that mean?"

"Mr. Jacobin, I wish I knew."

I lead him around to the back of the house, where a really old cable box bristling with severed wires is mounted next to my little deck, close to the baseboards of the slightly raised house. Culver scratches his head, making his dark hair twirl up.

"Well," he rolls out. "This is all gonna have to go. I'll just put in a new box and wire everything up fresh, so you just tell me where you want your plug-ins and I'll get you set up and put in a router for you. I can help you hook up your TV, too, if you want."

"I can manage connecting one cable to the box, I think," I say dryly. "But thank you."

Yeah, I'm getting better at this.

At just being thankful with how easily everyone in this town offers to help, even when you don't really need it—and even if the person offering a hand weirds me out.

I leave him to do his work and head inside to change out of my work clothes, making sure to close the curtains in my bedroom first.

When I settle back in the kitchen to scope out my dinner options, I can see him through the back window. My cupboard's already a little bare and I need to head to the grocery store since I didn't put enough thought into my first shopping trip here.

Even though I try to focus on my own business, I still find myself watching Culver.

I don't want to rush him, but I don't want to leave with him here, either.

And what makes me uncomfortable is that every time I glance out the window, he's glancing in at *me*.

He holds eye contact too long before he grins and ducks his head back to his work.

Hillfolk don't eat people, you chicken, I remind myself, staring at those massive Neanderthal teeth that look too capable of cracking bones to suck the marrow out.

God, I hate this.

This whole thing with the Xs, Lucas' history with the Arrendells, it's making me paranoid about everyone.

But I'm relieved when my phone rings, offering a little contact to break the surreal atmosphere.

I stop wandering between the living room and kitchen and dig my phone out of my messenger bag on the dining room table.

When I see Lucas' name on the caller ID, my heart skips.

"Hey," I say into the phone—just as Culver looks up again, his head bobbing up over the edge of the windowsill.

All I can see are his eyes. The rest of his face is hidden, but he's watching me.

"Hey," Lucas says. Just the sound of his voice is enough to warm me. I don't know how I tripped into falling for this guy, but now I'm tumbling pretty hard. "You busy tonight?"

"No, not really, just trying to figure out what I can make for dinner with half a loaf of stale bread and some olives."

"Well, you're in luck," Lucas drawls. "Because I was actually calling to ask you over for dinner. My place, tonight, around seven?"

My breath stops.

I can't take it anymore.

I have to turn away from those dark eyes drilling into me. I give Culver my back, even if that still makes me feel vulnerable.

"Sure," I whisper. "Honestly, I'm glad you called. I don't want to be alone right now."

"Why's that? Lilah, is somebody there with you?"

I hesitate.

I don't want my dumb overactive imagination to worry him. I'm sure he'll laugh at me too for getting so freaked out by a guy who's just a little awkward.

"I'm fine. Just hungry enough to eat a tire."

"Then get your fine ass here as soon as you can, Miss Lilah. Food'll be waiting."

"I'll be there!"

"With bells on?"

I giggle.

"A little more than that." Even with Culver still peeking in, Lucas always makes me smile. "Talk to you later."

He mutters my name softly in acknowledgment and hangs up.

I make myself turn, glancing out the window.

This time, Culver has his head down working, rather than staring in like the world's most obvious Peeping Tom. I linger, not really processing much, just turning over the little things I need to do to get ready for work tomorrow so I can make time for Lucas tonight.

That's when it hits me.

Something's not right outside.

There's a shadow looming around the tree line past my fence that wasn't there before. The shape blends into the leaves and earthy bark.

A man.

A man with a familiar silhouette, sunlight gleaming off his sandy-brown hair, face hollow-eyed and sunken as he stares at my house with burning eyes.

Roger?

Holy shit, Roger!

It happens so fast.

My breath chokes off.

My chest caves in.

My fingers clench my phone like a brick, right before I drop it with a clatter.

Without thinking, I sprint through the back door out of the kitchen. The screen bounces with a wild squeal as I fling it open, heart racing, and tumble out onto the deck.

There's no one there.

No one standing in the trees at all.

No one but me and Culver Jacobin, who jerks his head up with a yelp of surprise, dropping the wire clippers he'd been holding.

"Uh." He stares at me, wide-eyed and flustered. "Ma'am, everything all right?"

"There was a..." I don't finish, pointing limply at the fence instead. "I think there was a man in the trees. Did you see him?"

"No, ma'am." Culver shakes his head slowly, then turns his head, squinting over his shoulder in the direction I'm pointing. "Ain't seen nobody out here, and I got good eyes." Then he peers at me. "You feeling okay?"

"Sure," I whisper weakly, but I'm definitely not.

I'm just frozen, imagining Roger Strunk staring at me in broad daylight.

I swallow hard and back up.

"Sorry for startling you," I say over my shoulder. "I'm fine."

Culver's eyes trail me as I bang the kitchen door shut and press my face into my hands, trying to calm my pulse.

It isn't helping, and why should it?

Just one day.

One little day of peace is all I want, and I'm not going to get it.

I'm cracking now.

Totally losing it.

But maybe I need dinner with Lucas more than I thought for all the wrong reasons.

I need something when I can't be alone.

XIV: REDDER HERRING (LUCAS)

$\mathcal{I}$ don't know what has me so damn fidgety.

The fact that in five minutes, Delilah Clarendon's going to blow into my house, eat my cooking, take up space in my life—or the fact that she wouldn't tell me why she didn't want to be alone.

She was acting real cagey on the phone.

Talking low like she didn't want to be overheard. And when I asked her if someone was there with her?

She just mumbled something back without a real answer.

Damn.

There I was, fixing to go tearing out there, my head rattling with all these dark possibilities.

Montero Arrendell holding her at gunpoint, forcing her to act like nothing was wrong, or maybe his snot-nosed son. But she didn't *sound* like she was lying, exactly.

What the hell?

I had to believe her.

Trust her.

And hope she'll actually show up tonight.

Also, I've never cooked to impress a girl before.

I'm no fancy chef. I'm good with boiling some pasta and

making a little homemade Bolognese sauce, or throwing a roast in the oven with some chopped up potatoes soaked in a marinade together.

Better than living on sandwiches and takeout like other bachelors I know, or relying on your grandparents to cook for a little girl like certain *other* bachelors I know. Captain Grant would be lost without some help.

Tonight, I've gone all-out.

Panko-crusted crab cakes dusted with seasoning.

Seared asparagus tips in a thick sauce of caramelized cooking wine with sliced mushrooms and almond slivers.

A cheddar pasta bake with bacon and little garlic bread crumbles crusted on top.

For dessert, we've got hand-rolled cinnamon nut bread dots with dipping sauces—cream, icing, caramel, strawberry.

I'm standing over the stove, watching a YouTube video on my phone and reading the captions about how long to simmer the wine sauce on low so it thickens just right without going sour when my doorbell rings.

I check the temperature on the stove, then whip my apron off and drape it over the back of a chair before speeding to the door.

Yep, I've got it bad, huh?

When I open the door and see Miss Delilah standing there, I have my answer.

She's not just pretty as a picture.

She *is* the whole damn picture, simply gorgeous in a dark-grey thigh-skimming pleated skirt, an oversized sweater in light green on top. It's almost see-through over a pale strappy camisole. Stylish black leather ankle boots with scrunched-up white socks and pale-green trim that matches her sweater complete the look.

The girl knows how to look like sex on a stick without even trying.

Hell, she doesn't *need* to try hard when she carries herself with the confidence to pull off wearing any damn thing she pleases.

Her hair's half up in a knot, half down, and it shimmers over her shoulders in black ripples. She raises the bottle of wine in her left hand and a six-pack of bottled stout hanging from the other.

"I didn't know what would fit better," she says with that little grin that makes her eyes glitter and my heart pound like a freight train. "So I brought both."

"Smart lady." I peel back to let her in, smoothing my hands over my simple white button-down shirt. It hangs over a dark t-shirt with jeans, like she'd give a good goddamn about one wrinkle somewhere.

"Both works for me. We'll have wine with dinner and beer with dessert. Hell, might be interesting to see how the beer complements the sauces."

"What sauces?" She steps inside with a little sashaying stride, this playfulness that makes her so wicked as she hands over the goods. "What did you make?"

"You really want to spoil the surprise already?"

"Have you cooked up the culinary wonder of the world?" Her eyes round in astonishment.

"Come find out, brat." Laughing, I toss my head toward the kitchen. "Should be about done."

"Awesome timing."

"Or I timed the recipes for when I figured you'd show," I say with a snort.

She just snickers.

I lead her into the kitchen, suddenly painfully conscious of my house, wondering what she must think of it.

The building is a two-story alpine-style cottage. My great-grandparents built it over seventy years ago. It's dark grey on the outside with ornate white trim framing the black-shingled roof and applied in intricate patterns under the eaves, framing the windows and doors.

Inside, it's all wood and neutral greys, giving the house this nice moody feel like a misty morning.

It suits me.

A lot of the rooms are smaller like they always are in old houses, but plenty of tall windows help make up for it—and the main living area is one big space with minimal accents.

Doesn't need 'em with the ash wood. Grain and knots are subtle decoration enough.

I'm a fan of simplicity.

While I've long since replaced furniture that wore out over the course of my lifetime, I kept the same minimalist focus on comfort that my parents and Celeste had: soft cream linen upholstery, natural wood tones, furniture with deep cushions.

All stuff meant to be lived on, rather than being show pieces.

It's been my home since I was born, and there's still a picture of me and Celeste above the fireplace, right next to another framed photo of my entire family when our folks were still alive and I was just a swaddled-up baby.

I wonder what Delilah sees as she soaks the place in. Her curious gaze turns with each step she takes in my wake.

Does she see a house that's full of light, love, and memories for generations?

Or does she just see a lonely asshole, clinging to a bygone past he can never bring to life again?

Her small smile gives away nothing as she follows me into my homey kitchen that's all quartz-topped wood counters everywhere, a big butcher block island, and a massive six-burner range.

Right now, it's filled with mingling scents of the food. I turn the burner off on the asparagus before pulling on my mitts and opening up the oven.

The pasta bake looks good, and the crab cakes have been sitting pretty and keeping warm so they'll taste like they're just out of the pan.

I glance at Delilah.

"Island or table?" I ask, nodding at the barstools around the butcher block, and the dining table tucked against the window on the far end.

"Hmmm. Island?" she says after a moment. "Anything I can do to help out?"

"You can pour the wine, if you want. Glasses are on the rack over there." I jerk my chin toward the rows of wineglasses hanging upside down from the rack built into the bottom of one row of ash wood cabinets.

With a thoughtful sound, Delilah retrieves two glasses and then climbs up on one of the tall wooden hardbacked stools.

She pops the cork with a practiced twist, easing it out carefully without even needing a corkscrew.

The delicate, tart aroma of white wine joins the smells of the food.

It's only after a second that I realize she picked the stool I draped my apron over.

After she finishes pouring the wine, she gives me a mild look and picks up one of the strings on the apron, tugging it over her shoulder.

"Nice," she says offhandedly. "Think I could see you in it? The ruffles suit you."

"Very fucking funny." Rolling my eyes, I sling out two plates and start loading up. "It was Celeste's. The strings are just long enough for it to fit, so I never saw much need to buy a new one."

Delilah sobers, her eyes flickering with chagrin.

"Oh, I'm sorry. I shouldn't have—"

"Lilah," I interrupt gently, scooping up the cutlery before taking everything to the island. I slide a plate in front of her and finish setting silverware before I say, "I loved my sister. Still love her. After our parents died, she was all I had. But she's not a forbidden subject in this house. She'd have laughed just as much at me wearing her apron, frills and blue checks and all." With my hand free, I catch a strand of Delilah's hair and tweak it, teasing the tip against her cheek. "You didn't say anything wrong."

She releases out a slow breath and smiles.

"Good." She lightly touches the back of my hand.

Smiling like a damn fool already, I settle in across from her with my own plate.

"I don't fuck with formality, so if you're hungry, dig in. Unless you want to do the obligatory small talk like it's a real date. Y'know, the kind where you're in a fancy restaurant being awkward with each other while you wait for appetizers."

Delilah had started to reach for her fork, but now she stops, giving me a wide-eyed look. Her cheeks stain in delicate red.

"...is this a date?"

Oh, shit.

Here we go.

I feel like some awkward-ass kid again, all bones, too big for myself.

I clear my throat. "I mean, yeah. If you want it to be. I—"

"Lucas, it's a date!" Her eyes ignite and she grins in a way I've never seen, all sweetness and warmth. "Just call it a date, dude. Because you're *really* cute when you blush."

"You really are a goddamned *brat*," I grumble, pointing my fork at her.

"And you," she says merrily, "must be a great cook. Because just *looking* at this makes me hungry, and it smells amazing. You really went through all this trouble for me?"

"Wasn't no trouble," I lie.

"Lucas?"

"Yeah?"

Her lips press together as she tries to suppress her laughter. "I think you left your cooking video playing."

Shit.

I glance back at my phone, still propped up on its little stand next to the stove. Sure enough, the video flicked over to the next in the queue even though it's on mute.

Oops.

There goes my secret.

Muttering, I ignore how hot my face is and get up. I snag the phone and shove it in my pocket, then drop down in the chair and point at her.

"You saw nothing."

"I don't know what you're talking about, Officer." She laughs, biting into her crab cakes. "Yum. Also, I totally didn't just watch a man being adorable, looking up recipe videos to cook for me. I'm not flattered at all. Or even slightly impressed." Then she takes a bite and drops that teasing tone as she lets out a low groan, her eyes slipping half-closed. "I'm lying. I'm completely impressed. This is so *good*."

"Yeah?" My chest warms and I savor my own bite before swallowing. Didn't turn out half-bad. "I used to do all the cooking around the house even before my little stint on galley duty. Cleaning, too. Celeste was always too busy working like hell to take care of us, so I tried to tackle the household crap. Whatever I could do to make it easier on her, but I guess it made me a little too self-sufficient. Sorry if you were hoping to find a beat-up man cave."

It's almost strange how easily it slips out.

Just talking about my sister casually, recalling the good times instead of the pain.

With Delilah here, when I think of Celeste, I just smile.

I don't fall down that pit of hatred and grief, constantly churning around the unanswered question, *Where the fuck did she go?*

Hell, just being near Delilah Clarendon soothes the raw edges off old wounds and lets me feel something besides pain.

She's watching me thoughtfully now, like she can see what I'm thinking, before she takes a longer look around the kitchen.

"So, this is where you grew up?"

"Yeah." I duck my head. "Been in the family for a long time. Figured I should keep it. For a while I let the Bowdens rent it out, back when I was gone. Felt weird, though, with tourists living in this place that belonged to the folks I love."

"It must be lonely," she says. "There's so much *family* in this house, the way it feels, the presence... but for you it's like being surrounded by ghosts, isn't it?"

She has no clue.

Or maybe she *does,* and that's the problem.

It's strange to have her look at me this way, and for me to feel so real.

Like she already knows me inside and out with this presence we have together. I don't need to bare the painful gristle of my heart when she can already touch it so gently.

Fuck, my mind goes places it shouldn't.

"Maybe one day I'll fill it up with family again," I say without thinking.

Delilah gives me a startled look, tucking her hair behind her ear with a shy smile.

"You never know." She pauses for another bite, clearly enjoying the grub. She won't look at me as she murmurs, "I've always wanted kids myself someday, but..." She shakes her head, staring at her plate. "I think deep down I'm afraid I'll damage them. I never had a stable household with someone who really wanted me around. I don't know what good parenting feels like. It's different from taking a few child psychology courses. I've just got so much *bitterness* there. So I'm worried I'd be a bad mom and end up hurting them when I just want to love them." She shrugs. "Plus, I'd probably have to go to a sperm bank to find a dad I wouldn't want to strangle within a week."

Jealousy darts through me, no matter how absurd.

"Don't think you'd hurt them one bit," I growl. I try to be gentle—this is a heavy thing for her—but I can't. "You're the talk of the whole town right now, you know."

"I am?" She blinks at me.

"Well, yeah." I turn things over through a few more bites, rewinding my brain to earlier in the day, remembering fragments of conversation. "When I was picking up groceries earlier, I overheard a few parents talking in the store. Their kids are

fucking in love with you, Lilah. They think you hung the moon."
I smile. "Grant said Nell talked about nothing else from the
second he picked her up. She said you tell the best stories, and
you're really smart and real pretty. She already wants to grow
her hair out long like yours."

Delilah sputters on her next bite, snagging her napkin.

"Oh, my," she strains out, red-faced. "Well, at least I made a
good first impression, right?"

I watch her fondly, giving her a minute to collect herself.

"You really don't know what to do with compliments, do
you, woman?"

"*No.* So stop it." Inhaling sharply, she balls up her napkin,
giving me a warning look that tells me it could be sailing my
way soon if I step out of line. Then she abruptly changes the
subject. "Did I ever tell you why my hair's so long? It's this silly
little thing..."

"Tell me the little things. I'm greedy as hell when it comes to
you."

That earns me an unguarded look, surprised and wide-eyed.
"Okay. But only if you tell me a little thing after."

Damn, she's good.

"Deal," I throw back.

"I didn't cut my hair from high school until I met my mom
again," she tells me immediately. "That's why I still wear it long.
At first it was just carelessness, no one noticing I was getting a
little shaggy as they passed me around from family to family,
nobody wanting to make my hair their responsibility." She
shrugs again and catches a fine strand of black hair, drawing it
over her shoulder to stroke down its length. "Somewhere in this
mess, I still have the same hair I had when I was with my
mother. That was the best day of my life." A soft smile flits
across her face as she twirls that lock around her finger. "It's still
there. The same hair she brushed with her hands when she
hugged me so hard it almost left me sore. Same hair she hadn't
touched since I was a baby."

Damn, this girl.

I reach across the island to catch that lock of hair, coiling it in my fingers. "You love her to death, don't you?"

"Yeah. During the bad times, Mom was all I had, even if she was just a distant memory. A fantasy, even. I loved her my whole life without knowing her, even when I thought she abandoned me. It's like the connection just stayed." She shakes her head, then wrinkles her nose in a cute little scrunch when I tickle the tip with her hair. "I should call her. Tell her all about Redhaven. She'd like you, I think." Grinning, she bats my hand away, reclaiming her hair. "Mostly because your mouth is as bad as mine."

"So she's got a fondness for sarcasm, huh? I'm sure we'd get along fine."

"She gave birth to a shit-talker, didn't she?"

"That must've hurt," I say slowly, well aware I'm taking my life into my hands. "Squeezing out a chubby little cactus."

"*Lucas!*" Yep, there it is.

That balled-up napkin boinks off my face while she scowls at me, her lips still curling up at the corners as she laughs.

"I'm not a freaking cactus—*okay, maybe I am.* Hmph."

Picking up her fork, she aims it at me before savagely hacking off a few asparagus tips.

"Your turn, mister. Little thing. Now."

"You want a dirty secret? Fine." I think for a moment. "I've seen every Disney movie ever made."

The skeptical look she gives me is enough to make me grin.

"...you? Disney?"

"Look, Grant's off raising little Nell by himself. Most of the time his parents take her when he's got to work, but sometimes they can't, so that girl's grown up half in the police dispatch office with all of us as her babysitters." I blow out an exasperated sigh, even though I love that kid like she was my own. "If we don't distract her, she will abso-goddamn-lutely hop on one of the dispatch computers and raise hell. Don't know how she

NICOLE SNOW

breaks past the access restrictions. She's sharp as a whip, that's for sure. So there's an entire collection of DVDs in the back room at the station, and since I hang out there when there's no patrols scheduled on my shift, I've seen 'em all. Pretty sure Henri isn't far behind me, though."

Delilah laughs, her eyes glittering. "I bet it's not as good as my collection."

"You're into 'em, huh?"

"The music rocks, okay?" She's flustered now, trying to preserve her tough-girl image. "I mean... I usually watched them with the kids when I was doing my training in New York. They just became a fact of life. But there's something *emotional* about the songs, you know? And I like any kind of movie that makes me feel things that strong, no matter what age it's meant for." She points her fork at me, a bit of asparagus still clinging to it. "And before you ask, yes, the lyrics to 'Let It Go' are burned into my brain forever."

A shudder of black horror runs through me as she grins.

In the back of my mind, I hear the familiar melody and shake my head violently.

"*Don't*. Don't you dare start singing it, New York. Little Nell wouldn't stop for six damn months. I swear that song plays in hell's waiting room. If I gotta hear it one more time—"

"Gotcha!" she says. "See, now I know how to threaten you if I really want my way."

I drop my fork and raise both hands. "You think you have to threaten me? Anything you want, it's done."

"*Aaan-y-thing?*" She drags the word out, a slow smile growing on her face.

"Don't like that look in your eye."

"After dinner," she announces firmly. "Let's watch movies. You've got streaming, right?"

I snort. "I give you free rein and that's your first wish?"

"Oh, I never said that's *all* I'd want." There's something sly in her smile, something that makes my blood blaze. "That's just for starters."

"Miss Lilah," I say slowly, "I think you're looking for excuses to stay over."

"And if I am?"

"Fuck the excuses," I answer, and goddamn, sometimes I have trouble just saying what I feel, but this comes out so easy. "I was hoping you'd want to."

There's a long, warm look between us, one that leaves me damn near sighing with the potential in it.

We finish dinner, chasing our food with white wine.

Sometimes we tease, mock-bicker, and I get another napkin chucked at my head for my smart-ass comments.

Mostly, we're just quiet, and it feels good.

Once we're done, I load the plates in the sink, snag the beer she brought, and head out to the living room.

I'm still feeling a little warm from the wine, but not quite buzzed. Delilah seems steady as she trails me and then drops down on the sofa with a little swing of her legs, watching me while I hunt for a remote I rarely use, feeling between the couch cushions.

"So Culver Jacobin came to my house today," she says abruptly.

"What?" My head comes up so sharply I almost give myself whiplash.

"He was there when you called. He was also hanging around when I hallucinated my ex standing outside my house."

"Culver Jacobin? What the hell was he there for?"

"He's the cable guy, I guess." She folds her arms tight, leaning back against the sofa. "He messed with the crime scene. I'm sorry, I just wasn't fast enough to stop him. He *licked* the blood, Lucas."

Delilah grimaces, her whole face screwing up, and I don't blame her one bit.

"What the fuck?" I just stare at her. "I got nothin'. The Jacobins are weird as hell, but that's nasty, even for them."

"Unsanitary for sure. Good thing no one saw him, or you'd probably have a few new cannibal rumors around here. But get this." Her voice drops a little. "He said it's pig's blood. He could tell by the taste, supposedly, because they sell the blood down at the butcher's shop."

"Pig's blood. Huh." I finally unearth the remote from between the cushions, then go grab dessert and settle in next to her. I try to get my appetite back after what she just told me with the nut bread bites perched on the coffee table in easy reach, flanked by cups of dipping sauces. "Guess that makes it more likely it was just a sick prank. Kids fucking around."

"I guess. Anyone could buy a carton of pig's blood from the butcher's, right?"

"Yeah." I frown, turning that over. Somehow, it still doesn't sit right. "What was that about your ex, though?"

"Oh, I... I looked out the kitchen door and I could've sworn he was there, hovering around by the trees. There was a lot of shadow. It could've been the way the light fell, I guess, because when I ran out there..." She trails off and shakes her head slowly. "Nothing. Not even swaying branches like someone just fled. Culver said he didn't see anything, either. I think I scared the crap out of him."

"That's a nice change for once." I stroke my chin.

I don't know.

It's possible, I suppose.

She's been putting on a mighty brave face, but anyone would get spooked and start seeing things out of the corner of their eye if they lived through half the shit she's experienced since coming to Redhaven.

"I guess that makes sense. If it happens again, I'm adding surveillance cameras to your place."

"Oh, cool. Next it'll be robo-gun turrets and killer drones," Delilah teases with a little laugh. "That reminds me, though—the motion sensor lights didn't come on when we were moving around the yard today."

"They won't by daylight. They're solar powered, so if they're gonna conserve and store energy they can't turn on all the time. Only when the light sensors know it's dark."

"*Ooh.*" She purses her lips. "Fancy. You really went all out."

"Anything for a New York-sized pain in my ass."

There it is again.

That cute little falter, the way she can't handle it when someone's real with her.

She gives me an uncertain look.

I fucking love the way she blushes.

This is how it should've been before we went hog wild ripping each other's clothes off. These quiet moments, getting to know each other, figuring out how we fit.

And she fits real damn nice against me as I stretch one arm along the back of the sofa, offering a place against my side.

Delilah doesn't hesitate to tuck herself against me, pulling her legs up onto the sofa to snuggle into the crook of my arm. Her scent wafts up like perfume, drenching me as I flick the TV on and scroll through the selection until she insists we do *Hercules.*

I know this one word for word.

Nell's in love with Megara and wants to be her when she grows up, assuming Delilah hasn't stolen Meg's place in her heart.

Apparently, Nell's not the only one. Delilah loses herself in the story, watching so transfixed it's almost innocent, bringing out the sweet young woman under the hardened New York boss girl she tries to be.

While she watches the movie, I'm watching her.

Goddamn, does my heart skip when she sings along, mouthing, *At least out loud... I won't say I'm in love.*

Yeah, Miss Lilah.

Me too.

I give her a little surprise of my own, belting out a flawless rendition of "A Star Is Born," even if the high notes kill me.

It does the trick when she flops over laughing.

It's so warm and cozy, and by the time the movie's close to ending, we're teasing each other more than we're paying attention, halfway sparring and half feeding each other bites of dessert.

Then, as the closing credits roll, she kisses me.

I suddenly forget all about the son of Zeus even if I've got his thunder in my vein when she slips over my lap and straddles me.

My cactus girl melts me with that hot little body, her thighs struggling to even fit around me, that little skirt so tempting I want to rip it the fuck off.

Only takes an instant to turn me into a monster of pure lust.

When I slip my hands under her skirt, digging into her ass cheeks, pulling her closer, kissing her, I'm intoxicated.

Judging by the way she's breathing, she's drunk on me, too.

She just holds on tighter, wrapping her legs around my waist.

I lift her up and carry her to the stairs.

This dizzying young woman stays with me all night, long after I tumble her down into the sheets and worship every inch of her body until she screams herself hoarse.

XV: RED BLOODED (DELILAH)

*I*t's not fair.

It's so not fair for Lucas Graves to be this effing *cute*.

It's probably no surprise that date one led to date two.

We kind of already got the wild monkey sex out of the way—and now I guess we're realizing that we can actually *stand* being around each other without going to war.

Since he did dinner for our first date, he left date two in my hands. But since I don't know much about Redhaven yet, I'm not exactly bursting with brilliant ideas.

I do, however, have a great view of the lake from my house. Including a little boat launch and its hand-painted wooden sign with rental prices for the tourists.

Considering it's offseason, getting a reservation is as easy as a quick phone call.

Which is how we end up here.

Floating on the center of a lake as smooth as glass.

Still Lake earns its name honestly.

The rowboat gently bobs in the slow, almost invisible current. The sun beats down on us, warm and soothed by the cool breeze skimming over the water.

Lucas sits across from me, completely soaked, his hair plastered into his eyes and his dark heather-blue t-shirt clinging to him like a second skin.

It's almost obscene how it outlines every carnal delight of his body, accenting every muscle that strained over me in hard, flexing thrusts just last night.

I'd be turned on just looking at him, if only I wasn't trying not to laugh until I snort.

With his mouth set in a grim line, Lucas lifts both hands and pulls his wet hair aside like he's pulling back curtains.

"Glad you find this so entertaining," he grumbles.

That's it.

I lose it again.

I go down in a laughing fit, clapping my hands over my mouth, but all that does is make it come out in little spurts while I laugh until my stomach hurts.

"I'm sorry!" I mumble around my fingers. "But I told you not to stand up."

"Yeah, yeah. Boat's too big for me; you're too small to counterbalance. You'd think I'd remember how to handle a fucking tiny skiff like this after being a sailor." He snorts in disgust, but his eyes glitter warmly. "Laugh it up, New York. I really did think the picnic basket was about to go over the side."

I bite back another giggle, clearing my throat and trying to plaster on a straight face. "It probably would have, if you hadn't decided to take its place. You saved our lunch. My very own Herc."

"You wanna get wet too?" he growls and lunges toward me, rocking the boat.

I squeal, holding my hands up.

"No, no, no, you'll tip us over!"

He mock-pounces.

I tumble back against the edge of the boat, gripping the sides.

The water slaps and splashes as it sways frantically, but Lucas catches both edges, stopping himself mid-lunge and grinning at me far too wickedly for a man who just dumped himself in the lake a minute ago.

"Gotcha," he practically purrs.

I widen my eyes—then sit up and scramble for the picnic basket.

I dig around inside until I find one of the crumpled-up napkins and lob it right at his dripping wet face.

The napkin hits him square between the eyes, and he bursts out laughing, sinking back onto the opposite seat as the boat slowly begins to calm.

"Guess I deserved that."

"Only a little," I grumble, but I'm still grinning.

I can't help myself.

Shaking my head, I lean forward to dig around until I find the blankets I folded under our lunch just in case Lucas wasn't keen on boating and would rather picnic on the shore.

I wouldn't have minded. We had a lovely slow morning hike here, taking in the late summer air, the birds, the shimmering green leaves.

But this is nice, too.

Just us in our own little world in the center of the lake. Too far from the houses on the shore to be anything but a speck, half the perimeter ringed by thick walls of trees.

Ever since I've moved here, I've felt watched.

That's why it's nice to feel safe and alone out here with Lucas.

I shake the two blankets into my lap, then bend my finger at him.

"Come here. *Carefully* this time."

Lucas quirks a thick black brow at me before he moves across the boat, stretching his body out and laying his head down in my lap.

I smile down at him as I brush his wet hair back, gently scrubbing it with a corner of the blanket before dabbing at his cheeks.

"You could stay like this," I say.

"Thought you promised me dessert," he says, lacing his hands together over his stomach.

Every last one of his abs is outlined like he's just naked and painted blue.

"Dessert's finger food. So if you hold still..."

"What? You're saying you'll feed me?" A slow smile grows on his lips.

"Don't get used to it. I'm not playing harem girl, feeding the Emperor grapes every day."

He wrinkles his nose. "I don't even like grapes."

"It's a metaphor. But how do you feel about strawberries?" Bending over him, I rummage around in the basket again. "Voil—*ah!*"

That yelp?

It comes out because while I bent over him, Lucas nipped the underside of one of my breasts.

I yank back, blushing furiously, the little basket of strawberries and sealed tin of chocolate dip clutched against my chest.

"*Lucas!*"

He grins up at me unrepentantly. "Thought you were offering me a strawberry. Whoops."

"Why are you such a giant dick?"

"Mainly?" His grin widens. "'Cause you like this big dick so damn much."

I huff. "Don't get too cocky, mister, or no strawberries for you."

I don't know how it's possible for his grin to get any wider, and it looks good on his perma-grump face.

His lazy, half-lidded eyes gleam with an amusement that stops my heart.

"You want to talk metaphors? You want to know what strawberries are a metaphor for in some of the older books I read? 'Cause I think I just got a mouthful."

Yep.

I'm going to spontaneously combust and it's all his fault.

"I'm going to murder you." I stare at him flatly.

"That's a Class One felony in North Carolina," he teases. "Threatening an officer of the law. Minimum sentence, not being allowed to leave my bedroom for at least a week."

"*Psssh!* They'll never catch me if you happen to accidentally choke on a strawberry here." I smile sweetly as I pry the lid off the chocolate sauce, dipping a fresh red strawberry in before I hold it to his lips. "Feeling lucky today?"

Smirking, Lucas runs his tongue over his lips—then slowly sinks his teeth into the strawberry.

Seriously. I've never seen anyone make biting down on fruit look so sexual. But the way his teeth part the red skin one little bit at a time, exposing the soft flesh inside, his lips moving against the slick red exterior...

I think *I'm* going to choke to death instead.

I just stare at him, forgetting how to breathe, how to blink.

My breaths shorten and my entire body feels way too hot.

The spot where he nipped me through my loose, translucent tank top and light lace bra throbs.

Actually, all of me throbs, from the tips of my toes to the ends of my fingers to the tips of my, uh—strawberries.

"Hate you," I whisper as he nibbles his way up to the stem clutched between my fingers.

"Liar," he teases, flicking his tongue out to lick the last of the strawberry juice, catching my fingertips. "You want to try to choke me again or what? Got a few other ideas for what you can put in my mouth."

Before I can curse him, he reaches up and plucks the stem away from me, tossing it over the side. He eases the strawberries and the tin of sauce away from my unresisting fingers. Lid on the chocolate sauce, food disappearing back into the basket, and then, I feel him.

First, it's his hand against the back of my neck.

His strong, hot fingers weaving through my hair, bunching it up in loops against my neck, pulling me in.

I should tell him no.

Even if we're far from the shore, we're here in the open beneath the bright-blue blazing sky.

I'm so powerless against him.

Powerless against that lazy, arrogant smile.

Against the confidence and desire building in his eyes.

Against Lucas pushing his steaming body against mine and capturing my mouth in a kiss that never ends.

He teases and bites me the same way he treated the strawberry, taking me over a little bit at a time until I feel like something so hot, so sweet and perfect he has to possess.

I'm burning so hot I feel like I could evaporate the entire lake in this rough giant's hands.

And I belong to him completely as he pushes me down to the bottom of the boat.

The blankets tumble in a mess around us as his body covers mine.

"Lucas!" I can't help gasping his name, tugging at his clothes, forgetting that we're in a flimsy boat when all it takes is a touch for me to *need* him desperately.

And God, does he touch me.

His fingers slide under my tank top, caressing my skin like he's branding me into his brain through tactile contact.

I dig my fingers into his hair, biting his mouth as he teases my nipples.

Whispering for more, more, more as he shoves my thighs apart and pushes between them.

I can already feel him through his jeans, thrusting against me like he wants to ruin me so good.

The man loves to tease.

And he doesn't stop until I'm helpless and rocking under him, grinding against his cock with a hunger that makes me forget everything but Lucas.

My desperation tilts the boat violently for just a second.

I get a glimpse of my own lust-crazed reflection in the ripples over the side.

Heart flipping, I wrap my arms and legs around him, shrieking. "Oh my *God*—"

"Steady, *steady*." His voice is rich with repressed laughter. Lucas goes still on top of me, looking down with a warm, gentle smile. "Maybe we slow down. If you *can*, darlin'."

My eyes narrow.

"Or maybe we should save this for when we're back on dry land," I reply breathlessly, but of course, I don't really want to.

Not when this feels too right.

Not when I'm ignited.

Not when I can't stand to wait another second.

It's like he knows it, too. He leans down, brushing his nose to mine, then his lips.

"You sure?" he whispers. "Your little pussy tells me something else, Miss Lilah. Don't think that's the lake getting me wet as hell."

I bite my lip, flushing.

My skirt's up around my hips and I want to tell him he's wrong, that he's just dealing with soaked denim. But I'd be lying through my teeth when all it takes is one more hard nudge of his cock and I'm sucking sharp breaths, trembling, ready to take every inch of Lucas Graves.

"I could be convinced," I whisper.

He gives me another heart-stopping smile.

"Then I'd better do some good convincing."

I barely get a second to catch my breath before he sets about *convincing* me a little too well.

Suddenly that slow, deliberate way Lucas talks feels different.

It's the same as the slow, relentless way he takes me.

Stroking me like I'm something precious, fucking me intently, kissing me all over until I'm the one who's got to rein myself in as he makes me arch, makes me thrash, engraves his kiss all over me.

I know the feeling of his lips everywhere—from my shoulders to my breasts to my stomach.

From my inner thighs to the throbbing pearl between my legs.

He tastes me, invades me with his tongue, and makes me come again and again with domineering lashes that claim me in ways I didn't know I could be owned.

Holy, holy shit.

When he pins me down to lick me harder, growling against my pussy, seizing my clit between his teeth, there's nothing left but Lucas and his heat and the sound of my own barely muffled scream.

I'm so close as he slows down wickedly, teasing me until I squirm.

My voice flies over the quiet lake, soaring into the clear blue sky.

When my ears start working again, the water slaps and sighs against the side of the boat in echoing rhythm.

I swear, it's like the entire world syncs up to me as Lucas takes me higher, higher.

Oh, God, *higher.*

I think I can touch the sun.

"Fucking come for me," he whispers.

I stare down blankly, trembling as I see the feral look in his eyes, and obey.

I'm coming *again.*

His broad shoulders part my thighs until they quiver.

Until I'm a prisoner for every last sugar-lash of his tongue, and soon, every stroke of his slow, punishing cock.

Until I don't think my nerves can take any more of his magic.

Until he proves I *can.*

He's a force of nature, a summer storm made flesh, grunting like a bull as he rocks the boat.

There's as much choice as a leaf gets before the wind rips it off a tree.

I can only surrender and be swept away as Lucas crashes through me again and again, pillaging me from the inside out, leaving me absolutely spent.

I don't know how I come one more time, but I do when he thrusts so deep.

His body flexes and he releases with a vicious, "Fuck!"

Yes, yes!

I hold on so tight I can't feel my fingers, both of us one exploding pulse, feeling him fill me as his cock swells and heaves again and again.

We'll worry about how we forgot the condom later. For now—

Holy hell.

Holy hell, I'm more content than I've been with a man in a very long time.

No, more than ever.

Possibly happier than I'll ever be again.

* * *

WHEN HE'S DONE torturing me with heaven, we curl up in the boat to rest and enjoy the lazy afternoon.

I feed him more strawberries and he reads to me from a fantasy novel he brought along.

I'm thrilled that he's resting so easy, so calm, after turning my bones to jelly.

This man really is too much.

While he reads to me, I run my fingers across his brow, watching the intent concentration in his forest-green eyes.

I'm not really processing the words about knights and dragons.

Not when I'm so focused on *him*.

There's something about Lucas that's inherently good, kind, and I almost feel like—

No. Don't go there.

My reverie breaks as he stops, tilting his head, looking at me upside down. "Hey. What're you staring at me for?"

"No reason." I duck my head, tucking my hair behind my ear.

"Bull. You only say 'no reason' when you're trying to pretend you don't like me, Miss Lilah."

Scowling, I poke his nose. "Maybe I *don't* like you."

"After that? You serious?" He catches my hand and draws it in to kiss the center of my palm. "If you coming fireworks wasn't liking me, then I can't wait to see what it looks like when you finally do, gorgeous. You're falling hard as hell and I wish you'd just admit it."

I gasp.

My heart stalls.

My mouth goes dry.

I can barely fumble a response. "You... you think I'm going to fall in love with you that easy? C'mon."

"Not easy, no. Nothing worth having is *ever* easy." His lips trace back and forth over my palm, ticklish and sweet. "So don't be easy on me, Miss Lilah. Make it fucking hard. You're worth a heaping lot of hell and then some."

No words.

I can't even identify this wild feeling throbbing through me, lighting me up from the inside more breathlessly than the fizz and pop of champagne.

So I just smile, curling my fingers around his and drawing his hand in to kiss his thick, coarse knuckles.

"Stop flattering me and finish the chapter," I tease softly. "I want to know what happens."

"Do you even know what happened? Swore you zoned out there."

"...a little," I admit. "I—"

I can't name the thing that cuts me off, that makes me stop cold.

It's a feeling, this heavy sensation I've had of being watched that's haunted me so many times since I came to Redhaven. It's like a thick blanket thrown over me, blurring my vision, coating my skin with this awful feeling and turning the colors of everything around us wrong.

I jerk my head up, holding my breath, heart thudding as I search the shore.

Lucas goes tense in my lap.

"Lilah, what's wrong?"

I swallow hard, feeling naked in my thin clothing. I reach for the blanket, drawing it around me tightly.

"Sorry. I just felt like someone was watching all of a sudden." I stare at the tree line along the far edge of the lake, much too close to my house. "Somewhere over there."

Lucas sits up and turns, his expression hardening as he follows my gaze.

Of course, there's nothing there.

I can't see anything.

He shakes his head. "Probably one of the damn Jacobins coming out to fish."

"...that doesn't make me feel any better," I whisper. "I know, I shouldn't overreact, but Culver was just *weird*."

"What, you've never licked a little blood off your wall?" Lucas says dryly. "Think that merits being a little freaked." His arm wraps around me then, pulling me into the shelter of his body. "How about we head on in? Getting a little sticky out anyway, and the mosquitos'll be showing up in force soon."

"Sure," I whisper.

Honestly, I hate that I feel like my paranoia just put a damper on this lovely afternoon. But if Lucas is disappointed, he doesn't show it.

He just holds me tighter, giving me an easy, reassuring nod that tells me it's okay.

NICOLE SNOW

I'm learning he has a body language all his own, unspoken gestures and long looks that say so much more than words.

And every last one of those things is full of kindness.

So are his hands when they settle me against the seat on the opposite side of the boat. Then he takes up the oars and starts rowing us back to shore.

My eyes are glued to him the whole time.

His body flexes powerfully as we glide across the water, looking over his shoulder and aiming for the rental dock once we're in range.

The muscles in his neck strain, hard and hypnotically rhythmic.

"Tell you what," he says, just a hint of breath in his voice from the tiring work. "If you don't feel okay going home, you stay over at my place tonight."

"Lucas Graves, you're just trying to get me back to your lair," I tease.

"Damn fucking right." He faces me again with a grin. "I also want to take care of you—if you'll let me."

"Lucas," I say softly, relishing the red streaks growing across his face, "I'm starting to think there's nothing I wouldn't let you do."

"Yeah?" His eyes light up. "Careful what you tell me, darlin'. I might just do it."

I glance away, unable to help laughing. "Yeah. You might."

We say nothing then.

We don't need to.

There's just the soft sound of the oars dipping in and out of the water, mingling with our own breathing.

And that's okay.

But as we draw in closer to shore, I scan the trees near my house.

I swear.

I *swear* I catch a glimpse of something pale. Just a dusty light-brown blur, disappearing through the trees before I

286

can blink, blending in invisibly as if it was never there at all.

But I'm stuck on that color.

Sandy.

Glimmering strands reflecting sunlight a certain way.

Too much like the color I used to see shimmering in the morning sunlight, back when Roger and I faced each other over breakfast and smiled like we thought we'd be in love forever.

Another time, another place, another life I just can't escape.

And I don't know what it means when it feels like we're just playing some terrible game of cat and mouse now, where I don't even know who's the hunter and who's the hunted.

* * *

I HATE that I feel so shy, so nervous, coming back to Lucas' house when I was just here last night, enjoying myself.

I was here, curled up safe in his arms, and yet...

There's something different in the air tonight.

Something about the way he looks at me.

Something about the soft, slow silence between us as he leads me upstairs with our fingers twined, to that broad, open loft space with his massive bed.

Last night, he made me scream his name all over again.

Tonight, he doesn't give me the chance.

Not when his lips never part from mine.

Not when he lays me down on his bed like I'm something precious and kisses me like he could never stand to let me go.

I'm lost in this haze with him and I never want to come back.

Soon, I'm not even thinking about the deeper reasons why I stayed over tonight, the danger and weirdness looming.

Tonight, nothing exists but us.

Not the Jacobins. Not the Arrendells. Not my creepy ex.

Not even the dead girl who won't stop haunting my mind.

There's just me and Lucas.

There's just his touch and light and heat.

There's just his all-consuming eyes drinking me in and big capable hands that strip me bare.

They make me gasp with the coarseness of his calluses against my skin.

God, I love those hands.

And there's just him stealing soft cries from my lips, tasting me over and over again as he shows me everything.

What could be mine, if I'd just open up and admit I'm falling helplessly in love with this man.

If I'd admit that all the things I've always wanted are right here in front of me.

It feels like he could give them all to me, if I'd shut my fears up and trust him.

If I could let him inside more than my body.

If I could invite him into those deep, hollow places of my heart he already touches in some intangible way, even as he fills me.

He gathers me against him possessively, enveloping me against his chest, holding me close as he takes me so high and never, ever lets me come down.

Foly huck.

I'm gone.

Captured.

Addicted.

I'm so dizzy I can't breathe.

I'm—

Goddammit, yes.

I'm in love.

And I'm so wrapped up in watching his body shudder and the pure, raw erotic pleasure on his face that I almost miss it when it hits me.

That sudden surge, that jolt, my body tumbling down faster than my brain as he makes me feel things I never thought possible.

He pulls me up against him, my thighs straddling his lap, my body moving over his.

His hand claps my ass, adding just the right sting to our pleasure.

I gasp again as he hits some new place inside me, striking deep, marking me from the inside out.

He consumes my senses, crashing over me like the wave he is as our pleasure rips me apart.

I come harder than ever, crying his name.

Like if I say it enough times, everything will be all right.

Like I'm chanting his name and hoping it has some power to bind him to my heart.

* * *

I'M NOT surprised that I sleep hard in Lucas' arms.

There's something about riding this emotional insanity that's so thrilling it drains you. So I curl up against him happily and pass out, snuggled into the sweat-slicked warmth of his bulk.

He's a human shield.

I sleep like the dead, dreamless and content.

Until I blink awake in the middle of the night with my mouth dry and cottony.

Squinting at my phone on the nightstand, I see it's just past two o'clock.

Lucas is a snoring, motionless lump against my back.

I twist around to face him, just watching him illuminated in the moonlight. The way he turns his face into the pillow until there's just a twitch of dark brows, the dip of his upper lip visible on one side.

My heart strums sharply.

Part of me doesn't want to trust this.

How many times have people who told me they cared ever really meant it?

Basically just once with Mom.

But there's a lonely, aching piece of me that wants to believe Lucas is genuine. The real deal behind his cocky smirk.

I want to think that big brutish body might be powered by an equally mammoth heart.

That he actually *cares* and he is what he says.

I turn over restlessly.

I shouldn't dwell on this right now, anyway. Especially when I'm about to wake him up by choking on my own parched throat.

Gingerly, I pry myself out of his arms and slip out of bed.

The shirt he was wearing earlier is draped across the back of a chair in the corner, and I steal it for a nightshirt, shrugging it on over my naked body and shaking my hair loose from the collar before padding downstairs to the kitchen.

I fill a glass of water in the sink and drink, easing the itch in my throat.

Then I wander out into the moonlit living room, pacing around. It gives me something to do until I can head back upstairs and snuggle up with my human furnace again.

But as I pass the coffee table, something catches the corner of my eye.

Red.

The same blood-red dress I saw my first day here, spilled across my floor.

Emma.

The crime scene photos, taken the day I found her body.

I nearly spray water, choking, and start to cough, gasping as I rub my throat.

Jesus.

What the hell?

I glance over my shoulder at the stairs, but there's no sign of Lucas.

Biting my lips, I look back at the coffee table. The photos are on top of a stack of papers in a rumpled file folder. The case file, I'm guessing.

I know, I know.

It's official police business and all.

I really shouldn't.

But how can I help it when I'm drawn to this mystery—drawn to her—and I need to flipping *know.*

I just want to know what happened, if a beautiful girl with so much to live for truly died of an overdose and nothing else.

I find a coaster—*I'm not a heathen, okay?*—and set my glass down before settling on the edge of the sofa to thumb through the photos.

Okay.

Deep breath.

Obviously, I'm not a forensics expert, but the closer I look, Emma looks like she was *flung* there. Something about the way she's tilted just isn't right, and it's easier to notice in a photo rather than panicking over finding her very real body.

It just doesn't look like she passed out on her own and dropped dead.

She's too—I don't know—neat?

Yeah, neat.

Shouldn't there be froth coming out of her lips or something if she ODed? Maybe more than spit.

I don't know.

I'm thinking too hard, and seeing her like this jolts me.

After staring another minute, I make myself put the photos down.

I start paging through the case report instead.

It doesn't take me long to find a toxicology summary from the county coroner.

Wow, that's a lot of cocaine in her system.

Sure, I might be grasping at straws, thinking something else happened here.

Maybe Lucas is, too.

But I wonder if the old, raw hurt of losing his sister is

blinding him to the bitter truth: that a girl came to Redhaven for a party and made her own trouble, no dirty deeds required.

It would still be an awful tragedy if that's the case, but at least it wouldn't mean we might have another one with a killer on the loose.

"Is that it, Emma? Am I right?" I whisper. "Are you still so restless because you did this to yourself accidentally?"

Of course, there's no answer.

Somehow, that's the most disturbing part.

I flip through a few more pages, then stop, frowning at a footnote on one page.

Lucas' handwriting. I'm starting to recognize his big blocky chicken scratch.

Do not contact next of kin.

Wait, what?

Another chill knifes through me—and an odd sense of betrayal, sudden and sinking down to the tips of my toes and making me feel heavier than lead.

I don't understand.

He'd said he'd tell them... didn't he?

He swore up and down he'd give Emma's family closure.

But why would he lie to me about that?

And if he lied about that, what else is he holding back?

XVI: RED WITH RAGE (LUCAS)

*M*y bed feels like a chasm.

I wake up to it empty and I can't say I'm happy about that.

More, I wake with unease, this gut punch vibrating through me the instant I roll over and find Delilah's spot cold. Barely any wrinkles in the sheets telling me she was ever there.

With everything going on these days, I don't feel safe when I don't know where she is.

I listen intently, but the house is so quiet it hums.

No light under the upstairs bathroom door, either.

Fuck.

"Delilah?" I call softly.

No answer.

I slip out of bed with an alarm ringing in my skull.

You're being paranoid, asshole. Who the hell would break into a cop's house to get to her?

But this is Redhaven.

Whenever something weird happens, it never operates by normal rules.

I head for the stairs, moving lightly on the floor.

No light coming up from downstairs either.

I tread down silently as I make my way to the living room.

Only to see that dark head of hair on the sofa, bowed over something she's looking at.

An explosive breath turns into a laugh as it leaves my lungs. "Jesus Christ, Lilah. You damn near gave me a heart attack, being all ridiculous with that—"

I stop when she goes stiff, looking over her shoulder at me.

Those sad blue eyes are bursting with *hurt*.

Pain.

Accusations.

I'm really fucking confused till I step closer and see what she's holding.

The case file.

Emma Santos' file.

Fuck me.

I forgot I left it out after reading through it before I went out to meet her today. That still doesn't give her any goddamned right to—

"What are you doing with that?" I demand.

"Why didn't you call Emma's family?" she flings back without missing a beat.

I scowl. "You don't know I didn't—"

"It says it right here! I saw your note. You're full of crap." She stands, brandishing the folder like a knife, pages and photos bristling from the edges. "Lucas, you promised—you promised me—and right here it says you didn't do it and you told other people not to!"

Damn.

The girl has a point, but why's she losing her shit over this?

I drag my hand over my face. "Lilah, listen, there's heavy shit going on that I can't tell you—"

"Like what?" She throws the folder down on the sofa. Those terrible pictures of that poor girl go fanning out across the cushions while Delilah glares at me, her eyes scalding coals. "Like the fact that my house is *still* the site of an active murder investigation? Like the fact that you *suspected* me?"

"I was still working a few angles. I told you about Celeste—"

"Yeah? Maybe you think I went back in time and hurt her, too, since apparently you think I could've murdered Emma. Holy shit, you—" She stops. Her lips tremble. Worst part is, I fucking know how she feels, even if that jab about Celeste was low. "So what was your grand plan? Fuck me into complacency, and then get me to confess?"

"There was no grand fucking plan, woman. I—goddamn, look, I *had* to do my job as a cop, okay?" I bite off, clenching my fists helplessly. "It was early in the case. I had to consider every possibility. Wasn't trying to get into your pants for police business, and if you think that, you're not as smart as I thought. I can't believe you'd stand here and fucking think I don't—"

It's my turn to seize up.

I want to tell her I'm crashing, going down, falling madly in love with her.

I want to tell her I'd never hurt her.

I want to tell her everything, including why I broke my promise until I can give Emma's folks *real* peace with concrete answers that tell the truth.

I want to tell her how it makes my heart bash my ribs like an angry caged-up bird to see her in my shirt with her eyes all lit with emotion.

I want to tell her I need her.

That I'll protect her.

That it was just due diligence.

That I never ever seriously thought she could hurt anyone.

Only, I'm all thorns and edges right now, too hung up on fighting words and the blue razors in her eyes that are still aimed at me.

Maybe you think I went back in time and hurt her, too.

Before I can stop it, my temper leaps ahead of my brain.

"You can't fucking blame anyone but yourself for what you

find when you go digging around in other people's shit, Delilah. You were never meant to see that. That's confidential police material," I snap.

She stares at me, then lets out an incredulous laugh. "That's it? *That's* all you have to say? 'If you're upset because I lied to you, it's your own fault for finding out about it. Next time, sit down and shut up like a good little girl.'"

"That's not what I mean and you know it." Growling, I grind a hand against my forehead, struggling to keep my head on. "I told you, this case is complicated as hell. You *know* that. I had my reasons, but I didn't fucking lie for nothing. Emma's family *will* know. It's just not the right time yet, not when there's still loose ends to tie up and assholes standing by with scissors, waiting to cut the truth out forever. Fuck, I didn't tell you because I was trying to protect you."

"Did I ask to be protected?" Delilah's eyes are hard, but the shimmer of impending tears darkens them. She folds her arms around herself in that defensive stance she has that aches so much, walling herself off. "And I sure as hell never asked you to lie to me and stalk me like I'm your property." She swallows, looking away from me pointedly. "I don't want to stay here with you. I want my things, and I want you to take me home."

I reach toward her helplessly. "Delilah—"

"I said I want to go home!" She pivots on her heel, stalking toward my door in nothing but my shirt. "Fuck it, I'll walk."

"No—shit, no." Sagging, I scrub my fingers over my face, wishing I could climb out of my own damn skin. "Let me get your clothes. I'll drive you. It's not safe alone at night."

Delilah doesn't say anything, and thank God she doesn't fight me over that.

She won't even look at me now.

I can't stop staring at her.

I don't know how the hell this shit blew up so violently so fast, with me and my clumsy fucking mouth.

I tried to explain and it came out all wrong, making everything a hundred times worse.

That's called life when you're tromping around with enough grief and frustration in your heart to trip up ten good men.

I guess she doesn't want anything to do with me now. So I turn away and trudge upstairs to fetch her clothing.

Guess that's it.

We're over before we had a chance to find out what we could ever be.

XVII: RED AS A BEET (DELILAH)

here are few things more mortifying than being driven home like a kid from soccer practice by the man you just dumped, still sore from him fucking the life out of you, with your mouth still bruised and tender from his kiss.

Before Lucas turns down my street, I stop him, sitting stiff as a board in the passenger seat. "Just let me out here."

He eases his truck to a halt at the corner, a block from my house.

God, this sucks.

I won't look at him, but I can feel his gaze crushing me like it weighs a thousand pounds. "Delilah, it's only—"

"I'm fine right here."

Yes, I'm holding back tears.

I'm so not fine.

I don't want him to see me cry.

So I fumble for the door handle and tear it open, practically falling out onto the sidewalk.

"Delilah!" he growls after me.

"I'm *fine*," I snap back, stalking away. "Go home, Lucas."

I half expect him to follow me, giant overprotective idiot that he is.

But there's only the rumble of his idling engine, growing quieter with every step I take. Louder then softer as he does a probably illegal U-turn at the corner.

His headlights sweep over me one more time, spilling down the darkened street before dimming.

Then he's gone.

Leaving me standing there on the sidewalk, digging my fingers into my sides as I hug myself until it hurts. Like maybe I can hold myself together by sheer force until I can get inside, lock the doors, and ugly cry myself to sleep.

Alone.

My grief threatens to spill over even now as I speed up the sidewalk to my gate.

You never expect something so good to derail this abruptly any more than you climb behind the wheel expecting to have a semi plow into you.

Where did it all go so wrong, so fast?

Except I know.

For Lucas, Emma's death is still an open case. He'll never let it go the same way he never let Celeste go.

I know he's still investigating. I get that.

It makes sense that he wouldn't tell the family in case they said anything that could tip off Emma's murderer—if there is a murderer at all.

I still don't know why I got so spitting mad.

But actually I do, and it's only partly about Emma.

It's Lucas being so close-mouthed with me, even after everything we shared.

Especially after everything.

I started to feel like I was getting to know him, opening up, trusting him, and this tiny, vulnerable part of me that's somehow survived a lifetime of cynicism and hard knocks was hoping when it shouldn't.

Hoping he'd meet me halfway.

But now I know he's happy to keep me at arm's length,

forever reaching, always naïve and stupid enough to think he's within my grasp.

Screw that.

So much for thinking I'd killed my idealism.

Hardened big-city girl my ass.

Yeah. I should've taken a lesson from Roger and stopped bothering with men.

Sniffling and still choking on the knot in my throat, I unlatch my gate and shuffle up my pathway.

No, really. I'm not stomping or dragging my feet at all.

If only the kids could see me now.

I'm way more sulky and sad and petulant than a third grader throwing a tantrum.

I know I'm overreacting.

I'm just taking this too hard.

All because I wanted a fresh start. I wanted this to be as amazing as it felt, instead of human and complex and messy and doomed from the start.

As I draw closer to the porch with a heavy sigh, the motion sensor lights Lucas installed snap on, flooding the porch with illumination.

The glare highlights what I couldn't see in the dark.

My heart sputters to a dead stop and I freeze midstep.

Another red X.

This time, it's splashed across my front door in vivid warning. *Thou shall not enter.*

My pulse thunders in my ears until it's deafening. Talk about amping up my panic.

I still try to climb the steps, willing myself not to trip like the dumb lead in every bad horror movie.

It's fresh, I think.

Paint this time—probably—at least I can smell the acidic undertone of spray paint. But there's something else, too.

Thick. Metallic. Meaty.

Not more blood?

For the love of God...

There's something else, too. A small shoebox on the front mat, spattered in stray red droplets.

Amana Ray shoes, the brand name reads. Some oddly calm part of my brain draws a connection.

Roger was obsessed with Amana Ray. He freaking refused to wear anything else whenever he trained for 5Ks and 10Ks and charity runs.

Numbly, I pick up the box.

It's not that heavy, but it's not light either.

There's something sliding around inside with a loose, shuffling sound, and many smaller things striking the sides of the box.

I find out what those smaller things are when I lift the lid with shaking hands.

Photographs.

What looks like over a hundred in their stiff little white square frames. My own face stares up at me from all of them.

"Jesus!" I whisper-scream.

My lungs won't work.

I go stumbling backward, heart lodged in my throat, on the verge of blacking out.

Brute shock stabs through me. Everything tingles like an electric current.

The box slips from my grasp and plummets to the porch, scattering the photos everywhere. As it lands with a heavy *thump!* more of them erupt, spilling all over my front mat.

"Idiot," I mutter to myself.

With a sigh, I drop to my knees, pawing through the mess, picking one up, staring at it, throwing it aside, grasping for another, slowly choking on my own fear.

This can't be happening.

Oh, but it is.

One photo after the next shows my life in gloriously boring detail.

There I am, curled up on the sofa reviewing lesson plans, the light from the TV reflecting on my face, the entire scene so glassy through my living room window.

Me, just past the half-closed curtains of my bedroom window, sleeping and unaware and vulnerable.

Me again, standing at the head of my class, taken from just far enough away that I can tell the photographer was somewhere in the school courtyard—probably hiding in the trees the children like to play around. They caught me with one hand pointing at a map of New England while I was helping my young readers sound out state names.

Getting into my car just outside the school, caught mid-motion as I toss my purse on the seat and slip behind the wheel.

At the convenience store, picking out wine and a case of beer to bring over to Lucas' for that first date dinner.

A glimpse of my naked profile from that night as I stripped down to shower, shivering at the thought of seeing him again.

That one hits the hardest, turning me into a hyperventilating wreck, sucking on my own chest in awful rhythm.

The photograph goes jittery in my vision with the force of my trembling fingers.

Roger. It had to be!

He was there, watching me in my most intimate moments, and now the wonder and happiness is so—

Tainted.

I feel tainted.

A wet splatter hits the photograph. For a second, I think it's the tears overflowing my eyes—*fuck this entire night*—until it hits me.

It's red.

A thick, ugly drop of red, staining the picture, obscuring my naked breasts as I turn away from the camera.

Then another falls, striking the scattered photographs on the mat like a rusted rain.

Another and another and another, a sickening splatter of unholy blood falling down from—from—oh *God!*

I don't want to look up.

But I can't stop myself.

Something terrible and invisible cranes my head, cranking it back like I'm a puppet. I can't stop how it pulls my strings even as my heart, my shivering hurting body scream *no, no, no!*

I blink away the tears blurring my vision as I stare at the eaves of the porch overhang.

Right on time for the biggest shock of my life.

Roger Strunk's corpse has been laced up against the underside of the overhang, his entire body gutted and hollowed out like a butchered pig.

His bulging blank eyes stare down at me with the same ugly accusation as the emptiness in Emma's dead stare.

You.

I'm dead and it should have been you.

The horror hits me in the head like a concussion, jarring my whole body.

I only have one second to struggle, to process this, to fail so miserably before the world starts reeling.

A scream tries to claw up my throat, but never makes it out.

Everything is distant and muffled and so far away.

That invisible puppetmaster of my own blinding emotion wheels me to the side, jerking me back into the night.

Before I understand anything, I pass out dead on my porch.

XVIII: RED HAZE (LUCAS)

*F*uck, shit, and damn.

I never should've let Delilah go home alone.

I've barely made it back to my place before the call comes in.

Another dead body at that little blue house.

This time, there's no doubt it was murder—and the victim? Delilah's ex-boyfriend.

What the actual *fuck*.

I'm out the door in a flash, not even bothering to change into my uniform. All I can think about is Delilah.

If she's hurt, if anyone threatened her, if she's okay after stumbling on another corpse.

If she threw herself into a bad situation because of my big fat fucking mouth.

Too many *ifs*.

My heart is a tangled nest of thorns.

Whatever the fuck's going on here just got ten times worse.

When I pull up to the house, every squad car in town lines the sidewalk, lighting up the night in whirling blue and red carnival colors.

Yellow tape circles the fence like a deadly bow on a gift no one asked for.

Everyone's here but Chief Bowden—go fucking figure.

Micah, Grant, Henri, all of them roaming the scene in uniform.

Henri photographs something by the front door while Grant paces the property with a flashlight, muttering into his radio and throwing down evidence markers. Micah, he's talking to a small and ragged Delilah.

Her hair is a mess like she's scratched it raw, or shaken it into a wild mane.

The moment I see those smears of crimson on her bare arms, staining the dress I just ripped off her hours ago, I bolt from the car, my gut vibrating pure regret.

"Lilah?" I gasp, nearly vaulting over the fence. "Did he hurt you? Did he—"

Her head comes up sharply, silencing my words.

It's not half as bad as the look plastered on her face.

It stops me in my tracks and rips the words from my throat.

She stares at me like *I* did this.

Like it's somehow my fault.

The hurt that knifes through me is a force of nature, hoisting me up and body-slamming me back into the pavement.

"Stay away from me," she whispers, her voice trembling—and she edges around Micah, putting his tall put-together albino ass between us. I can't blame him for looking puzzled, his pale eyes worried as he stops scratching things down on his notepad. "Sorry, I don't... I don't want to talk to him, Officer Ainsley."

I must have the damnedest look on my face.

Because the look Micah gives me is the same sympathy you show a puppy in a kennel when you can't take it home.

"She's not hurt, Graves," he tells me. "She fainted and landed in some blood. Maybe you should go talk to the captain and take a look at what we've got?"

Fuck.

I don't know what to do.

What to say.

What I could ever give up to hold my shattered heart together.

Does she trust me so little after that fight?

Did one shitty dumb omission on my part annihilate whatever fragile faith she ever had in me?

Or does she just blame me for her ex-boyfriend's death, when I've been so obsessed with tracking the Arrendells that I went blind to something else popping off right under my nose?

I don't notice the harsh fist I'm holding at my side until my hand stings from the tension.

I stay frozen while Micah leans down and mutters something to her. Delilah nods slowly, then looks up, looking past me like I'm made of glass at the sound of a car door slamming and a worried call.

I tear my gaze away from her to see the Bowdens' personal Durango pulling up to the curve—but it's not the chief who steps out.

It's Janelle.

"Delilah!" Janelle calls, fretting as she nearly flings herself against the fence. "Oh, honey, I came as soon as I heard—are you all right?"

Sniffling, Delilah rubs one eye. "...no, not really, but I'm ready to get out of here. He said they just need to photograph me and take my clothes for evidence. But I can't go back in that house."

"Don't you worry, hon. I brought you something fresh to change into, and the neighbors staring through their windows will be happy to let you change next door," Janelle says cheerfully. "Then you can come right home with me. Your room at The Rookery's all freshened up."

At least they have Delilah taken care of.

Which means I need to stop standing here, feeling my heart bleed out all over the grass, and go do my damn job.

I drink in one last look at her, but she's so pointedly pretending I'm not there she might as well be screaming at me.

It fucking guts me that I can't just walk over and hold her.

Still, the one thing I won't do tonight is make things worse.

Stay away, she said.

So I do, tearing myself away and making my way up the front walk, stepping around a couple of evidence markers as I go.

On the porch, Henri crouches down in front of a few scattered photographs, next to a fairly new-looking high-end shoebox, all of them splattered with blood. His nitrile-gloved fingers click away with his phone camera.

I frown, my gut churning with confusion.

"Where's the body?"

I stop as Henri throws a grim look over his shoulder, then looks up pointedly.

No way.

No fucking way.

I crane my head up and feel my heart turn to ice, this frozen asteroid floating in the dead space in my chest.

Roger Strunk's dead, empty eyes stare back at me.

He's been gutted. So neatly and efficiently hollowed out it could only have been done by machine at a slaughterhouse. The man's just a hollow cavity of meat and bone now.

If I didn't have a stomach for this kind of trauma, I'd be heaving my guts out on the ground.

His arms and legs have been wedged into the support beams underneath the roof, spreading him out like he's bound to a kite.

"Motherfucker," I spit, sickness roiling through me. "Who the fuck does something this sick?"

"You tell me," Henri drawls. "I'm not from around these parts. Who do you know that's real good at butchering?"

Henri doesn't need to say it.

Neither do I.

We both have one guess.

No one else in town has the kind of sweeping farm and slaughterhouse operation like the Jacobins.

Fuck.

"It had to be done somewhere else. Not here," I say. "Grant find any of the organs in the yard?"

"Nada. No sign."

"There's not enough blood," I growl, hunkering down next to Henri.

I position myself away from the slow drip of blood still trickling down from above. If the photos weren't evidence, I'd rip the damn things in half when I see them.

Textbook stalker shit.

No wonder she's so worked up.

No wonder she doesn't want to see me, when the way I've been shadowing her probably makes me seem no better than everybody else making her life miserable.

"They did it somewhere else," I say again. "Killed him and did their work, then brought him here."

"What you thinkin', Lieutenant?"

"Two possibilities." I frown, rubbing at my chin. "Either one of the hillfolk's been stalking Delilah this whole time, slashing those nasty red Xs to send her a message, taking those photos, and now killing Strunk like it's some big gift to her, or..." I trail off.

"Or?" Henri urges.

"Or Strunk was behind the stalking," I say, and there's a feeling of *rightness* to that. "The Xs, the photographs, whatever. Only, somebody else didn't like it. He wasn't worthy, so that somebody decided to get him out of the way. They killed him because they were protecting Delilah."

Henri stares at me for a few seconds with his brows trying to crawl off his forehead.

"That's some fucked up protection, all right. But about that." Henri lowers his phone, giving me a grave look. "Got something to show you, Lucas, and you ain't gonna like it."

* * *

IF I COULD CUT off my right arm and make her talk to me again, I'd do it in a heartbeat.

I fucking hate leaving Delilah behind, but it's got to be done.

By the time Bowden finally comes waddling up to the crime scene, still in his pajama top over his uniform slacks, Janelle's got her bundled into a change of clothes and whisked away to The Rookery.

At least I know she's safe with someone.

Henri and I leave the others to keep working the crime scene while we head back to the station to log evidence, handing it over to a pale, shaken Mallory.

I put in a quick call to Raleigh.

We need more than a coroner this time. A few forensics people would be nice, whoever can get that body down without damaging the evidence, plus a few more spare officers, too.

Before we left, Grant said he wanted eyes on the crime scene at all times.

I don't blame him, but there's just not enough of us here to do that.

The air was suffocating as I read Delilah's testimony from Micah's scratch pad on the drive back—and it stays thick as mud in my mind while Henri drags me over to Grant's desk and the computer we all steal for our workstation.

"So, after that tip about the pig's blood," Henri says, clicking through files and chewing at one corner of his mouth in concentration, "I called Rick down at the butcher's shop. Asked for his security tapes for the last week. Y'all put me on graveyard shift like the pig fuckers you are, and I figured I could do something to pass the time. That's how I found this."

He opens a video file.

The media player window shows us a high angled, grainy shot in washed-out color, looking down on the neat, clean, folksy interior of the town's butcher shop.

A few people wait in line in front of the register, while a few more browse the big glass displays with red cuts of fresh meat, ground sausage, sweetmeats, you name it.

"See there?" Henri taps the screen over the second guy in line.

I squint closer.

I recognize the build immediately.

He's tall, lanky, wearing a hoodie and sunglasses.

As he turns a little, looking warily over his shoulder, I glimpse his profile, his mouth, the nervous angles of his face.

"That's him," I mutter grimly. "Roger Strunk."

"Mm-hmm. And look what he's buying."

Strunk's turn at the register comes next. He says something I can't hear, but jolly old Rick smiles behind the counter and comes back with a large waxed paper carton with a plastic lid.

Through the plastic, I see red liquid washing up the sides, staining the interior of the cup.

"Goddamn." Cursing, I sit back in my chair. "Pig's blood." I glance at the timestamp. "Four days ago? The timeline adds up then."

Henri nods, pausing the video. "We also know he was alive four days ago, though the corpse is fresh enough that I could've guessed that. No decay or bloating. No smell. It looks like your second theory was right, mon ami."

The implications almost knock me down.

"Yeah. We've got *two* stalkers after Delilah—and one didn't like the competition." That sits real fucking uneasy with me. If I had a choice I'd have her under guard in a safe house twenty-four seven. "You know our next steps, don't you, Henri?"

His eyes narrow. "We don't have a warrant yet, Lieutenant. We don't even have probable cause. Just because they've got butchering facilities doesn't mean anything. It's circumstantial. Same logic makes Rick a suspect, too."

"We'll find our probable cause," I snarl. "Let's get the fuck out there and keep an eye on the Jacobins."

* * *

NOT SEEING Delilah for over twenty-four hours eats a hole in me like a cigarette burn.

But Micah promised me she was fine when he volunteered for tonight's stakeout.

She's holding up bravely, doing everything she could to help the investigation by scouring her memory for details when he dropped by to check on her this afternoon.

I wish it was me.

I wish it was me checking up on her, comforting her, dragging her into my arms.

Offering an apology.

I was wrong.

I'm not one hundred percent sure of that even now, but it's slowly settling in bone deep.

Maybe I was right about Montero Arrendell killing my sister, but there was something totally different going on with this case.

I let my own bullshit cloud my judgment. I missed the warning signs.

I almost got Delilah *killed.*

Hell, she's been terrorized thanks to my blind spots.

I owe her an apology for that.

But she doesn't want to see me. Even my texts go unanswered.

I try calling once.

Of course, she doesn't pick up.

Fuck it.

I'm not heaping more stress on her when she's already upset and dealing with coming home to a dead body for the second time.

So I'll do the next best thing.

Find out who the fuck has been stalking her and lock him up in the deepest damned hole on Earth.

I slouch behind the wheel of my patrol car, watching for any movements through the trees. It was a bitch for Micah and me to maneuver this damn thing off-road in the woods.

Now we're parked on a good vantage point at the top of a hill, looking down through the fireflies over the Jacobin farm. The place is nestled in its own little valley, ringed on all sides by trees.

We're likely not going to be able to back out of this little alcove without making a hell of a racket, but by then it won't matter.

It's one o'clock in the damn morning.

So it's a little fishy that they're up and working, no matter what kind of early-late hours farmers usually keep.

In the passenger seat, Micah leans forward, folding his arms on the dash and lazily resting his chin on them. The moonlight through the windshield reflects off his white-blond hair, dappled by the shadows of the leaves overhead.

"Now that's interesting," he whispers. "What do you think is in those crates?"

I watch as the entire family—a whole tribe, really, some two dozen men—works to fill the backs of several open-top cargo trucks with unmarked crates. The wooden slats are packed so tight I can't make out a glimpse of what's inside.

"Could be corn, jared preserves, fresh fruit heading up to market. Any number of other things. Or..."

"Or it could be a big batch of that battery acid they call moonshine," Micah fills in softly. He's narrowed in on them with his usual predatory intensity. Sometimes it makes him look more like a battle-hardened sniper than a junior cop. "Maybe even something else. I think we've got enough suspicion to land ourselves a search warrant, though."

My lip curls viciously.

It's a technicality.

I know it is.

But I've seen too many convictions tossed out because someone didn't do things right.

That's why we *will* do this by the book, no matter how much it slows shit down.

I snap a few more photos on my phone, catching the movement below, the unmarked crates, the trucks. My gaze lingers on Culver Jacobin.

In town, he's always smiling and ambling along, a little too friendly sometimes but harmless, coming off like the town goofball.

Not tonight.

Now, he's dead serious, grim and focused.

It's like he's peeled his mask off, showing something cold and disturbed underneath.

Delilah said she caught him staring in town too many times, and the encounter she described when he came to install her cable box—fuck.

I'd like to find out just how much Culver Jacobin knows about butchering pigs.

"C'mon." I start the engine. "Let's head back in."

The sound of the patrol car echoes over the hills. Everyone down in the valley goes tense, stopping in their tracks.

Neither of us breathe, just waiting.

There's a flurry of motion, coordinated movements like a flock of crows. It doesn't take them two minutes to vanish.

Crates flying from hand to hand, disappearing into a massive barn. Doors and windows snap shut.

They're gone like they were never there.

Just empty trucks with no one behind the wheel and nothing in their beds.

Footsteps in the packed dirt belonging to no one.

"Eerie as hell," Micah mutters.

"Tell me about it. Let's get the hell out of here," I say, backing the patrol car through the trees faster than I should.

* * *

I HAVEN'T SLEPT or gone home in at least a day.

By the time Chief Bowden and Captain Faircross call a meeting the next morning, I've been staring at crime scene photos till my eyes hurt.

The incident reports with the vandalism and those Xs. The rumors of Roger Strunk around town, someone peering in Delilah's window, Emma Santos' body.

It's all here, but what the hell am I still missing?

I need something to make this all make sense. *A motive.*

Did it happen because Culver Jacobin is obsessed with Delilah?

I guess he could've heard about her before she arrived, done a little Googling, gotten himself all worked up in his crazy-ass mind. Maybe he started scheming in advance, and his plan included kidnapping an Arrendell piece of arm candy and leaving her dead in Delilah's house to kick things off.

She did say she saw someone running away from the house that first day, after all.

Could've been Culver, leaving the body.

He'd fit the description pretty damn well, too.

"Everyone here?" Grant calls.

I lift my head sharply, reaching for my cup of half-cold coffee.

Grant stands in the middle of the room. Even Chief Bowden looks small next to him today, while Micah and Henri drape themselves over chairs nearby. They've got the backup from Raleigh out guarding the crime scene.

I don't notice Grant clearing his throat loudly or looking my way. "And by that, I mean are you fucking awake, Graves?"

"Give me a few more sips, Cap." I guzzle my coffee, draining half of it in one gulp. "Okay, now talk."

"The theory we're working with right now," Grant says, "is that Culver Jacobin is the most obvious suspect. With how secretive they are, we don't know who handles the butchering for the Jacobins, but he'd likely have seen how it's done. Also, he's shown some interest in the target, so he could have a motive."

"Trouble is," Henri says, "that kind of suspicion's not grounds to arrest him."

"Maybe not," Grant answers. "But we can sure haul his ass in for questioning, anyway."

"We *sure* it's Culver?" I rub at one gritty eye. "I don't know. Something's not sitting right. Emma Santos was found killed before Delilah even showed up. Before Culver ever met her. Yeah, it's possible he could've searched her or heard about her around town, but that doesn't explain the instant obsession."

Bowden frowns, resting his hands against his large belly. "Emma Santos wasn't killed. She died of a self-inflicted overdose. That case has nothing to do with this one."

"I have a theory that—"

"—that you've got a bug up your ass about the Arrendells. We know. You'll do anything you can to string these two cases together and shackle it to them," Bowden replies impatiently. "Give it a rest, Lucas. If you can't be objective about this, I'll pull you off the case."

Goddamn.

It's probably the first time in ages I've ever heard that useless lump exert his authority in any meaningful way. I work my lips helplessly, casting a glance at Grant, but he only shakes his head, his eyes hard with warning.

Not now. Let it go, man.

My guts twist.

There's a waiting silence in the room.

Gritting my teeth, I look away and force myself to say it. "Yes, sir."

This isn't over.

Also, *I'm* not the asshole who brought up the Arrendells.

What if I wasn't wrong after all?

What if—

Goddammit, something stinks and it's right in front of my nose. Close enough to smell it and sour your stomach, but almost too frigging close to see clearly.

What the fuck am I missing?

* * *

THE MEETING ENDS after working over a few more theories and divvying out assignments to follow up on the case.

Henri goes off to bring in Culver.

I wind up on stakeout duty at the house, keeping me far away from the station when they bring that little hill rat in. That was the chief's decision.

I don't think it's a coincidence.

As I get up to head out, Micah catches my arm, leaning in close.

"She's okay. You don't need to worry," he growls.

A knot I hadn't realized I've been holding on to all day loosens in my chest. "What, you saw her?"

"On my way in." Micah nods. "Captain gave approval for me to fetch her things, take them from her house to The Rookery. She's holding up all right. Stubborn as hell, that woman." He smiles. "The two of you are a lot alike. No wonder you fight like wolverines over the dumbest damn things."

"It was a pretty dumb fucking fight." I smile faintly.

"Most fights are. We get ourselves all worked up, then later, we realize it was all egos and useless crap that got in the way of time we could've spent together." He sounds like he's talking from experience, and he gives me a long look, letting go of my arm. "Give her time. She'll talk to you again."

I hope like hell he's right.

I'd give anything for a chance to make it right again and bring my pretty Lilah home to my arms.

XIX: CHERRY RED (DELILAH)

*S*leep? Impossible.

Every time I try, I just see him again.

Roger.

Spread open like a rack of lamb, his vacant eyes cutting and sharp.

Like he blames me.

Oh, I know it's not my fault.

He never should have stalked me to this cursed little town.

If he'd just gotten the help he needed and stayed in New York and called me a bitch to his drinking buddies like a normal ex-boyfriend, he'd still be alive.

I sigh.

What's really keeping me awake is the great unknown.

Wondering who would *kill* my stalker ex-boyfriend just to send a message.

Who could possibly be that focused on me?

The walls of The Rookery feel too thin tonight, even though it should be the safest place in town. But even knowing the chief of police and his wife are close doesn't help.

I've never been more alone, and when you're alone, you can't feel totally safe.

I want Lucas so bad it kills me.

I miss his heat, his wall of a body just waiting for me to curl up, to burrow into him, to hide against, but my head's gotten him all tangled up in this mess.

My feelings are all spikes, ready to stick anything that gets too close.

If I saw him right now, I don't know if I'd kiss him or scream until I throw out my voice.

But Lucas isn't some stalker freak killer making my life a living hell.

My problems with him are mostly *me*.

I'll even admit it's not totally about Emma or the fact that he lied.

Not about some vague promise that was never fully broken, just delayed for the purpose of the investigation.

The truth? I'm afraid.

I'm a bitter, screwed up little mess who'll find any excuse to push away a man who could be too good for me. We were getting too real, and he was so close to rewriting the stain of my past.

Deep down, that terrified me.

So I found my excuse to run without realizing it until later.

Now, I glance at the clock with my heart hanging low.

It's after eleven p.m. Seven more hours alone.

I can't stand it.

I snatch up my phone and stare at the screen with his last text.

Lucas: *Can we talk without going nuclear on each other, darlin'? Give me five minutes.*

God, I almost do it.

I almost mash the call button and reach for what I really want in that scared, flighty little hollow in my heart buried under so much grief.

I almost call out to him.

It's not pride that stops me.

It's the fact that I don't even know what I'd say. How to explain why everything just spiraled when my feelings are so tangled into Gordian knots I can't begin to sort them out.

Call it a delayed trauma reaction or something.

And that was before I found my creepy ex-boyfriend mangled and dead on my roof.

Roger was warped and so sick he might've hurt me, but he still didn't deserve that.

He should've had his day in a courtroom like anyone else.

Just like Lucas Graves doesn't deserve my clumsy flailing around now.

So I'll talk to him.

After I get myself sorted out and I can find the right words, we'll sit down for a heart-to-heart chat.

When I stab at my contacts with tears in my eyes, it's not Lucas' contact I'm mashing with my fingertip.

It's my mother's.

Mitsi Clarendon is the kind of night owl you can only be when you spend twenty years running your own all-night diner, so I'm not worried about waking her up.

"Delilah!" she chirps as bright and cheery as ever. "I've been on tenterhooks waiting to hear from you. One text when you arrived? *Really.*" She clucks her tongue in mock disapproval, but her voice is overflowing with warm laughter. "How are things with your new job? With everything? Are you all settled in?"

"Oh, Mom. You don't even want to know. Mom, I—" That word stops me every time. It's been years, and it still gives me that little hitch of breath, having someone to call *Mom.* I exhale and start over again. "Mom, I think I really fucked up."

"What's the matter? Is the job not working out, love?"

"The job is the *only* thing that's working out." I roll over and bury my face in the plush pillow of my borrowed—well, technically free—bed, mumbling around it. "Don't get me wrong. The kids are great. The school is nice. I love the staff, and they seem to like me. But I think I accidentally stumbled on a portal to hell. Redhaven is one bad never-ending thriller film."

"Really? But it has such wonderful reviews!"

I can't help smiling. My mother loves her nosy little neighborhood apps like NextDoorish that let her snoop around on the neighbors.

"Some things don't get reported to the police or NextDoorish," I say dryly, propping my chin up and staring out the window. I can't tell her everything that's been happening.

She'd explode into Mom-bits with worry.

The woman does that.

It's like she's trying to cram eighteen years of missed parenting in all at once.

So I divert with a question. "What do you put on a police report for a broken heart, anyway?"

"Oh, Lilah." She clucks her tongue in sympathy. "You always attract the worst men. Stop that."

I laugh.

"That's the hell of it, Mom. This time... this time I actually got a good one, and I went and screwed everything up. I just—I can't let myself trust him enough to be genuine. He made mistakes too, but I wouldn't even give him a chance to apologize." It hurts to say it, somewhere down low in this heavy place in my chest. "I was an asshole. I let my temper come out to play and I hurt him. Bad."

"Are we talking unfixable?"

"Maybe?"

"You aren't telling me everything, baby girl. What else?"

There it is. There's the mom voice that always makes me smile.

I sigh, dragging a hand over my face. "...he wants to talk. He's tried. Even after I went off hard enough to level the whole town, he actually wants to talk to me."

"Then why don't you let him?" Mom asks innocently.

Oof.

"What do I *say?*" I sputter. "We've got issues, Mom. We bang heads a lot and then my gasket blows. Why would anyone want me when I'm just this porcupine?"

I can't bring myself to use the cactus analogy when that belongs to him.

"Because I want you around all the time," she points out softly. "And I'm quite familiar with your temper after watching you nearly pin a diner's hand to a table with a fork for smacking your bottom."

I can tell she's trying not to laugh at the memory.

My face turns into a tomato.

I'm just trying not to crawl under the bed from sheer mortification.

"Lilah," she continues gently. "If I've seen your temper and still love you, it's because that fire is part of you. I know you're always working to rein it in. It's part of what makes you so strong. If this man's any good, don't you think he can see it, too?"

"I don't know." My heart rattles. "Mom, I don't even know if it's love with him."

"I think you do," she whispers confidently.

Crap, she's right.

She always is.

Like it or not, I'm in flipping love with Lucas Graves.

And I don't know how to handle love without burning it to ashes.

My eyes sting with panic.

I press my fingers to my lips, steadying my voice. "I... I gotta go. I have to teach in the morning and it's crazy late. Those little monsters wear me out."

"But they love you anyway, don't they?" She laughs. "So do I, sweet girl. You be safe out there, all right? And call if you need anything else."

"I will."

Yeah, right.

Real safe with dead bodies everywhere.

I didn't even hint at why Redhaven still might eat me alive.

But I'm smiling anyway, and I don't want to worry her this late.

"Love you too, Mom. Good night."

"Good night, sweet girl."

The call ends and I sprawl out sideways across the bed, staring at the room with my heart in a knot.

That was helpful and entirely awful, making me look at things I've been refusing to admit.

Like the fact that I love Lucas Graves.

Just what the hell am I supposed to do with that?

* * *

BY MY LUNCH break the next day, I'm still as confused as ever about Lucas and turning some things over about Emma.

About Roger.

About this gory mess, and why it seems to revolve around me.

I nibble at the little finger sandwiches I threw together this morning, scrolling my phone as I search *Emma Santos Instagram model.*

The results immediately bring me to her Insta account.

Only, it's been taken over by someone else.

Her mother, I think, and all of the most recent posts are—*oh.*

My heart can't take this.

All of the most recent posts are desperate pleas for any information on her whereabouts. She's asking for recent sightings, tips, offering a cash reward that sounds like it's all they can afford.

God.

Emma looked so much like her mother, Marina Santos. She's a tall, slim woman with a pointed chin and a heart-shaped face and soft brown eyes that look as liquid as Emma's probably did when she was alive.

In one photo, she's holding a huge piece of poster board with a blown-up color photograph of a smiling, laughing Emma taped to it. Below it, big blocky Magic Marker letters are colored in with a phone number and email listed.

Have you seen my daughter?
Help my baby girl come home.

WRECKED.

I'm about to start bawling right here in the break room at school.

I linger on the number, temptation itching in my fingers, but I make myself scroll past to older photos. Emma's photos aren't the sort of staged perfection you'd expect from Instagram influencers, but instead they're candid shots of her just living life.

Always in motion, this vibrant thing who always seems like she's mid-laugh, mid-turn, never quite holding still, her eyes bright and sparkling clear.

She was so beautiful.

So full of life.

It's hard for me to think a girl like her would have overdosed so easily. The patterns in her posts don't reflect that at all.

Fitness, lifestyle, healthy foods, taking pleasure in so many simple things. I can't see where she'd even be a drug fiend, but I guess you never know what demons people are really fighting behind closed doors.

I keep scrolling, unsure what I'm looking for.

It's not like she's going to have an old photo posted with any of the Arrendells—let alone Culver Jacobin.

Also, my battery's at 9%. My break's almost over and I should just give it up.

I start swiping the app closed, but accidentally flick to another photo instead.

Emma again, this time dancing in a club. The colored lights play beautifully off her gold skin. I can't make out her dance partner in the shadows.

But I can see the bracelet glimmering on her wrist, shining rose gold against disco spangles.

A simple bar. A delicate chain.

Xs engraved on the familiar bar.

Holy shit!

It's the same bracelet I stuffed in the bottom drawer of my dresser, hoping to never look at it again after what Lucas told me about Celeste and Montero Arrendell.

Only mine has seven Xs.

Emma's...

I think Emma's has *six*.

Every muscle seizes up. I stare at her slender wrist, at the look of joy on her face, my lungs slowly filling with cement.

No. No fucking *way*.

Oh, something is very, very rotten in the state of Denmark—especially when I'm sure she wasn't wearing that bracelet when I found her body.

And I've got 8% battery left to do something about it.

Inhaling sharply, I start to punch in the phone number—when my phone buzzes in my hand, nearly making me shriek.

I jump back like I'm holding a palmful of bees.

I stare at a number I don't recognize.

Local area code.

The only local numbers I have saved are Lucas, Ulysses, Nora, Janelle, and the furniture shop that delivered my bed, and it's not any of them.

Heart thumping, I swipe my thumb across the green answer icon.

"Hello?"

"Hello, Miss Clarendon."

Montero Arrendell.

His voice oozes coolly through the phone, this stone-cold thing that feels like a bone-stripping wind biting the back of my neck.

My racing heart goes painfully still like a rabbit that's just come eye to eye with a wolf.

It's like he *knew.*

"Mr. Arrendell," I force out. My voice sounds like it belongs to someone else, someone completely numb. "What can I do for you?"

"Actually, I called to find out what I can do for *you.*" Over the phone, without the force of his physical presence and commanding charisma, his friendly tone sounds phony. "All these wicked things continuously happening, you poor thing. You must be scared out of your wits."

I swallow roughly.

"I don't scare that easily, sir." And my voice chooses right then to crack, making a liar out of me. I'm petrified right now, and I realize I'm scared of him. Of the connections my mind strings together with that bracelet in Emma's photograph. Of how it could all be tied to me, to Roger's death. "But I'm fine. Really."

"You don't have to put on a brave face, Delilah—may I call you Delilah?"

No.

The very idea is nauseating, and I have to force words off my tongue. "If you want to."

"Then I insist you call me Montero. I don't want you feeling the need to be so formal with me. I'd like to offer you more protection, if I may."

I frown. "What kind of protection? The police are doing a good job."

"There are a number of things I could do," he says. "Assign

you a personal guard detail. Hire a private investigator to handle affairs. Our house, we have plenty of suites we could spare if you'd like to—"

"That won't be necessary," I rush out. Every word he speaks feels like a Venus flytrap slowly closing around me. "You're very generous, but I wouldn't dare impose. I'm sure I'll be fine."

"So independent. I admire that. Are you certain there's nothing I can do to change your mind?" he coaxes.

"I'm sure," I bite off.

I'm also sure I'd rather eat live cockroaches slathered in ghost pepper sauce than let him lure me into that house.

At least my defensiveness calms the frightened panic shooting through my veins. I manage to sound steadier when I ask, "Ulysses said you wanted to meet with me?"

"Oh, that. Yes. Administrative matters, nothing more. We can talk about it when you're more settled in and this terrible business has passed."

I'm actually a little surprised he didn't pressure me to see him. But maybe that would be too obvious—or he can sense how spooked out of my skin I am.

I want off this call now.

He's not the one I want to be talking to, and the longer we speak, the more I worry I'll give away something that'll make him suspicious.

"I'm so sorry. My battery's about to die and my lunch break's almost over."

"Don't you dare apologize, Delilah. I called you in the middle of your workday," Montero responds firmly. "Do what you need to do. I just hope you know you can call on me for anything— anything at all."

There's a silky-sour undertone there. A touch of weird innuendo that leaves my stomach turning inside out. I choke back the horror in my throat.

"Thanks," I force out, polite but stilted. "Bye."

"Goodbye, Delilah."

He makes my name sound like a slime-coated leaf flapping around.

I hang up with my throat stuck together.

Then I stare at my battery indicator.

6% left.

Fuck.

Pulse jacking, I swipe back to the photo of Marina Santos with one hand, scrabbling in my bag for a pen with the other, and I—I *don't have anything to write on.*

Awesome.

So I scribble down the number in blue ink on the cheap particle board of the break room table.

Oops.

I hope that'll come out.

Christ, why didn't I just write it on my hand or something?

I get the last number down just as my phone beeps and dies with a cheerful chirp and a flash of the logo.

It's just me, my dying phone, and that number on the table.

And I've got six minutes until my break's over. I can hear the children shrieking around the courtyard, their laughter drifting through the windows.

It's so normal versus the weird, crushing atmosphere in here.

My heart skips in an accusatory rhythm, demanding action.

My fingers shake as I tuck my hair behind my ear and glance at the old corded break room phone mounted on the wall. I don't know if the thing's even connected.

Only one way to find out.

Now it's more important than ever that I talk to Marina Santos.

Before I can talk myself out of it, I rocket to my feet, skitter over to the phone, and press the handset to my ear. There's a dull tone, and I crane my head to see the numbers on the table before punching them in. I hold my breath and wait.

After a few rings, a soft voice picks up. "Hello?"

The déjà vu that hits is intense.

327

No matter their pitch, their age, their accent, I know that voice.

Every mother worried for their daughter sounds the same. It's almost like hearing my own mom speaking with a Spanish accent.

"H-hello? Mrs. Santos?" I try to get my voice under control. *What am I doing?*

"Yes, this is she, with whom am I speaking?" She sucks in a breath. "Have you... have you heard something about my Emma?"

"No, ma'am," I blurt out.

Then I smack my palm on my forehead.

Dumbass, why did you lie?

This is why I called her, isn't it?

To tell her the truth, so she can stop this agonizing searching.

But something jerks me back. I don't know what it is just yet, but I already told her no and now I don't know how to break the news.

I don't know if I can hurt her, even if it's more painful not to let her know her daughter is dead, delaying the inevitable.

I scramble for something to say.

"My name is Mitsi—" I stop. My eyes dart around the room, landing on an unopened box of tape on the supply shelf. "Mitsi Scotch. I'm a reporter with the—" Red ballpoint pens. Legal pads. "—Red Ledger, out of North Carolina. Listen, I heard about your missing daughter online and I was hoping to find out more about her. Maybe a story in the paper could help you spread the word."

Yep, I'm going straight to hell.

But maybe she can tell me something that makes the insanity of Redhaven make *sense*.

Maybe I can help her help me fix the gaping hole in my heart I won't let Lucas Graves fill.

She's quiet before she slowly whispers, "North Carolina?"

"Yes, ma'am. Does that mean anything to you?"

"No—well, no, I don't think so. What did you want to know?"

"Mostly, if Emma's behavior had changed before she disappeared," I say. "Like was she spending time with people who weren't her usual crowd? Abandoning old friends? Any different moods or erratic behavior? Being secretive?"

"It's hard to say," Mrs. Santos says with a sigh. "She's such a fast-moving girl, always doing something, trying new things. You never know where you'll find her next. Rock climbing one day, ballroom dancing the next. She's never met a stranger in her life. Everyone's a friend to my girl." The fondness, the love in her voice rings so clear it strangles me. "But come to think of it, there was one thing a little different..."

I lean forward like I can strain toward her through the phone, bracing a hand against the wall. "Yeah? What was that?"

"She was so happy about something, but she wouldn't tell me what. She was always trying out for modeling jobs, acting gigs, looking for her big break. I thought maybe she had a lead on something but she didn't want to jinx it by telling me. But when I think about it, she was almost acting like..." She trails off.

"Like?"

"...like she was in love." The woman says it almost reluctantly, and I remember Lucas talking about Celeste, how she changed and she'd gone all starry-eyed the way young women do when they find a bad thing that seems so good. "Emma was blushing at everything all the time, drifting off in her own little world. Hardly eating some nights, hardly sleeping. It's like she was living on air and glowing with sunshine."

"But she never mentioned anyone? You never saw her crush?"

"No—oh, you know how girls her age can be, acting like it's Romeo and Juliet and they're sneaking off to the next great romance. It's more exciting when it's forbidden."

I frown. "Or would she keep him secret because she thought you might disapprove? Forgive me, but did Emma have a history of dating anyone more... sketchy?"

Like me.

Me and my bad luck that's less bad luck and more not knowing what real love looks like until I've had my heart trampled on.

Or until I've trampled all over him.

"How did you know?" Mrs. Santos whisper. "Frankly, I blame her father. I never should have brought that man into my home, but he gave me Emma. Terrible deadbeat, cruel, running around on me all the time, never could hold down a job, and sometimes —" She stops and draws a breath. "Sometimes, he was so mean to my Emma. Always playing games with her just to get her hopes up and then crush them to pieces. She stopped letting him get under her skin by the time she was sixteen, but..." Marina sighs. "I still don't know how she grew up so sweet with a prick for a father."

"I'm sure you had a lot to do with it, Mrs. Santos," I say softly. "Mothers always do."

There's a hitched sound.

I think she's trying not to cry.

Oh, no.

"Does this help? Can you do something to find my daughter?"

"I'll try," I promise.

I'm lower than a gum wrapper right now. I'm such a coward.

But I can't tell her.

What if I say something that screws up the investigation? Everything Lucas and his men are trying to do to get real justice for Emma.

He was right to keep it a secret, I realize with a sickening weight in my belly.

I never should have called.

But the bell rings, trilling through the whole school and telling me I'm out of time.

"I'm sorry, ma'am. I have to go. Thanks for your time today."

"Just bring her home." The urgent way she speaks feels like

she's reaching through the phone to grasp my hands, holding tight, pleading. "Please, Miss Scotch. Bring my Emma home."

"I will, Mrs. Santos," I whisper, fighting the jagged lump in my throat. "I'll do everything I can to find out what happened to your daughter."

That, at least, is the only truth I can offer her.

* * *

BY THE TIME class lets out, my head is spinning—and the very last person I want to see is anyone named Arrendell.

Guess who's waiting when I step outside and head to my Kia.

Ulysses leans against a gleaming, brand-new BMW—*what happened to the Benz? Already bored with it?*—with his hands ever so casually tucked into his slacks. He's practically striking a dramatic GQ pose that's too deliberately accidental to be real.

Ugh.

I hope my expression doesn't give me away when I'm so not in the mood for this.

I flash him a swift smile and quickstep past like I'm assuming he's there for someone else. As if I can even look at him without feeling a ring of fire around my wrist.

That bracelet is branding, a ghostly echo of Emma's fingers around my arm, tugging me impatiently toward answers.

"Hey, Delilah!" he calls.

I suppress a flinch when he lifts a hand, hailing me.

Okay.

Act natural.

Don't act like you suspect his father of cold-blooded murder.

I throw on my brightest smile, turning to face him as he jogs toward me. "Ulysses, hi. Here for another boring meeting?"

"Meeting ended twenty minutes ago, actually. The principal's fishing for a bigger budget for 'grounds beautification,' but what he really wanted was a new HVAC system since his office gets beastly hot. No idea why he had to beat around the bush. He could have just asked." He stops in front of me with a wide smile. "Just like I should ask you—would you come up to the house?"

I blink. "Um, the house? Why?"

"I should have started with that first." Laughing, he offers me his arm. "Walk with me. Let's have a coffee."

Jesus, no.

I don't want to touch him.

I don't want to go anywhere with this skeezy man.

But I also don't want to give myself away or make him suspicious. I also don't fancy getting fired for insulting my boss' boss after everything I've already suffered to keep this job.

"Sure," I clip.

My smile feels like a frozen grimace as I slip my arm into his.

The coffee shop is just up the street from the school.

As we walk, he fusses over me, attentive and always seeming to know just a little too much about what's going on in my life. When I ask how, he chalks it up to the town gossip vine.

But he knows all about Roger and how I'm staying at The Rookery.

He's oh-so-worried about all the terrible death I've witnessed, too, and please don't let it ruin my impression of the town.

It's not Redhaven giving me a bad impression, despite everything.

I also don't know what to say about Roger.

I've hated him for so long that I haven't figured out how to parse my feelings about his shocking death, or the guilt I feel for it, so I'm just—not parsing right now.

Not processing at all.

Shoving it all aside, I try to talk as normally as possible. Ulysses is happy to treat me like I'm a wilting damsel, two seconds away from collapsing on the pavement in grief.

I've had enough by the time we place our coffee orders and settle in at a little table outside the café.

"So, what was that about coming up to the house? Are there

little Arrendells in need of tutoring?" I flash a smile and change the subject.

"No, no. If I could, I'd keep you for that, but we boys are all degenerate rakes who won't give our darling mother any grand-children." He flashes me a bone-white smile over his Cortado. "Do you remember I said my brothers were coming home, and we were throwing a big welcome bash? It's a charity gala, really, but my brothers love stealing the spotlight. My father thought perhaps a night out under the lights with good music and five-star food might take your woes away. He sees himself as the protector of this town. Go figure. He's pretty chagrined over what a time you've had ever since you moved here." He leans closer, almost conspiratorial. "Just between you and me, I think he wants to make a good impression."

Yikes.

I'm going to vomit.

The man who killed Celeste Graves—who possibly murdered Emma Santos—wants to *make a good impression on me?*

And after Montero's own attempt at luring me to his lair failed earlier, now his own son is trying to reel me in.

"Will you walk into my parlor?" said the spider to the fly.

I shudder, hating how I read that poem to the third graders earlier.

But I'm no damselfly.

I shake my head, locking my eyes on his. "I've heard about your parties. Famous people everywhere and star-studded entertainment, right? That's just not my jam. A street rat like me wouldn't fit in."

His smile vanishes as his brows pull together. "What? Oh, no. We can't have you thinking of yourself that way, Deli—"

He breaks off as his phone buzzes from somewhere in his pocket. With a sheepish smile, he says, "Excuse me. I hate how these damned phones make everybody rude these days."

I really wonder if he's actually so mild mannered, or if it's just part of his cultivated act.

"Go ahead. I don't mind." I take a sip of my frozen latte and smile.

With a grateful nod, he retrieves his phone and swipes the lock screen.

It's definitely not the brain freeze that seizes my whole body when I see the top window on his screen right before he tabs away to his text messages.

It's only there for a second, but it's unmistakable.

Instagram.

A glimpse of the exact same page I was looking at over lunch. *Emma Santos.*

Shock, panic, and a thousand other things dart through me.

What the actual fuck?

Why was he looking at Emma's Insta profile?

I must have the craziest look on my face.

Ulysses glances up a second later and chuckles softly. "Relax. It wasn't a girl. Just Robert."

Holy hell.

My stomach flips over again.

Does he seriously think I'm *jealous? Of him?*

Woof.

Roll with it, Delilah. Better than him figuring out what you're really thinking.

I swallow the mouthful of coffee slush I left sitting on my tongue.

"Robert?"

"Yes, that one. From Hollywood. He always fusses over what to wear." Ulysses shrugs. "Speaking of attire, if that's what you're so worried about, don't. I have people who handle the fashion end. All you have to bring is your own fine face. It's this Friday night. The party won't really amp up until after eight when my brothers arrive, but you're certainly welcome earlier." He watches me intently. "Don't let me down, Delilah?"

He gives me a miserable hangdog look.

Everything in me screams *no, no, no.*

Don't do it.

Don't even think about it.

But I've already made up my mind.

If I can get inside that house, maybe I can find a clue. Something damning that links Montero Arrendell to Emma. To Celeste. To that Ethan guy. Maybe even to Roger.

It's like she's over my shoulder, whispering to me, and she sounds too much like her mother, Marina.

Do it.

Find answers.

Find justice.

Call me a huge idiot. Yes, I know I'm being reckless, making the same mistake every dumb overly brave girl does in the movies and books, but this is real life.

I have an advantage Ulysses Arrendell doesn't.

The posh vulture sitting across from me doesn't know what I know.

I'm smiling like I'm skittish and shy when what I'd really like to do is slap him across the face.

"Well... I guess. I've always wanted to meet a superhero—or a guy who plays one in the movies."

"Fantastic!" Ulysses beams at me like a little boy who just found out he's taking a NASA field trip. "I'll find something darling for you, don't worry—you'll just need to accessorize. You still have the bracelet?"

"Yes." I clear my throat, glancing away. "I just left it at home. It's so pretty, so delicate, and I was worried one of the kids might break it."

I'm a little proud of the way I'm casually lying through my teeth without stumbling over words.

A light touch to my wrist brings me back.

I almost have to nail myself down to keep from flinching away from his hand as I meet his avid, drilling green eyes.

"Say you'll wear it," he whispers, something so intense in his voice it makes me shudder. "I'd love to see it on you."

My bones are ice.

My lips feel numb as I mutter, "Oh, yeah. Sure."

Yeah.

Sure.

Why do those two words feel like putting a noose around my own neck?

Somehow, I can already feel it closing as he smiles so brightly it's almost blinding.

XX: RED STRING OF FATE (LUCAS)

S omewhere along the way, I went and got myself good and addicted to Delilah Clarendon.

Not seeing her for days, not being able to make it right, eats a hole in me like an acid spill.

I feel her absence like I'm fucking fiending, this gnawing sensation in my veins, making me desperate for her.

And I just *know* if we sit down and talk, put our tempers aside, let ourselves calm the fuck down and put our feelings on the table, we can sort everything out.

That's the way this works.

There's no such thing as a relationship where people don't fight—little tiffs, disagreements over the direction of the toilet roll, a shitty comment causing hurt, stress building up until someone explodes.

For two normal people, it's impossible to fit your rough edges together without a little friction now and then.

What makes shit work is being willing to sand those rough edges down and work together to get past the grit.

You have to talk it out and remember why you still love each other.

That's what I want with Delilah. With our tempers, there's no way we'd never fight again, even if we made up tomorrow.

But I want my tomorrow.

I want a chance to hash it out after we've both cooled down and realized how ridiculous we're being, only to laugh and kiss each other and forget about it till one of us brings our spikes out again.

Trouble is, I can't get to tomorrow when I'm stuck worrying about today.

About this whole damn *week*.

The planned raid on the Jacobins that the captain signed off on is looming. Both their farm and—if we can find it—wherever they've set up their still.

All we've got is circumstantial evidence. No real grounds for arrests that won't get laughed out of court in ten minutes.

Still, I want on that property and I'll turn over every fucking stone and hay bale and five hundred pound hog if I have to.

If it means finding evidence that one of those redneck zombie assholes killed Delilah's ex to scare her to death.

As much as it kills me to say it, this is more important than going to Delilah and ripping out my heart right now.

This is about keeping her safe.

Every day I throw myself into planning with my team, and the small squad sent in from Raleigh, I remember that.

We're poring over a hastily drawn-up map of the hills around town, marking the best spots for a vantage point, plotting timing, entry and exit points.

If we're being honest, we have no fucking clue how many of them are up there.

The Jacobins are their own clan and they're secretive as hell. Some of the people out there are probably not even related by blood—at least, I hope, since they seem to marry among themselves.

They might as well be a whole separate village on Redhaven's periphery.

We're heading into uncharted waters, and I'm going to have to trust Grant, Henri, and Micah.

If we function like a team, we just might pull this off.

The problem is finding that fucking still.

If we're chasing actionable evidence, it's going to be there.

I know damn well Chief Bowden has some idea where it might be. That's part of his whole thing with kindly looking the other way when a little bootleg whiskey isn't something worth calling in a SWAT team or causing a big ruckus.

Of course, he's out sick from work now.

Like he ever does anything, but the second we started talking about the raid, he staggered out like he had the fucking vapors.

The heat, he said. Getting too old for this late summer swelter.

Uh-huh.

Maybe I'm too suspicious, but that sure as hell doesn't hold water with me.

I don't have time to think about it, though.

Two more days.

Two more days till we go in hot, tactical gear and all.

I'm nervous as hell—and after Grant caught me at his desk again, going over the map for the fiftieth time, he kicked me out to do a coffee run for everyone.

That's how much of a pain in the ass I'm being.

I've been demoted to coffee boy.

Then again, I guess a little fresh air won't hurt, so I head out, squinting against the midmorning sun.

It's Saturday—I think?

I feel like goddamned Gollum coming out of a dark cave, shrinking away from the blinding sun.

Just living feels real weird right now when I've been up in my own head for days with this case, and when I'm not working it, I'm working myself in circles over Delilah.

Days.

Days without a word, though I've seen her now and then

around town. Her car passes by the station on her way to and from school. I've also seen her when she's on her lunch break in the café with Nora.

Or with Ulysses fucking Arrendell.

Yeah, don't like that, and I can't help but wonder.

Does she feel so unsafe in this town, with *me*, that she'd turn to him for security?

I don't want to believe it.

Especially when every time I see them together, Delilah looks as stiff as a board.

I don't think Ulysses even notices, chattering on like the entire universe revolves around him and his every word is a gift to the little people.

It's the third time I've seen them together in under a week, and always at this little coffee shop or walking around the town square.

I'm no psych profiler, but I'd bet my house that Ulysses Arrendell is a classic narcissist—and I think I'd win.

Some narcissists are just charmers with huge egos. Nothing much to worry about as long as you don't believe the bullshit they spout off about themselves.

Malignant narcissists are the ones you've got to watch out for. They'll do anything to feed their sense of superiority and control. Anything to shore up their self-image and tighten their grip.

Anything.

Which makes me wonder what he's getting out of his Delilah fix when she's not the kind of girl who'll dole out endless flattery to stroke his ego.

Hell, she barely tolerates his presence with awkward smiles and glassy eyes.

I know I shouldn't be staring that hard with knives spinning in my veins.

I'm just a jealous fucking addict.

I keep going back for more punishment, even when it's like a stick to the eye every time she looks through me.

We always seem to notice each other before we make eye contact, like a sixth sense.

Just like I know she's there before I even see her through the café window today.

She's too pretty, this delicate thing you wouldn't guess could take a man out in half a second with that wicked tongue.

Her hair's completely loose today, cascading over her shoulders in waves, this beautiful dark cloak that makes her the regal queen she is in my eyes.

I stop across the street with my heart tangled up, this hunger throbbing away as I watch her poking her straw in and out of her drink. She's looking at Ulysses without quite making eye contact.

All while he smiles at her like a fucking doofus with a crayon drawing his teacher just told him was a Picasso masterpiece.

I can't hear their conversation, of course.

And I don't need to know the words to have the flaming urge to bust in and drag her away from him.

Can't blame Ollie for everything, though. All evidence points toward Culver Jacobin as Delilah's stalker.

She shouldn't be in any real danger from him, at least in theory. Especially when she knows he's just baiting her, bringing her to his twisted fuck of an old man.

I'm not worried she'll fall into Montero's clutches.

I'm confident Lilah's too smart to let that happen.

Just as long as she still believes me.

As long as she hasn't branded me such a liar that she's dismissed everything I ever said about Celeste.

Fuck, no.

I won't get tied up in that again, or else I'll talk myself out of making a real attempt to talk to her when the time is right.

Soon.

If she still won't take my texts and calls then, I'll show up on her doorstep. I'll see if I can convince her to listen to me one more time, to remember what we had before that argument was something worth fighting for.

Today, I'll be the man.

Better than the jealous little monkey hopping up and down inside me.

I'll go with my better instincts and *wait*.

Grumbling, I prop my shoulder against one of the trees planted next to the sidewalk, resting in the shade, mentally working through the plan of attack again.

No one's seen the Jacobins in town since the night we staked out their farm, but they're up there. A little long-range surveillance on foot with binoculars confirmed that, and now and then we've seen their trucks on the roads moving in and out of town.

Damn odd.

I don't have long to ponder that, though.

After a few minutes, Ulysses stands, bowing to Delilah as he says something that involves checking his phone. He beams at a limp wave of her hand, her smile so strained it might break.

I hate this shit.

If he annoys her so much, why is she with him?

That the cop in you talking, Lucas? Or your fucking inner monkey?

Not sure there's much difference right now.

Ulysses leaves, stepping out into the sunlight. He doesn't glance in my direction before he sets off down the street toward the town square.

Delilah lingers inside the shop. Her false, tight smile fades slowly, leaving a pensive expression as she frowns down at her drink, slowly swirling her straw without taking another sip.

The longing cuts me off at the knees.

That need, that gravity, almost pulls me across the street so I can throw my arms around her, even if it'd win me nothing more than a searing slap to the face for my trouble.

I only stop myself as she lifts her head, glancing around, and then turns to the big front window. She's obviously checking for Ulysses.

She's seriously not buying your shit, fella.

I smirk to myself.

With a sweep of her hair over her shoulder, Delilah gets up, shouldering her bag and tossing back the last of her drink before heading for the door. Something on her wrist glints with the movement, catching my eye with a shimmer of rose gold.

Huh?

It can't be.

Oh, but of course it fucking *is*.

My vision goes flashing red.

And even as she steps onto the sidewalk with the door chiming, I'm moving, stalking across the street like a charging tiger.

There's nothing else in my head except for the fact that *she's wearing that shitty bracelet.*

The same type of bracelet my sister wore the night she disappeared.

The mark of murder.

Every hint of reason and patience flies out the window.

My higher brain isn't functioning when all I can see is Delilah wearing that death curse like it's just a flippant fashion accessory.

Like it isn't a prophecy waiting to be fulfilled, damning her to the same fate Celeste suffered.

"What the hell do you think you're doing?" I snarl, planting myself on the sidewalk in front of her.

I throw myself into her path so fast she nearly smacks into me.

Whatever, call me a dick.

I'm done with this tiptoeing around shit.

She stumbles back a step, flashing me a hot-eyed look of irritation before it shutters and turns distant. "Last I checked, Officer Graves, I was walking down the street. Did I violate some obscure small-town ordinance, or are you back to harassing citizens again?"

"Don't you 'Officer Graves' me. You know what I'm talking about, Lilah." I can't take the cool sarcasm in her voice when she was so open for me before, so warm, that connection between us burning hot. I also can't stop myself from snatching her arm just above the wrist, holding it up between us till that bracelet chimes in soft accusation. "Why the fuck are you wearing his mark?"

"His mark?"

Delilah yanks her arm away.

Goddammit.

I may be mad as hell, but I'm not trying to hurt her.

She retreats out of my reach, glowering up at me with those wild blue eyes full of fire.

"You controlling, possessive, arrogant *dick*," she bites off. "That's how you think about everything, isn't it? Who's property, who isn't. So now I can't wear a flipping bracelet without being someone's pet?" Her eyes narrow. "It's just a piece of jewelry, Lucas. I don't belong to anyone. Not to him. Definitely not to you. So, if you'll excuse me, I don't owe you a single word."

I pull up short, staring at her in shock.

My whole heart crashes through my shoes.

Is that how she sees me?

No better than every other controlling fuckwit who ever tried to own her? Just like the crazy asshole ex who stalked her here and got himself killed?

My lips work helplessly.

We're standing in the middle of the street and people are staring, but I don't care.

I just meet her furious glare, searching for words.

"It's not about that and you know it," I growl. She's almost winded me with shock, taking my temper with it. I guess I finally found out how many stabs it takes before a cactus makes you bleed. "You *know* what that bracelet means, Delilah. Don't bullshit me. I told you what happened to my sister. If you let them keep sucking you in, you'll be next." I swallow. My throat hurts like it's full of pulverized glass. "Don't do this to me, woman. Don't fucking make me have *you* as my next case. I couldn't stand it."

Her mouth pulls open, but she doesn't say anything.

I scratch the back of my neck, praying for a second of inspiration that'll make her listen.

"Look, this is coming out all mangled. I'm trying to tell you I can stand losing you because we fought. Because you hate me now. Because you think I lied. Fine. What I can't stand is knowing I lost you 'cause I couldn't stop them from hurting you."

She stops short, looking at me with her eyes so dark, her expression unreadable.

I don't see anger anymore.

There's something I don't understand written on her face.

Something lost, full of so much hurt, and I don't think it's all because of me.

"I know what I'm doing," she struggles out. "And I don't need you to come rushing to my rescue. I'm not the one who needs saving, Lucas. If you can't figure out what happened to Emma Santos—*I will.*"

What does that mean?

Before I can ask, she leaves me standing there.

I'm too fucking stunned for words, aching to reach out and stop her, chase her down, but knowing I have no right. She'll only hate me more if I try.

Her hair lashes behind her like an angry cat's tail, black and rhythmic, as she walks away with her head held high.

I watch her fade out of sight in a protective swarm of fireflies with a sickness churning in my gut and one question lashing through me over and over.

What the hell is Delilah Clarendon planning? And why do I get the awful feeling those fireflies won't be enough to save her?

XXI: ROSES ARE RED (DELILAH)

*S*omebody remind me again why I ever wanted to work things out with that ginormous asshole in uniform? I'm having trouble remembering.

I glare at myself in the mirror perched on the vanity of my room at The Rookery. I only make myself stop because it's a little hard to put on wing-tip eyeliner when you're giving yourself premature wrinkles.

Ugh.

I try shoving Lucas out of my mind for the hundredth time, just focusing on my makeup and hair and nothing else.

I have no earthly idea how to dress for tonight, let alone how to act for a party full of celebrities, but I should at least make an effort pretending I do.

I finish lining my right eye and stop, studying my reflection in the mirror.

The makeup isn't the problem.

There's something lodged in my throat. That's the only reason it hurts so terribly right now.

Yeah.

Not because for just a second, I saw a horrible coincidence as I stared at my own reflection.

I look like Emma Santos.

My black hair piled up into an intentionally messy chignon just like hers was when I found her.

My skin might be tanned, not naturally dark like hers, but both of us are golden-kissed and slender-boned.

And that bracelet on my wrist...

The one I've been wearing on our last two meetings at the café, so Ulysses will actually think whatever he's trying with me will work and won't question me abruptly agreeing to Montero's invitation to the party.

Don't do this, Delilah.

I can't tell if that voice in my head is mine, some echo of my mother's, or what I imagine Emma sounded like.

For an instant, I swear there's someone behind me, a thin figure with sad eyes.

But when I whip around, searching behind me, searching the room, there's no one.

Apparently, I've gone from imagining ghosts to seeing them.

And Emma Santos is definitely begging me to find out if Montero Arrendell killed her, but not if it means getting myself killed in the process.

God.

I should've told Lucas.

I should've told him what I was planning and brought him on board. But I'd might as well ask for a flying unicorn to ride into the party on.

I've been avoiding him so Ulysses won't get upset, won't get suspicious or feel like Lucas is male competition. If Ulysses gets rattled and jealous enough to drop me, this whole thing falls apart.

It cuts me in half, pretending like I can't even see him, because I never know who might be watching and reporting back to Ulysses.

Or worse, to Montero.

I can't stand the idea that the Arrendell patriarch might

destroy Lucas the way he hurt Celeste, just to get him out of the way.

I also can't stomach sitting around and waiting for that to happen.

So I have to end this *now.*

But when I saw Lucas earlier, for the briefest moment my heart leaped into my throat, this brilliant burst of joy.

How could it leave any doubt in my mind?

I'm definitely in love with Redhaven's messiest, most sarcastic dick in uniform.

Until he had to go and open his mouth.

He came storming over like a raging bull, snarling at me over the bracelet and being the possessive butthead he is. My temper flared and next thing I knew, we were shouting at each other in the street and I was too mad to try to reason with him.

How does he do it?

How is it this man makes me see nothing but red... and somehow I still love him?

I almost enjoy being pissed at him.

But I enjoy the quiet moments where he looks at me like I'm the only thing that matters infinitely more.

That's us.

We fight so furiously it's no wonder we fuck so passionately. And I have a feeling, if this would all go away and we actually had a chance...

We could figure out how to be amazing together to fight our way back from the brink and still care for each other.

It would only make us stronger.

Frowning, my fingers clench the eyeliner stick.

I stare at my phone on the vanity next to my glittery black clutch purse.

I should call him. So we can both apologize and break through our caging pride. So I can tell him what I'm doing—

But I know he'll try to talk me out of it.

He might be right, too, when what I'm about to do would

land me on a Too Stupid to Live Heroines list, if this were a romance novel.

But I *need* to know.

When I talk to Lucas again, I want to give him the proof that he was right all along.

Proof that he can get justice for his sister.

Proof that I can get justice for Emma.

I will my fingers to stop shaking, finish my eyes, and touch up my lips. Just as I'm finishing up the last accents on my deep, smoky red eyeshadow and making sure my foundation blends into my hairline, there's a polite knock at the door.

I smile.

Only Janelle Bowden would knock like a guest in her own bed and breakfast.

"It's open!" I call, tucking my makeup into the purse in case I need it later.

In the mirror, I see the door creak open.

Janelle peeks in past the crack like she's checking to see if I'm decent before she squeezes in with a rustling black garment bag draped over her arm.

She carries it like it's the most precious thing. Past the bottom, I can just make out a fringe of something shimmery and red inside.

Red dress.

Just like Emma, I think with a cold dread that makes my skin crawl. *Or maybe I'm just cold.*

The summer heat has finally broken and there's a crisp bite of autumn in the air, but that's not the real reason I shrivel up.

"You mean they really sent me a designer dress?" I ask cheerfully.

"I wouldn't make a fuss out of it if they didn't," she says dryly, laying the bag on the bed. "I do believe it's Mrs. Arrendell's. She'll never wear a dress twice, so it'd go to waste if she didn't give them to gorgeous young women who need a little dolling up."

"No, that's not weird," I mutter, mostly to myself. "Invite me to a fancy party in his mother's dress..."

Janelle gives me a shrewd look. "I suppose it would be strange, if this were a date with young Ulysses," she teases knowingly. "*Is* it a date? I see the way he looks at you, hon."

Revulsion hits like a sucker punch.

Just as strong as the rising urge to run out into the night, find Lucas, and throw myself into his arms.

But no.

I could never want someone like Ulysses Arrendell.

He's a pale, dead ember to the fire of Lucas Graves.

I clear my throat, hoping she didn't notice the little falter in my smile.

"I really don't think it's a date, Janelle. More like... I don't know. Schmoozing the new teacher? Honestly, I think Ulysses is just trying to be nice after all the bad things that've happened."

"Oh, yes, he's like that. He's a kind boy behind all his flash." She clucks her tongue and fiddles with the zipper on the garment bag. "Now, let's get you pretty and dressed up. Their butler called and I think he said they'll be sending a car for you in about twenty minutes."

Any response I might've had dries up in my mouth as she unzips the bag and exposes the dress waiting inside.

No matter how weirded out I am, the dress is drop-dead gorgeous. Strapless with a scalloped bodice, a deep shade of crimson.

From chest to hips, the fabric is shirred in a wrap style with subtle gemstones studded throughout. They're as small as glitter chips and so carefully laid they're only visible when they catch the light.

The skirt that flares out from the tight sheath comes in rippling layers, cut so that when I put it on, it'll skim my knees in the front, but sheet down around me in a train that nearly goes to the floor in the back.

I feel too ordinary for a dress like that.

And if I'm going to be beautiful wearing it, Ulysses Arrendell definitely isn't the one I want admiring me.

Another girl in a red dress.

I shiver, curling my arms around myself.

I guess Janelle takes that shiver for awe or nerves because she gives me an indulgent smile. "Let me help you into it, dear. The zipper in the back might be a bit tricky."

"A-ah, yes. Thank you."

I let her coax me out of my towel.

She teases me about my sleek lacy underthings, but I don't really hear her.

I'm prickling with goose bumps as the dress slips over me in silky layers, then zips up tight as a binding cage.

My heart keeps pounding.

For the first time, I'm actually scared.

But when have I ever let fear stop me from doing something bold?

Once she's helped me adjust the fit, Janelle holds me at arm's length with a fond smile.

"There you go," she says. "Pretty as a picture!" She turns me gently toward the mirror. "Have a look."

I don't want to.

For some ungodly reason, I don't want to really see myself in this dress.

Maybe I'm worried I'll see Emma's face staring back at me.

I instinctively balk, but before I have to explain myself, there's a loud honk from downstairs.

Janelle releases my shoulders, glancing at the window. "Oh, I believe your ride is here!"

"I'd better get moving." I offer her a smile and snatch my purse, slipping the phone inside it. "Thanks for the help. You're a dream."

"Of course, Delilah. After everything you've been through, you deserve to be a princess for one night."

Bless her heart.

I mean it.

Only, I don't feel like a princess as I scramble away. More like a soldier marching into combat.

I flash her another smile, then gather up my skirts, slip my feet into my strappy black heels, and dart outside.

I'm expecting a town car waiting at the end of the walk. More likely just a black sedan with blackout windows—I don't know, I have a strange idea of what rich people ride around in.

I'm definitely not expecting the full-blown stretch limousine parked on the curb, complete with a suited driver wearing white gloves. He stands next to the back door, just waiting for me.

Holy shit.

I stumble to a halt.

What's weirder is, I've never seen this man in town at all, and I've been around long enough that I'm starting to recognize people by faces, if not by names.

I wonder if there's a whole village up at that massive manor, house staff who exist solely to make the Arrendells' lives easier with no roots in Redhaven at all.

I'm hesitant as I draw closer to the gate and push it open.

Part of me thinks this can't possibly be meant for a girl like me, growing up and getting passed around like a worn hand-me-down. Now here I am climbing into a limo in a dress that probably costs more than my annual salary.

The man even bows.

"Miss Clarendon," he says, opening the car door for me, leaving no mistake.

I'm almost expecting Ulysses to be inside, but it's empty.

The interior is a plush, deep, velvety grey with seats like butter.

I settle inside, making sure to gather my skirts, and smile at the driver.

He just nods respectfully and shuts the door before rounding to the driver's side.

The last thing I see as the car pulls out is Janelle. She's

standing in the gold-lit open door of The Rookery, waving to me like my very own fairy godmother.

It's a strange feeling, gliding into Redhaven in a limousine.

It's already late, so most people are tucked away at home. But there are enough families still milling around on the sidewalk.

I catch a few quick double takes before the limousine turns onto the winding paved lane that climbs up the hill to the Arrendell house.

From a distance, I knew the house was massive, but up close? It's imposing.

An enormous baroque beast of stone at least five stories tall, all narrow glowing windows and climbing pillars with a cobblestone courtyard.

A fountain centers the circular space, turning it into a roundabout.

Shimmering lights in crystal fixtures illuminate steps at least a hundred feet wide, climbing at least a full flight up to the arched doorway.

As we draw closer, I realize there are a few more limos on the lane ahead of us, and pulling up to those steps—my stomach flips over as I realize I'm looking at the star of the latest big superhero action film.

Her blonde hair glows in the night as her driver helps her out at the foot of the steps before driving her limousine away.

I am so hopelessly out of my depth here.

I watch a few more movie starlets and a couple of well-known tech industry billionaires exit their limousines before it's my turn.

I feel like an insect with this giant house looming over me like a living thing.

Easily crushed.

Effortlessly erased.

My chest caves in, but I gather my courage and look down at the bracelet on my wrist.

Emma, give me courage.

I wrap my fingers around it, pressing it against my skin until the rose gold warms, hot as flesh.

I can do this.

For Emma.

So I put on my best smile as the driver ushers me out of the car, gesturing to the base of those steps.

The night feels warm after being in the limo's cool interior. It heightens the chills running down my spine.

I tell myself it's just the temperature change—not the man who appears at the head of the stairs like he's been waiting for me and counting down the seconds.

Ulysses Arrendell.

For a moment, I think it's Montero.

It's the way they carry themselves, I think, their similar builds. Something equally arrogant and knowing in their body language. The confidence of wealthy men that strides across generations, I guess.

With his face shadowed, it's only the glint of the crystal lights off his blond hair that tells me I'm dealing with the younger one.

I want to shake him.

I want to scream in his face and ask, *how much do you know?*

Are you just as complicit, or are you nothing but your father's patsy?

But the words stick in the back of my throat as he struts down the stairs like the peacock he is, obviously presenting himself for my approval.

He's wearing some strange hybrid tuxedo-suit, precisely tailored to his frame.

Objectively, he looks nice.

I'm just not interested.

"Delilah." He nearly purrs my name as he draws into reach, holding out both hands. "You are a vision tonight. I'm glad as hell you decided to come."

"I thought I could use a stress-free night. A little champagne never hurt a girl," I answer, hoping my reluctance doesn't show as I slip my hands into his. "Thank you again for inviting me."

"You'll have to thank my father. It was his idea. I am *infinitely* grateful to him, though." Jeez. There's something a little too intimate about the way his eyes flash over me, lingering on the bracelet as he clasps my hands, then lets go to offer me his arm. His eyes glitter with warmth. "Come. Let me introduce you to a few movie executives. Just as long as you promise not to let them steal you away from me for their next blockbuster."

I snort, slipping my hand into his arm.

"No actress aspirations here," I say. "That ended when I was sixteen."

I don't mention that I'm planning to put on an Oscar-worthy performance tonight.

It's overwhelming when Ulysses leads me up the stone steps under that towering archway.

The entry hall of the house alone is larger than my entire cottage with its black-and-white patterned marble floors. A black velvet runner rug leads even deeper into the cavernous home.

Everything is all white stone, antique bronze fixtures, expensive odds and ends with naked cherub statues and bronze sculptures and draperies, all strewn around with fresh flowers tucked in every corner.

White. Lilies of the Valley, I think.

Don't those flowers usually mean death?

That's a little on the nose, or else it's just my awful imagination.

Several hallways and staircases snake off from the entryway. Ulysses leads me down a tall, narrow, black-carpeted hall, past several closed doors of weathered oak so ancient it's nearly black.

The entire time he says nothing, but he looks down at me like he can't get his fill.

I struggle not to flinch away.

NICOLE SNOW

I keep my head bowed like I'm just shy. I distract myself from the weirdness, watching the small cluster of people up ahead, only to blink as one man turns his head and I catch his elegant, sloping profile, spectacles, distinctive jaw, and wild hair roughed back in a ponytail tonight.

I actually stumble.

"Is th-that...?"

"In the flesh. He needed a break from the bruising defamation case with his ex-wife. Such a circus," Ulysses answers dryly. "No Oompa-Loompas or pirates with him tonight, I'm afraid. I might be able to introduce you, but he is a tad prickly. He might be kind, or he might keep you all night boasting about his next film project. He's like that."

I can't help laughing. "I'm fine with watching from a distance, thanks. I've seen enough of that drama on Twitter and TikTok."

"Can't blame you. He may be an interesting man, but he is *exhausting.*"

I won't lie.

Even if I'm tense, scared, putting on an act, I'm legit starstruck by the company the Arrendells keep.

By the time the carpeted hallway opens into a grand ballroom with ceilings so high I can barely see them in the shadows, I've seen half the Billboard Top 20, the entire cast of the latest MCU TV franchise, and a quiet, unassuming man in a finely tailored suit who personally owns about ten percent of the world's global worth.

It's so dizzying it's a minor miracle I don't barf.

So is the sheer scale of the ballroom.

The center floor is already swirling with people dancing, black suits and bright dresses making a kaleidoscope of grace.

All around me, people lounge at tables in cozy groups with chaises and divans and other comfortable places to stretch out and perform their art of looking effortlessly beautiful.

I just about choke on my own breath when one of the highest

paid supermodels in the world glides past, glances over me, and gives me a cool but sweet smile.

"Banging dress," she murmurs before she floats by.

"I—" I swallow. "I can't tell if she meant that or not."

"Oh, she did. Her face is just frozen that way, and it's impossible for her to not sound like she's mocking you." Ulysses chuckles. "Don't let it overwhelm you. They're ordinary people behind their status, just like you, I promise."

"The hell they are," I mutter.

Too loud.

That actually makes him laugh. "You are a *delight*, Delilah."

"So," a smooth voice says behind us. "Is this the one you and father won't shut up about then?"

Ulysses' mouth thins.

He rolls his eyes and mouths, *"Brace yourself"* before we turn to face the speaker.

I instantly recognize Xavier Arrendell from Google. He's a carbon copy of Ulysses, but a few years older.

A bit taller and coarser, his hair shorter and his saber-sharp cheekbones undercut by a slightly unkempt blond beard. He looks me over with cool green eyes, his mouth curled cynically.

His navy-blue suit sits on him handsomely, shimmering faintly in the light from the crystal chandelier overhead.

With a sigh, Ulysses says, "If he can bother to mind his manners, Delilah, I'd like to introduce you to my older brother, Xavier."

"I can bother my manners just fine, but can you mind your dalliances?" Xavier says flatly. "You make too many headlines, *brother*."

I sputter, shaking my head quickly.

"We're not together," I say. "I'm the pity invite. The new schoolteacher. I'm not cut out to be part of your world."

Ulysses makes an odd sound that actually sounds a little hurt.

Xavier gives me the strangest look.

His gaze dips down to my hand on Ulysses' arm—the

bracelet on my wrist. There's something bitter and hard in his eyes.

"Is that what you think you are?" he asks.

Eesh.

I don't even know what to make of that. But I don't get a chance to fumble for a reply to that oddly ominous statement when a whirlwind of color comes sweeping into us.

A tall, slim blond man with a long shower of hair and a blinding violet suit wraps his arms around Xavier's neck from behind, resting his chin on Xavier's shoulder.

"Don't be an asshole, Xav," the man—must be Aleksander Arrendell, couldn't be anyone else—says. "Ulysses brought the most darling toy to play with. Be nice." Merry green eyes fix on me, set in a narrow porcelain-like face. "I'm Aleksander, but you can just call me Sandy."

"No one calls you Sandy," Xavier grunts in disgust. "Not even you. Now get the hell off me!"

Ulysses quirks a brow and gives me an almost conspiratorial look. "Now do you see why I spend so much time in town, while they go gallivanting around the world?"

"They're charming," I say dryly. "Really."

But the way they look at me makes me uncomfortable.

Like I really am just a toy.

Catnip, maybe.

And these brothers are very hungry, intimidating cats.

Ulysses exhales. "If they're done staring, Delilah, let's go mingle." As a waiter walks past, he reaches out and snags a champagne flute for me. "Champagne?"

"Please." I take it quickly. "I think I should be drunker for this."

But not too drunk, a little voice screams. *Keep your guard up.*

Xavier snorts at me and mutters a "Nice to meet you," but he's already walking away.

Aleksander lingers, looking at me thoughtfully.

"You're different," he says slowly.

I frown. "Different from...?"

"Oh, never mind," he says quickly, bending at the waist in an exaggerated bow. His silky hair pours over his shoulder. "A pleasure to meet you, Delilah Clarendon. We hope to see more of you."

Ulysses coaxes me away. "Come. I promise I won't let anyone here eat you."

"Not even your brothers?" I joke, following him and pressing my mouth to the rim of my glass—but I don't drink.

God, I wouldn't mind a little something to take the edge off right now, but I can't dull my senses.

The temptation is almost too much, though, as Ulysses whirls me through his social groups.

Five minutes later, I feel more like an accessory than a person, but I'm kind of okay with that when no one seems to expect me to say more than a few friendly words.

I've said 'nice to meet you' more times than I can count after I've met over a dozen people so famous they don't even bother introducing themselves. They just assume I know who they are —and they're right.

It's almost a relief when someone taps me on the shoulder, pulling me and Ulysses away from yet another dizzying introduction to a man who spends his time trolling the internet when he's not launching more rockets than NASA.

But this man needs no introduction.

Montero Arrendell.

The entire time Ulysses spun me through the people mill, I've been scanning around for the patriarch and matriarch of the Arrendell empire, but haven't seen them.

So it's disconcerting to suddenly be looking up into his inscrutable green eyes.

He watches me with a small smile, oozing his Clark Gable charm with his black hair parted and waxed neatly to one side, his slim mustache groomed, his suit impeccable.

"Delilah," he says warmly, reaching for my upper arms.

My skin tries to crawl right off me.

It's insane how hard it is to force a smile.

"May I steal her?" He glances at his son.

Oh God, oh God.

Ulysses looks less than pleased. His gentlemanly smile never wavers, but his mouth goes tight and twitchy.

"Lady's choice," he clips.

Yikes.

I know I'm supposed to refuse right now. I'm supposed to flutter around and say I want to stay with Ulysses, lean on his arm and cling just a little harder.

But this is my chance.

This is my chance to get closer to Montero and see if he gives away anything I can use.

So I flash Ulysses an apologetic smile, then turn a warmer one on Montero as I slip my hand free from Ulysses' arm and step closer to his father.

"I'd love to dance."

"You delight me, young lady." Montero rolls the words with that lyrical accent that smells like old money, offering his arm.

I slip away with a repressed shudder and let Ulysses take my untouched champagne flute.

One last look back at Ulysses now.

I'm playing my part, acting like I'm missing him already—and then it's straight into the devil's arms.

I let Montero lead me through the tangle of flowing, perfectly statuesque bodies and out onto the dance floor.

The crowd parts and a little space clears for us, making us the center of attention as he takes both my hands and guides one to his shoulder, pulling me into a waltz.

Ugh.

I've never waltzed in my life.

But Montero makes it feel so effortless. All I have to do is follow his steps and try not to barf at the nauseating feeling of being in this man's arms.

He's watching me shrewdly tonight.

I wonder what he's looking for, my heart thumping nervously, until he continues as if he'd never left off.

"Like I said, you delight me, Miss Clarendon. But not nearly so much, I think, as you delight my son."

There's a long silence between us, filled only with the music of the live orchestra in their dim corner, the movements of our feet, the sounds of conversation and laughter all around us.

Before I look away pointedly, trying to make myself blush even though it doesn't seem to be cooperating when I feel so cold.

"I don't know what you mean, Mr. Arrendell..."

"I think you do." His fingers tighten on mine. I look up into a gaze burning like a cruel green sun, like he's trying to drag me into his undertow by the sheer force of his personality. "Ulysses is smitten with you. I can't help but wonder how you feel about him."

Sweet Jesus.

There's something so *off* here.

On the surface, he sounds like a man curious about a girl his son might be serious about, just asking probing questions to protect his family.

But there's a different edge to it.

Almost like he thinks I owe him an answer, something *personal.*

Maybe I'm imagining it, but I wonder if this is how a man would sound if the girl he's been stalking and terrorizing was paying attention to anyone but him.

Especially with how his hand rests just above the small of my back, skin to skin where the plunging back of the gown leaves my spine exposed, leaving me feeling slimy everywhere his hand touches.

It's almost possessive.

I don't like it.

I don't like anyone touching me that way but Lucas.

I choke down pure revulsion, searching for an answer that doesn't blow this whole thing.

"Yes, he's been lovely to me ever since I moved here. Always doing his best to take care of me, despite..." I let my voice hitch. "Despite everything, really."

Montero nods gravely and leads me into another turn.

"Ah, yes. I don't blame you, my dear, if you're still upset over such grisly business. You've had quite the run of bad luck. When we spoke before, I meant to convey my condolences regarding the young man who died. You were acquainted, were you not?"

This time I'm not faking the way my breath sucks in.

It hurts.

Yes, Roger was a creep, but he still shouldn't have wound up gutted in a town he didn't even know.

"Yes." I swallow hard. "He was my ex-boyfriend. I didn't—we didn't have anything between us anymore. I broke up with him, but..." Licking my lips, I lower my eyes. "I just wish he hadn't died like that."

And I wish I wasn't in the arms of a possible murderer.

I *know* all signs point to the Jacobins, but that doesn't rule out Montero having a hand in it.

There's something running deeper here, and the bracelet on my wrist feels like the key.

"Shameful. Just as shameful as the fact that the police haven't come close to identifying the perpetrator yet." He *tsks*, his eyes hardening. His grip draws me in closer until our bodies are almost touching. I fight not to cringe away from the crawling heat of his skin. "We'll need to have a talk at the next budget meeting with Chief Bowden, I think. I'm concerned where they're allocating their resources."

Defensiveness snaps inside me and I force it down, keeping my voice neutral. "They're trying. I can't imagine they're used to dealing with anything like this in a town as small as Redhaven, right?"

"This town does have its surprises, but you're correct,"

Montero muses. He looks at me for a long, strange moment, his mouth tightening before it relaxes into an easy smile. "I think I feel eyes burning a hole in the back of my head. Perhaps my son would like to cut in." He spins me around until I see Ulysses, loitering against the wall and watching us with his mouth set in a broody frown. "He doesn't like to share."

Before I can remind him that I'm not Ulysses' to share, Montero bends closer.

Too close.

His breath feels wet and hot near my ear as he whispers, "But I do delight in watching him enjoy himself."

I'm frozen.

Struggling not to *shove* him and give myself away—but he pulls back slowly. His jaw brushes my cheek and he releases me with an almost triumphant smile.

My tongue is ice.

It's so bad I'm actually a little grateful for Ulysses coming to save me. He crosses the dance floor to take my arm.

"I take it your dance is over," he says, giving his father a flinty look. He glances down at me, handing over my champagne. "You look like you need to sit, Delilah. Would you mind if I took a moment to speak with my father while you rest?"

"No, that's fine," I say weakly.

Actually, that's perfect.

Even as the two men walk away with their heads close together, I take quick stock of my surroundings before making a beeline toward a weird flower-covered circular sofa. I picked it for three reasons.

One, there's no one else on it.

Two, it's out of the way, tucked off in a darker corner where no one will notice me.

And three, it's close to a winding staircase of dark, glossy wood that looks like it leads up to the private chambers of the house.

This is my chance.

I settle down on the sofa, pulling myself together for a moment and resting my champagne on the wooden top of the little upholstered pillar in the center.

No way I'm touching it now, especially not after leaving it unattended with a rich weirdo I barely know.

For a few minutes, I watch the glitterati swirling around.

This isn't anywhere I want to be for much longer, anyway.

Glances are turning more heated.

A few people are breaking into spontaneous make-out sessions on the dance floor, a few I even know are married or seeing someone who isn't the person in their arms.

Some of the seating arrangements become petting zoos, hungry hands sliding under skirts and down pants.

This may be a charity gala, but people are definitely here to give away more than their money.

Not my scene.

Not my circus.

I can't see Ulysses or Montero anymore, but I wait a little longer just in case. Ulysses has a bad habit of materializing out of nowhere.

When the crowd shifts enough so they're a barrier between me and the rest of the floor, it's go time.

Gathering my skirts, I dash to the stairs.

I've got to be quick. This red dress makes me a beacon in any normal lighting.

Glancing over my shoulder every other step and trying not to trip, I race upstairs.

No one looks at me. Nobody notices.

They're all drunk on booze and lust.

I don't stop until I'm behind a pillar, flattening myself against the striated marble, breathing hard.

Okay.

Okay.

I look around again, then eye the dark, narrow hall leading

off the small railed walkway circling the ballroom and over-looking the main floor.

Try to be as quiet as possible.

I kick my shoes off and hook two fingers in them. The velvety carpet helps, making my stride stealthier.

With one last glance over my shoulder, I slip into the hall and let the shadows envelop me.

This place is a labyrinth.

I'm not even sure what I'm looking for as I peek into one room after another.

Of course, there are a ton of bathrooms, a music room, a billiards room, a study, and what looks like guest rooms with adjacent servants' quarters.

I'm surprised I haven't bumped into any of the house staff, but I guess they're all too busy taking care of the crowd downstairs.

It's like they have specialized rooms for everything from playing darts to reading. The library is such a dream I actually linger, unable to help being impressed.

All those old books.

Their smell rolls up my nostrils like ancient perfume.

Lucas would love it.

So do they have a special murder room, too? I wonder.

I snort at myself—and nearly choke on it when the next room I peek in, there's the starlet I saw getting out of her limousine when we pulled up.

Only now she's snorting a messy line of cocaine off a very attractive young man with his waiter's uniform open, making a table out of his washboard abs. Stifling a squeak, I jerk back before they see me.

Definitely not my crowd.

I creep past the doorway, but they never notice me. *Thank God.*

After checking a few more rooms, I finally reach the end of the hallway and another stairwell leading up to the next level.

That's where I find it.

Lavish multiroom suites take up entire wings of the building. Some of them are unoccupied, but a few are clearly being used by the family.

If I can find the one belonging to Lucia and Montero—assuming they even share living quarters—I might be able to find something. Emma's phone, something personal of hers that maybe he'd have kept like any serial killer keeping a trophy from his victims.

But I stop as I open one door on a luxurious suite decorated in walnut wood and burgundy velvet.

I know it's Ulysses' room immediately because I recognize some of the fine suits thrown casually over the sitting room furniture.

He's got the most expensive tastes with so many fine collectors' items, including the bits and pieces of women's jewelry scattered on dressers.

On the table of the vanity, against one wall, too.

My throat closes as I step closer. My own washed-out reflection stares back at me with the image of my own sick realization, my horror, on full display.

But I'm not looking at a reflection or at myself.

I'm stuck on a photo tucked in the mirror's corner.

A shot of Emma Santos, but not one from her Instagram.

Because in this one?

She's wearing the same red dress I found her in. It swirls around her, captured mid-spin, just as she's turning to look coyly back at the photographer.

My insides twist in a knot.

Holy shit.

Holy shit.

...it wasn't Montero at all.

It was *Ulysses.*

Ulysses killed Emma Santos.

And if that red dress is any hint, he intends to kill me next.

"I wish you hadn't done that," Ulysses growls behind me with weary impatience, his voice so close it shivers down the back of my neck.

I start to whirl—

But I never get the chance.

Something cold stings the side of my neck, and it's not my heart turning into brittle ice.

I barely catch a flash of soulless, empty tea-green eyes before I collapse, before my legs go numb and drop me down a bottomless abyss.

XXII: BLOOD IS TOO (LUCAS)

J've gotta keep my head in the game.

Tonight's the night.

Come hell or high water, we're going to close in on the Jacobins and get some answers about what happened to Roger Strunk.

We've got our map of the farmstead and a tactical blueprint for storming probable entry points to the still. Took a little bullying from the whole crew for Chief Bowden to cough up their last known location, all while he just sat there mumbling and clipping his damn fingernails.

The chief insisted we didn't need to go this far, just find 'em another way without risking our own necks in a raid.

There are days when I really wonder about that man.

I think he knows lots of shit and just looks the other way because he's that desperate to avoid trouble.

Right now, though, he's absent.

It's just me, Grant, Henri, and Micah bent over our red-marked map in the back of the station, all of us clustered over Grant's desk. The Raleigh team is outside in their SWAT van, waiting for orders.

We have our own desks, by the way. They're just gathering dust because we always congregate here before a ruckus.

Tonight, we're decked out in black like burglars. Mostly tactical gear that's years out of date when we don't get the kind of new, fancy equipment you find in the big cities. No need out here for more than a little basic armor.

Can you imagine us going in like a hostage crisis team over some loose hogs?

Too bad we'll be facing down another different kind of pig real soon.

I need to focus, and I fucking can't.

My brain stays glued to Delilah, Lilah, and more Lilah again.

Every time we see each other, it just short-circuits a little more.

All I ever wanted to do was make it right by her.

I also haven't been able to stop thinking about what she said.

Has she been getting herself in deep with the Arrendells intentionally to dig up info on Emma?

That stubborn-ass woman's gonna get herself killed.

Another pretty dark-haired girl gone missing.

Fuck, I can't stand it.

"Lucas. *Lucas.*" Grant snaps his fingers in front of my face. "You with us?"

"Cap, yeah." I blink, coming back to reality. All the guys are staring, wondering what fucking planet I left my brain on. "Sorry, just mulling over the Santos case."

Grant frowns. "You think we'll find fresh leads on that with the Jacobins? You think they're connected?"

"Maybe," I deflect. "Can't hurt to keep an eye out, can it?"

"Primary target first, but if we catch anything of interest, we definitely won't overlook it," Grant agrees. "Now if—"

Mallory interrupts us suddenly, wheeling her chair back from the dispatch computer and pressing the button to mute the mic on her headset. "Would one of you boys mind talking to Mrs. McLeary? She's real agitated and says she won't hang up until she talks to a 'real cop.'" She rolls her eyes, pursing her lips with an irritable snort.

We exchange questioning glances, and then every eye in the room lands on Henri.

He holds his hands up. "All right, all right, I'll do it. Don't know why that woman always wants to talk to *me*."

"She's got a thing for Cajun accents." Micah smirks.

"She's *eighty*." Henri shoots him a scorned look.

"Not a day past seventy-eight," I throw in mildly. "Still in her prime. Don't be so closed-minded, 'mon ami.' That's age discrimination."

"I hate all of y'all," Henri says, but he snags the desk phone, glancing at Mallory. Mallory nods and taps something on her switchboard, the phone lights up, and Henri lifts it to his ear. "This is Officer Fontenot. What can I do for you, ma'am?"

We sit back and wait.

Henri's part of this crew—not just comic relief—and there's no point in going on with the planning if he's not listening.

His eyes glaze over.

His voice maintains the same pleasant drawl, but we watch him as he closes his eyes and pinches his nose. Then he opens one eye and flips us all off.

"Yes. I'm sorry, ma'am. We'll see what we can do about the noise—yes, ma'am. Yes, it is a travesty, ma'am. Highly indecent. I absolutely agree. Good people should be in bed right now." He makes a choking noise, his eyes widening before he scowls at us all, his face red and mouthing, *I really fucking hate y'all.* "No, ma'am, I've got my own bed to go back to, but thank you very much. You have a good night now."

He drops the phone like he's been burned, glowering. "Next time, one of y'all take it, 'cause fuck that."

"What'd your girlfriend want, Henri?" Micah grins wickedly.

"She ain't my—" Henri sputters, dragging a hand over his face. "Noise complaint. Guess the big house is throwing another charity bash and all the Hollywood weirdos and bigwigs are kicking it up. They're getting damn loud up there, I guess. She wanted us to know it's indecent and rude, and demanded we put a stop to it." He quirks a brow. "So, we gonna put a stop to it or what?"

Grant grimaces. "Any other night we could do a quick drop-in, knock and ask them to keep it down politely, but now's not the best time. They wouldn't listen, anyway. We cite the Arrendells, they'll just laugh it off and take it out on us at the next budget session. So forget it. Mrs. McLeary will wear herself out fuming and fall asleep in the next hour, anyway."

"We've got bigger things to worry about than a little racket," I point out, but I can barely hear my own voice coming out so distant.

Another party.

And Delilah was with Ulysses, wearing that bracelet, wasn't she?

She told me she was going to solve Emma's murder, and I—

Fuck!

I have to find her.

Suddenly, I think I have a pretty good idea what she's planning, and I can't go through it again.

I can't let history repeat itself.

Last time I saw Celeste, we fought like alley cats right before she ran out the door into Montero's devil arms and now it's happening *again.*

"Lucas?" Grant frowns. "You're white as a goddamned sheet. What's going on?"

"Maybe nothing. Maybe everything." I push back from the desk.

My intuition jackhammers like a migraine, and there's pure dread crawling up the back of my neck. "I gotta go check on something real important. I know the plan. If I'm not back in half an hour, I'll meet you there."

Folding his arms over his chest, Grant gives me a long,

measured look. "Now isn't the time for personal business, Graves. I need you with me."

"I will be, I just—" I take a shaky breath. I can't stand to explain this—especially to him, of all people—only to have him tell me I'm crazy and can't get over my shit with my sister, so I just shake my head. "This could be life or death, Cap. Please."

Grant grinds his teeth, considering it, then nods. "Radio if you need backup."

There's something knowing in the way he looks at me.

Something heavy.

Fuck, maybe he understands after all.

There's just no time to explain right now. I only nod sharply and head for the door, stomping out on the sidewalk.

I need to find Delilah *now*.

I need to stop her before she becomes the next lifeless girl in red.

* * *

THE ROOKERY IS silent and dark when I show up—a ten-minute walk from the station, five minutes at my ground-eating run.

Looks like Janelle's already shut down for the night. I try the front door, but no luck.

Dammit.

I circle the building manically, looking for Delilah's room, hoping she's staying in the same suite as before. It's not that hard to remember which one it is when there's a faint pink echo of the X that was sprayed below her window, now pressure-blasted off and waiting to be painted over.

I peer up at the window, but it's as dark as the lobby.

"Delilah?" I call softly—then ask myself what the fuck I'm doing. I've got a phone and her number.

Snorting at my own dumbassery, I reach into my pocket, turning away.

Then I freeze.

There's a presence behind me.

Just the faint scuff of a footstep moving real quiet. So close.

I whirl around, my hands coming up defensively.

Right in time to see Culver Jacobin's broad, toothy grin as a shovel comes slamming at my face.

A big black square of *fuck you* plows into me.

My head explodes with pain, with darkness, with rattling angry stars mocking me.

Too late.

You're too late to save her.

The last thing I remember is stretching out a hand like I'm reaching for Delilah as I keel over and knock the fuck out.

* * *

Let's be real.

I wasn't expecting to wake up again.

Definitely wasn't expecting to wake up seasick and nauseous with my skull ringing like a church bell and my eyes crusted shut with what I'm pretty sure is blood.

I can't see a fucking thing.

Everything hurts.

I don't know if the ground is actually swaying under me or if that's just the concussion screwing up my vision. I think I hear the faint sound of water, maybe smell it, but it's hard to smell anything past the scent of my own blood caked in my nostrils.

Groaning, I scrub at my eyes till I can open them, blinking away ugly red shapes.

When I peer up, there's nothing but the night sky yawning overhead and the distant silhouettes of trees.

Everything looks blurry as hell. I think I need medical attention ASAP because blood loss is a motherfucker. But I manage to sit up slowly, every part of me protesting, my head reeling as I turn around to take in my surroundings.

Big mistake.

I'm immediately clutching at the sides of the little rowboat swaying under me with the movement, struggling not to hurk up my lunch into Still Lake.

What the fuck?

I'm out in the middle of the lake in the same damn rowboat I'd been in with Delilah on our date.

Only this time I'm alone.

There are no oars stowed in the oar locks, either. I feel around clumsily and bend over to look, making myself dizzy all over again.

I think I get what was supposed to happen here.

Culver Jacobin knocked me out, threw me in this boat, and pushed me out onto the lake to bleed to death long before anyone would find me.

Guess it's a good thing I'm too stubborn to die.

This is not how I wanted to find out I'm right, that he's the asshole who killed Roger Strunk. Can't think of any other reason why he'd do this, except he realized we were hot on his trail.

What scares me is that he found me at The Rookery.

He was probably already there looking for Delilah.

Obsessive stalker types get real crazy when they're cornered.

Some of the more extreme cases in criminal history have killed the object of their obsession because they felt like they were about to lose them, so murdering their prey becomes the only way to keep them according to their warped logic—and to make sure no one else could ever have them after the perp gets caught.

I bet the plan was to get to Delilah before we could stop him, but he tripped over me in the process. Which means—

Fuck.

Fear socks me so powerfully it's like a fist of pure grief.

Almost like mourning somebody before I even know she's gone.

I dig at my pockets and—motherfucker, my phone's not there.

That bastard took it.

With my luck, he probably threw it in the lake, and now it's sitting useless at the bottom.

I'm well and truly fucked until someone finds me.

If I try to swim out of here in my current condition, I'm definitely going to drown. Swimming and concussions pair with massive blood loss about like red wine pairs with pork rinds.

Maybe I can use my hands to paddle.

It'll be slow as hell, but better than nothing. Adrenaline gives me urgency and—

—and some kind of God must be with me tonight because I see *lights* through the trees.

Then I hear laughter, young and rowdy.

Shit.

There's someone out there on the lakeshore, and they're coming closer.

Straining toward those sweeps of light, I watch several high school kids come tearing through the trees by the pier, carrying coolers and zigzagging their way along, using their phones for flashlights.

They should all be at home in bed, but hell, when I was their age I snuck out to drink at the lake and raise hell, too.

I lean toward them, raise my arms, shouting as loud as I can, even if it makes my head ring.

"Hey! Hey!" I call, and they freeze, staring. "Little help out here?"

XXIII: RED AS SIN (DELILAH)

kay.

So.

Maybe I deserve my spot on the Too Stupid To Live Heroine List because I'm still not sure why I'm surprised I wound up in the situation I'm in now.

I threw myself in the thick of it like a *dumbass*, thinking I'm going to be all kick-ass Nancy Drew and solve a murder my stupid cop boyfriend couldn't even handle.

Right.

More like I'm about to be the latest Redhaven case file.

That's my first thought as I come to slowly.

My limbs and brain feel sluggish, and I think I smell—*is that animal flesh?*—manure, meat, blood.

Strong blood.

Fresh and potent, but it's mixed with another smell, too.

A strange one, something like... hot metal?

My arms hurt like hell. I don't even need to open my eyes to know I'm dangling from them, the full force of my weight pulling me down, making my shoulders burn.

Ugh. He injected me, didn't he?

And what did Ulysses poison me with?

376

Ulysses.

It was him all along.

Right under my nose, but I couldn't see it.

Like Lucas, I was hung up on the notion that whoever killed Celeste Graves also killed Emma Santos, and that couldn't have been Ulysses when he'd have been about twelve or thirteen at the time of Celeste's disappearance.

Maybe it's a *like father, like son* situation.

I don't know.

My head is spinning.

All I know is I need to figure out what the hell's going on and get out of here ASAP.

I carefully pry one eye open, trying to assess my surroundings without giving myself away.

I don't know how I avoid screaming bloody murder when I realize I'm surrounded by carcasses. Red meat and marbled white fat lines the walls surrounding me.

My eyes pinch shut again. I hold my breath until my heart calms, then slowly pry my eyes open again for a braver look.

Yep.

Pig carcasses.

I'm in some kind of shed with a dirt floor. Something that looks hastily constructed except for the sturdy wooden support beams with chains embedded in them, and hooks dangling from those chains—and *I'm* dangling from one of those hooks, I realize.

Whatever has my wrists tied, it's caught on the hook. The rest are embedded in the pigs that were slaughtered and left in various stages of butchering for market.

All around the walls of the shed are wood and metal worktables cluttered with tools.

Not just things for meat processing, but what looks like machining and electrical tools, too.

I see him bent over a stool, working at something that shoots up bright sparks.

377

Culver Jacobin?

...I am so confused right now.

If Ulysses was the one stalking and threatening me, the one who killed Roger, then why am I tied up in a shed with weirdo hillbilly Culver Jacobin right now?

Culver straightens, studying his handiwork. That's when I get a glimpse of what he's been working on.

The bracelet.

Holy hell.

Its weight is missing from my wrist, and he's etched another delicate X in it with the red-hot engraving pen in his hand.

The eighth X.

For me.

Cross my heart and hope to die.

Okay.

We can figure out the what's what and who's who later.

For now, I have to operate on the assumption that *someone* wants me dead, and I don't want to die.

So I need to focus less on the *who* and more on the *how* I'm getting out of here.

When Culver stands, dusting off bits of metal powder from his overalls and turning toward me, I slam my eyes closed and pretend to be out again.

Not fast enough.

He lets out a long, hooting whistle and the most awkward laugh I've ever heard. "Soo-wee, the little piggy's gone and woken herself up, huh?"

Fuck.

No point in faking now.

If I try to play dead, he'll probably touch me, maybe slap me around a little, anything to get a reaction.

So I open my eyes, staring at him with raw hatred and disgust flaring inside me.

"It was you," I bite off. "You killed Roger. And now you want me dead, too?"

Culver blinks at me like I just mouthed off in Russian—then guffaws, slapping his thigh. "Oh, nah, missus. I may be a man of many trades, but *that* ain't my talent." He grins wide, a nasty sneer full of blocky teeth. "I stick to pigs. It's the boss who likes the ladies. Me, I just wipe up what's left. You just sit tight now, lady. I been working up these pigs, but your turn's coming real soon."

Pigs?

What the hell is he talking about?

I just stare at him as he turns away from me with a satisfied little snicker.

That's when I hear the *crunch* of loose earth underneath him. It looks like it's been spread around, almost like mulch to absorb the blood from the slaughter.

But it's not just dirt.

That's where the manure smell is coming from.

My eyes focus on the little white chips spread around, like small things that weren't quite fully digested.

I swallow a cactus lodged in my throat as I realize that's bone.

Oh, God.

I read somewhere that hungry pigs will eat just about anything.

And more than once, rural murderers have used them to dispose of dead bodies. Once the pigs get ahold of them, there won't be anything left but bone fragments.

The boss?

My entire body ices over with a fever of fear and horror sinking in.

Ulysses Arrendell is going to murder me for sport.

Then Culver will feed my body to the hogs, and leave nothing behind but that cursed bracelet, waiting for another girl to become a mark on Ulysses' belt.

Lucas, I'm sorry.

All I can see are his sad, angry green eyes skimming over a

case file. About all that's left of me, if they ever find any evidence at all.

Lucas was right about everything.

I came looking for answers.

Trouble found me instead, and now I'll never get to tell him that all I really wanted was for him to hold me one more time.

XXIV: RED WITH GUILT (LUCAS)

*T*here's almost nothing more humiliating than getting towed to shore in a rowboat by your friends with a rope looped between a little borrowed speedboat and your pitiful goddamned chariot.

Nah.

What makes it even more humiliating is the crowd, drawn by the ambulance lights after the kids I flagged down called 911 and told Mallory there was some idiot cop stranded in a boat and bleeding to death.

Now it feels like half the town has come out to rubberneck while Grant, Henri, and Micah force me to sit still in the back of the ambulance. One of our local EMTs checks my head wound and pumps me full of some shit to keep my brain from swelling.

At least I'm out of the townsfolk's sight inside the ambulance, but it's not helping how I feel right now.

I clutch the space blanket the EMT threw around my shoulders and glare at my team—and Chief Bowden, hovering just past the ambulance doors.

"I'm fucking telling you," I snarl. "Culver Jacobin smacked me with a shovel. He's the psycho shit who's been stalking Delilah."

Chief Bowden snorts.

"Culver Jacobin? You think he got the wits for that?" he says, gesturing toward the teenagers clustered on the edge of the crowd and gabbing away. "Do those kids have beer? Shouldn't we—"

"Fuck the beer," I spit through my teeth. "They saved my ass, Chief. Let 'em have a can or two of their daddy's lager. Listen to me, where are the Jacobins *now?* We have to find Culver. We have to find Delilah before—"

"Aw, you don't have to worry about her," Bowden says. "Janelle got her all prettied up and sent up to the big house for that party tonight. She's safe. That place is a fortress. Nobody's gonna get to her there."

Like hell.

That's called walking right into the lion's den.

"Graves, listen," Grant cuts in. "You're in no condition to—"

"I'm fine, Cap. I *will* be fucking fine." I bat the EMT away as she tries to slap a cold compress over my eye. "Quit worrying about me. We've got to do the raid, Captain, and we've got to do it tonight—but we might need to adjust the plan first."

"Go on," Grant says skeptically.

"We find Delilah first," I growl. "Then we split up. Considering Emma Santos' body was found at Delilah's house, that's a possible kill site if this is a fetishistic, ritual thing. One of us takes the house; one of us takes the main Jacobin farm; one of us goes up to the Arrendell house and checks for her there—and one of us finds the still. Keep the Raleigh crew on standby and call them in for backup, wherever we find her." I stare hard at Chief Bowden, who's suddenly avoiding my eyes. "By the way, that'll go a hell of a lot faster if somebody opens his trap and stops pretending he doesn't know *where it is.*"

Chief Bowden gives me a sour look. "I knew where it *was.* That was two weeks ago, and they don't tell me when they move. I just get real good at tracking them down. I haven't found 'em since. You can point fingers all you damn well want, Graves, but I got nothing and I'm not holding a thing back."

"Goddammit, Chief, you—"

I'm half a breath away from launching myself right at his frog-like throat—but Henri jabs a hand against my chest. That Cajun offers me a reassuring smile, though there's worry building in his eyes like a summer storm.

"I got a better idea, mon ami," he says. "You told us Culver took your phone, right?"

I nod—then wince, and this time I let the EMT press the cold pack to my throbbing skull. "Yeah. He might still have it on him if he didn't chuck it in the lake. I don't know."

"Then it won't be hard to find him at all." Henri grins and holds up his own phone. "'Cause I got you and the whole squad on GPS."

* * *

Yep.

Right now, I'm thinking I owe that Louisiana boy a year's worth of beer.

I hadn't thought much of it months ago, when Henri suggested we install a new app that lets us share our location with approved contacts via GPS, voluntarily allowing nonstop tracking.

It made it a hell of a lot faster to find our crew when responding to emergencies.

Now, that little trick might just help save Delilah.

Took a little work to convince Grant I could handle the mission after a blow to the head—but once he realized he'd have to throw me into the drunk tank and hide the key to stop me, he reluctantly gave his blessing.

He's off to the big house while Micah checks Delilah's place, and Henri's on his way out to the main farm.

Which leaves me, creeping silently through the woods with the GPS on Mallory's borrowed phone leading me to the coordinates where my phone last pinged a cell tower. It's still active, too, meaning it wasn't ever at the bottom of the lake.

North of town.

High in the hills.

Fuck, I'm so high on whatever the medics gave me I can't even feel the pain in my skull.

My sight's almost too clear as it catches a little starlight, too bright.

All the fine details grab my attention as I prowl through the darkness, my ears prickling for any signs I might've been spotted or heard.

There!

My heart drums harder as I catch a glimpse of light through the dense trees.

I drop down low, holding my breath as I inch closer, careful not to even let a twig snap under my feet.

Slowly, slowly, I stay hunkered down behind some low brush to take in the situation.

It's the still, all right.

A bunch of big metal tanks as large as small swimming pools, covered with tarps, but more than that, too.

They've got sheds. The kind you can take apart in minutes and flat-pack into the back of a truck.

There's also a hastily erected pen full of—pigs?

Yeah, I'm fucking confused till I remember a lot of brewers use manure to make moonshine. Something about the microbes helping cultivate the yeast.

So I guess they keep a segment of their pig stock at the still, whatever it takes to have a ready supply of fresh shit.

If they really need some more, there's plenty flowing down on the rest of us from the house up on the hill.

But what really gets me is the car parked on the narrow

beaten path through the trees opposite me, a path that says this site has been used many times before.

I know that car.

And I know what it means as I watch Ulysses Arrendell pull the door open to the only lit shed and step inside.

All this time, we've been spinning in circles because we've been looking for *one* guilty fuck.

Not two, working in tandem to throw us off the trail.

I can barely hold still, vibrating with pure rage, waiting till Ulysses moves inside so he won't spot me.

Then I dive toward the shed, keeping to the shadows and holding my breath, praying with everything in me that I'll still find her alive.

When I flatten myself against one side of the screened-in window and peer around the edge, listening to the voices floating through the mesh, my heart sinks.

Sure enough, there she is.

They've strung my girl up from a hook, surrounded by carcasses. Her feet dangle over the floor and a red dress sheaths her frame.

Culver hangs back like the gangly freak he is, watching with a mindless grin while Ulysses paces in front of her.

He's holding a massive cleaver in one hand.

I feel fucking sick as I watch him smack the blunt side of it against his palm again and again, smiling coldly enough to flash freeze hell.

"You must understand, Delilah," he purrs. "I do this out of love."

Rather than shrinking away from him in fear, Delilah's all spitfire, her blue eyes spinning wild and snapping as she snarls, "You don't love me. You're *sick*."

"But I do!" he insists, reaching up to stroke the edge of the blade down her cheek.

She tenses, jerking away.

The only thing that stops me from charging in like a bull is knowing he'll open her up right in front of me before I make it two steps.

Volcanic fury boils inside me as he continues, "The moment you sent in your application, I had to have you. Such pretty photos all over your social media. It's like you were *inviting* me, with those eyes full of such delicious anger." He smirks. "I knew the first time I saw you that you were waiting for me. This delicacy, begging to ripen, to grow rich and full with my love so that when you burst, you'll be the sweetest I've ever tasted on the very first bite."

Delilah's eyes widen with horror. "You—you can't kill me. You *can't*. People will come. They'll look for me..."

"People will believe the note found in your house," Ulysses says smugly. "You simply couldn't take the stress of Redhaven anymore, and you ran away. A tale as old as time. You were afraid of someone stalking you, so you decided to disappear, start a new life somewhere else, where you don't want anyone to find you. It's almost too easy. Your idiot ex gave me the perfect alibi. Perfect chaos." He practically pouts, inhaling sharply like he's getting hard and high off her fear. "I would've liked to let you ripen a little longer, though. But you had to go and be nosy, didn't you?" He shakes his head slowly. "Really, Delilah. Calling that Santos woman from the school phone? Don't you *know* we pay the bills and see all call records?"

There's a moment of silent dread.

My headache amps up to a droning pain. Hell of a time for those painkillers to fade.

"There's something seriously wrong with you," she whispers. "You're saying you posted that job ad just to lure a potential victim? Like this whole thing has been one big mind game to fuck with me. To enjoy frightening me. Is that why you left Emma's body at my house? To screw with *me?*"

"Emma," Ulysses says tightly, "was a mistake. And not *mine.*"

He doesn't look at Culver, but Culver cringes back anyway.

I see it now.

The shape Delilah saw running away from the house on her first day in town.

That was Culver goddamned Jacobin, sent to dispose of Emma's body after Ulysses killed her in Delilah's house.

Only, he was a day late and a dollar short, and he ran off—leaving the body behind—when Delilah pulled up to the house too soon.

I've got to get in there.

I've got to put a stop to this and save my Lilah.

It's two against one and I like those odds.

Even if I'm hopped up on enough meds that I could get run over by a tank and not feel it, and I'm not firing on all cylinders, I have to try.

There's no time to wait for backup.

I snag Mallory's phone anyway, punching in a quick message to the crew, hit Send, start to take stock of the interior, anything I can use for a tactical advantage.

Think, man.

Think.

But those shitty words keep coming, floating over me in waves of terrible memories.

"You're just like your father," Delilah spits. "You even like the same kind of girls."

Ulysses lifts his snotty blond brows. "And what kind of girl do you think my father killed?"

"Celeste Graves, for one." She glowers at him so fiercely I half expect her to go right for his throat with her teeth. "Your dad killed her, and now you're taking up his tradition."

Ulysses goes still.

His face turns into an eerie, wide-eyed mask, his pupils shrinking to pinpricks.

My heart leaps up my throat as he leans into her, halting the knife just under the tip of her nose.

"Shut up, cunt. I'll *not* have someone else take credit for my work," he breathes in an eerily empty voice. "Especially not my *first.*"

His first?

His fucking *first?*

I reel back like I'm shot, my entire body pulsing with a heart attack of shock.

My sister was his first murder and he's outright admitting it.

Before I can even try to process that, Delilah echoes the rabbit-thoughts circling in my brain. She stares at him, the color draining from her face.

"Your f-first? How? You would've been like *twelve—*"

"Don't you know?" He leans back from her with that crazed look still growing in his eyes. "The age for my rite of passage. She was the first strawberry I ever tasted, and my beautiful Celeste was *delicious.*"

"Jesus. Fuck." Delilah makes a sickly angry sound. "What is *wrong* with you? Why do you..."

"Delilah, Delilah," he says, swaying the knife under her chin, "don't you know that being rich and respected is terribly boring? A man must create his own thrills to escape so much responsibility. Luckily, I found mine early—and I wouldn't part with them for anything."

That's it.

He's a fucking dead man walking.

I never hear how Delilah responds through the raw indignation exploding up my spine.

Blood roars in my ears like a waterfall.

Ulysses Arrendell killed my sister.

Because he was *bored.*

"Now." Ulysses growls again, raising the knife and aiming it at Delilah's sternum. "Enough idle talk. I've worked up a terrible thirst keeping you entertained."

Any thought of caution, of control, of common sense disappears, burned to ash in the inferno of my rage, my grief, my need to end this before the monster-fuck in front of me kills again.

Before he kills her.

I only know one thing—no cleaver can hurt more than the truth tonight.

Before I waste another second thinking about what I'm doing, I hurl myself through the flimsy aluminum wall of the shed and fling myself into Ulysses Arrendell's teeth.

XXV: IN THE RED (DELILAH)

*S*o, this is how I die.

I'm still turning over the risk factors in trying to *headbutt* Ulysses Arrendell without impaling my throat on that knife and whether or not I can bounce hard enough to knock the chains around my wrists free, unlooping them from the hook.

I'm definitely not expecting the entire wall of the shed to start caving in.

It collapses like a car crash in a movie, but instead of a car it's—

"Lucas?!" I gasp.

The man becomes a giant blur before I can even blink.

He tackles Ulysses like he's going for a touchdown, hurling the creep flat on his back.

I stare, hope and shock and confusion thrashing around inside me in this tangled mess.

Ulysses hits the ground hard, grunting and swearing under Lucas' weight.

Holy hell.

I've never seen Lucas so furious.

In this moment, he's not human, but this creature of thorns and naked outrage.

His eyes flash like green lightning as his fist plows into Ulysses' wrist and sends the cleaver flying across the dirty floor.

I have one blurry second of sick realization—*oh God, Celeste Graves' bones are probably mulched in the dirt*—before I realize Culver's moving.

He tries to climb over Lucas as they tumble around at my feet, tearing at each other like rabid wolverines.

Ulysses is sharp and quick and agile. His thinner frame helps him dodge Lucas as his fist crashes down again and again like a sledgehammer.

"Oh, no, you don't!" I hiss.

My arms may be bound, but my legs aren't.

Hoisting myself up by the waist, I clench my inner core and lift my legs, snapping them around Culver's neck, dragging him backward.

I so wish I'd done more Kegel exercises.

It's like trying to ride a bucking bronco as Culver howls, grappling at my legs and trying to force them open with brute strength.

Crossing my ankles, I squeeze like I'm smashing a pumpkin, crushing my thighs against his neck, trying like mad to push down on his windpipe in just the right place.

Come. On.

Definitely awkward.

But I'm glad he's facing away from me and not getting a mouthful of—you know.

I'd never live this down.

But he's stumbling around now, straining for air, snarling and flinging me around everywhere.

I feel like a fish writhing on a hook.

My body flops and stretches painfully, but I just keep squeezing my thighs, doing my best to hold on until he's out cold, gritting my teeth until they hurt.

I've only seen this in the movies. Does it even work in real life?

When it happens, I'm not expecting it to be so sudden.

Culver lets out this weird garbled wet noise and staggers away from me like a dog trying to break its leash, stretching me almost horizontal.

The pressure on my knees threatens to break their death grip.

Then Ulysses bucks Lucas off him, sending Lucas stumbling into Culver.

His weight throws Culver back toward me.

My calves crush tighter, and I pray to every muscle I've developed on my daily runs that I can just knock him out before it's too late.

But then Ulysses surges to his feet and charges at Lucas.

Shrieking like mad, I act without thinking.

I use my viselike grip on Culver to push his unsteady bulk, swinging my hips with just enough force to toss him at Ulysses.

Over two hundred pounds of gangly, oxygen-deprived hillbilly goes flying into his boss.

Their skulls knock together like coconuts, heads rocking back on their necks like Pez dispensers.

Fighting for survival isn't supposed to turn into slapstick comedy.

I'd be laughing like crazy if it wasn't our lives on the line.

Lucas pauses for a breathless moment, glancing at me.

"Thanks, New York," he rattles out.

"Behind you!" I cry.

He swings around just in time to duck as a very pissed off, very bewildered Ulysses swings a wild roundhouse kick at him.

From his crouch, Lucas plows right into Ulysses' midsection and steamrolls him across the room.

It's marvelous to watch, this freight train of a man barreling along while Ulysses bangs his fists helplessly on Lucas' head and shoulders.

I've still got Culver flopping around against me like a stranded fish, but he's weaker now, making these harsh gagging sounds.

And if I twist just right—*there!*

I think I'm about to dislocate my freaking shin, but I've got my knee against his trachea.

The adrenaline rush gives me the strength I need as I *push*—only to almost lose my grip at another loud crash from across the room.

I jerk my head up, spitting a tuft of my own hair out of my mouth.

Just in time to see Lucas slam Ulysses into a worktable.

"You filthy, unworthy *cur*—" Ulysses grinds out.

It's all he gets.

Because Lucas grabs him by his messy hair and smashes his head down on the metal so hard there's a bright burst of blood from his temple.

Ulysses' eyes roll back, blinking in disbelief.

Then he slumps down, unconscious, his body pouring limply onto the floor.

Lucas straightens, fierce and strong in his black tactical gear, legs braced, staring down at Ulysses with raw vengeance in his eyes, his chest heaving.

God, he's too gorgeous for life.

The kind of dark knight you only see in fairy tales.

My hero.

My protector.

My broken beast.

My everything, even when I didn't know I needed anything like him.

He's also got two good working hands and I don't.

"A little help here?" I call out, even as Culver straightens up and makes another clumsy lunge away from me.

Ow. My hips are going to be aching for a week.

"Huh?" Lucas' head jerks up, his dazed eyes clearing.

He stares for a second before he strides across the room.

After Ulysses, it's just cleanup.

One more powerful backhand puts Culver out like a light.

His head slips down like a jack-in-the-box slinking back into its hole.

Gasping, I let my legs drop, just dangling as exhaustion crashes over me.

Holy hell... thank God."

"Sorry it took so long, Lilah," Lucas says sheepishly. He reaches for me, his hands skimming up my arms toward the chains. Even as sore and exhausted and frazzled as I am with the rush of fear and adrenaline, it feels so undeniably *good* to have him touch me again. "Let me get you down before you—"

The sudden sound of a shotgun jacking cuts him off mid-sentence.

Multiple shotguns jacking.

Oh, God.

We both freeze before Lucas pulls me against him, gathering me protectively against his body as he positions himself between me and a new threat we don't have a prayer against.

About a dozen hard, grimy bearded men in overalls surround us, pouring in through the broken wall of the shed and the open door.

They're aiming their guns right at us, all headed by that creepy scarecrow, Ephraim Jacobin.

No one says anything.

Eerie silence stretches on.

"Don't even think about it," Lucas warns in a feral growl, his body hard and battle-ready against mine. "This is official police business. We've got your boy dead to rights on attempted murder, Ephraim. Drop your guns."

There's a breathless moment where multiple sets of fingers hover over triggers.

Eyes narrow, sighting down the lengths of barrels, ready to end us both in a thunder of death we won't even hear. Bullets travel faster than sound.

I'm almost too tired, too sick, too sad to be afraid.

I've almost died so many times tonight that if they're going to shoot me, whatever.

We tried.

Still, that silence is far more unnerving than any threats.

Until a new sound splits the night, this wailing like a hundred angry ghosts.

Sirens.

Loud. Shrill. Fast approaching.

Enough of them to know there's some major cavalry riding up on the hillfolk.

There's a frozen moment as every head in the room snaps up.

Right before the Jacobins abruptly vanish.

I wouldn't believe it if I wasn't seeing it with my own eyes.

One minute they're standing there, menacing as ever.

The next, they just melt away into the shadows like grizzled ninjas.

No.

More like cockroaches, scurrying off at the first hint of light.

Lucas slumps against me, then catches my chin in his fingers, tipping my face up to his so gently.

His lips brush mine.

I moan, whimpering the hot relief that rushes through me, the last of my energy collapsing, leaving me limper than a worn dishrag.

"Hey. *Hey,*" he whispers with a weary smile and a new shine in his warm, spring-green eyes. "You okay, Miss Lilah?"

"Best I've ever been. Who knew I just needed a fight and a bunch of guns in my face?" I joke, then jerk my arms, rattling the chains. "Now, if you could get me down from here..."

* * *

FOR ABOUT FIVE SECONDS, I almost murdered Lucas Graves myself.

If only because that sarcastic, sweet, overprotective, dumbass man thought it was *funny* to make jokes about how kinky this could be before he unhitched me from the meat hook and put me down on my own two feet—only to catch me as my legs collapsed under me.

Whatever strength my survival instinct gave me disappeared.

And now, as I sit on a padded examining table at Redhaven's tiny medical center, I realize I've likely still got some kind of sedative swirling in my veins.

I'm so ready to pass out.

It's been the longest night of my life and now it's just a blur.

Telling Lucas what happened, hearing his side, then repeating it all for Captain Faircross while he jotted down notes and asked questions that helped us piece everything together.

The nurses fussed over us the whole time and gave Lucas a well-deserved reaming when apparently he'd already taken a head wound from Culver Jacobin while he was out looking for me tonight.

Shit.

See, I should've choked him *harder*.

Kegels.

Next time, I'll snap his flipping neck.

At least it's finally quiet, though.

Neither of us can go home yet when we're waiting for the toxicology report to find out if I was injected with anything worth worrying about. As soon as they have an ambulance ready, they say they're dragging Lucas off to Raleigh for immediate head X-rays at a larger hospital just to make sure he doesn't have a skull fracture.

I know he doesn't.

He's more hardheaded than a cantaloupe.

Of course, if he hadn't been as stubborn as a bull to come after me, I wouldn't be alive right now.

I keep thinking that over as we sit in the exam room, waiting for the nurse to give us the all clear.

I'm definitely going to the hospital with him.

I haven't been able to let go of him except when the nurses forced us apart for exams, and right now we lean against each other, our hands twined and resting where our thighs press together, his thumb stroking over the lower edge of the bandages on my wrist.

We're both a total mess.

Filthy, torn-up, bandaged, bruised, and we badly need showers.

Yet somehow, I've never been more content in my life.

"Missed you, jerk," I whisper. I've got to be honest. I've got to tell him how I feel, put the thorns away when I know I almost lost my chance to talk to him forever. "These days haven't been right without you. I don't know how everything went so wrong—"

He touches his fingers to my lips. "They went off the rails because we're both big headed and stubborn as hell, darlin'. Convinced our way's the only way. We blow into everything temper first. You know what that means?" He chuckles. "We're too much alike, Lilah, and I like it that way. Means nothing will ever get boring."

I smile until I break.

"Honestly... after tonight, after the last few weeks, I could use a little boring." I tilt my head to his shoulder, looking up at him. "But I don't think I could ever get bored with you."

"So are we back together or what?" he asks with a hopeful look.

I laugh, rubbing my cheek on his shoulder.

"We weren't really broken up before, dude. I was just waiting for you to wake up and grovel."

"Ah, hell. I'll remember that for next time. This a New York ritual you never told me about?"

"*Don't* you start with that New York crap again." I poke his ribs, then wince when he cringes, letting out a pained hiss. "Oops. Sorry!"

"Damn. Think maybe they need to X-ray more than my head."

"My bad," I mumble, snuggling in closer to his side. "You really took a beating tonight—and it's all my fault."

"Woman, it was worth it, and it wasn't your fault. The real assholes responsible will be waking up in handcuffs very soon." He rubs his stubble-darkened cheek to my hair. "Fuck, Lilah. I finally *know*. I finally know the truth—and I got to knock that fucker out for killing her."

"Closure," I murmur with a nod. "For Emma and for Celeste."

"For me." Lucas exhales heavily. "Thank you. I'd never have found it if you hadn't been the most reckless dumbass girl on the planet. Still can't say I approve, but I'm grateful as hell."

I only smile again.

I'll kill him for calling me a dumbass later.

He gets *one* free pass tonight for saving my life. I'm not a total bitch, right?

Quietly, I bring my other hand over to cover our clasped fingers, holding on so tight.

That comfortable silence is back between us again, that thing that always tells us we *fit* so easily. So perfectly.

And it's all right to be together without saying a word.

I'm so close to dozing off on his broad shoulder, but I remember the nurses warned us to stay awake, considering our conditions.

It's a challenge.

In here, there's nothing but the faint sounds of equipment moving, people talking outside, the night wind, soft crickets outside the windows.

"Delilah?" Lucas whispers.

"Mmph?" I murmur, stirring against him to stay awake.

"Fuck, I'm just gonna say it. I love you," he rumbles, his voice heavy with such heartfelt emotion.

My heart does the sweetest somersault as I turn my head to nuzzle his throat, feeling his pulse. It's racing just as fast as mine.

"You do? Brave man," I whisper back, tilting my head up to find his lips for a kiss. "I guess it's a good thing I love you back."

XXVI: TIE A RED RIBBON ON IT
(LUCAS)

*D*elilah Clarendon loves me.

Days later, I still can't get over it.

And those are busy damn days as we wrap this thing up and bring some peace and normalcy back to Redhaven.

Days of pouring over the reports Grant wrote, making sure the information's accurate right down to the last dotted i.

Days of writing up my own reports, reopening my sister's case file, creating brand-new evidence files linking the murders of Celeste Graves and Emma Santos to Ulysses Arrendell and Culver Jacobin. Plus, several other missing persons over the past twenty years.

They're all poor dark-haired girls with sad eyes whose disappearances bear investigating when those Xs on that bracelet say there's at least six more trophies on Ulysses' hellish kill list.

Fuck, we haven't made any headway on the Ethan Sanderson case, either.

There's a new energy to Captain Faircross these days, a new focus I haven't seen now that he has a lead on his best friend. I hope like hell that sooner or later, he can get a little closure, too.

We can guess what really happened, even if Ethan's body

hasn't turned up yet. I'd bet my bottom dollar the poor boy got mixed up in some dirty business with Ulysses Arrendell.

Of course, the interviews are a disappointing dead end.

The Arrendells are all horrified and disgusted by their son, but everyone from Montero to the brothers swears they had no inkling that their precious Ulysses was a serial killer.

They work their press people to the bone, sending out appropriate public condemnations and sincerest apologies to the media.

I'm thinking it'll hurt their business in the circles they move in.

Still not enough.

I don't believe a word of what they say either, but there's no fucking evidence to poach the rest of the family, hiding behind the best A-list lawyers and PR people big money buys.

I swear they're coaching Ephraim Jacobin to stay out of hot water, too. The old man swore the same 'I know nothing' line about his son, Culver, insisting he only came in guns blazing because he thought trespassers were attacking his property.

Fuck everything about that.

As young as Culver is, someone else *had* to be behind the people-eating pigs before he took up the gruesome business. A kid couldn't wrangle a herd of monster hogs all by himself.

The only thing that keeps me sane and probably prevents a heart attack from rage is one hard fact I can cling to.

Both Ulysses Arrendell and Culver Jacobin are rotting away in a Raleigh prison, awaiting arraignment and then trial.

Culver even flipped and spilled his guts in interrogation—feeding the girls to the pigs, helping Ulysses with his sick games, engraving that bracelet that was passed from one victim to the next, carving open Roger Strunk's body after Ulysses killed him with a drug overdose they snuck him at a bar—and then pinning it all on Ulysses.

Culver swears he'll cough up descriptions of more girls in exchange for a lighter sentence.

What the fuck ever.

Even though we might never recover Celeste's body, I'll have a headstone put up for her in the town cemetery. I think she'd like that.

Recognition that she lived and died in Redhaven. A marker that there are people who still remember her. Still love her, and always will.

After all this time, she deserves a proper burial, even if it can't include her remains.

Maybe I deserve a day off, too, but I've still got a mountain of evidence to scrape through so when the state goes in to prosecute, they'll have an ironclad case for seeking maximum sentences.

Murder and attempted murder for sure.

Then there's the matter of the cocaine brick we found when we tore apart Culver's little workshop, but he got real silent about that. Especially when we asked where Ulysses got the cocaine he loaded into Emma to hide the traces of what really killed her from toxicology.

Old Ephraim Jacobin just shook his head and muttered something about corrupting city influences.

I don't believe *that*, either.

I don't let things go easy. Not when they matter.

I've been patient this long. I can wait. Whatever's still waiting out there with Montero and the rest?

We'll find it.

Of course, Ulysses denied everything. It's his word against Culver's in court, but we've got our evidence.

The photographs we recovered from Ulysses' room. A few pieces of jewelry that can be tied to Emma and the other missing women. Tons of testimony from Delilah.

It'll go through and he's cooked.

It *has* to go through.

Once Ulysses Arrendell falls, then I'll knock that entire fucked up family off their pedestals one by one.

Yes, it'll take time.

Every journey starts with a single step, and if the man who killed my sister is bound for jail, that's a damned good first step.

Someone nurtured Ulysses into what he is.

Someone enabled him.

I'd almost pity him, if he was already 'initiated' into murder at age twelve. He never stood a chance at being normal.

Then again, pity's for people who don't have a body count.

For Ulysses, there's only hard contempt and horror.

Plus the grim satisfaction that he's going to rot behind bars.

Emma Santos keeps helping us from beyond the grave, too. The new evidence got the county coroner to re-open her case and do a deeper toxicology run.

This time, they found the same stuff in her veins that was in Delilah's, once her tox screenings came back the other night.

A nasty little benzo that's normally used as an antidepressant. One hefty dose in the neck knocks a person out.

The cocaine was added to Emma's bloodstream immediately after death to cover Ulysses' tracks, when that second look at toxicology showed the real cause of death was a benzo overdose.

Ulysses has a pattern. The coke perfectly concealed the other crap in Emma's posthumous blood tests. Further forensic investigation into the substance found at the still confirmed human DNA was also in the bone chips recovered from the digested material.

Now we've got the county DA authorizing us to reach out of our jurisdiction and subpoena footage from venues where Ulysses and Emma were seen together in Los Angeles.

Yep.

That fucker is going *down*.

I'll finally get some peace.

And if I'm lucky, a nice long stretch of quiet with the amazing woman who helped me find it.

I stretch my arms out, leaning back in the desk chair, glancing around the back office of the station.

I'm the only cop on duty right now, except for Mallory on dispatch. She's on her phone passing time, whipping through another dirty little interactive story.

I smile and glance at my folders and case reports.

That shit can wait for tomorrow.

I'm still recovering from a traumatic brain injury after all, even if I only stayed in bed for one day.

What really kept me there was Delilah.

I hope she's still there when I get home.

She's been staying with me, ordered on bed rest and to watch for negative side effects of the drug. She's been recovering fine so far, this restless bundle of energy, pouting at me every morning about missing her class.

I bet the kids miss her, too.

I've just about made up my mind to call it a day when the desk phone rings with a Raleigh area code. I roll my head, cracking my neck before I pick up.

"Officer Graves, how can I help you?"

"Officer Graves? This is Officer Karl Everett, Raleigh PD. Do you have a minute? It's important."

I sit forward.

Tell me those fuckers didn't get out on bail.

Tell me the Arrendells didn't find a way to pay their way out of the prison system entirely.

"What happened?" I growl.

"It's the suspects you turned over to us last week," Everett says hesitantly. "Ulysses Arrendell and Culver Jacobin. They're both—well, they're both dead."

Dead?

I rock back in my chair, too stunned to think.

"How?"

"Suicide, I'm afraid. Both of them," Everett confesses reluctantly. "Apparently, Arrendell hanged himself with his bedsheets in his cell. As for Jacobin, it almost looks like an accident, but we think he did it deliberately. He wadded up a bunch of paper napkins from the cafeteria, shoved them down his throat, and choked."

What the fucking fuck?

I'm so lost for words my vision blurs.

I don't even know how to feel. I sit there so numb I can't feel my legs.

They didn't kill themselves.

I know those fucks wouldn't.

Ulysses is too much of a narcissist chickenshit, and Culver, he was desperately hoping that throwing Ollie under the bus would grant him some immunity and lighter sentencing.

This stinks like a cover-up.

The Arrendells, tying up all their loose ends, murdering their own son and his minion before—

Before what?

What do they have to hide that they were afraid would come falling out in court?

"Officer Graves?" Everett cuts in. "You there?"

"Yeah. Sorry." I drag my hand over my face. "Any video surveillance?"

"That's the thing. There was a power outage for a few hours. No footage at all." He sighs. "If you think it's fishy, so do I. I've had our technical specialists check everything three times. If there was any tampering, we've got no proof. Not one damn bit."

My gut churns.

My worst suspicions are confirmed.

I chew on the news until I feel sick before I say, "Well, thanks for letting me know. I'll inform my captain. You should call it in to the DA since this will need to go on the case record."

"Will do," Everett says. "Thank you."

We hang up, and I just sit there a while longer, fused to the chair with my fingers laced together, processing as much as my brain physically can.

How the hell do you even start to hash this out?

I should be livid.

Furious that they managed to evade justice.

Only, I know they didn't take themselves out.

Someone else did.

The whole thing bleeds shades of Jeffrey Epstein, and considering all the powerful dickheads the Arrendells rub shoulders with, I wonder if they took them out the same way.

It's so fucking ironic an acid laugh rolls out of me.

What they stole from others has now been taken from them.

Before those bastards died, they knew how it felt to stare death in the face and know someone else was pulling the strings, giving them no choice.

It's a twisted kind of poetry.

The man who killed my sister suffering the same fate.

Is that justice enough for me?

I shake my head.

No, not forever.

For today, it'll have to do.

* * *

WHEN I GET HOME, Delilah's waiting for me, curled up on the sofa in one of my shirts.

That sight normally drives me into a frenzy, but today my thoughts are heavy.

She knows it as soon as I hang my belt and holster up and settle down on the couch. She instantly shuts the TV off and scoots over.

"Something happened," I grind out.

"But are you okay?" Dark indigo eyes look up at me, worried and sweet. She curls her hand against my arm.

"A lot happened." I sigh, wrapping my arm around her shoulders and gathering her against me. "They're fucking dead, Lilah. Both of them. Ulysses and Culver offed themselves in their cells, supposedly. Of course, I don't believe a damn word of it."

"What?" Her eyes widen.

"Yeah. It's been a day." I smile wryly. "Aside from the obvious complications, I can't bring myself to get too choked up over it."

She buries her face in my shoulder. "Honestly, I hope they're getting poked in the ass with burning-hot irons by demons who look just like Emma and Celeste."

I can't help laughing.

She always does that.

"Very creative. The kids must love your story time."

"I mean it," she says fiercely, but then stops with her gaze turning thoughtful. "I guess that's it then? No chance of them wiggling out of it now. Real closure."

"For me," I point out. "Not for Emma's family."

"Oh." Delilah studies me curiously and brushes my cheek. "Are you ready for that?"

"It's long past time. I can't let her ma suffer any longer now that I've got some real answers for her." I take a deep breath. "Stay here with me while I do it?"

"Sure," she says without hesitation.

No more doubt.

No doubt at all that no matter what happens, my girl's got my back.

I mean, hell, would your girlfriend choke a guy out with her thighs to stop him from jumping you?

The memory almost makes me smile, but it's not quite in me right now with the somber job ahead.

I drag my brand-new phone out of my pocket—same model as my old one, creature of habit, all my information synced and loaded from the cloud. Marina Santos' number has been saved in my contacts for weeks, just waiting for me to give her the news.

Waiting for this dark, fateful moment.

Exhaling heavily, I punch in her name, then lift my phone to my ear and wait while Delilah wraps her hand so tight in mine, leaning into me.

She's all the silent encouragement I need.

Even so, my heart almost cracks in two as a woman answers.

"Hello?" Her voice is weary.

"Hello, Marina Santos?"

"Yes. Who is this?"

"My name—" I stop. This is the part of the job I hate more than anything. "My name is Officer Lucas Graves. I'm with the police department in Redhaven, North Carolina. Ma'am, I'm afraid I have some news about your daughter."

Her hitched, broken breath says she already knows before I say a word.

She's on the verge of tears as she whispers, "No. No, no, don't say it—"

"I'm sorry," I force out. "I'm so sorry, Mrs. Santos. I wish I didn't have to."

There's no answer but the chaotic sob of a mother falling to pieces.

I close my eyes, feeling Delilah stroking my arm, holding back her own tears as we let Mrs. Santos cry for as long as she needs to.

It feels like days, but it's only a few awful minutes where there's nothing but her muffled grief, slowly fading into spent gasps.

"I knew. Oh, God, I knew it," she says softly, her voice so scratchy. "I just didn't want to face it. It's been so long..."

"I know, ma'am. I was the same way with my sister. The men who hurt your daughter also hurt my sister, but they're gone now. They can't ever hurt anyone again. I'll send over all the information." My lungs shudder on my next breath. "We never found my sister's body. But Emma, she's waiting for you here, ma'am. You can bring her home and put her to rest. If you want to make arrangements, we'll help you get that sorted, too."

Fuck, I'll pay the expense myself to fly her home.

My heart sags to my knees when I hear Delilah fighting back tears.

A pained whimper sounds over the phone. "These men—they killed my Emma?"

"Yes, ma'am. That's correct."

"And you... you stopped them? For your sister. For my daughter."

My fingers tighten on Delilah's so damn hard, and she nuzzles into my shoulder.

"Yes, ma'am. I had to for them—and to save the life of someone I love."

"Th-thank you," Marina Santos strangles out. "Thank you for fighting for my baby girl."

Goddamn, that hurts.

I can't accept her thanks.

Not for this.

But I won't reject her warmth, her gratitude, the only thing she can offer me.

I only ask, "Is there anything else I can do for you, ma'am?"

"Tell me?" she answers with a desperate hope. "Tell me everything that happened. Help me understand. I don't want to wait."

So I do.

I give her the whole ugly story, everything we know.

How Ulysses lured girls into his web.

How he got his venom into poor Emma with his glitz and charm, using her high hopes for life against her.

How he took advantage of her.

How he murdered her to satisfy his own depraved bloodlust.

How a mistake with Culver made Emma the key to ending his terror.

How we never would have stopped him without her body, without the clues she left us.

Finally, how he stalked Delilah and almost killed her.

Lilah shivers against me as I recite that part, kissing the back of my neck gratefully.

I leave nothing out.

Mrs. Santos deserves the full blackhearted truth.

When it's over and I've drained it out of me like lancing some horrible abscess, she's quiet.

Another minute passes before she says, "...twelve. My God. He started doing this when he was *twelve*... how could a child be so monstrous?"

I wish like hell I had an answer that made sense.

"Some folks change as they grow up," I offer. "But other folks are born broken in ways that can turn destructive if they aren't controlled."

"I just wish someone cared for him more. Protected him, so he wouldn't have... it doesn't matter." She trails off, and when she speaks again, her voice brightens. "Thank you, Officer Graves. Please keep protecting those you love."

"I'll do my very best, Mrs. Santos," I promise, looking down at the little firecracker curled against me. "Thank you."

I mean it with my entire heart and soul.

After we hang up, Delilah and I sit quietly together for about an hour.

Then, without a word, she takes my hand, rising off the couch and leading me toward the stairs, the upstairs loft, my bed.

She knows I don't want to think.

She knows what I need.

She gives me the comfort of her body, the wordless promise in kisses, in caresses, in the way she arches against me as I tear off our clothes and fuck the pain away.

We're still so battered.

We still go at it like the flesh-starved beasts we are.

Every kiss, every stroke, every taste of her throat and every twist of her hair in my fist brings us together in perfect rhythm.

It's slow but fast.

Deep yet thin.

Sweet but so damn dirty when it ends with me clutching her little ass in my hands until my fingers ache, flinging her up and down on my cock, jerking myself off in her pussy until I erupt inside her like a volcano coming undone.

"Lilah, fuck! Fuck!"

She comes for me real sweet, ass bobbing and perfect tits swaying in my face.

Her lips peel back, crying my name till I smother them again.

Delilah Clarendon has never tasted better than she does today.

And it's all because I know nothing will ever steal her away from me again.

She's mine down to the soul.

So fucking mine it vibrates through me as my cock pumps with claiming strokes, filling her to overflowing.

She crashes down in my arms, both of us a mess of pure sweat and come and the sweetest relief.

I never could have imagined this kind of sex happening when we first met, claws out and teeth bared as much as our hearts.

Now, it's a high I can't imagine living without.

This cynical wildcat trusted me enough to let me inside her heart, let me bask in her warmth, in the dreams she holds and the sweetness she guards behind her barbed wire.

Life without my Lilah would be empty.

As I peel her up from the bed, I wish I could tell her with more than my body how much she fills my heart.

Just like the way I fill her tight, clenching flesh until I can't.

We're timeless together.

Silent.

Wordless.

You never need words to say the shit that really matters.

The only thing I need to say is *"Delilah"* as I claim her lips with my teeth, taking us both to the pinnacle we can only reach together.

* * *

It's sunset by the time we settle quietly into the afterglow.

With Delilah still curled in my arms, I walk my fingers lazily over her shoulder.

"I'm sorry, you know," she murmurs. "I don't think I ever said that out loud. Sorry for not trusting you. Sorry for being so defensive. I wish I'd never shut you out."

I smile drowsily. "I know. Thanks for saying it out loud, though. For the record, I'm sorry for being such a rhino ass, too."

"...you're not sorry for that. You still *are* an ass," she teases, and I laugh.

"Guilty as charged." I hold up my hand.

She playfully swats it and thumps my chest.

"Dork. Mmm, you know, though..."

"Yeah?"

"I wouldn't mind you being my dork for a good long time."

The feeling that spreads through me is like melting sunlight on a spring day.

"Yeah? You mean it?"

"I trust you," Delilah says simply. Those words carry as much weight as *I love you*, when I know—I know how life has treated her, all those hard knocks giving her a mighty rough time with people. "It's been a long time since I trusted anyone. Not just to be with me—but to *stay*."

I get it now.

The way people abandoned her again and again, told her she was too much trouble, not worth fighting for, not worth keeping.

Hell, I'd push folks away to avoid that pain, just like her.

I catch her hand and bring it to my lips, kissing her palm. "I will stay, Lilah. As long as you'll have me. I love you, and I need to see how far we can take this."

"Deal. We'll see how long I can tolerate you," she whispers. Her eyes glitter and her lips are warm as she pushes up to kiss me. "Because if you'll fight that hard to save me, Lucas, I hope you'll fight that hard to love me as much as I love you."

XXVII: RED LETTER DAY (DELILAH)

Months Later

I love the smell of a bright summer day.

Even better, the smell of a summer day with my munchkins yelling "Miss Clare! Miss Clare!"—because half of them can't say Clarendon yet—as they scamper around.

They come charging in with a thousand questions, plying me with everything from the wonders of pinecones to flowers to four-leaf-clovers.

I can't help but smile.

They're all thrilled to be on this summer field trip, hiking through the hills along the lakeshore. Every last kid treats what they find in the forest like it's a tiny miracle.

That's why I truly love this.

Through their eyes, I get to see the magic of life again.

They're so open, so innocent, and it's a total joy just watching them indulge their curiosity.

"So, 'Miss Clare,'" a deep voice drawls at my back. "How much further to this campsite?"

I spin around, lacing my hands together behind my back and smiling impishly at Lucas.

He's bent over with the weight of our camping gear, though it's easy to tell he's exaggerating when it's not that crushing for him. Just light summer tents and a couple backpacks.

It's not even enough to make him break a sweat, though I wouldn't mind watching his skintight white t-shirt turn translucent.

Of course, the big lunk insisted on carrying everything, leaving me and the kids free to run ahead.

"Close enough to keep you from complaining," I tease, poking him in the nose.

He snaps his teeth at me with a mock-growl that seems more feral.

I think it's because he's grown his scruff out into a proper thick beard since winter, making him look more rugged and sinfully handsome than ever.

Or maybe I'm just swooning that hard for this man.

Everything he does makes me love him a little more.

Well.

Not *everything*.

If he leaves the toilet seat up one more time, I might scream loud enough to burst his eardrums.

But considering that's one of the only things I've had to complain about over the past few months of normalcy in Redhaven...

Yeah. I'd say things have turned out pretty sweet after all.

Life has calmed down tremendously.

No creepy stalkers. No more dead bodies.

I rarely see the Jacobins in town ever since the big dustup, and neither does anyone else. The Arrendells either avoid me like the plague or talk to me with such strained courtesy you'd think I was royalty.

I'm good with that.

They can stay away. *Far, far away.*

Sure, they still sign my paychecks at the school.

But I look at that as the town paying me, not them. And this town has given me a mountain of goodness to be grateful for, now that I'm really settled in.

Wonderful classes full of bright, eager students.

An amazing friend in Nora. Not to mention Janelle, who knew nothing about Ulysses' true intentions and was horrified for accidentally delivering me into his hands.

A happy life settling in with Lucas.

Oh, and Lucas himself.

Those spring-green eyes always look at me with such wild adoration. Like I'm something precious he would never dream of throwing away.

He's looking at me that way now as we make our way to the camp—a common spot for hikers with a cleared fire pit, good flat areas to set up tents, and lots of old logs to sit on.

Together we wrangle up the kids and turn them loose so they can help us set up. Lucas handles the tents with a little help from me when I'm not chasing rug rats down.

He's technically here in an official capacity as the police department chaperone, but it's nice having him along to do the heavy lifting, too.

It's also nice that every time I glance up from anchoring another tent post in the ground, he's just watching me.

Always with this lopsided half smile like he's still trying to figure out how exactly we happened.

The heat in his eyes speaks so much louder.

It says he doesn't know, but he doesn't mind one bit.

That goes double for me.

I keep catching myself smiling back shyly as long as I can before another little hand pulls me away.

It's a total circus, getting these mini monsters settled and then prepping dinner.

It's grilled cheese toasted over the fire tonight, and then roasted marshmallows for dessert.

There are *oohs* and *ahhs* and excited chatter when I break out the s'mores.

Good thing we remembered wet wipes to take care of all the chocolate-smeared fingers and faces.

When we settle in for story time, I'm not sure if we should be telling ghost stories, but the kids insist.

They wind up shrieking themselves silly when Lucas holds a flashlight up to his face and tells them the story of a monster in the lake. I struggle not to laugh.

Still Lake isn't big enough for monsters. Not even the Loch Ness kind.

And now, neither is my life as long as I'm with him.

Even if a few of the kids look nervous, by the time Lucas finishes his story, half of them are nodding off. While I gather them up to usher them to their tents, Lucas bends to kiss my cheek.

"Just gonna go do a quick check for things that go bump in the night," he says, gripping his flashlight. "Stomp around a bit. Scare off any cougars."

"Cougars?" little Nickie Spelman mumbles as I lift him up into my arms.

"Don't worry," I say. "You're too big for any cougar snack."

Lucas chuckles and slips off into the woods while I get the kids settled. He's still not back by the time I tuck the last munchkin in with a promise the scary lake monster won't get her while she sleeps.

So I linger by the fire for a bit before I retreat to our shared tent, stretching and rolling my shoulders. I lean down to rub calves sore from hiking so many steep inclines.

A silhouette against the tent wall warns me just before Lucas ducks in. "Hey. Think you can leave the rug rats for five minutes? Something I wanna show you."

I chew my lower lip, frowning. "Is it far?"

"All in earshot and still in view. If anything happens, we'll be back in two steps. I promise." He offers me a warm, inviting hand and the biggest grin.

God, it's so nice to see this bear of a man smile.

How could I ever say no?

"As long as we're quick." Smiling, I slip my fingers into his and let him pull me to my feet and out into the night.

It's lovely out for late June.

Hot and sticky as a cinnamon bun, sure, but with the sun down, it's a pleasant warmth, almost like a hot tub that wraps you up. We're silent as we walk hand in hand through the trees.

I tilt my head up at a break in the branches, trying to pick out the constellations.

"Close your eyes, lady," Lucas whispers, bringing me to a halt next to him.

I give him a curious look and comply, closing my eyes and trusting him to lead me through the night.

Honestly, I trust him with so much more than that.

It's just a few more steps, right past the feeling of leaves brushing against my bare arms before he says, "Okay. You can look now."

I do—and the sight steals my breath away.

We're standing in an open field surrounded by thick forest, tall grass dotted with little juniper bushes and blooming fronds of lilac.

But the entire field is lit up with a galaxy of green-gold stars. Fireflies.

They burn so bright and luminous and pretty my chest goes tight with awe. My lips part on words that never come as I turn slowly, taking in the light show.

"Holy hell," I whisper.

There must be hundreds of the little bugs out here. The whole night glows with this miracle of nature.

Lucas caresses my chin, gently tilting my face to the sky again.

"As above, so below," he whispers.

My heart flips over at the beauty.

It's like the stars have come down to Earth, and I can reach out and hold them in my hands.

"I knew you'd love it," he says proudly.

I'm too awestruck to even sass back.

Laughing with delight, I gently cage a firefly with my fingers so I can watch its glow light up my palms before letting it free again.

I've never been this much in love.

Spinning with sheer exhilaration, I spread my arms out— only to stop as I face Lucas again.

He's watching me with his heart in his eyes, so clear it makes my throat knot with a shiver of sweet emotion.

"Lucas? What's up?"

"Lilah, you make this so hard when you're that damn pretty," he breathes, and then, "*Delilah.*"

He steps closer, catches my hands, taking them in his own and squeezing so tight.

"I've been working up to this for a good long while," he says, looking at me intently, his hands so warm in mine. "Just didn't know how to do it. I didn't want to just throw you a ring—"

A ring, oh God!

My heart soars, so high and bright, bursting with color like the fireflies.

"That makes me think of *them*. Of how they use shit like that bracelet as marks. I want to possess you, woman, but not like a thing stuck with my gold. I want you to be mine because you want to be. Because you chose me. Because you trust me." He swallows roughly, a hint of nerves breaking through that almost blows me down. "I also wanted you to have something to remember this by, too. So every time you see fireflies, you think of this—of what I know is right for us, when you're the only thing that's ever been true and real in my heart."

Oh. My. God.

Even as my answer flutters on my lips, shivering with the thrill of it along with the rest of me, he drops down to one knee.

I'm freaking *shaking* as he holds my hands in his, looking up at me with so many promises so bright they shame the stars.

"Marry me, Miss Delilah Clarendon."

I can't tell if it's a question or a statement.

I don't care.

"Took you long enough!" I rush out—then throw myself against him, sealing my high-pitched *"Yes, yes, yes!"* to his lips with a kiss.

His startled joy is drowned out by the messy crush of our mouths.

We kiss like we're dying of thirst. Like we can never get enough.

"Pace yourself, darlin'. We've only got the rest of our lives." He chuckles.

I barely let him finish before attacking his mouth again.

Oh, the heat feels so wild, so frantic, exploding with wonder and beauty and sheer, overwhelming happiness.

It's a kiss that feels like closure. The end of the worst chapter of my life—and the beginning of a book that can only be my new favorite.

His mouth moves hard against mine, claiming and desperate and yet so reverent. I know he'll never hurt me.

Not this man.

Not on his life.

Not the one who touches me like he can see how fragile I really am.

Not the beast who shows me he's the one who'll never throw me away.

He loves me.

And I flipping love Lucas Graves.

Enough to trust him with my heart, my soul, and my future.

I could never be happier than I will be as his wife.

He's such a big, gorgeous, adorably annoying asshole.

More importantly, he's a gentle, thoughtful, wonderful man with a heart bigger than the sky.

Beneath that sky, I kiss him with my all.

I promise the fireflies that we'll be together for the rest of our lives.

* * *

Months Later

WE GET MARRIED among the fireflies, too.

It's not an extravagant wedding.

It doesn't need to be.

I also barely notice the late summer humidity making the night sticky. We chose a late hour to say our vows for a reason.

Our love will always have a touch of darkness along with the fireflies and stars.

And it's even more glorious than I could ever imagine with everything we truly need.

Family means so much to us.

All that really matters is having everyone we consider family here with us on our big day.

My mother drove down from NYC the second she could. Although she's met Lucas before, she hugs him like she's seeing him for the very first time.

Nora's there too, hugging me until I nearly pop out of my corset.

Of course, all the boys from the police station show up too.

Grant Faircross looks like he's about to burst out of his tuxedo as he stands in as best man, while his girl Nell is our charming little flower girl.

I couldn't ask for a more perfect wedding in this intimate cluster of people and so many amazing tiny lights scattered around. A reminder of the night we made our real promise to each other, not so long ago, only now it's floating there in the open for everyone to see.

I don't think anyone walks off to the reception with a dry eye.

There's this sweet, heavy moment right before the ceremony starts where a few night birds perk up in the trees, pulling my gaze up.

I swear, it feels like Emma Santos is here, too. Wishing us well among the fireflies.

And Celeste Graves.

I'll never meet her, but somehow I know she's watching over us in the stars and chirping crickets, giving her blessing from the Great Beyond.

The ceremony feels sweetly informal and that's totally us.

We don't need pomp to make it real.

When the music swells, when I step out of the little alcove in the trees where Janelle was fussing with my hair, when I see Lucas standing there looking so handsome in his three-piece tux on the other side of the field with a universe of fireflies between us...

Yes.

God, yes.

I promise I'll never ask for anything else when this is all I want.

I can't take my eyes off him as I start down the makeshift aisle that's really just a narrow lane of flowers between the packed rows of our friends.

He's my Hercules to the end.

He's perfection itself.

He's—yelling?

"Delilah!" My name flies out of his mouth as my heel catches the soft earth and I pitch forward, nearly flinging my bouquet.

Everyone around me gasps.

Lucas runs forward, hand outstretched, but I catch myself in time—*just barely*—and pull myself up, clearing my throat and flushing hotly.

The wedding march is still playing and my face is redder than a fire engine.

Everyone stares, even Lucas.

Then it happens.

I laugh.

I just laugh and laugh until I can't stop.

I don't know why, but it feels right.

Me tripping over my clumsy feet, turning something solemn into pure whimsy.

Thankfully, everyone relaxes with huge sighs of relief, grinning and laughing along with me.

Lucas eyes me with concern for a few more seconds before a slow, warm smile spreads over his lips. Then the priest beckons, clearing his throat with gentle amusement.

"Slowly now," he teases. "We don't want any accidents today."

No way.

No accidents.

Only a very deliberate choice to spend the rest of my life with Lucas Graves.

I'm extra careful as I continue the procession up the aisle, though.

Nell traipses around me with high-skipping steps, throwing flower petals everywhere. When I reach the spot where Lucas waits with the priest, Lucas holds his hands out, his eyes glittering.

"You in such a hurry to get to me you can't walk straight, New York?"

Smiling, I slip my fingers into his. "Don't get too full of yourself, dork."

"Can't help it." He grins. "Prettiest girl in the big city's about to be my wife. I must be pretty hot shit to have a babe like her falling for me."

I roll my eyes, trying not to laugh.

The priest clears his throat again with a chuckle, giving Lucas a mild look.

"Language," the priest teases. "We are technically in the middle of a religious ceremony. Are we ready?"

Lucas nods firmly.

"I've never been more ready in my life," I breathe.

That earns me a gentle look from the priest and a fierce one from Lucas, right before the priest begins.

"Dearly beloved," he says. "We are gathered here today..."

Gathered is right.

Friends, family, people I never imagined having in my life when I'm so used to being alone and unwanted.

Yet this man wants me, and so do they.

In sickness and in health, till death do we part, yada yada yada, you know the rest.

Mom first showed me how amazing it felt to know someone loves you.

Now, Lucas shows me just what it means to love someone and want them right back—and trust them to take that feeling, to hold it, to cherish it and make it theirs forever.

I don't remember repeating our vows—even if I stumble over a few words and make Lucas mess up, until the priest makes us repeat it again.

Oops.

We're so wrapped up in each other's eyes we're only half listening to what we're supposed to say.

Until the very last.

Those perfect final words.

The fireflies live in his eyes tonight, dwelling in those stark depths. And the way he looks at me in my summery white dress with my bouquet of flowers picked by all my students...

Wow.

I really do feel like the most prettiest girl in the world tonight.

His smile says he knows what's coming, asking if I'm ready.

We're going to fight.

It's what we do.

We'll have sick days and bad days and tragic days where life and death becomes more than bickering over what type of potato salad to bring to the police picnic.

But as long as we always love harder than we fight, we'll always find our way back to the light.

We'll find our fireflies.

And we'll always kiss away the wounds we claw in each other before carving sweeter ones with the way we crash together in bed.

That's who we are.

It's who we need to be together.

It's what makes us stronger, when we never crumble, never waver.

And there's no waver, not a crumb of doubt, when the priest says, "Do you, Delilah, take Lucas to be your lawfully wedded husband?"

"*I do,*" I answer.

That's the one thing I can't trip over when I mean it so sincerely.

When what I'm really saying is, *I love you and I always will.*

Lucas answers the same question, growling his "I do" with a powerful glance that binds us together with the force of its certainty.

The rock-solid promise that he'll love me right back.

Tonight.

Tomorrow.

Always.

For a trembling moment, the whole night goes still.

We share this silent second, this great *stillness*, our first instant as husband and wife while the stars and the fireflies and loving eyes look on.

Then Lucas sweeps me into his arms.

My husband draws my lips to his for the very first time.

There are a thousand ways to describe that kiss, but only one that matters.

His warmth reaches down inside me and plucks all my strings with a wildness and fervor that belongs to me as surely as mine is his.

His kiss proclaims he's my husband, my protector forever, and *I am his wife.*

We're no longer broken when our love made us whole.

I don't know how I'm still standing as he breaks away.

We're just one big beating heart of the reddest passion that's so wrong it can only be right.

With the fireflies as my witness, I swear we'll never be lonely again.

FLASH FORWARD: RED LIKE MY HEART (LUCAS)

Years Later

I never thought I'd see my house full of this much light and laughter ever again.

Except it's not my house anymore.

Now, it's *ours*.

This once lonely home is bursting with family warmth. My family. *Our family.*

The family Delilah and I have built together, and we're far from done.

Along with several *other* families, considering the fact that our backyard is currently full of screaming children chasing each other through the sprinklers.

They're splashing themselves silly in the giant kiddie pools I hauled in just for this special occasion—our daughter's fourth birthday party.

Four is a big deal.

It's the age where she'll form memories that last, and damn, if I'm not determined to make every last one of them happy.

I can't help stopping to watch them all with a lazy smile hanging on my face.

I'm standing just inside the kitchen door, looking through the window at the brightly colored mess of toys our yard has become. It's a lovely, weird chaos when you're a father.

I half forget the tray of frozen orange creamsicle pops in my hands.

Homemade, too. Being a dad means you've always gotta up your game in the kitchen, and of course I aim to please.

It's a sight out there.

We've got streamers everywhere, a big custom-printed banner announcing *Lily's Four Years Old Today!*, and so much glitter blowing around it could choke a pixie riding a sugar high.

The bouncy house against the back fence shakes like it's alive from all the jumping little feet bopping around inside. A few of the parents who came out today are clustered by the refreshment table, sipping their beers and sodas and chatting while they keep a close eye on the munchkins.

Not Delilah, though.

My girl is in the thick of it, standing over one of the pools, lifting Lily in and out of the water while our firstborn baby girl kicks and shrieks with laughter. She splashes like a dolphin, getting Delilah's black hair soaking wet, delighted by whatever this little game is they've made up on the fly.

I wouldn't even guess.

I can never tell with those two.

They've got this secret bond that lets them speak their own language. Most of the time I'm confused and have no damn clue what's going on.

But hell, I don't need to.

I don't need to know their every thought to love my daughter and her mama so much my heart could fucking explode. A feeling that's grown too big to be confined to my chest.

It's a heavy, wonderful love, weighty enough to keep a man's feet on the ground.

This is my life now, and I'll choose it every day I'm still breathing. Maybe after, too.

Sure beats the hell out of chasing after Redhaven's latest weirdness and someone's brush with the reaper. It's been a wild ride the last few years.

Those are stories for another time, though, and I'm not getting caught up in them today.

Right now, I can't take my eyes off them—or off the tiny little creature clinging to Delilah's chest in her little papoose carrier, strapped in snugly. She's so tired she doesn't even mind her sister's manic kicking that splashes water all over her.

Our second girl, Melanie, isn't even a year old yet.

And if we both have our way, by the time she's four, she'll have a whole mess of siblings.

My wife never fails to surprise me.

I've never seen anyone blossom into parenthood the way she has. All of her old fears were unfounded.

From the moment she found out she was pregnant for the very first time, she just erupted with joy, nearly glowing. Even when the pregnancy hormones kicked in and I'm pretty sure I came close to being the next Redhaven murder case every time I even thought about getting on her nerves.

Kids love her like bees love honey. The pack of rugrats from her classes that showed up today is proof, circling around her in an adoring spiral even now, shouting out questions when they can.

Delilah loves kids with the fullness of her soul.

She loves *our* kids just as much as I love her.

Yeah, I know I'm heavy on the cheesy shit today, but damn.

If loving your family makes a man soft, then call me butter.

The sound of the front door creaking pulls me from my reverie, right before a warm, merry voice sails through the living room.

"Grandma's here with the cake!" Mitsi Clarendon calls, then falters. "Oh my, where did everyone go?"

"Out back!" I call, pulling away from the back door to meet her at the threshold between the kitchen and the living room. "Pool party's already started, Mitsi."

Even as I say it, there's another loud splash from outside followed by excited yipping.

I glance outside and watch our husky puppy, Wolfie, go thrashing into the pool with the kids, making a mess everywhere.

Great.

Now the house is destined to smell like wet dog for a week.

Still smiling, I turn my attention back to Delilah's mother.

Sometimes it's jarring when I see Mitsi and she looks so much like Delilah—just older, rounder, her eyes a paler shade of that indigo-blue.

As I trade my small tray of popsicles into her hands and take over the larger cake box, she catches me when I bend and kisses my cheek.

"Lucas," she says with a warmth that always makes me ache for the mother I lost a long time ago. Yet it's a distant thing when there's so much kindness in this woman who looks at me like I'm her own son. Her hand cups my cheek. "It's so good to see you."

"You make it sound like you haven't been camped out in our guest room for a week." She always does that every time we see each other again—even if it's only after ten minutes. Like she's startled I'm still *here*, but then she's a lot like her daughter with that fear of abandonment.

I grin, tossing my head toward the door.

"C'mon. Let's go chase them out of the water and give 'em a little time to settle down before they overload on cake too fast."

Mitsi laughs as we head out into the bright sun together.

The instant we appear, there's a riot.

The kids know what's in the big box like a dog smelling a hidden bone.

With shrieks of *"Cake! Cake!"* that could shatter glass, a whirlwind of children descends on us.

I forge through the churning mass of tiny, squirming bodies to the picnic table, where a few of the other parents step up to help with amused laughs, glancing at me as if to say *First time?*

They herd their own kids away to sit down and a few others start setting out rainbow-colored paper plates and forks.

I put the cake box down in a safe spot away from pawing hands while Mitsi keeps those hands busy, pressing creamsicles in them to keep them occupied until we can light the candles and cut the cake.

My wife—my gorgeous, patient wife—and daughters come running over breathlessly with a very drenched puppy bouncing around their ankles with his tongue lolling out.

Delilah's flushed, and it's such a beautiful look on her.

The animated light that shines in her eyes is so different from the hard, closed, wary looks when I first met her.

But then I'm different, too.

I can't imagine the man I was back then ever doing what I do now—sweeping her close with baby Melanie caught between us and catching her up in a kiss while everybody watches.

I'm not surprised our daughter's the first one to shout, "Ew, cooties!" even though the other monsters pick up Lily's refrain until they're nearly chanting it.

Chuckling, I hold Delilah close for a moment longer, looking down into those starry eyes that promise me later, tonight, when we're alone, there'll be cooties everywhere.

We'll be trading them till dawn.

For now, though, I sweep Lily up and tickle her ribs.

"That's right, Daddy's got cooties—and now I'm giving them to you!" I blow a raspberry on her little belly.

Lily bursts into screaming laughter, grabbing at my hair.

"No cooties, Daddy! Cake, cake!"

"Well," Delilah says, "if the birthday girl wants cake, the birthday girl gets cake."

I glance up, watching as Mitsi finishes setting four tall, slim sparkler candles in the big sheet cake printed with a sugary *Inky the Penguin* airbrush.

Everybody's favorite cartoon pen pal penguin is a big hit. The books were around when I was a kid and I think I've read them at bedtime to Lily two hundred times. I know it won't be long before my little girl starts sending her own letters to Inky, just like damn near every kid in Lilah's class.

"Up you go, princess." I heft Lily up onto my shoulders, and together we take our daughters up to the head of the table.

There's so much fidgeting and squirming going on, it's like watching a bunch of puppies trying to treat train, waiting for the command that says they can *eat*.

Trust me.

I see this a lot.

Wolfie never lasts more than ten seconds.

He's a work in progress just like Lily.

I swing Lily down in front of the cake, and Delilah produces a lighter, quickly firing up the candles and setting them off sparkling and crackling.

Lily looks up at it in wide-eyed wonder, her little mouth hanging open.

"All yours, tiny monster." I give her a nudge. She wasn't old enough to really understand this last year, but we blew them out for her after she gave a few tiny halfhearted puffs, but this year it's all her thing. "Blow out your candles, big girl, and then we can all have some cake."

Lily's broad grin mirrors her mother's.

She puffs up her cheeks, leans in, and blows out the candles in one big huffing rush.

The table erupts into cheers and laughter and clapping.

Cries of *Happy Birthday!* so infectious that baby Melanie giggles, too, even though she doesn't know what's going on. As we start to cut the cake and pass out slices, aided by the other parents, Delilah tugs on my arm, coaxing me to lean down where she can whisper in my ear.

"You realize after this big show, we're going to have to outdo ourselves three times a year from now on," she murmurs.

For a second, it doesn't register.

I blink, puzzled.

"Three? But we only have two ki—oh."

Oh, shit.

I'm about to fall over, clutching the party plate in my hand. I almost drop it when, with a sly smile, Delilah drops another slice of cake on it.

"That's *your* party present. Enjoy," she sasses, tucking herself against my side while I grin fit to crack my face in half.

Inside, I'm lit up just like those damn sparklers.

Another kid.

We're going to have another kid, and our house, our *life*—

It will never, ever be lonely again.

I'll never be lonely again.

Somewhere, I hope Celeste is smiling down on us.

I hope I've done her proud.

The life my sister wanted for me, the happiness, there's no question.

And I'd like to think that somewhere, she's at ease, finally able to rest now that the man who killed her is gone.

I know I'm at peace, too.

I can finally let go.

I look forward to every day that follows without living in the darkness of the past.

Not when every new dawn is another chance for me to live.

Every single day, I'll find new ways to love Delilah Graves more than I did yesterday.

ABOUT NICOLE SNOW

cole Snow is a *Wall Street Journal* and *USA Today* bestselling athor. She found her love of writing by hashing out love scenes on lunch breaks and plotting her great escape from boardrooms. Her work roared onto the indie romance scene in 2014 with her Grizzlies MC series.

Since then Snow aims for the very best in growly, heart-of-gold alpha heroes, unbelievable suspense, and swoon storms aplenty.

Already hooked on her stuff? Visit nicolesnowbooks.com to sign up for her newsletter and connect on social media.

Got a question or comment on her work? Reach her anytime at nicole@nicolesnowbooks.com

Thanks for reading. And please remember to leave an honest review! Nothing helps an author more.

MORE BOOKS BY NICOLE

Knights of Dallas Books

The Romeo Arrangement

The Best Friend Zone

The Hero I Need

The Worst Best Friend

Accidental Knight (Companion book)*

Bossy Seattle Suits

One Bossy Proposal

One Bossy Dare

One Bossy Date

One Bossy Offer

Bad Chicago Bosses

Office Grump

Bossy Grump

Perfect Grump

Damaged Grump

Heroes of Heart's Edge Books

No Perfect Hero

No Good Doctor

No Broken Beast

No Damaged Goods

No Fair Lady

No White Knight

No Gentle Giant

Marriage Mistake Standalone Books

Accidental Hero

Accidental Protector

Accidental Romeo

Accidental Knight

Accidental Rebel

Accidental Shield

Stand Alone Novels

The Perfect Wrong

Cinderella Undone

Man Enough

Surprise Daddy

Prince With Benefits

Marry Me Again

Love Scars

Recklessly His

Enguard Protectors Books

Still Not Over You

Still Not Into You

Still Not Yours

Still Not Love

Baby Fever Books

Baby Fever Bride

Baby Fever Promise

Baby Fever Secrets

Only Pretend Books

Fiance on Paper

One Night Bride

Grizzlies MC Books

Outlaw's Kiss

Outlaw's Obsession

Outlaw's Bride

Outlaw's Vow

Deadly Pistols MC Books

Never Love an Outlaw

Never Kiss an Outlaw

Never Have an Outlaw's Baby

Never Wed an Outlaw

Prairie Devils MC Books

Outlaw Kind of Love

Nomad Kind of Love

Savage Kind of Love

Wicked Kind of Love

Bitter Kind of Love